BLOOD & BONES: SHADE

Blood Fury MC®

Book 6

JEANNE ST. JAMES

———

Photographer/Cover Artist: Golden Czermak at FuriousFotog
Cover Model: Tyler Bland
Editor: Proofreading by the Page
Beta readers: Andi Babcock, Sharon Abrams & Alexandra Swab, Author Whitley Cox
Blood Fury MC Logo: Jennifer Edwards

———

**Sign up for Jeanne's newsletter: https://www. authorjeannestjames.com/
Join her FB readers' group for the inside scoop: https://www.facebook.com/groups/JeannesReviewCrew/**

Sign up for my newsletter for insider information, author news, and new releases:
https://www.authorjeannestjames.com/

Content Warning

WARNING! While I usually don't do trigger warnings, I figured since some of the memories/flashbacks involve a child, this book might need one just to prepare readers before diving in. Please note, this story includes:

Sex/child trafficking (memories)
Kidnapping/child abduction (memories/prologue)
Physical and sexual abuse of a child (flashbacks/memories)
Attempted suicide (memories)
Murder

Blood & Bones: Trip (Book 1)
Blood & Bones: Sig (Book 2)
Blood & Bones: Judge (Book 3)
Blood & Bones: Deacon (Book 4)
Blood & Bones: Cage (Book 5)
Blood & Bones: Shade (Book 6)
Blood & Bones: Rook (Book 7)
Blood & Bones: Rev (Book 8)
Crash: A Dirty Angels MC/Blood Fury MC
Crossover (Book 8.5)
Blood & Bones: Ozzy (Book 9)
Blood & Bones: Dodge (Book 10)
Blood & Bones: Whip (Book 11)
Blood & Bones: Easy (Book 12)

Character List

BFMC Members:

Trip Davis – *President* – Son of Buck Davis, half-brother to Sig, mother is Tammy, Runs Buck You Recovery

Sig Stevens – *Vice President* – Son of Buck Davis, mother is Silvia, three years younger than Trip, helps run Buck You Recovery

Judge (Judd Scott) – *Sgt at Arms* - Father (Ox) was an Original, owns Justice Bail Bonds

Deacon Edwards – *Treasurer* – Judge's cousin, Skip Tracer/Bounty Hunter at Justice Bail Bonds

Cage (Chris Dietrich) – *Road Captain* – Dutch's youngest son, mechanic at Dutch's Garage

Ozzy (Thomas Oswald) – *Secretary* – *Original* – manages club-owned The Grove Inn.

Rook (Randy Dietrich) – Dutch's oldest son

Dutch (David Dietrich) – *Original* – Owns Dutch's Garage, sons: Cage & Rook

Dodge – Manager - Crazy Pete's Bar, did time with Rook in jail

Whip – Mechanic at Dutch's Garage (formerly known as the prospect Sparky)

Rev (Mickey Rivers) – Mechanic at Dutch's Garage (formerly known as the prospect Mouse)

Shade (Julian Bennett) – works at Tioga Pet Crematorium (formerly known as the prospect Shady)

Easy – works at Tioga Pet Crematorium

Tater Tot - *Prospect*

Possum - *Prospect*

Stella – *Trip's ol' lady* - Crazy Pete's daughter, owns Crazy Pete's Bar

Autumn (Red) – *Sig's ol' lady* – Accountant for the club's businesses

Cassidy (Cassie) – *Judge's ol' lady* – Manages club-owned Tioga Pet Crematorium

Reese – *Deacon's ol' lady* – Civil law attorney

Jemma – Cage's ol' lady – Hospice Nurse, Judge's younger sister

Former Originals:

Buck Davis – *President* – Deceased

Razor Stevens – *VP* - Deceased

Ox – *Sgt at Arms* – Deceased

Crazy Pete – *Treasurer* – Deceased

Tin Man (Tinny) – Deceased

Others:

Tessa – Trip's younger sister, Cage and Jemma's house mouse

Reilly – Reese's sister, works at Dutch's Garage

Henry (Ry) – Judge's son

Daisy – Cassie's daughter

Syn Stevens – Sig's sister
Saylor – Rev's sister, Judge and Cassie's house mouse
Silvia Stevens – Sig's mother, Razor's former ol' lady
Tammy Davis – Trip's mother, Buck's former ol' lady
Bebe Dietrich – Cage & Rook's mother, Dutch's former ol' lady
Clyde Davis – Buck's father, Trip & Sig's grandfather, deceased
Lizzy/Billie/Angel/Amber/Crystal/Brandy – Sweet butts
Max Bryson – *Chief of Police* – Manning Grove PD, Bryson brother
Marc Bryson – *Corporal* – Manning Grove PD, Bryson brother
Matt Bryson – *Officer* – Manning Grove PD, Bryson brother
Adam Bryson – *Officer* – Manning Grove PD, Brysons' cousin, Teddy's husband
Leah Bryson – *Officer* – Manning Grove PD, Marc's wife
Jet Bryson – *Officer* – Manning Grove PD, Adam's sister
Tommy Dunn – *Officer* – Manning Grove PD
Teddy Bryson – Owner Manes on Main, Adam Bryson's husband
Amanda Bryson – Max's wife, owner Boneyard Bakery
Carly Bryson – Matt's wife, OB/GYN doctor
Levi Bryson – Adopted son of Matt & Carly Bryson (birth mother: Autumn)

Prologue

STOLEN

THE SWEETNESS of the chocolate and vanilla swirl coated his tongue as soon as he took a lick.

He loved ice cream.

His mommy knew just how much, too. It was why every time she dragged him to the big building with all the busy stores, and the even bigger parking lot, she bought him an ice cream cone.

Because he'd been a good boy.

He hated this place, but sometimes it was worth going with her just to get his special treat. It had to be a swirl.

He followed his mommy out the doors and into the night, his sticky fingers leaving marks on the glass. His mommy had taught him to look both ways before stepping out into the street so he didn't get smashed by a car.

This wasn't really a street, but cars still drove on it. Sometimes really fast.

Most of the time she made him hold her hand so he'd keep up. She told him it was because he got "distracted." He didn't understand what she meant.

Tonight her hands were so full with bags, she couldn't hold his.

One time when she wasn't holding his hand, he forgot to look. She grabbed his elbow, jerked him back onto the sidewalk, yanked his arm straight up and swatted his butt really hard.

He didn't like that.

It made him cry.

She cried, too, and tried to hide it. But he saw it and it made him cry more.

He didn't like when his mommy was sad.

When Daddy left, she cried all the time.

He'd climb into her lap and put his hand on her wet cheeks and ask why she was crying. Did she miss Daddy?

She'd hug him close and never answer him. But the hug felt good, because he missed his daddy, too.

Julian didn't know what he did wrong to make his daddy never come back. His mommy would tell him he didn't do anything, but Julian didn't believe her.

Maybe he'd been bad. Maybe Daddy was mad at him.

Now Daddy was gone, Mommy always brought him with her to this place.

The place with all the people and cars.

The place where he sometimes got spanked, but also got ice cream.

His favorite kind.

He looked both ways again because he couldn't remember if he already did. Maybe that was what Mommy meant by him being "distracted."

Sometimes he had to think really, really hard to follow what she said or remember what she taught him, so he wouldn't get a spanking.

She always said those spankings were for his own good. So, he guessed that was okay.

He wanted to be good for his mommy so she wouldn't leave, too.

Because if she left, he'd be all alone.

He didn't want to be alone. Being alone was scary.

If he was alone, no one would talk to him.

Without his mommy, he wouldn't get any more chocolate and vanilla swirled ice cream.

When he saw no cars coming, he jumped off the sidewalk onto the lane where the cars drove. Where he could be smashed.

He ran to catch up to his mommy.

She was talking on her phone and walking so fast! Why wasn't she waiting for him?

He couldn't run and lick his ice cream cone at the same time. He had to walk slowly and be careful.

The ice cream began to drip, so he stopped and licked his hand. When he looked up again, he knew he had to catch up. She'd be mad if he got too far behind.

"Julian, let's go! It's late." She was still walking and talking. She wasn't waiting for him.

With a last lick of his cone and another lick at another fat milky drop on his hand, he began to run again and his shoelace started to flap. Mommy needed to tie it for him.

"My sneaker—" He stumbled when he stepped on his lace. He almost fell but caught himself so he didn't skin his knees. It always burned when he did that.

When his arms went out like an airplane to stop from falling, his ice cream cone tumbled from his fingers. His mouth made an *O* as he watched it plop upside down onto the pavement.

He stared at the mess it made, and his ice cream began to make brown and white octopus legs around the cone as it melted.

His eyes began to sting just like when she spanked him. "I d-dropped my ice cream, M-mommy!"

"Julian! Hurry up!" She sounded mad now.

But he dropped his ice cream! He wasn't done with it.

With every step his mother took, she got farther and farther away.

She always spent way too long inside the big building. Way too long inside those stores.

Sometimes it wasn't worth the ice cream.

Like now.

Because he dropped it.

He squatted down and picked up the cone, but none of the ice cream came with it. It was almost all a muddy puddle now. The cone had broken, too.

"Mommy!" A sob bubbled up his chest and he let it out. He didn't care if anyone thought he was a baby. "Mommy!"

His heart was beating so fast and he had a hard time seeing Mommy since he was crying.

He stood up and, with one last look at his ruined treat, he began to walk again, trying not to trip. His lace whipped around like a snake he saw at the zoo. He watched as it flipped back and forth with each step.

Flip. Flop.

It was fun.

"Mommy!" he called. He couldn't remember where their car was. He could never remember. "Mommy!"

"Julian, come on!" she called out as she stepped back out from between two parked cars. She was no longer talking on her stupid phone and the bags were on the ground at her feet.

He tried to run again but almost tripped. "Mommy, tie my shoe," he shouted.

As he got closer, she disappeared again between what he finally remembered was their van and another big black van, a lot bigger than theirs.

He stopped and stared at it.

Stranger danger.

That was what Mommy taught him about big vans like that. To stay away from them. To never get in a car with a stranger. To scream if someone tried to get him inside a car or a van.

But their van was parked next to it. That was where Mommy was waiting for him. He didn't have to worry about the black one. It belonged to someone inside... He stopped and turned to look at the big building. The mall. That was what she called it. He had a hard time remembering.

He spotted his spilled ice cream again, even though the parking lot was full of shadows. He took a breath so big it sucked his belly in and then he pushed all the air back out so he wouldn't cry again. He rubbed the back of his hand over his eyes and his nose.

Mommy hadn't seen him crying yet. He didn't want her to know he wasn't a big boy. That he was a crybaby. If he told her what happened, maybe she'd stop on the way home and get him another one.

That was what she'd do! Because Mommy loved him. Not like Daddy.

He spun and ran, doing his best not to fall, to the spot where she disappeared.

He stumbled to a stop.

Two men were standing with his mommy.

She looked really scared.

She was crying and her eyes went wide when she spotted him.

Julian didn't like the way she looked.

He didn't like the way they were holding her.

She didn't look happy at all. She looked really upset.

She looked like this after Daddy left.

He couldn't understand what she was saying because of the man's hand covering her mouth.

"Mommy?"

The side of the black van was open, and they were trying to put her inside.

Her arms were moving and her feet were kicking. She didn't like what they were doing. *Stranger danger!*

She was fighting them so much, it took both of them to shove her into the van.

"Jul—"

A needle appeared in the one man's hand.

He hated needles! He hated going to the doctor to get shots.

They always gave him ouchies.

He ran over to them to stop them from giving his mommy an ouchie, too.

"Mommy!"

He was too late. The bigger man with the baseball cap and the bushy beard pushed it into Mommy. The other man who was short and fat turned toward Julian.

"What the fuck?" he shouted so loudly, Julian wanted to cover his ears.

"What are you doing to my mommy?"

"Fuck, asshole. She's got a kid."

Julian ran to the opening of the van and saw his mommy now lying on her stomach and not moving. There wasn't a seat in the back like in their own van, she was right on the floor.

Was his mommy sleeping?

Was she dead?

She wasn't moving. She wasn't crying. She wasn't screaming any more. She wasn't scared.

"Mommy!" He reached for her and the fat man grabbed his arm and yanked him away.

"What the fuck are we gonna do with this kid?"

The tall man shrugged. "Leave him here?"

"We leave him here, someone's gonna find him and this will be reported."

"Then we take him with us."

"And do what with him?"

"Who fucking cares, asshole! We can dump him some-where, or let the boss deal with him."

"Don't think he was part of the deal."

"Just get the fuck in the van before someone sees us and calls the cops."

"You told me to take her car." He held up a set of keys and shook them, making them jingle.

"Then get in her minivan and shut the fuck up. Gonna call the boss and ask what he wants done with him."

"He's gonna be pissed."

"Maybe not. This kid's the right age. He's probably worth something."

"Maybe we can get money for him ourselves."

"Fuck that. I'm not risking that shit. We'll let the boss decide."

"Get in the van, kid," the tall one demanded.

"I don't wanna get in the van. I want my mommy!"

"Get in the damn van!" The fat man jerked on his arm. Julian winced. "Ow!"

Stranger danger.

What did mommy say he was supposed to do?

Yell!

Julian opened his mouth and let out a loud shriek.

A hand clamped over his mouth, stifling his yell. He bared his teeth and bit as hard as he could.

"Fuckin' A, you little asshole!"

Julian was struck alongside his head.

"Look, kid. We'll kill her if you don't cooperate. You need to be a good boy or you'll never see your mommy again."

What? He'd never see his mommy again?

Tears began to leak from his eyes.

"You think he understands any of that, asshole? He's what? Three?"

"He ain't three. Are ya, kid?"

No, he was four.

That was what his mommy told him when he blew out the candle on his birthday cake. It was ice cream, too. Chocolate and vanilla with chocolate crumbles in between.

But he couldn't answer, the man's hand was covering his mouth.

"Doesn't fucking matter how old he is. We got something to tie his ass up?"

"Need to keep him quiet, too. Can't be driving and hearing his ass screaming."

The fat man's big belly jiggled when he laughed. "Now I'm glad I'm driving her car. Wouldn't want to listen to that."

"Let's get him tied up and gagged then."

"We need to tie her up, too, in case that shit wears off."

"It won't."

"You wanna risk it?"

He tried getting loose, he tried biting the man's hand again. Nothing was working.

His mommy still wasn't moving.

She couldn't help him.

She couldn't.

He was supposed to fight and shout, "Stranger danger!"

But he couldn't.

He hated the mall.

He never wanted to come back here.

Mommy would have to get him ice cream somewhere else from now on.

He wasn't coming back here again.

He wasn't.

He needed to wipe his eyes so he could see. He needed to wipe his nose so he could breathe. Snot was filling it and the man's hand was smearing it.

He was thrown onto the dirty floor of the van and before he could scream again as loud as possible, something was tied tightly around his mouth. It tasted yucky. He'd eaten dirt before and that was what it tasted like.

His arms began to hurt because they were yanked behind his back and his hands couldn't move anymore. He couldn't kick because the man tied his legs together.

The big side door slammed shut and the back of the van got darker.

He no longer heard the men talking.

He couldn't see the front of the van. He could only hear another door opening and slamming shut. Someone starting the van. The rumble of the floor beneath his wet cheek.

He stared at his mommy's face, making a wish just like he had with his birthday cake. He squeezed his eyes shut really, really hard and wished and wished and wished.

He wished Mommy would help him.

He wished she'd tell him what was happening.

He wished she'd open her eyes.

She didn't.

None of that happened.

Not until much later.

Chapter One

Shade's boots crunched on dead leaves as he worked his way through the woods. Since he knew the area inside and out now, he no longer needed to refer to his hand-drawn map. He no longer needed to refer to the marks—the symbols and numbers—he'd made on that map, either.

He should probably burn it since it was evidence. It was always best not to keep shit like that around.

Which was why he was dragging tonight's catch behind him down the mountain instead of leaving it behind. He didn't care that it made more noise than his footsteps.

Tonight he hadn't needed to go all the way up to the main clearing. Instead, he stumbled upon a "guard" close to the bottom. The Shirley clan had set up a few since the last time the Blood Fury went up Hillbilly Hill to bring home one of their own.

The first time, last November, it had been to retrieve a pregnant Autumn, aka Red. Sig's ol' lady.

Then last week, they all went up again to take back more stolen Fury property. The hillbilly inbreds had knocked Jemma out and taken Cage's baby girl, Dyna. Then had the balls, or the lack of brains, to use her as a tool for an ambush.

The Fury wasn't playing anymore. They had warned the Guardians of Freedom, a sovereign nation otherwise known as the Shirley Clan, not to fuck with them after the first time.

They dared to fuck with them again.

Now the Fury was fucking them up the ass without any lube. Not even with a little bit of spit.

They were doing it quietly.

Carefully.

Slowly.

While Judge, the sergeant at arms, along with their prez, Trip, were in charge of this undertaking, Shade was the main player.

He asked them. They agreed.

Shade had nothing to lose.

Nothing at all.

Not like some of his brothers who had families, like Cage and Judge, or ol' ladies, like Trip, Sig and Deacon. Or siblings, like most of the rest.

Shade had no one.

If he fucked up and something happened to him, it would be no loss. No one would mourn. Except maybe his brothers.

And anyway, out of all of his club brothers, he was an expert with knives. A quiet, efficient way to cull the herd of hillbilly goat fuckers.

While the rest knew how to handle guns, Shade did not. He stuck with what was familiar. What felt natural in his hand.

What he'd used in the past to keep himself breathing. What he'd also used when he was too tired to breathe anymore.

But that was only one time during a moment of weakness.

He'd been stolen once. He decided he wouldn't let those people steal him again by forcing his hand to do something drastic.

So, he didn't let them.

Just like he wouldn't let the Shirleys get away with stealing women or children. Or injuring his brothers, like they had with Ozzy and Dodge.

Thank fuck both of them got off easy.

Unlike the Shirleys.

He glanced at the man behind him, who was now dirtier from being dragged through the undergrowth of the forest than when he'd been standing on two feet.

The fucker had been holding an AR-15 and casually smoking when Shade came upon him. He'd also been taking a lot of nips at a flask tucked in his dirty cargo pants. It was the smoke that gave him away while the moonshine made the man numb and dumb. Dumber than normal.

He was Shade's perfect target. Snagging the man wouldn't raise the alarm. They were too far from the compound.

It had been way too easy.

Shade stood hidden to the left of the man and threw a rock to the right.

Easy distraction. The Shirley was too stupid to realize it.

As the hillbilly turned to look toward the noise, Shade snuck up and made a clean slice under the man's thick beard before he even knew what was happening.

Standing behind the fucker until Shade was sure the job was done, he couldn't see the man's face, but he was sure it was full of surprise since he dropped the hand-rolled and the AR-15. Then the Shirley slowly collapsed to his knees, his own hand trying to stem the flow of blood rushing from the ear to ear slice.

Not that anything could stop it. Fuck no, it was too late.

Once his target's heart stopped and his lungs went still, Shade slung the semi-automatic rifle over his back using the strap to secure it there. He grabbed both ankles and began to hoof it down the short distance to Copperhead Road, where he'd left the van.

Black, windowless. Just like the one when he was four.

But this one was used for Tioga Pet Crematorium, one of the club's businesses. It was only used to steal Shirleys. Not women and children.

At least, not yet.

They still hadn't decided what to do with the kids—forty of them and growing—in the compound. Or the women.

They decided to only worry about the men first. Once everyone with hair on their balls was extinct, they could decide about the rest.

A decision no one really wanted to make.

Truthfully, Shade didn't, either. He preferred to leave the kids with their mommas. Especially since he never had that chance.

He ground his back molars and pushed onward.

After a few more minutes of dragging the dead weight, he saw the van where he'd hidden it on the opposite side of Copperhead Road in the woods. He had built a "screen" of branches and brush to hide the van from any eyes. Especially pigs.

He didn't want any of them greeting him in the middle of the night with his bounty. Not only would that be fucking awkward, it would raise some questions.

Just a few.

Ones he wouldn't answer.

He'd gotten away his whole adult life never spending a minute behind bars, unlike most of his brothers, and he wanted to keep it that way.

He'd spent too much time in a different type of prison. Ten of his thirty years.

A whole fucking decade.

He reminded himself now was not the time to revisit that shit...

That was the past. He'd spent the last sixteen years trying to move past it.

He hadn't. Never would. But he tried not to give it more than a fucking minute of his time, at least while he was awake. He spent too much time in the past while he slept.

Or tried to sleep.

Shade glanced both ways before crossing the dark road to make sure no vehicles were coming. He dropped the body at the bottom of the mountain lane, jogged across the road and down fifty feet. He quickly uncovered the van and drove it back to the bottom of Hillbilly Hill.

He could have dragged the man behind him, across the pavement and to the van, but that would leave evidence.

Blood. Hair. Skin. Pieces of clothing.

He shoved the van into Park, jogged around to the side and threw open the sliding door.

He tucked the AR-15 into the van under a tarp. He'd put it in his secret hiding spot, where he was putting all the weapons he came across. His spot wasn't on the farm since Trip didn't want them there. Most of his club brothers were ex-felons, a couple still on probation or parole, and if the pigs—local, state or feds—found a stash of weapons on the club's property, it would cause issues.

Trip and Judge had told him to put them elsewhere. If Shade left them behind, the Shirleys would find them and use them against the Fury.

The less men, the less weapons, the better.

Even so, Shade didn't want to destroy them, just in case the Fury needed to arm themselves in the future. They'd been outgunned the last time. They couldn't let that happen again.

All the Shirley's weapons were untraceable for the most part. Not registered, no serial numbers, nothing. Good for the Fury if they got into any kind of war.

He spread out another tarp over the floor of the van, and once he wrangled the bled-out redneck onto it, he wrapped it securely around the body.

Just like when he picked up dead animals for cremation.

Not dogs and cats. But like pigs and goats and the rest of those livestock animals he wasn't sure why people made them pets.

Wasn't his business.

Running the crematorium made the club scratch. It made him scratch.

Money he'd been stashing away.

He slammed the side door closed, ran around to the driver's side and didn't turn on the headlights until a half mile down the road, preferring to use the light of the moon to guide him in the direction of Tioga Pet Crematorium.

Best fucking club purchase Deacon, the club's treasurer, ever recommended.

But then Deacon was fucking smart.

Unlike Shade.

SHADE SHOVED the van's shifter into Park and twisted his head toward the passenger seat. "Ready?"

With a quick glance over at him, Cassie gave him a single nod. "Yes. I swear this never gets easier."

That was because she had a fucking heart. She cared about people and their pets.

To Shade, this was just a part of the job. Of him being a part of the Fury. He did what he had to do for his club and for himself. To him, this was just another day in the many days since he arrived in Manning Grove and became a prospect. Since he proved himself last fall and earned his patches.

He carefully formed his next words. "Don't gotta do it. Could teach me how."

Judge's ol' lady shook her blonde head and stared out of the passenger side window to the house they were parked in front of.

The house wasn't huge, but it was well-kept.

Most people who could afford it preferred to put their pets "to sleep" at home.

They hired them because they wanted their pets treated with respect, even after they were dead. Cassie made sure that happened. Their customers' pets got treated better than a lot of humans.

He didn't quite understand it, but then he'd never had a pet. At least not one with fur and any kind of intelligence. He'd named a few spiders and other kinds of bugs that had lived with him in...

No. Not now.

He switched mental gears back to real pets. Like Jury and Justice.

He saw how Deacon and Judge interacted with their American Bulldogs and that always caught his attention.

Maybe he should get a dog.

He'd rather have a loyal dog for a bed companion than one of those sweet butts. Not that he'd be doing the same thing to his dog as a sweet butt.

That would be just wrong. He knew that now.

But when he was a boy he'd seen things...

No. Not now.

He reminded himself to concentrate on the present.

Cassie sighed softly and pushed open the van door. "Can you grab my bag?"

Of course he could. He always did.

Whatever Cassie wanted, Shade did.

He liked and respected Cassie a lot. She was a kind soul. Funny, too. But she was always trying to get him to talk more. She was always asking him questions, trying to figure him out, trying to discover his secrets and what made him tick.

Shit he didn't share with anyone.

One time she just came out of nowhere and gave him a bear hug, scaring the shit out of him.

When he pulled free, he asked, "Why'd you do that?"

"Because it looked like you needed one," was the answer she gave him with her pretty smile. Though, that time it was tinged with sadness. Then she simply walked away.

Judge did good with Cassie. Daisy, on the other hand, was debatable. The six-year-old could be a sassy little shit. But the club's enforcer doted on the girl and he was the one who had to live with the kid, not Shade.

He needed to get out of his fucking head and focus on the job ahead. His thoughts drifted a lot, and it took an effort sometimes to keep them on track.

Like today.

But then, he was tired, which made it worse. He'd started the large animal furnace last night at two a.m. and it didn't automatically shut off until early this morning. After it cooled down, he had to collect the ashes and put them in a container for disposal.

He hid that container until he found a chance to spread the ashes in one of the far fields on the farm. Eventually those ashes would be turned with the dirt when the Amish came with their plows and draft horses and their pretty daughters.

He might not be smart, but he certainly wasn't as dumb as Sig and Cage for touching an Amish girl. Sig and Cage's last names could've been Shirley after those dumb shits fucked up and almost screwed up the relationship between the Amish and the club. That pissed off Trip to no end.

Shade wouldn't make that mistake. He kept his hands to himself. No pussy was worth getting his colors stripped.

He went to the back of the van and grabbed Cassie's bag with the things she'd need to humanely put down the homeowner's pet.

A cat.

That was what Cassie said.

In truth, she could've come by herself. She could handle a cat on her own. But Shade didn't like her going out on calls by herself if he or Easy were available. Not with all the Shirleys who were still breathing.

Judge appreciated his diligence. But he didn't do it for Judge, he did it for Cassie.

He walked up the flower-lined brick walkway to the porch of the small two-story house. It was a simple red brick home with a black-painted door, black shutters and plain white trim. It had a two-story, two-car garage attached that almost doubled the size of the house.

He stood on the porch, staring at the door, wondering if he should knock.

He never should've let Cassie go inside alone. He raised his fist, but before he could rap on it, the door swung open.

A young woman stood on the other side. Pretty. Maybe about twenty or so. Long, straight legs. Too slender for his taste. No tits or curves to her. She had to grow up a little more. Become a woman. She needed more dips and valleys yet.

Her big brown eyes were red-rimmed, and her strawberry-blonde hair was pulled up into a long, straight ponytail, the same way he was wearing his. Her nose was also red and running since she was sniffling.

Obviously, she'd been crying. That happened often on these calls.

The owners cried. Sometimes a lot. Sometimes too much.

"Come in," the girl said with a thick voice, swinging the door open wider. "Cassie said you were right behind her."

He gave her a nod and stepped into the tiny tiled foyer. The staircase to the second floor was in front of him, a room was on his left, another one to his right.

He wasn't sure which way to go.

"In here." The girl pushed past him and headed to the right.

"There he is," Cassie said with relief when she spotted him. "Mrs. Goodson, this is my helper, Shawn."

Shawn. It was a name she came up with on the fly months and months ago, the first time they both went to a customer's home. She didn't think his road name Shade was a good way to introduce him. It might cause questions, especially if he wore his cut. Which he didn't. Cassie didn't allow it during working hours when dealing with the public.

Shade didn't care. She could call him whatever. A name was just that, a name. It didn't define who he was.

Only his past could do that.

So, he went with it.

"Shawn, this is Rachelle Goodson. She..."

Shade was focused on another girl sitting on the floor holding a cat wrapped in a blanket. She looked just like the twenty-year-old, but younger. Maybe seventeen or eighteen. He wasn't sure.

Not that it mattered.

Naturally pretty, though. Boys probably were drawn to both girls. Sisters, most likely.

That one had a tissue crumpled in one hand and tears running unchecked down her face.

"Hello." The greeting was husky but feminine. Also tinged with sadness.

He glanced up from the teenager holding the cat and

focused on the woman standing next to Cassie. The one with the voice that caused his gut to heat up when he heard it.

Cassie was curvy as fuck. She had a surplus of tits and ass, plus thick thighs that would cushion a man's hips just right. Judge's ol' lady was like prime rib. Just enough fat to make the meat tender, where some of the sweet butts were like gnawing on a porkchop bone. No meat, no fat, no flavor.

The woman standing next to her was curvy but not Cassie curvy. She also wasn't as tall as Judge's woman. She wasn't petite, but her legs weren't as long and thick, either. However, they were shapely, not straight sticks. More like a drumstick worth nibbling on.

He blinked slowly as he took her in, then let his gaze slice over the two younger women.

They could all be sisters.

Maybe.

Though the older one wore glasses and everything about her looked more mature. Her eyes held more wisdom, too.

She'd lived a life. She wasn't just starting out.

No, not a sister.

Mother.

Same strawberry-blonde hair, same big brown eyes.

"Shawn?" Cassie prodded like she always did when he disappeared into his head and forgot to talk.

He shook himself mentally.

What did she want him to say?

Oh yeah. "Nice to meet you... Mrs..." *Fuck,* he forgot her last name already.

"Rachelle. Most people just call me Chelle." She took a deep inhale and held out her hand. "I wish we were meeting under better circumstances."

He raised his gaze from her feet, which were tucked into fancy flip-flops. The toenails were all painted a light pink. Nothing flashy like the nail polish the sweet butts wore.

"Sorry," he muttered, taking her fingers in his. Not shaking her hand but just holding it.

Her skin was warm and soft, her grip firm. Confident.

He liked that.

She had a strong backbone. This wasn't a woman who'd fall apart at the slightest thing.

No.

He fucking *really* liked that.

"Me, too," she said softly, staring at him with her brow dipped low as she attempted to subtly extract her hand from his.

For some reason, he didn't want to let her go.

But if he didn't, she'd think it was weird. That something was wrong with him.

Plenty of things were wrong with him, but he tried not to make it obvious. So, he released her hand, dragging the tips of his fingers along her palm when he did so.

He caught her soft, ragged inhale and the curl of her fingers into her palm, like his touch had hurt.

Would never hurt you, he assured her in his head.

"You let us know when you're ready," Cassie told them, pulling his attention back to the room.

"We're ready," Chelle said as a single tear rolled from the corner of her eye. A couple creases marked both sides.

Yeah, not a sister.

Definitely their mother.

Maybe late thirties, early forties.

She wasn't what he'd call pretty, not like the younger ones, but beautiful.

Yeah, she was fully grown. She already lived through a lot of mistakes. Her daughters still had a lot of mistakes to make yet.

He took a quick glance around the room and his eyes

landed on a bunch of framed photos on the fireplace mantel. One photo was of a bride and groom. The bride looked just like the twenty-year-old who greeted him at the door and the young man wore a uniform. Had to be the mother when she was younger. When she got married and added that *Mrs.* to her name.

He wondered why the husband wasn't with his girls. Maybe he was at work.

Or didn't give a fuck about the cat.

He thought carefully about his question before he asked it, "We waitin' on anyone?"

Chelle shook her head. "No. We're all here."

"Mom," the one on the floor said. "I'm not ready." Tears were now dripping off her chin and her nose was running unchecked.

Chelle gave her daughter a lopsided smile that didn't reach her big brown eyes behind those glasses. "I know, sweetheart, but Pumpkin is ready. We don't want him suffering anymore."

Shade glanced at the orange tabby in the girl's arms. Only its head was visible from the blanket.

"It old?" he asked.

"Eighteen," the older girl answered, moving to join her sister on the floor. "Can we hold him while you do it?" she asked Cassie.

"Yes, if that's what you'd like. You can comfort him. It'll be painless. I promise."

"And then what happens?" the younger one asked.

"Then he'll go to sleep," Cassie said.

That wasn't quite what happened.

"Forever." The youngest glanced up at her mother. "Then what, Mom?"

"We already decided this, Josie." The words came firm, but gentle. Like a mom should sound.

Josie sniffled, nodded and hugged Pumpkin to her chest. The cat gave a weak meow.

The older girl put her arm around her sister and glanced up at Cassie. "Okay."

"Do you want to join them on the floor?" Cassie asked Chelle, holding out her hand for the bag Shade still held.

"No, I'll let them..." The woman's words faded off as her mouth wobbled. She was trying to remain strong, trying not to lose it in front of her kids.

Cassie nodded in understanding and got on the floor with the girls, opening up her kit and doing her thing.

Shade stared at the mother. She was struggling not to bawl.

Over a cat.

Shade glanced at the animal while Cassie quickly shaved a spot on its leg to prepare it for what came next.

Cassie wasn't crying yet. She always did her best to wait until after they left the house. But sometimes she couldn't help it.

It was who she was. She felt things deeply.

This was probably not the best job for her.

If she would train Shade to do it, he'd get it done quickly, efficiently and without one tear.

Shade stopped watching Cassie, because he knew the procedure, and watched Rachelle Goodson instead. He could tell what stage Cassie was in the process just by watching the woman's face. He could read it even though Chelle tried to hide it.

He was good at that. Picking up on other people's emotions.

He was once told it was a gift.

He was also once told that it was surprising that someone so stupid like him could be gifted like that.

But his skill at observation made up for his lack of conversation.

Chelle's mouth tightened as she rolled her lips under when her daughters both began to sob. Her fingers flexed like she wanted to hold them, which she probably did, but she waited.

She let her girls have the time they needed to say goodbye to their pet.

A member of their family. That was what all their customers said. Their cat or dog or parakeet was a member of their family. Their child.

Their pets were treated better than a lot of children.

When their pets suffered, they could make a decision to end it. Most children who suffered didn't get that choice.

They had to bear it. Live with it. Let it shape them and their future.

He didn't know how long he stood there. Frozen in time. Watching. Observing the woman standing not ten feet from him.

Eventually she lifted her gaze from the activity on the floor to him. She quickly hid her confused expression but didn't look away.

No.

She fucking held his gaze. Strong. Brave. Unwavering.

Something about her soothed his soul. Made his thoughts calm and clearer.

He couldn't look away, even if he wanted to.

It wasn't only the big expressive eyes with the thick black lashes that held intelligence, it was the length and shape of her nose. The curve and thickness of her lips. The shape of her eyebrows. The color of her hair. The way it fell loosely around her shoulders but looked a bit disheveled. Like she'd been running her fingers through it out of habit. Or out of worry.

Her hair fell just past her shoulders but wasn't as long as his. Hers was straight for the most part while his was curly, went past his shoulders and fell down his back when he didn't have it pulled up. He put it up when he needed to keep it under control and out of his face. Like when he rode his sled. Or when he was working.

But he'd always kept it long. It began to grow out of control after that day in the mall parking lot. No one ever cut it. Not one of them. They let it go. They loved the length. The curls. The way they could manipulate his head by using his hair. The way they could use it as a leash. The way they could use it to dole out pain and, on a rare occasion, pleasure.

At seventeen he had it shorn down to the scalp, so no one could control him with his hair again. But he hated it. He felt too exposed without hair. He immediately let it grow again until it felt comfortable. Until he went back to feeling like himself.

Or at least, who he thought he was.

By growing it back out, he took that control back. Not letting them rule his life in any way. If he wanted it long, he would keep it long. No one else would dictate the length.

Fuck them all.

Even though he preferred it long, he never wanted anyone touching it.

Never again.

Angel, one of the sweet butts, tried to touch it one night and he almost broke her wrist. He didn't realize how tightly he had a hold of her until she began to cry.

Sig wasn't happy that he'd left a bruise on one of the sweet butts when she hadn't asked for it. The VP said that if Shade needed to create bruises to get off to find a woman who was willing to take them.

That wasn't what it was about, but he didn't bother to explain it to Sig. Shade let it go. So did Angel, but she never tried to touch his hair again.

For some unexplainable reason, he wanted the woman

standing before him to touch it. To run her fingers through it.

He wanted to see his loose curls against her tits when he sucked them. Against her thighs when he touched her down there with his mouth, too. He wanted his hair to curtain around their faces as he sunk his dick deep inside her, so it was just her and him, hiding from the rest of the world. Her wet warmth surrounding him, comforting him.

Giving him solace and peace.

Something sex had never done for him before.

It was strange...

He believed being with her would give him that.

He had no idea why.

He just knew.

Her lips parted and her eyes widened slightly behind her lenses, her pupils dilating. Not enough for anyone else to notice, but he did.

Even from where he stood, he could see the rapid pulse in her neck as she swallowed, and the change in the pace her chest rose and fell.

He flared his nostrils and inhaled slowly, deeply, to pick up the slight change in her scent.

Subtle. For him.

A reaction to his attention.

She was fighting it. As she should.

He was only there for a job.

Her now permanently sleeping cat.

Her body jerked sharply, their gazes broke and they were both pulled from the strange spell when Cassie's voice invaded his head. "Uh... *Shawn?*"

He forced himself to glance her way. She was still sitting on the floor, but now frowning up at him.

"Shawn... Can you take Pumpkin out to the van?"

Usually the family spent time with the pet after it was gone. Talking. Petting. Crying.

Had they done that already?

Had he been so lost in *her* he hadn't noticed how the time had slipped away?

He gave Cassie a nod and took the cat from the older daughter's arms. It was still warm, the body still flexible, but even wrapped in the blanket he could tell it had been mostly skin and bones.

It seemed like that was what happened to old pets, they began to wither away to nothing. Eventually they'd probably turn to dust, but Cassie helped them get there quicker. Didn't let them suffer any longer than necessary.

He knew Chelle followed on his heels, because he could pick up her scent swirling around them in the air as they walked. Nothing heavy. Nothing floral. But more like...

Vanilla, maybe.

Cinnamon.

Apple pie?

Mixed with the slightest scent of woman. A woman who was enjoying what a man was doing to her.

Not the scent of fear.

Had he caused her arousal?

He ignored it and kept moving but as he reached the front door, she pushed past him, her arm brushing his. She opened the door for him, not looking at what he carried in his arms, but staring at him instead.

Trying to figure him out.

Trying to see what lurked inside him.

He wasn't worried she'd succeed. No one ever had.

She cleared her throat and that movement under the delicate skin of her long neck caught his attention.

Fuck. He wanted to touch her throat. He tightened his grip on the cat to avoid doing just that.

"I'm sorry. I didn't have a chance for a last goodbye," she said in a broken whisper.

He kept his voice low, too. "Didn't wanna break down in front of your girls."

Relief from his understanding filled her eyes. "No."

He jerked his chin toward the road. "At the van. Away from the house."

She nodded and once they stepped outside, she closed the door behind her.

He hoped Cassie stayed with the girls a little longer. They'd need her. Then they'd need their mother.

That meant his time with Chelle was limited.

He strode quickly to the back of the van and she followed right behind him.

When he got there, he opened one side of the back double doors, then turned. "Wanna hold him? Or you want me to put him down?"

"If you could hold him, please. I'll say a quick goodbye."

He didn't understand the point of saying goodbye once something stopped breathing, but he let her have this. It was what she needed.

It also gave him a few more minutes with her. Something he needed.

She uncovered the cat's head and leaned in, her reddish-blonde hair brushing against his chest, sweeping over his arms. Tempting him.

He wanted to rub the silky strands between his fingers, lift them to his nose.

"Goodbye, Pumpkin. You've been a good boy." She kissed its head.

You've been a good boy...

No. Not now.

Shade did his best not to grimace. Not because of what she said, but because she put her lips on a dead animal. And not the kind served on a plate.

Her fingers wrapped around his forearm as she straightened and she stood closer than he normally liked, but her proximity didn't bother him. In fact, he liked it.

He more than liked it. He wanted to be even closer. She wasn't close enough.

"Thank you," she whispered and her sob turned into a little hiccup.

Shade closed his eyes, concentrated really hard, and slowly recited the speech Cassie had taught him. "Thank you for choosin' us in your time of need. If we can be of service in the future, please don't hesitate to contact us."

He opened his eyes to see Chelle frowning up at him.

Didn't he get it right?

It sounded okay in his head. Which words did he screw up? Did he just show her how stupid he was?

Fuck. He should've let Cassie say that part. But he didn't want Chelle walking away.

Not yet.

"I screw up?"

She reached under her glasses to wipe away a tear clinging to her long eyelashes with the back of her knuckle. But her lips were curved up slightly in an amused smile. "That sounded rehearsed."

She didn't say if he got any of the words wrong. "You understood?"

Surprise filled her brown eyes. "Yes, of course. You said it slowly enough. I understood you just fine. What you said, though, sounded like a canned response."

Because it was. "Yeah," he said, relieved he hadn't fucked up the speech.

"It doesn't fit you."

"What fits me?"

Cassie joined them. Thank fuck because he hadn't wanted Chelle to answer that. Cassie's head swiveled back and forth from Shade to Chelle and finally landed on the woman's hand on Shade's arm. "We'll deliver his ashes back to you in the wood box you already chose."

Chelle nodded. "Thank you."

Shade knew one thing. He'd be the one delivering those fucking ashes.

Chelle removed her hand and stepped back, breaking their connection. "When will I get him back?"

"It takes a couple of—"

Shade interrupted Cassie with, "Tomorrow." He ignored her raised eyebrows. "Will bring him back tomorrow. What day?"

"You just said tomorrow, Shawn," Cassie reminded him with a pointed look.

For fuck's sake, he had rushed to speak and chose the wrong word. He tried again. "What time?"

Fuck. Fuck. Fuck.

"Uh... I should be home from work a little after three. So, four? Or is that too late?"

"Will be here at four," he said more carefully.

Chelle gave them both a little smile as she moved from behind the van back onto the sidewalk. "Thank you both for being so compassionate. It made such a difficult time a little easier. Pumpkin hated going to the vet and..."

When her lips stopped moving, he realized he'd been staring at them.

Cassie elbowed him in the ribs. "Shawn."

"Tomorrow," he repeated.

"See you tomorrow," Chelle answered. "Thank you."

With one last look at Shade and then the cat in his arms, she turned and went back to the house.

"Do what you need to do with Pumpkin and let's go," Cassie said with a sly grin.

No tears today.

She threw her bag in the back and went around to the passenger side.

Shade did what he had to do to secure the cat. Once he closed the rear double doors, he turned to glance at the house. He hadn't been expecting to see Chelle standing on the porch, watching him.

Maybe she thought he was a freak.

Maybe she was now worried about her daughters' safety.

Maybe she'd call Cassie tomorrow morning to tell her she didn't want Shade delivering the ashes.

She lifted her hand slightly in a sort of wave.

He jerked up his chin at her in response and headed to the driver's door.

Or maybe he'd see her tomorrow at four.

And maybe she'd smell like warm apple pie and an even warmer woman.

Chapter Two

HE WAS TOO FUCKING tired to head up the mountain tonight. He'd gotten no sleep last night since he had processed the last Shirley he bagged in the Easy Bake oven.

He spent the day cremating Chelle Goodson's cat, along with two other pets. After scooping up Pumpkin's ashes, he placed them carefully in the small carved box she ordered.

He had no idea why people wanted to keep ashes.

He didn't get it. Probably never would.

Now, he needed sleep.

He also needed to make sure he got sleep. To do so, he headed out to the pavilion where it was quieter than the bunkhouse or The Barn.

It was certainly quieter out there than Crazy Pete's.

The darkness of night guaranteed he could sit unseen for a little bit. Though, Easy knew his hiding spot and wandered out from The Barn and joined him not ten minutes later.

He hadn't said much when he came out. Once he settled on top of the picnic table next to Shade, he broke out a hand-rolled. Between puffs on his cigarette, he'd hold out his hand for a hit off Shade's joint.

If anyone knew Shade best, it was Easy since they worked at the crematorium together. His club brother didn't push him to have unnecessary conversation just to fill the void. He didn't prod Shade about his past. Most likely so Shade didn't ask Easy about his.

They all had secrets. Every fucking one of them. That was why he liked it here. Unless you wanted to share, you didn't have to. As long as you worked and were loyal to the brotherhood, you were good.

Judge didn't trust him at first and ran a background check on him. But that was all right. He'd only had minor scrapes with the law, nothing where he'd done any time. That was because he was always really fucking careful.

Really fucking careful.

He reached behind him and picked up the Mason jar he brought back on one of his trips up the mountain. He'd found a hidden stash up there. The moonshine the clan made was potent and helped numb his brain so he could sleep without dreaming.

"Where'd you get that?" Easy asked.

Shade passed it to him and, after a whiff, Easy took a sip. "Holy fuck. Shit tastes like apple pie with a toxic twist." He took another sip and grimaced.

The mention of apple pie had his thoughts turning to Chelle. He couldn't get her out of his brain.

If the moonshine and pot didn't knock his ass out, then he'd use the vision of the strawberry-blonde imprinted on his brain to help. Not many women caught his interest. But there was something about this one...

He had no idea why.

He looked forward to seeing her again tomorrow when he dropped off the cremains, but afterward he needed to scrape her from his thoughts.

She wasn't for him.

Or more like it, he wasn't for her.

She had a husband, if the photo on the mantel was any indication. Divorced women usually didn't keep photos of their ex around. Not unless they were still stuck on them.

Even without the husband, she had two daughters that he knew of. A family.

Probably a good life.

She wouldn't want to get involved with anyone who could disturb that good life.

So, yeah, he needed to forget the way she looked, the way she smelled and her soft touch on his arm.

He couldn't go there. It was best if he kept his sex life simple.

Easy exchanged the Mason jar with the joint in Shade's hand. He took a sip, while Easy sucked a deep lungful of pot and held it for what seemed like forever. But then Easy was a smoker, unlike Shade.

Shade hated cigarettes, but then, he had a reason.

The moonshine seared his gut and warmed his blood.

"That him?" Easy asked, jerking his chin at the cardboard box that had held the ashes of the former hillbilly.

Shade grunted his answer and took another sip.

"Need to burn that box," Easy said. Something Shade already knew.

He'd done it before. He'd do it again. He had a system now.

He didn't bring them all off the mountain, only when he could. Sometimes he dragged them deep into the woods and buried them under leaves and branches until the animals could get to it.

Like the coyotes. Rodents and vultures. Whatever creatures would enjoy an easy meal. Whatever they didn't eat, the worms and maggots would.

Eventually the Shirley would go back to the Earth, where they came from.

Still too many to go...

He was also worried they'd bring in more. From Ohio. Or wherever. He had no idea how extensive the Guardians of Freedom were. They probably had clusters all around the country like the KKK, another clan that needed to be wiped clean from the Earth.

He was leaving the current clan leader for last. If he took that guy out first, they would just replace him. So, he decided to leave the head of the snake intact and chop away at the body, working from the tail up.

"Fuck," he muttered as a slender figure worked her way through the dark to where he and Easy sat.

Easy glanced in the direction he was looking, then clapped him on the back. "Someone's out huntin' tonight."

"They all were. Why I came out here."

Easy let out an easy laugh. "The more you resist, the harder they work you, brother. Just give 'em a little and they'll go away."

He tried that and it didn't work.

He was not like his brothers who needed to get their rocks off just about every night in one way or another.

It wasn't that he didn't like sex. He did. It also wasn't like he needed it to mean anything. He didn't. Usually it was just mindless motion. A primal itch needing to be occasionally scratched.

But there never had been a woman in his life he'd wanted to hang onto for the long haul. Not like his brothers who had found their ol' ladies.

Even if he was looking, he wouldn't be looking in The Barn. He had a bit of a thing about sticking his dick where another man's cum might be lurking. Though, for the most part, he was pretty sure his brothers wrapped it up tight when it came to the sweet butts. Or at least, he hoped to fuck they did.

Wraps were one thing Trip made sure stayed in stock in the bunkhouse. And a lot of them. Before meeting Cassie,

Judge had always used his own. For whatever reason. Some of the other guys did, too.

Brandy, whose momma named her after the color of her hair, stopped in front of the two of them, with a tilt to her head and hands planted on her slender hips. "Why are you guys hiding out here in the dark?"

"Nobody's fuckin' hidin', sweetheart," Easy said, the smoke from the premium Kush rolling out of his mouth. "Just chillin'."

Brandy's head swiveled back and forth between him and Easy.

Yeah, she was on the hunt to fill her cunt.

"I know how to help you relax a little more."

Easy grinned. "Yeah? How?"

"However you want, baby," she answered, dropping her voice an octave lower in an attempt to make it husky and her more tempting.

Chelle's voice had that natural huskiness to it. She didn't have to force it. She also didn't have to force his attention. It had been stuck on her from the second he saw her.

"What are you drinking, Shade?" Brandy snagged the Mason jar out of his hand and took a big gulp before he could stop her. She coughed and shuddered. "Yuck! That tastes like apple-flavored turpentine."

Easy threw his head back and laughed. "It'll put hair on your chest." He grabbed the jar from her and took another swig.

"You don't even have hair on your chest," Brandy huffed. "And this one," she ran a hand up Shade's thigh from his knee toward his crotch, "never takes his shirt off for me to see."

Shade snatched her wrist before her hand reached its target and gripped it tightly, making her gasp.

"Gotta ask him first, sweetheart," Easy reminded her, "you know the rules."

Shade released her before he hurt her by mistake and she stepped back with a frown, rubbing her wrist. "He's the only one with that rule."

That was bullshit and she knew it. None of the sweet butts could touch a brother who'd claimed an ol' lady. Unless they had permission first. From what Shade saw, not one of them had given any of the club girls permission to touch them.

Especially since none of the women who'd been claimed at the table would put up with it. Not a damn one.

Ozzy told him late one night that the Originals were never faithful to their ol' ladies. He'd been a member in another club out in the Midwest, or somewhere, for years where it was a pussy free-for-all, too.

At this point, any relationships in the Fury were new. Shade figured that might change down the road when those relationships began to wear thin.

Even so, he didn't care where his brothers stuck their dicks. Wasn't his business.

Just like it wasn't theirs when it came to where Shade stuck his. Plus, everyone thought he had the club's colors inked into his back like the rest of them.

He didn't.

On the rare occasion he snagged and bagged one of the sweet butts, he made sure to keep his shirt on. His jeans, too. Otherwise, questions might be raised. Questions he didn't want to answer. Whether with the truth or a lie.

"Don't matter if he's the only one with that rule. Need to follow it," Easy warned her.

"He can speak for himself, E."

"He shouldn't have to say shit, you know his fuckin' rule."

Shade picked up on his brother's slight annoyance. It was pretty hard to piss off Easy. Like his road name indicated, he was pretty fucking easy-going. He had a lot of tolerance until he didn't, but it took a lot to get him there.

Brandy sidled up to Easy, pressing her tits into his arm and trailing her fingers up his thigh. "You don't have a rule."

Easy let her stroke the denim covering his dick. His irritation quickly disappeared. "Yeah, sweetheart, you know I don't."

Easy reached into his cut and pulled out a small metal container, similar to one most of the guys carried for their hand-rolleds and joints. He flipped it open and plucked out a half-spent joint and tucked it between his lips. He held his palm out and Shade handed him his Zippo. After lighting it, he said, "C'mere, sweetheart."

He turned the joint around, putting the lit end into his mouth, and, snagging Brandy's arm, pulled her between his cocked knees. She leaned in and put her lips over his as he shot-gunned the smoke into her mouth.

When they were done, he combed his fingers into the side of her light brown hair above her ear and gripped it tight, pulled her in for a short kiss, then yanked her head away, making her look at him. "He might not want you right now, but you touchin' me made me hard. What you gonna do about it?" He ground what was left of the joint, which now was pretty much only a roach, between his two fingers, then flicked the pieces into the dark. "Brandy."

"Yeah?"

"What you waitin' for? Asked you what you're gonna do." He leaned back a little bit to give the sweet butt room to unbuckle his belt and unfasten his jeans.

Shade was about to get a show.

Nothing new around here.

None of his brothers cared who watched. None of his brothers cared if another brother joined in on the action. As long as the woman was kept in between them, they were up for just about anything.

"Want your knees on the wood bench while you're doin' it," Easy said. "Like you're a naughty Catholic girl, prayin' for forgiveness."

Brandy was wearing a short skirt, typical for most of the sweet butts since it gave the brothers easy access. Most of the time, they didn't even bother to wear panties.

Shade figured her kneeling on the wood bench in between Easy's legs would be a bit uncomfortable on her bare skin.

As Brandy went willingly into that position, taking Easy's hard dick in her hand and wrapping her skilled lips around it, Shade began to feel that discomfort in his own knees. The pressure on his joints. The pain. The eventual loss of feeling in his legs.

Sometimes for his punishment. Most times for someone else's pleasure.

Usually for a few minutes. Occasionally for a few hours...

No. Not now.

He reached for the open Mason jar sitting on the table between him and Easy. He gripped it tightly between his fingers, swallowed a mouthful and swished it around trying to wash away the taste of that memory.

He forced his eyes to remain open because if he closed them, he'd go back there...

He spent the last thirteen years trying to move forward. But they kept trying to drag him the fuck back.

Back to a life he no longer lived.

No. Not now.

He bit the inside of his cheek until the metallic taste of blood touched his tongue.

Sometimes that worked.

Most times it didn't.

He took another hit of the joint forgotten within his fingers, wishing its effects would hurry the fuck up.

He stared at Brandy's head bobbing in Easy's lap. He had one hand gripping her hair like a ponytail to control the pace, the other propped on the table behind him. He jerked his chin at him. "Missin' out, brother."

Before he could answer, another sweet butt came out of the dark and joined them under the pavilion.

Christ, he'd have to find a new fucking hiding spot.

"What you doin', Crystal?" Easy asked the platinum blonde with the gray-blue eyes.

Tonight her hair was almost white, tomorrow it could be blue or pink. Or even pitch black. She wore frayed Daisy Dukes that were so short the white lining of the pockets peeked out. Shade was pretty damn sure, if she turned around, most of her ass would be hanging out, too. Unlike Brandy, Crystal had a little meat on her bones. That meant her ass was worth smashing. She was good with her mouth, but that ass kept her busy with his brothers.

Shade had it once. While she made a lot of noise during that quickie, it was all fake like a soundtrack from a cheesy porn video. That didn't do shit for him. He quickly shot his load, then scraped her off.

At least if she was sucking him off, he didn't have to listen to her fake moans and cries. Or at least they were muffled to a bearable level.

"I was looking for Shade," Crystal finally answered Easy after watching Brandy go to town on his dick for a few moments. She licked her lips like she was ready to tag in.

Easy turned to him. "You lookin' for Crystal?"

His brother already knew that answer, but he gave it anyway, so Crystal could hear it. "Nope."

"Sorry, sweetheart, he ain't in the mood."

She pouted. "Nobody's around inside. Rook grabbed Billie and disappeared. Lizzy went to The Grove Inn to be with Ozzy. Dodge is working... Angel's entertaining Whip... Not sure where Rev's at..."

"Don't wanna be alone?" Easy asked with a groan, both hands now wrapped around the back of Brandy's head as he fucked her face. Not gently, either.

Shade bet if he looked, Brandy's mascara was now smeared from how deep Easy was giving it to her. He expected to hear a few gags from her soon. The girls could take it deep, but only for so long.

Every time he heard one of them gag or made them gag himself, he felt that reflex at the back of his own throat.

Because of that, he always did his best not to drive that hard.

Even so, watching that action almost made Shade want to tell Crystal to get on her knees on the bench, too. He was going to blow a load tonight no matter what, whether it was by his own fist or from Crystal's mouth.

Shade considered his options as that skilled mouth said, "No. I don't want to be alone tonight." Her fake whine made the decision between his fist and Crystal's mouth an easy one.

"Well, then you can help Brandy keep me company," Easy suggested.

Her eyes lit up but she shot a glance at Shade, who didn't encourage or discourage her from taking Easy's offer.

"Sure you don't want none of this, brother? Willin' to share."

Shade shook his head as Easy grimaced when Brandy's pace increased.

"Why don't you show us your tits, Crys. Sooner I come, the sooner the three of us can go inside so Brandy and I can give you the attention you're lookin' for."

Crystal didn't even hesitate to rip off her top, squeeze her tits together and play with her nipples.

Shade's dick was finally paying attention. He took

another swig of the moonshine and ignored it. He already had his fantasy picked out for tonight. Doing Crystal might ruin it.

Anyway, he needed sleep. Crystal was sometimes hard to get rid of afterward. He was too tired to deal with that shit tonight.

"Fuck," Easy groaned, then grunted, as his hips surged up and he pushed Brandy's head down.

Crystal laughed when Brandy gagged hard.

Shade shook his head and took a long drag off the joint which was almost down to a roach. He held the smoke deep within his lungs while he watched Brandy disengage and wipe the strings of spit from her mouth with her hand.

"Now, sweetheart, give Crys a kiss. Let her taste what's she's gonna get shortly."

The two women didn't even hesitate. Their mouths locked together and Shade could see the exchange of tongues.

Then he heard Crystal's over-the-top noises.

Yeah, he would stick to his fist tonight. And thoughts of a strawberry-blonde that he was pretty sure didn't come in a box, like Crystal's color.

After the ladies were done kissing each other and teasing Easy, his brother adjusted himself and his jeans and climbed off the table.

"Hope they ride me so hard there ain't nothin' left of me in the mornin'. So, might be late to work tomorrow. Just sayin'."

"Hear you, brother," Shade answered.

"Oh, yeah, guaranteed you'll be hearin' us all night." He grinned.

Great.

He'd have to put in his earplugs tonight. He was pretty sure Easy and the two women wouldn't be the only ones making a racket in the bunkhouse. Most nights it got pretty fucking loud. Especially when Billie was ripping someone a new asshole.

That was one sweet butt Shade avoided. He had no fucking clue how she ever ended up being Whip's girlfriend, even for the quick minute she was.

The young brother was almost as quiet as Shade. Almost. But the baby-faced biker certainly didn't look like a guy who'd like his sex rough or kinky. Or his woman to dominate him.

But then, what the fuck did he know.

With that said, Billie was a good addition to the stable since, every once in a while, his brothers liked to get their hands dirty. Or they liked to play the way Billie wanted to play.

Whatever they were into.

Didn't matter to Shade. Everybody had their thing.

Easy tucked a lit hand-rolled between his lips, draped his arms over both women and, with a last jerk of his chin to Shade, headed toward the bunkhouse.

Shade picked up the empty box that had contained the Shirley cremains, tossed it in a nearby fifty-five-gallon drum, poured a little moonshine on it and lit it with his Zippo.

He stood and watched the thing burn, making sure all the evidence was reduced to ashes just like the man he'd scattered in the far field.

One more Shirley down. Too many to fucking go.

Chapter Three

CHELLE HEARD the motorcycle before she saw it. She expected it to speed by, even though she lived on a quiet street on the edge of town. She had come home from work, changed quickly and decided to head outside to weed the front garden while waiting for the man from the crematorium to deliver Pumpkin's ashes.

Damn cat.

She'd cried almost all night over him. Her eyes had still been red and baggy when she arrived at work this morning.

All because of a cat who lived a long life. Eighteen spoiled years.

He'd been around Josie's whole life. Most of Maddie's, too.

Her husband never liked cats, but then he hadn't been around when she brought the kitten home from the animal shelter.

Pumpkin helped teach her girls responsibility and also how to be kind to animals. Though, sometimes they fought over whose bed the orange tabby would sleep in. However, that wasn't their choice. Pumpkin always made that one on his own.

Chelle knelt on a foam gardening pad while pulling some stray weeds. She couldn't afford to hire someone to do it for her. She used to make the girls help for some spare cash, but now Maddie was busy with college and her job. And Josie was busy with high school, her part-time job and her extracurricular activities. Ones Chelle hoped would get her into a good college and maybe even land her a scholarship to help pay for that education.

She and her husband thought a college degree was important for their future, so they'd started funds for both girls as soon as they were born. Luckily, her daughters always had a good work ethic and worked summer and part-time jobs when they could. Though, any money they earned went to their cars. Chelle couldn't help pay for both.

Not on her salary.

It would've been cheaper to find a spot to bury Pumpkin instead of spending the money on cremating him, but...

She wasn't ready to let that damn cat go.

She used the back of her wrist, avoiding her dirty gardening gloves, to wipe away the sting in her eyes.

She was done crying over that damn cat.

She sniffled. *Damn it.*

Pumpkin had managed to wrap his little paws around her heart the second she saw him in the cage with his littermates.

She ripped out the next dandelion from between the flowers with more force than necessary and tossed it into the five-gallon bucket next to her. Then, with a groan, she rose to her feet.

God, once she hit forty it seemed everything on her had started to fall apart. Forty seemed to have been some magical number. Now she was forty-one.

And still alone.

Hell, more alone now that her girls were almost all grown up.

She took a deep inhale and turned with a frown when the motorcycle slowed and pulled into her driveway with a deep rumble.

What the hell?

Her heart began to race as she realized the rider was wearing one of those leather vests. The ones the members of that MC, based right outside of town, wore.

She couldn't see the man's face which made it even worse. It was covered from the nose down with black fabric that made his face look like the bottom half of a skull. His eyes were covered with dark sunglasses and his hair covered in another piece of black fabric, similar to a do-rag.

She quickly gauged the distance between her and the front door. Could she make it?

She had stupidly left her cell phone inside.

Maybe she could scream and a couple of her neighbors would help.

She should run now.

Now.

She should...

The bike became quiet and her frown deepened when the man yanked down the face covering and removed the one from his head.

Wait.

She recognized that hair. She'd only seen that color, that length, those curls on one man.

Shawn from Tioga Pet Crematorium.

What the hell?

With her heart beating in her throat, she began to move toward the porch steps anyway, keeping one eye on him.

Did that MC own the crematorium? She knew they owned a few businesses in town.

While none of them had ever caused problems in Manning Grove recently—that she knew of—the whispers in town had also hit her ears. A couple decades ago, the MC had caused a lot of problems. Murder and mayhem, people said.

And, of course, working in the local school district, she heard *all* the gossip.

"Shawn?" she called out, causing those sunglasses to turn her way.

In the slight hesitation before he jerked up his chin at her, she could've sworn he'd been checking her out from head to toe.

Huh.

Did she have dirt on her face? She glanced down. Or did she get her clothes stained?

He removed his vest and draped it inside out over the seat of his motorcycle. Why would he do that? To hide what it said on the back? Too late, she had already recognized it.

She had seen some of their members around town. Especially at Dino's Diner, so she knew what—or who—those vests represented. She'd also seen a big, bearded man wearing one while dropping off Daisy Lange some mornings at school.

There seemed to be quite a few now. Just a couple of years ago, there hadn't been any. Most likely because she'd been told the club had disbanded a long time ago.

She had no idea what changed. Why they seemed to be everywhere now.

Still... This man... the man from the crematorium wore one of those vests and was riding what looked like a Harley.

So...

He was in that motorcycle gang.

Shawn turned, dug into one of the black leather bags hanging on the side of the bike and removed a small wood box along with what looked like paperwork.

Pumpkin.

The man was delivering Pumpkin just like he said he would.

She hadn't realized it was four o'clock already. She must have lost track of time while she weeded.

She forgot to breathe as he moved up her walkway. His gait was long, but smooth, his hips loose. The worn black T-shirt he wore pulled tightly over his broad chest and shoulders. His arms—what she could see of them—were completely tatted up. If what she saw was any indication, he had two full sleeves. She also wondered if the rich color of his skin was from the sun or what he was born with. With his skin tone, the color of his eyes, his hair, and the shape of his nose, plus the dark facial hair, he looked like he had some Spanish in him. Or Portuguese. Or Greek... One of those warm places. Exotic.

He wasn't huge but looked solid.

She released her bottom lip once she realized it had been tucked between her teeth.

And why did any of this matter?

It shouldn't. She shouldn't be checking out some biker who worked at a pet crematorium.

No, that wasn't right. She shouldn't be checking out a biker. Period.

Especially one who had to be at least ten years younger than her.

But, *my oh my*, watching the way he walked up to where she now stood on her porch made her a bit... thirsty.

She hadn't had someone like him quench her thirst in a long time...

She closed her eyes and groaned at her own thoughts. Right now, she was no better than her girls when checking out cute boys, elbowing each other and giggling.

What the hell, Chelle? Were you out in the sun too long?

"You okay?"

Holy cannoli, that voice, too. Honey-coated gravel. Smooth, with just enough grit.

Gutter, meet Chelle. She needs to remove her thoughts from you.

She opened her eyes and had to look up slightly since he now stood almost toe to toe with her. She wasn't quite short, but he was definitely taller than her.

"Yes." *Oh my God*, that came out way more breathless than it should have. Heat crept into her cheeks.

He slowly removed his sunglasses and hung them from the neck of his T-shirt. His dark brown, almost black, eyes, surrounded by thick black lashes a woman would kill for, traced every inch of her face.

"Do I have dirt on my face or something?" she whispered, her hand coming up automatically to wipe away whatever it was.

"No," he said almost as softly.

"Then what are you looking at?"

"You."

Thump. Thump. Thump.

She wasn't sure if that was her heart or her pussy making her body thump like that. "I'm... fine."

"Not why I was lookin'."

"Why were you looking?" And still looking? *And* causing a flutter in her belly?

"Appreciate beautiful things."

She had watched his full lips carefully form each of those words.

"Me?" got caught in her throat. He was calling her beautiful?

"You."

Damn it, he must be a player. "Um... thank you?" She hated men who thought they could manipulate women easily, simply with compliments and pointed looks.

She'd be disappointed if he was like that. He didn't seem to be yesterday.

Today?

Maybe it was because Cassie Lange wasn't with him.

Wait.

She hadn't put two and two together. Was Cassie Daisy's mother?

Crap, that made another connection between the club and the crematorium.

Didn't matter. Pumpkin had been all that mattered. In truth, both Cassie and Shawn had also been nothing but kind.

She gathered herself and concentrated on the whole reason Shawn had shown up in the first place. Not to give her compliments. Not to make her weak in the knees.

"Come inside. I still need to pay you." She walked up the steps to her door and held it open for him.

He hadn't moved from the base of the brick steps. "Cassie said you can mail the check."

She shook her head. "I can pay you now. Especially since you delivered the ashes so promptly. I can't thank you enough."

After a long pause, he took his time climbing the steps but instead of walking through the door, he held it for her, giving one of those little chin jerks toward the interior of her home.

She went ahead and he followed her in. However, the sound of the door latching behind her sent a shock up her spine.

Should she be frightened of being alone with him inside her house?

Honestly, nothing about him scared her. Even the knowledge of why he wore that vest.

She would've heard if the biker gang had been wreaking havoc on the town and its citizens. Plus, Manning Grove had a great police department. She couldn't imagine the chief, who she knew, would tolerate a gang going wild in his town. A town Max Bryson had grown up in and was now raising his own family in, too.

"Where you want it?"

She found it interesting, like she had yesterday, that he spoke slowly and deliberately. Like he thought carefully about each word before speaking.

Not only had that habit caught her attention, so did when he had screwed up his choice of the words *time* and *day*. Like he'd gotten confused when he had rushed to answer.

She wanted to ask him about it, but that would be inappropriate.

He was a stranger.

Only here in her home to drop off Pumpkin. In a few minutes he'd be gone and she'd most likely never speak to him again.

Maybe she'd see him around town. Maybe not.

"Mrs. Goodson?"

"Huh?"

"The cremains." He lifted the box, his face a blank mask.

Was he really laughing on the inside how much of an idiot she was acting? *Good lord*, he'd turned her stupid.

Only one other man had turned her stupid like that and she'd married him. "Oh... yes. Uh... On the mantel for now, I guess. Let me grab my checkbook."

"Don't gotta pay..."

She heard his sigh as she rushed from the entryway into the kitchen where her checkbook was tucked in a drawer. "I know I don't!" she called out.

When she headed back toward the front of the house with her checkbook and a pen in hand, he no longer stood at the front door. She looked left and saw him standing in front of her gas fireplace. The small carved box had been tucked between two framed photos in the center of the mantel.

He didn't turn when she approached. He was too busy studying her family photos.

Some of them were of just the two girls. A couple were of her and Brendan. But Shawn's fingers had connected with the frame holding a photo of her and her daughters, the day Maddie graduated from high school. Not so long ago.

It had been the perfect day weather-wise and all three of them wore huge smiles as bright as the sun. Not an ounce of melancholy could be seen on Chelle's face, even though she was sad that Brendan couldn't see the day his oldest daughter graduated high school. Wouldn't be around to see her graduate from college. Get married. Have their first grandchild...

Even so, the three of them celebrated the day Maddie had graduated with honors and had been accepted to three universities, all offering scholarships. Thank goodness.

The picture was one of her favorites. Right next to the one of her and Brendan's wedding photo. She'd been just a waif of a girl back then, hardly a woman. And unaware she would soon learn the hard way that life wasn't fair. Sometimes it was even downright cruel.

"Just the two," he murmured, his index finger sliding along the bottom of the silver frame.

The two?

Oh yes, he turned her stupid. "Uh... Yes. Just Maddie and Josie."

"Beautiful, like their mom."

"I..." The rest of her response disintegrated. "Do you have the bill?"

He turned and the intense look in his dark eyes surprised her.

Maybe it should cause some concern.

For some crazy reason, she wanted to reach out and touch his curly hair, which hung loosely around his shoulders. Yesterday it had been pulled back into a ponytail.

She'd never been one to be attracted to men with long

hair, but his fit the rest of his features. He could be a pirate, getting ready to board his enemy's ship.

That was a weird thought.

Even so, his hair was so long it almost reached his nipples, which she noted were pebbled beneath the snug, soft cotton. Hard, unlike his hair which she wanted to run her fingers through to see if it really was as soft and springy as it looked.

She had the strange urge to press her nose to it.

Let that silky cloud tickle her inner thighs.

She blew out a shaky breath.

"Okay?"

Heat flickered up her cheeks. "I'm... fine."

"Sure?"

"Yes." She needed to shake loose this reaction to him she kept having. It didn't make sense.

Her response to him, her thoughts, were crazy.

She'd be surprised if he was even thirty.

And he was a biker, she reminded herself once again.

She certainly didn't date younger men and certainly didn't entertain the idea of one who had a questionable past or future.

Well, she should've just stopped at *she certainly didn't date.* Because that was truer than anything.

Manning Grove was a great town. For the most part safe. The school system was good. The people friendly. The taxes and cost of living reasonable.

But for a single woman in her forties, it didn't give her much of a dating life.

She refused to date any single teachers—if any even existed at this point—because she didn't want to deal with the awkwardness if anything went wrong.

She also didn't hang out at bars.

In truth, she didn't hang anywhere. She went to work

and came home. She looked after her girls. The two most important people in her life.

Her brother had tried to set her up a couple of times, but both of those blind dates had been a disaster.

Maybe she wasn't meant to find anyone.

Maybe Brendan had been the only one for her. Her soulmate.

She'd never know for sure since they didn't get enough time together.

Shawn held out the paperwork and she took it from him. One item was the invoice, the other an envelope which felt like a card. She assumed it was a sympathy card.

She had read too many of those in her lifetime. She wasn't sure if she was ready to read another. But it was thoughtful and appreciated, anyhow.

She placed the unopened card on the coffee table and perched on the edge of the couch to fill out the check, relieved payday was just a couple of days away. This unexpected, but necessary, expense had dug into this week's grocery funds.

"What you gonna do with them?"

"What?" she asked, distracted as she finished signing the check.

"The ashes."

She glanced up. He still stood by the fireplace, but he was no longer looking at the photos, he watched her, instead. "Oh, I don't know. Whatever the girls want to do with them."

"Where are they?"

"Who?"

"Your girls."

She frowned, wondering again if she should be concerned with his interest in her life. And her daughters. He might be too young for her, but he was too old for them.

Maddie was twenty and, at just seventeen, Josie was only a senior in high school.

"Josie has Spanish Club after school and Maddie has an evening class."

"Evenin' class?"

"At Mansfield University."

He glanced back at the graduation picture. "She's smart, then."

"Both my girls do okay," she kidded with a smile. "I'm not sure who they got their brains from, me or their father."

"Got their looks from their momma."

"Yes, sometimes people think the three of us are sisters. It always makes me laugh."

"True, though. At first, thought you were sisters."

Chelle always took that as a compliment. "Thank you."

He shrugged. "Don't look old enough to have two grown girls."

"Well, they might look grown, but most of the time they don't act it. Sometimes they act like my students."

"Students?"

She rose from the couch and held out the check. "Please tell Cassie thank you."

He tipped his head.

"Speaking of students, is Daisy Lange related to Cassie?" Now that she thought about it, they looked a lot alike. Both blonde and outgoing. Cut from the same cloth.

"Her girl. How do you know that hell-on-wheels?"

Chelle grinned at the description of the six-year-old girl. She'd only met Daisy a few times so far but she'd left an impression. "I work at Daisy's school."

"As a teacher," he concluded on his own.

"No, the librarian. I saw Daisy's father dropping her off the other morning. He wore the same vest as you."

His mouth became tight. "Noticed my vest?"

"Hard to miss it."

"Ain't supposed to wear it at customers' homes."

"Well... you did."

"Wasn't thinkin' you'd be outside waitin'."

"It's a beautiful day. Figured I'd work outside until you arrived."

"Makes sense."

"Don't worry, I won't tattle," she kidded him.

His head tilted as he studied her.

The way he looked at her, the questions and comments. The way he spoke. None of it actual flirting. But all of it should disturb her.

It didn't. It made her curious. The same way he was about her.

Maybe that was just stupid of her. But then again, being near him was making her as irrational as a hormonal teenage girl. And she was far from that.

"Tell me about it," she urged before she could think better of it. He had the check, she had Pumpkin's ashes, no reason remained to keep him there.

"About what?"

"The vest."

He stared at her, his expression cautious. "Shouldn't have worn it."

"But you did."

"Habit."

"So, now that the cat's out of the bag—" She grimaced at her choice of idiom. It was bad timing. Not for him but her. "I'm curious. Is it a secret?"

"No."

"What is it then?"

"A brotherhood."

"And the vest represents that brotherhood."

"Yeah. It's a cut."

"A cut," she echoed, finding that a weird name for a leather vest.

"Our club's colors."

She frowned. "What do you mean?"

"The colors that represent our club. Our patches."

"The ones on the back."

He tipped his head.

"Is your club dangerous?"

He stared at her for a few uncomfortable seconds, his face not only blank but his eyes turned hard and distant. His soft answer was anything but warm. "Only to our enemies."

"You have enemies?"

"Everybody's got enemies."

"Not everyone."

"Chelle, we all got enemies. Some we see, most we don't."

She wasn't sure if it was the familiar use of her first name or what he said that caused the shiver.

But he noticed it and frowned.

She pushed on. "I was told it disbanded a long time ago."

"Yeah."

"But now it's up and running again?"

A small grunt escaped him.

"Why do you call it a brotherhood?"

"Family."

"Your family is a part of the MC?"

"They're my family." He shifted, looking uncomfortable at her line of questioning.

Her check was now crumpled in his hand.

Shit. Had she pushed him too far?

Chapter Four

SHADE NEEDED TO FUCKING LEAVE, but he was having a difficult time walking away from Chelle.

She was like a goddamn magnet and he was steel. The pull toward her was weird. He didn't understand it besides her being a beautiful woman.

He'd seen a lot of pretty or beautiful women in his life, but none had caught his attention as quickly as her.

She was smart, but too curious.

He had no idea why she was digging.

He fucked up by wearing his cut in her driveway. Yeah, it was habit to wear it whenever he was on his sled, but he should've known better. And it was true, he hadn't expected her to be outside waiting.

But then, nothing about this visit was going as expected.

He thought he'd show up, hand over the box and leave. Not be invited inside.

Even though she now knew he belonged to the Fury, she invited him in, anyway. He first took that as a positive, but now... he realized he was fucking wrong.

Her questions were making him tense. Fury business was no one else's. Not that she asked for anything that wasn't common knowledge. But he had to make sure she didn't dig any deeper.

He didn't share secrets, whether the club's or his own.

So, yeah, he needed to leave, because every question she asked, he'd answered. It would be better to just part ways before he fucked up again.

Problem was, she wasn't the only one curious. The pictures of a younger her with her man made him want to ask questions, too.

In truth, the answers wouldn't matter. It wouldn't change a damn thing.

She wasn't for him.

He wasn't for her.

They were too damn different.

A fucking school librarian.

Jesus fuck. She'd be horrified if she knew the truth about him.

"Would you like a glass of iced tea?"

What? Why wasn't she rushing him out the door now that she knew he was a biker?

No, he didn't need a goddamn glass of iced tea. He needed a bowl of premium Kush and a pint of moonshine to scrub her from his brain. That was what the fuck he needed.

He should've let Cassie bring the fucking ashes. Or Easy.

Anybody but him.

But he said he would and he always kept his word. That was the one thing he had of value besides his club and his sled. His word.

If he said he was going to do something, he did his damn best to do it. He made no excuses. He expected the same from others. Though, in the past he'd been disappointed one too many times.

Until recently, at least.

Once he found his home on the farm with his club brothers.

Once he found his place in the Blood Fury MC.

Beyond that, he needed nothing else.

He especially didn't need to create a complication in his life by lusting after a woman not even on his level. Which was way under hers.

Educated. Smart. Well-spoken. Established.

Even married.

That last one made him come to his senses. He needed to get the fuck out of Mrs. Rachelle Goodson's house and never come back.

That was what he'd do. Leave and forget all about her.

"Is that blood on your boot? Did you hurt yourself?"

Every drop of his own blood froze in his veins. He followed her gaze down to his left boot and saw the dried smear.

Thick and dark red, noticeable even on the scuffed black leather.

Another fuck up.

Fuck.

He slammed the brakes on his spinning thoughts because if he rushed to answer her, to deny what it was, his words wouldn't be right.

They could come out very, very wrong.

"No." What else could red liquid be? "Paint. Must be paint."

The brown eyes behind her glasses lit up. "Oh, like art? Or walls?"

Fuck. He almost snorted at the idea of him being an artist. He never held an artist's paint brush or, *hell*, even a fucking crayon. "Walls."

"I..."

She what?

"I've been looking for someone to paint. The walls are

overdue for a fresh coat, especially now that the girls are grown. No more thumbtack holes in their walls from posters, crayon marks, and the rest. What would you charge me?"

He stared at her. *Say what?* She wanted to pay him to paint the interior of her home?

"I had gotten a couple of estimates from professional companies... but I... uh... was a bit shocked at their prices. I mean, I know they're probably worth it, but I just can't afford to do the whole house at once right now. Not with Maddie in college and Josie heading there soon. I figured I'd just hold off, but... I'd be glad to hire you if you could work piecemeal."

"Piece... meal?" What did she mean?

"Well, with being an elementary school librarian, I don't have a huge salary or bank account, of course." Her cheeks flushed red again. Like when she'd been checking him out earlier. "If you're willing, I could pay by the room. Professionals only wanted to contract the whole house. I'd buy the paint and any materials you need, but pay you as you go..."

He continued to stare at her and she fidgeted with straightening her glasses.

"I could pay you cash for each room when I have it. I mean, I would hire you for each room once I have the cash." She made a sound of frustration at the back of her throat.

He didn't know the first fucking thing about painting walls. He'd done some construction here and there in the past to earn scratch while he bounced from place to place. It was easy to get a job doing oddball shit like that. Especially when he'd hang out in the parking lot of home improvement stores to get selected for day work. No education or resume needed.

Crazy enough, none of those jobs ever consisted of painting.

He guessed it couldn't be too fucking hard. It was slapping paint on walls and not making a mess. But why the fuck would he want to do that?

He worked all fucking day at the crematorium and at night...

He was busy at night.

He had given his word to his prez and sergeant at arms. He was going to stick to the plan.

"I mean, if you don't want to do it, I'd understand. I can't pay much, but, like I said, I can pay you cash."

Extra scratch would be good. He could always use more.

When he was done dealing with the Shirleys, he needed to get back to his own plans. He'd need scratch for that.

Working at the crematorium didn't pay much since he was required to work there for the club. The majority of the money the business made went back to the club to help pay for expenses. For the farm, The Barn, the bunkhouse.

Trip only charged his brothers a minimum amount to live in the bunkhouse. Mostly to help cover the utilities, which they used a lot of.

The more the club made, the fatter the club account, the better. That way if anyone needed it for whatever reason, it was there.

Would it have to be paid back? Most likely. But Trip liked having that cushion, especially for emergencies.

The latest being Cage needing a home for him and his baby girl, Dyna. Cage couldn't shell out the cash, but now he could make payments back to the club in an amount he could afford every month.

The club having fat coffers was like having their own personal bank and it helped keep everything running.

Trip was a smart motherfucker, that was for sure. Shade wished he had half his business sense. Even half his smarts.

He didn't, so he was only a grunt who took orders.

And grunts like him painted interior walls of homes

owned by beautiful, intelligent women. They didn't hook up with them.

No reason remained for him to be standing in Chelle's home right now. He'd kept his word to deliver the cremains and he'd gotten the payment for their services. He needed to leave.

He shouldn't be considering painting her house so he could come back and spend more time with her.

Especially if she was married. Hubby wouldn't like some lowlife biker sniffing around his librarian wife.

"Gotta go," he muttered.

As he went to move around her, to escape, she reached out and touched his arm. Right above the wide black leather cuff he wore on his left wrist. "Wait."

His lungs seized and every muscle in his body turned to concrete at her touch.

She probably wouldn't stop him if she knew the truth about him. She'd demand he leave, lock her doors and probably draw her blinds.

Then she'd stand with her phone in her hand ready to dial 911.

But she didn't know the truth and hopefully never would.

If he left now, she'd always think he was a nice guy who did a nice thing by bringing over her cat's ashes. That was the best way she could remember him.

And, if he was smart, the only way.

But he wasn't smart. Him standing there and not continuing to walk out the front door proved it. "Don't got time."

"You mean now or for the painting?"

Both.

He inhaled deeply.

"It doesn't have to be right away..."

Fuck. Why the fuck did she want this? She could hire some college kid or neighbor, or, *hell*, head down to the nearest Home Depot parking lot and hire someone desperate for work.

"We can work on one room at a time."

He frowned. "We?"

"Well, if you do it on weekends, I can help."

That was even fucking worse. He'd be working in close quarters with her. "Ain't good at it."

The corners of the lips he wanted to taste curled up at the ends slightly. "I'm sure you're better than you think."

He dropped his gaze from her face to where her fingers were wrapped around his forearm. Right above where the wide strip of leather covered a reminder of his past.

That wasn't all he noticed. "Where's your weddin' ring?"

Her face paled and she quickly removed her hand, curling her fingers into her palm. "What?"

He wasn't expecting that reaction, but now he needed to know the answer. "Your weddin' ring."

"I... Why would you ask that?"

"Wonderin' why your hubby ain't paintin'." That wasn't why he wanted to know. He wanted to know where the fuck her man was. Why he'd been at her house twice in two days and hadn't seen him once or even heard him mentioned.

Why would a man let strangers come to his home and not be there to protect the ones he loved?

She took a step back with a frown. "Because he can't."

Something flickered behind her eyes. Pain? Sadness?

He wasn't expecting that. If anything, he expected her to get a bit bent about him asking. "You ain't wearin' a weddin' ring. He leave you?"

Yeah, he was being rude but maybe she would change her mind about wanting him to paint. If she changed her mind, he could walk away from her and out of her house a lot easier. He'd have zero reason to stay.

"I'm not sure what this has to do with anything."

"He might not want me paintin' your house." At least that part was true.

"I don't think he'll care."

"'Cause he's gone?" Why the fuck did he need to know so badly? It was more than trying to push her away, and that shit bothered him.

"Yes," she said softly, "he's gone. He's been gone a long time."

"Sorry." That didn't mean she didn't have a man in her life. Maybe not the same one as in the picture.

"I guess I could just do it myself. Maybe get the girls to help me..." Disappointment colored her words. She turned away with a sigh.

That heavy sigh got him in the gut, even though her changing her mind was what he hoped.

Right?

He hadn't liked when she was digging, but here he was doing the same. But his digging was painful to her and his intention wasn't to cause her hurt. He'd been trying to make her mad so she'd push him out the front door.

A flicker of guilt had him saying, "Can only do weekends. Saturdays. Not sure about Sundays."

Club runs were always on Sundays. They weren't every week, but whenever they could do them. Once a month for sure. And one was scheduled for this Sunday.

She turned back and nodded. Any grief he'd caused from his questions were now wiped away, relief replacing it. *Thank fuck.*

"It's no rush. I can stop at the paint store before Saturday and get everything we'd need."

There was that "we" again.

If he was smart, he wouldn't do this. He'd say no, walk out the door and never see her again. But he'd been told time and time again that he was stupid. Even called much worse. A name he wouldn't call anyone. Especially a child.

So, of course, he'd say yes.

Probably regret it, too.

He pulled his cell phone from his back pocket, unlocked it with his fingerprint and handed it to her.

She took it, surprised.

He always deleted his texts after he listened to them so he wasn't worried she'd see something she shouldn't. Like club business. Like something about the Shirleys.

"Put your name and number in it."

She smiled up at him. "That's a definite yes?"

Fuck, that smile sent blood rushing to his dick. "Probably gonna fire me after the first room."

She laughed softly, the corners of her big brown eyes crinkling behind her glasses. She dipped her head and entered her info into his phone. When she did, her long hair covered her face and he had to stop himself from tucking it behind her ear.

From rubbing those silky strands between his fingers.

From lifting them to his nose.

From gripping it in his fist, yanking her head back and taking her mouth...

When she was done, he snapped himself out of his fantasy and said, "Call yourself."

Her eyebrows, which were only slightly darker than her strawberry-blonde hair, knitted together. "What?"

"Call yourself. From my phone. So you got my number." He added quickly, "In case your plans cancel."

"Cancel?"

Fuck. Cancel wasn't the right word. "Change."

For fuck's sake, he was a fucking idiot. He knew better than to rush.

"Okay, I doubt I'll change my mind or cancel." She held out his phone and, when he took it from her fingers, his brushed hers. Color rushed into her face again and he could see her pulse beating in her delicate throat. "We didn't talk about your fee."

"Just... whatever you think's fair, Mrs. Goodson." He had tried to convince himself he was doing it for the extra scratch but, if he was honest with himself, that wasn't why.

"Chelle, please. I plan on calling you Shawn. Not that I know your last name, anyway."

She didn't know his last name.

Jesus fuck. She didn't even know his first name.

But that would be for the best.

If she paid him in cash, it wouldn't matter. She could continue to think he was Shawn.

"Gotta go," he murmured, tucking his phone into his back pocket again.

She followed him to the front door. "Again, thank you for dropping off Pumpkin and I'll see you Saturday."

He jerked his chin up at her. Because she was so close, he had to think harder about the word he said next. "Saturday." When it came out correctly and she didn't look at him funny, he opened the door and stepped out on the porch.

She followed him.

He kept going all the way back to his sled. He took his time to shrug on his cut, slide on his sunglasses, pull up his face covering and cover his hair with his skullcap.

Every one of those minutes, he struggled not to glance back at the porch. Where he knew she watched him.

Again, he figured it was more curiosity about the MC than anything.

After straddling his totally blacked-out HD Night Train, he started it. He let the deep rumble seep into his bones and bring him back to reality.

He belonged on his sled.

He belonged in his cut.

He belonged to the Fury brotherhood.

He did not belong in Chelle's house.

He definitely did not belong in her bed.

Now, he just had to make sure he didn't fuck that up.

———

HE HAD TEXTED her once he rolled out of bed Saturday morning to let her know when he'd arrive. It was later than he originally planned, but then his night up on the mountain ended up going sideways.

He'd almost gotten caught.

He had worked his way up past the main clearing trying to locate a male Shirley who was alone and accidentally stumbled across a bunch of the women working in a shed.

Making meth.

None of them wore any protective gear and, even as late as it was, a few young children were playing nearby with nobody watching them.

Mothers of the Fucking Year right there.

The shed was definitely not set up like a professional lab. They used everyday products they'd bought at Walmart, items like plastic sports drink bottles and allergy medicine. The technique they used was the most hillbilly, cheap way to make the drug.

Shade wondered who the fuck they sold that garbage to.

Manning Grove didn't have a bad drug problem from what he knew. But meth was a popular drug of choice for both country and city folk alike. It was a cheap, easily available high.

However, the clan had to have a way to distribute it.

He couldn't believe the local PD hadn't shut this shit down. Or brought in the DEA.

Maybe the chief and his crew hoped the Shirleys would blow up their own mountain with their stupidity. Shade knew making meth, especially the way they were doing it, was dangerous.

Just like the way they made moonshine. Liquor Control Enforcement would probably be interested in their shitty homemade stills. And if the Shirleys were careless, those stills could turn into bombs.

Maybe if they weren't selling it, like they were the meth, then the LCE couldn't give a fuck about the Shirleys' junkyard stills. While Shade had stolen some of their moonshine, he was damn sure he wouldn't pay a dime for it. But there was always a market for cheap booze.

Even if the Feds came in and hauled away the key players, the Shirleys would only make more Shirleys. There seemed to be an endless cycle of them. If the women were old enough to be fertile, they were usually pregnant or just had a kid.

At one point, Shade counted forty children, from teenagers to infants. He wasn't the best at counting but he knew that number was damn close.

The clan didn't need a lot of men to make a lot of babies. More than one woman for each Shirley male was completely acceptable. Even if they were related.

Unfortunately, while he was sneaking away from that shed last night, one of the little kids playing in the dirt spotted him and began to point and yell. That had the women scrambling and picking up weapons, which was a risky thing to do when working with highly explosive materials.

No one said the Shirleys were smart.

Shade escaped before the shed blew up, or had something more deadly than a little kid's finger pointed in his direction.

He slipped away successfully, but it had been close.

When he went up there, he wanted no one but his target to know he'd been on that mountain. And if possible, not even his target until it was too late.

Last night had been a failure on his part.

One that couldn't happen again.

He had come back to the farm, found a quiet spot out in the dark, smoked some bud and drank some of the Shirleys' own moonshine until he was ready to pass out.

Luckily, that didn't take long and once he did, he was out for longer than normal.

That stolen moonshine was probably killing the few good brain cells he had. He might have to switch back to drinking something not flirting with being poison.

Or paint thinner.

When he walked through her door, Chelle announced she bought real paint thinner, along with rollers, brushes, a few cans of paint, some plastic to cover the floors and furniture, blue tape and the rest of the shit needed to paint a fucking room.

Yesterday while things were quiet at the crematorium, he'd watched several YouTube videos on his phone from what he hoped were experts on how to tape off and paint a room. This way he wouldn't be totally fucking clueless.

He had tucked his cut into the saddlebag before entering her house and, as soon as he walked through the door, she had shoved a mug of black coffee at him. He'd taken it and sucked half of it down right away.

One problem with drinking himself to sleep some nights was that he woke up with a headache. But numbing himself so he could sleep was better than the alternative.

"I have a whole pot made, so help yourself. Plus, bottles of water and Gatorade in the fridge. Whatever you need, just let me know."

He wouldn't do that. Because if he let himself think about what he really needed, it would be Chelle naked on her back with him settled between her legs and his hips cushioned between her thighs.

After giving her a nod, he finished his first mug of strong

coffee instead. While he did so, he let his gaze sweep her from top to toe.

Her reddish-blonde hair was pulled up to the top of her head in a floppy loop-like thing which reminded him of a fountain. Her curvy figure was now, for the most part, hidden under an oversized white button down shirt with the sleeves rolled up to her elbows. Black stretchy pants—maybe what the women called leggings—covered what he could see of her legs.

And she was barefoot. Her pink-painted toes were surprisingly tempting. He'd never been into feet but if he was, Chelle's would be the type of feet he'd be into. Her toes weren't fat and stubby but long and delicate, just like her fingers.

"Gonna stay barefoot?" he asked after his last swallow of coffee. The caffeine was starting to kick in, *thank fuck*.

She shrugged. "Why not? The paint is water-based so it'll wash off. I paint my own nails so if my home mani-pedi gets messed up, I'm not going to worry about it."

Problem was, Shade might keep getting distracted by her sexy toes and the slender ankles that were exposed at the bottom of those snug leggings.

And the curve of her calves.

The swell of her hips.

Fuck.

Everything about her might distract him.

If he got distracted, he'd have to make sure he concentrated extra hard on the answers to any questions she asked. Otherwise, he was keeping his fucking mouth shut. It was the easiest way to avoid confusing himself and others with a wrong choice of words.

"Well, are you ready to get started? I figured we can get a good two hours of prep work in before breaking for lunch."

Damn, she was going to be a slave driver. While his brain

wasn't sure if he should be thrilled with that prospect, his dick had other ideas.

"You better pull your hair up," she warned. When she reached out to touch it, his heart tumbled heavily.

He never let anyone touch it. He even trimmed it himself when it got too long.

He forced himself to remain still and closed his eyes as she stroked the ends that laid against his chest. It was the gentlest touch, simply like petting Justice or Jury, and was gone within a split second.

He forced himself to breathe and opened his eyes. She was staring at him strangely, her expression a mix of confusion and embarrassment.

"I'm sorry. I shouldn't have..."

He shook his head. "Ain't a thing." Which was a goddamn lie since his chest had tightened painfully under her touch and his heart had tried to escape.

Trying to hide the tremor in his fingers, he dug into his front pocket and pulled out an elastic band, collecting the length of his hair and wrapping it into a tight knot at the back of his head. It would keep it from catching in the paint and making a complete mess.

He wanted to make sure he didn't go back to the farm with paint on him. That would raise questions.

This morning he'd dug out his oldest pair of jeans and a T-shirt that should've been thrown in a rag pile a couple of years ago. He figured he'd find a place after leaving Chelle's house to change into the clean jeans and tee he had tucked in one of his saddlebags, and keep the clothes he used for this job hidden. Once he was done painting whatever rooms she wanted completed, he could burn the evidence.

Nobody needed to know where he was or what he was doing. Or for who.

This shit was his business and not club business.

And, anyway, he didn't need his brothers riding his ass.

If any of them knew where he was and what he was doing, his ass would be sore and his patience thin.

Unlike some of his brothers, he wasn't one who crowed about who he stuck his dick into. He wasn't one who talked crudely about pussy, not only behind their back but sometimes in front of them, too.

None of the women who came to The Barn on a regular basis, or even on occasion by special invite, needed to be disrespected.

Yeah, it was their choice to put out. It was their choice how kinky they wanted to take it. It was their choice whether to do it out in the open or privately in one of the rooms, or wherever. It was their choice whether to take one or more brothers at the same time or same night.

But that was the most important thing...

Choice.

No one would stop any of the women who stepped foot on the farm, sweet butts or not, from leaving. If they'd had enough of his brothers' bullshit, they could walk away at any time.

Most of the women took everything in stride and actually loved the attention, the free food, the free booze and their choice of dick.

The only thing they had to agree to was keeping their mouth shut. They could not discuss what happened on the farm with anyone outside of the club. That was an important rule. Along with not shacking up in the bunkhouse.

Trip didn't want to see any women besides the ol' ladies in the morning. Come sunrise, all sweet butts and hang-arounds, male or female, better be gone.

Shade agreed with those rules.

He respected Trip a lot. That was why he was willing to head up that mountain and try to help control the threat to their brotherhood.

If the Shirleys would've let shit go after Sig got Red

back, none of this shit would've been necessary. It would be a case of *live and let live.*

But they didn't.

They fucking dared to take club property. A baby belonging to the Fury.

They used Dyna, an innocent child, in an attempt to ambush his brothers.

That shit was beyond unacceptable.

The Shirleys had to be aware by now that someone was going up there quietly and surgically removing their men. That meant the Fury needed to expect blowback resulting from those actions.

The clan wasn't going to sit back and take it quietly.

But Shade needed to reduce their numbers as much as possible before they did that, before they could rally and do damage to his club.

Shade had found proof one night of them making their own ammo, which didn't surprise him. They might not be smart, but they were resourceful. Most likely they were stockpiling it for another clash between the clan and the club.

That discovery was something he needed to discuss with Trip and Judge. The sooner, the better. Maybe he'd pull them aside tomorrow after the club run. Give them a rundown on current numbers and any new info he'd discovered.

But that was tomorrow. Today, at that very minute, he was standing in a school librarian's home. Someone who was unaware of the possible upcoming war between two groups of people in her town, which she assumed the local pigs kept safe.

None of Manning Grove's residents suspected the turmoil brewing. Especially the pigs. Both sides needed to keep it that way. Otherwise, investigations would begin and

Shade could end up doing a bid in a state or federal prison. And that bid wouldn't be a short one.

No, he'd find himself confined, not unlike when he was younger. But he couldn't escape an actual prison with armed guards, steel bars and razor wire like he might be able to with a makeshift one. He also felt really strongly about not letting anyone control his life like that again.

He would die first.

He glanced at his left wrist. Today he'd wrapped it with a blue bandana instead of his leather cuff. He had plenty of bandanas and didn't mind having to toss one if it got fucked up from paint.

"I had the girls help me move the furniture to the center of the room and then cover it. The floors are covered, too," Chelle said as he followed her into the room directly to the left off the foyer. "I hate the stark white. Everything was painted that color when I bought this place and, like I said the other day, now that the girls are mostly grown, it's time to paint it in colors of my choosing. Warm and welcoming."

Warm and welcoming.

"Gonna do the whole house?"

"Eventually, yes. But like I also said, I can't afford to do it at once. I figured we'd start in this room and work our way through the first floor."

He nodded and walked around the room. All the furniture had been shoved to the center and covered. Sheets of plastic were laid down over the wood floor and secured with more tape. But the windows and molding still needed to be prepped. That was going to suck. It looked like tedious work in the videos and he was sure it was worse when actually doing it. "Where are the girls?"

"They won't get in your way, don't worry."

He wasn't worried about that. But, in truth, they should be helping their mom out more than what they had. Any time a kid could spend with a loving parent, they should. One never knew when that time would get cut short.

He couldn't tell her that since it might open the conversation up to questions he didn't want to answer. Or even think about.

"They're both at work."

He could accept that answer.

"They both have a great work ethic."

That answer was even better. "Raised them right," he murmured.

She pushed an escapee from her loose bun, or whatever it was, out of her face and blew out a breath. "I hope so. I did my best."

He still wondered where that man in the photo was. He wanted to ask but she had gotten visibly upset when he asked the other day, so it was best to curb his curiosity. For now. That question might be answered while he worked side-by-side with her.

She went to the corner of the room and fiddled with her cell phone which was plugged into a speaker. "I hope you don't mind classic rock."

Slow Ride from Foghat filled the space between them.

"Won't complain."

She smiled and planted a hand on her hip. "Good. But if it begins to bother you, I have plenty of other playlists. You pulling up on that motorcycle the other day, and again this morning, made me in the mood for some good ol' rock."

One side of his mouth pulled up at her mischievous expression. The woman was fucking gorgeous. She had good taste in music, too.

Even better, she wasn't the least bit scared of him. Even though she should be.

She clapped her hands together. "Okay, well. Let's get started."

He smothered his grin. He could see her working with kids and getting them focused on whatever she got them focused on. He was sure working with children like Daisy was similar to herding cats.

Time and technique were necessary to be successful. Probably a lot of patience, too.

She began taping the edges of the windows while he taped the molding. He was right, every second of it sucked. But the music was good, the company even better, even when she just chattered away about nothing.

Sometimes sang along with the song.

A few times he had to stop what he was doing because she'd fuck up his concentration when she'd move to the music, rocking her hips and tossing her head around. A couple times she picked up a paintbrush to use it as a microphone.

Fuck yeah, just like he thought. It wasn't a good idea that he'd agreed to help her. The more time he spent with her, the more tempting she became.

When they were finally done with the endless taping, she smiled as she circled in place and inspected their prep work. "I think we're ready."

Hell yeah, they were. But what he was ready for had nothing to do with painting.

"After we're done edging, we can break for lunch. I hope you like chili. I have it heating in the crockpot."

Damn, this woman was organized.

Better yet, she made lunch. It'd been a long fucking time since someone else made him a meal. Other than a cook at a restaurant, like Dino's Diner. Or the sweet butts setting up a spread after a club run. That shit didn't count.

"Chili's good." He wasn't picky, especially with a home-cooked meal.

She brushed by him and he caught the scent of her shampoo or her soap, or whatever it was. He wanted to inspect it closer by sliding his nose along her skin or pressing it into her hair. He didn't.

Instead, he stood there as she strode out of the room, a woman on a mission, calling out, "The paint is in the laundry room, which is right off the kitchen. While I grab us a couple bottles of water, can you grab the Antique Rose? I figured that would work well in here. Warm, but not too dark."

Without a word, he followed her and she pointed toward the laundry room to the right as she headed over to the fridge.

He wanted to watch her as she bent over to grab bottles from the bottom refrigerator drawer, but forced himself into the small room off the kitchen instead. He froze when he spotted it.

Six cans of paint.

Six.

He went over to the cans where they were stacked on the floor along the wall and he sorted through them. Each had a dab of paint on the lid to identify what the color was, but he had no fucking clue which one was Antique Rose.

"Which one?" he called out.

"It should say it on the top."

Fuck. He closed his eyes and took a deep inhale through his nostrils. "Don't got my glasses on." It was a lie that had slipped off his tongue a thousand times and would a thousand more.

"Do you need to borrow mine?" he heard come from the kitchen.

He stood staring at the cans, ground his teeth, then squatted down to look carefully at the lids.

Antique Rose.

Antique Rose.

Antique fuckin' Rose.

He guessed the word antique could start with an A. He

knew the shape of an A. He knew the shapes of all letters of the alphabet. Though, sometimes he got them backwards and he always struggled to put the letters together to form words.

Maybe it was the only paint she bought which started with an A. He ran his finger over the lids of two cans where words were scribbled in black marker. Neither started with an A.

Goddamn it.

If none of them started with an A then he was screwed because that meant he was wrong on what letter the word "antique" started with.

He checked the other four cans. He needed to narrow it down. "How many cans did you get of Antique Rose?"

For fuck's sake, say four.

"Two."

He ground his back teeth again, his fingers tightening on the metal wire handle of one of the cans. He was fucked. Totally fucking fucked.

"I got two of that color, two Apple Core and two of the Baby Artichoke."

What color was a baby artichoke? "Sure you don't want the Baby Artichoke for that room?" he asked carefully. He recognized the shape of the B on the first two cans he had checked.

He jerked when her voice came from right behind him in the laundry room doorway. "No, I'm saving that for in here and maybe the hallway. I don't know yet. I figured I can test a spot first once we're ready to tackle those areas."

He turned and she was leaning a curvy hip against the door frame, her fingers wrapped around a half-empty bottle of water.

"Just one can for now."

Right. Just one can for now.

Easier said than done.

He grabbed one of the other cans. He had a fifty-fifty chance of getting it wrong.

"No, not that one. The Antique Rose."

And, of course, he picked the wrong one. *For fuck's sake.*

He froze when she closed in behind him, placed her hand on his back, using him for balance as she leaned over and snagged the can she wanted.

He hurried to put down the wrong one and took the right one from her. "Got it."

"I'll bring your water." She followed him out of the laundry room and back to the front room.

When they got there, she said, "Open the can, please, and I'll get it stirred."

As he used a screwdriver she'd handed him to pop the lid, he took a closer look at where the words Antique Rose were written.

He now recognized the Я. Rose must begin with an Я.

He took a picture of the two words in his mind and silently repeated the paint color name over and over to help recognize it the next time.

Unfortunately, he knew it wouldn't stick.

It never did.

Once the paint was stirred and poured into paint trays, she handed him a brush to work on the edges and corners and she grabbed a roller.

Then they got to work.

Chapter Five

AFTER A FEW MINUTES of stretched silence, except for the music, she asked, "You don't speak much, do you?"

"When I got somethin' to say."

A man of few words.

"Which isn't often." A shame since his honey-coated gravelly voice needed to be shared with the world.

She certainly would like to hear more of it. She'd like to hear more about him. She'd never been so curious about a man before.

He seemed to keep himself pretty closed up. While they had prepped earlier, she had chatted on and on. Besides a few grunts here and there, he really hadn't responded to much.

Not that she had talked about anything important. She had blathered on about television shows, movies, music. Things of general interest.

He jerked one shoulder up slightly. "Some people talk too much."

She laughed. "Like me. I bet you tuned me out after the first five minutes. I have a bad habit of talking to anyone, even when I shouldn't. But, to be honest, I talk to myself the most."

"Same. Just not out loud."

"That's probably for the best. I bet some people think I'm crazy when I'm having a whole conversation with myself. But it helps me concentrate, especially if I'm doing a task."

"Like paintin'."

She nodded. "Like painting." And to keep her mind from going back to her reaction—and his—when she reached out and stroked the soft ends of his hair.

She shouldn't have done it. It was inappropriate and she wouldn't want anyone touching her hair without asking first.

Not even after they asked, either.

The only one who she allowed to touch her hair were her girls, of course, and her hairdresser, Teddy from Manes on Main.

If a man reached out and touched her like that, he'd probably regret it.

While she'd apologized to Shawn, she still was embarrassed she did it.

Even so, when his breath had stilled, so had hers. When his heart thumped under her fingertips, so had hers.

The thrill that shot through her when she felt the soft ends, the urge to run her fingers through the complete length...

So very inappropriate.

She once again reminded herself of his age. And her own. She was tempted to ask him how old he was but, really, it wouldn't matter.

It wasn't just his age, but the fact he belonged to a biker gang. She had daughters, was a homeowner, and had a job at the elementary school. Even if he wasn't too young for her, he was not the type of man she should be interested in.

But he was pretty to look at. No doubt.

No matter what, she needed to keep her interest limited to looking. Not touching, tasting, or whatever else about him was tempting her.

She shook herself mentally.

It had been a knee-jerk reaction when she made the offer to him about painting. There was no real need to paint the house right now, especially when funds were tight with Maddie in college and Josie on her way after graduation.

She sighed at how Shawn had made her weak like a hormonal teenager. If she started giggling and winding and unwinding her hair around her finger while batting her eyelashes at him, she was going to smack herself in the face.

His "Okay?" made her jump.

"Yes, thank you. I'm fine. I'm just thinking about the chili." *And if you believe that, I have a bridge to sell you...*

"Smells good."

So did he when he first walked through the door. Now she could smell nothing but fresh paint, so she had no idea how he smelled her chili.

"I didn't make it too spicy..." She needed to go put herself in a time-out.

"Like spicy."

His short answers once again caught her attention. If he could answer in one or two words, he did. If he didn't have to answer at all, or a grunt sufficed, he took that route instead.

Maybe she was just used to being around a bunch of little chatterboxes all day at school. Her white noise.

The only time they were quiet—for the most part—was when she read to them during story-time. She loved watching their faces as she did so. Whether it was a scary part and they hid their faces behind their hands, or a funny part where they laughed loud and openly. She loved it all.

Reading to them out loud was her favorite thing to do right after helping a child pick out a book to read. Every time a child returned a book and begged for another one, her heart swelled. Their thirst for a good story, or even a non-fiction book on turtles or frogs or trains... Any interest in a book was encouraged.

She dealt with children of all reading levels. The ones who struggled and needed books with more pictures than words and the ones who were ahead of their age, who couldn't inhale a book fast enough.

Whether a child read only a few words or pages and pages of them, it expanded their horizon. Every word read opened up their world a little more.

And that made Chelle very, very happy.

Books had been her world ever since she learned to read. She only wanted to share that joy, which was why she became a librarian. It certainly wasn't for the pay.

With all the years she'd been a librarian and worked with children, she picked up on certain habits, mannerisms, responses, and speech patterns. While she wasn't an expert on learning disabilities, she'd done plenty of research in the past when a student needed help due to one.

Before she dipped her roller in the tray again, she paused and turned to study Shawn as he stood on her step stool and carefully painted the corner at the ceiling. He was slow and methodical, trying to be neat with the edges since she was leaving the ceilings white.

So far he had a steady hand.

Since his back was turned toward her and he wasn't paying attention, she let her gaze slide over him. A couple strands of his curly long hair had escaped the knot he'd wrangled it into. Luckily, those loose ends hadn't gotten caught in the paint. Yet.

She was tempted to ask him if the tattoos on his muscular arms had any meaning, but she doubted he would answer.

His shoulders were broad, his back long, his threadbare

T-shirt had pulled loose from the back of his jeans, probably from all the climbing up and down the step stool. His old jeans, now splattered with a few spots of Antique Rose, only hung onto his hips thanks to the leather belt cinched at his trim waist.

A worn leather wallet peeked from one back pocket and a metal chain snaked around his left hip where it was connected to a belt loop in the front. In the other back pocket, Chelle spotted the top of a cell phone.

His legs were long, slender and his jeans contoured the curves of his ass perfectly. His black leather biker boots disappeared under the ragged hems of his jeans.

His hair and his dark Spanish features—or whatever they were—had originally drew her, but his ass took a close second.

His voice was the icing on the very delicious slice of cake she was drooling over.

While all that certainly attracted her, it was not what made her curious about him.

No.

It had been his slow speech and the way he had difficulty figuring out which paint can to grab. His slow, carefully chosen words could mean he had a stutter he fought to overcome, but it didn't make sense that he couldn't read the clearly marked lids.

He couldn't read the clearly marked lids.

A task that should've taken seconds had taken minutes. Even then, it hadn't been done successfully. So, she doubted he had a speech problem, but more of a learning disability.

She chewed on her bottom lip.

Good lord, she should let it go and leave him be, but now she wanted to know. She needed to dig.

Why?

It wasn't like her to be nosy.

It wasn't like her to get into other people's business.

She had taught her daughters not to be gossips or judgmental. And to treat everyone, no matter who, with the same kindness and compassion. Everyone was unique in their own way, just like Maddie and Josie were, and should be celebrated for those differences.

But some of those more important differences could be improved upon, especially if it affected someone's quality of life. A lack of education was easy to change. A stutter not as easy, but possible to improve by working with a professional and using specific techniques.

However, she wasn't sure what Shawn's issue was.

Again, not your damn business, Chelle.

Whatever it was wouldn't affect the job she hired him for. That should be all that mattered.

Still, what if it was only the simple fact he couldn't read?

She was a damn librarian. Words were her life. How could she let something go that might be easy to fix? That she might have the capability of fixing?

A guttural noise had her heart skipping a beat and she realized he'd turned his head and was staring at her staring at him.

Damn.

He probably thought she wanted to quench her thirst by lapping at him like a cougar at a watering hole on a sweltering hot day.

Maybe that was true.

No maybe about it.

She always prided herself for her common sense. Something she passed onto her girls. But right now? She was questioning not only her common sense but her sanity. Because she'd lost her marbles, quite clearly.

She needed to find a container, collect her marbles, put a tight lid on it and shove it deep into a closet. Then close that door, lock it and move across the country.

That was what she needed to do.

Of course, that wasn't what she did.

———

Julian didn't know what was going on. They wouldn't let him talk to his mommy and they wouldn't let her talk to him. He asked for his mommy so many times they got angry and covered his mouth again.

He needed to ask her what was happening. Why they were in this big room in this big house. Why they were surrounded by men Julian didn't know. They weren't family. They weren't friends.

Strangers.

Stranger danger.

Why three ladies stood at the front of the room in a row, including his mommy…

He was at the back of the room and she probably couldn't see him there. She was awake again but wouldn't stop crying. He was crying just like his mommy, but no tears were coming out anymore.

Julian sucked a breath through his nose because his mouth was full of a dry, yucky rag. But it didn't stop the hiccup-sob coming from his belly and getting caught in his mouth where it couldn't escape. When his whole body jerked from it, the fingers on his shoulder dug deeper.

The man holding onto him was squeezing Julian's shoulder so tightly it hurt. When he tried to hit the man earlier, to get him to let go, the man again got angry and put something on his wrists that pinched his skin.

Mommy had once told him that bad people went to jail when he saw something like this on TV. Was he going to jail?

What did he do bad?

Was it the same thing he did that made his daddy leave?

Did he make the same mistake again?

Or did his mommy do something bad this time? Was that why she was standing up there with those other ladies? Because they were going to be punished?

He didn't want to see his mommy get punished. Maybe they could punish him instead and leave his mommy alone.

He looked up at the man who wouldn't let him move. The dark hair, shaggy like a dog's, the black scary eyes, the long nose. He was staring toward the front of the room.

He hated that man. He'd never forget his face.

Too many men were in that room to remember them all, but he wanted to.

Whatever they were doing was wrong. He just knew it. They were the ones who needed to be punished. Not him, not his mommy.

Suddenly, the room became quiet. He could see one of the ladies' head a bit better when she had stepped on a stool or something.

She looked scared. She was crying, too.

She had a rag in her mouth like he did. Why didn't she remove it? Were her hands tied, too? He couldn't see if that was true because he was too small and too many big men blocked his view.

He rose on his tiptoes to see if he could see any better. As soon as he did, the hand holding onto him shoved him back down.

"Don't move. Don't do anything. Just stand there. If you fight, you'll never see your mother again. I already told you that. Don't you want to see your mom again?"

Julian nodded. *Yes! Yes, I want my mommy!*

"Just be patient and you'll see her again soon."

He didn't believe this man. He was a big, fat liar.

But Julian wanted to be with his mommy no matter what, so maybe this time the man wasn't lying.

Lies were bad. Mommy said so. Maybe his mommy told the man to stop lying.

The room became louder when two other men began to cut off the clothes of the lady who could be seen above the crowd. One man had a knife and one a pair of big scissors. Things his mommy never let Julian play with. She said they could be dangerous and he could get hurt.

They cut away the lady's clothing and soon she was in only her underwear. And then, not even that. From where he stood, he could see she was now naked like when he took a bath.

Were they going to make her take a bath? Or a shower like his mommy did?

Julian didn't think she wanted to take a bath. She looked even more scared now. Her eyes, which had been wide, were now squeezed shut as they forced her to turn around in a circle, lifted her hair and let some of the other men touch her.

The room got even louder with what they were saying about her. How pretty she was. How young she was. About her private parts.

Some comments weren't very nice at all.

They were also touching her everywhere. Why were they doing that? Were they hurting her?

Soon the man standing next to the lady stopped the rest of the men from doing their "inspection," as he called it, and told everyone to step back and get ready to "bid."

Julian had no idea what any of that meant.

But he knew it wasn't good.

This was very bad.

He needed to escape the man who was holding him and get to his mommy and help her get away from the man holding her.

His mommy's eyes were moving back and forth. She was probably looking for him, but he couldn't call out to her or lift his hand to wave at her. He couldn't do anything so she'd see him.

He needed to get closer.

He tried to pull away from the painful hold, but the scary-looking man forced him back to his side.

"What did I tell you, brat? You want your mommy to get hurt because you're being a bad boy?"

No, he didn't want his mommy hurt.

He wanted to go home.

He wanted to go home with his mommy.

Why weren't they going home?

Why was he being forced to stand there?

Why was his mommy being forced to stand on the other side of the room?

The man next to the platform began to yell out for "bids."

The shouts of numbers came from men around the room. So quickly, that Julian couldn't keep up. All the big numbers began to blur in his head and he wobbled on his feet.

He hadn't eaten anything since those licks of his ice cream cone, the one he dropped in the parking lot at the mall.

His tummy now hurt. He needed a cup of water or juice because the rag made his tongue feel like he ate sand. He didn't feel so good, either.

Whenever his tummy hurt his mommy helped him by rubbing it. She also gave him ginger ale.

He needed to pee really, really bad, too. He didn't want to do it in his pants since he wasn't a baby. It had been a long time since he'd peed his pants and his mommy said she was proud of him.

He liked to make his mommy happy. When she was happy, he got things like ice cream or cookies. Or sometimes cake. Like for his birthday.

His tummy growled and it hurt.

He didn't know how long he stood there. He didn't know

when the lady on the stool, or whatever she was standing on, disappeared and the next one took her place. That one took a lot longer and looked a lot younger than his mommy and the other lady.

When the girl disappeared, his mommy was shoved forward next for everyone to touch her when she was naked.

Her eyes went wide when she spotted him, but only for a second before men moved again and blocked them from seeing each other.

He wanted to call out to her but couldn't. He thought he heard her screaming his name but he couldn't hear her very good. Not with that cloth in her mouth.

The mean man shoved him forward when the room got really quiet again.

He was finally going to get to see his mommy.

His heart began to beat really, really hard.

Maybe they'd let them go home now since whatever was happening was over.

The men all turned toward him as they made their way toward the front.

Every step took him closer to his mommy.

But the closer they got, he now couldn't see her at all.

She was gone.

Where did she go?

How could she leave him here? With strangers.

A room full of stranger danger.

She told him not to be alone with strangers.

She left him alone with strangers.

When they got to the front of the room, warm liquid soaked the front of his pants and dripped down his leg.

His mommy was going to be mad. But he'd rather have her mad at him than crying and sad. He never wanted to see his mommy sad again.

While the man was mad that Julian wet his pants, he also told everyone around them it didn't matter.

Julian realized why once they cut off all his clothes, too. Then shoved him onto what he could see now was a wooden crate upside down.

He didn't want to stand on the box naked. He didn't want strangers touching him. He didn't want them putting their hand on his privates.

He only wanted him and his mommy to go home.

Maybe if he closed his eyes and wished really, really, *really* hard, it might happen.

And if it did, he'd even promise to never ask for ice cream again.

Chapter Six

WITH THE POWER of his Night Train between his thighs, Shade gave his purring girl a little more throttle to make sure he stayed in formation and didn't drift out of line.

Unfortunately, he kept losing his concentration, kept disappearing back into his head. He kept replaying the nightmare that had woken him during the early morning hours. A nightmare, but also an unfortunate memory.

One of many that had the tendency to replay in his mind when he slept.

One of many that woke him up in a sweat.

One of many that caused him to lie awake at night.

One of many he wished he'd forget.

Especially of the one where his mother had been auctioned off to the highest bidder.

Then disappeared.

That was the last moment he ever saw her. That large room in the large house surrounded by strange men was the last place.

He had lost his father, then his mother.

Shortly after, he lost himself.

That day and for the next decade, he gained new "daddies" and "uncles."

That one large room turned into ten years of countless smaller rooms.

Different room. Same reason.

Different time. Same result.

One day blended into many.

Weeks blended into months.

Months into years.

He didn't know what sparked that particular memory last night. Maybe spending yesterday with Chelle, who was a mother. One he could tell would do anything for her daughters.

She loved to talk, even though he didn't, but that didn't stop her.

She was proud of her girls and talked about them a lot. What—or who—she didn't talk about was the man in the photo. The one standing next to her holding her hand while she wore a white dress.

While she wore his ring.

Before she bore his children.

He didn't ask because it wasn't his business. Shade was only there to make a little extra scratch for him to squirrel away. So he could get back to his plan. To his list.

The worn, folded piece of paper tucked in his wallet.

No. Not now.

He rode toward the rear of the pack, next to Easy. As Road Captain, Cage led the formation. Behind Cage, Trip rode with Stella wrapped around his back, holding tight, her long black hair with blue stripes pulled up and hidden under a purple bandana. Sig as VP rode next to Trip with Red, his ol' lady, holding on tight.

Out of everyone who rode with them on a run, Shade watched Autumn the most. Her red hair reminded him of fire and she hardly ever contained it. She liked the freedom of it whipping around her and her ol' man. Even though it had to become knotted like hell from the wind.

Seeing her so free on the back of Sig's sled did something to Shade.

Red was so strong—the strongest woman he ever knew—but they all looked out for her like she was the most vulnerable. It wasn't only Sig who would do anything for her...

Especially after they all went up that mountain and found out what happened to her. How she was kept, how she survived, what they did to her.

Fuck yeah, she was the strongest woman he knew. He also knew exactly what she'd been through. Though, her nightmare lasted about a year, unlike Shade's decade.

But a year was a year too long.

Red was free now. Happy.

Even though no one said this out loud, she probably saved Sig's life. She definitely motivated the VP to stay out of prison. That right there was a win for Trip. It gave the two half-brothers a chance to mend their relationship and become close again like they were when they were kids. It hadn't happened overnight but they were working on it. Slowly. With the help of Stella and Red.

In the next row, Judge and his cousin Deacon rode side by side with Cassie clinging to the club enforcer and Reese's cheek pressed to the treasurer's cut. As uptight as the lawyer could be, Deacon's ol' lady tended to loosen up during every run and always wore a big smile by the end. Riding on the back of Deacon's sled probably cleared her mind, just like spending time on his own sled usually did for Shade.

Those intelligent, strong women had caught the hearts and souls of Shade's brothers.

The rest filled in behind them. Rook, Rev, Whip, Dutch and Dodge. All ol' lady free like Shade and Easy.

Then there was Ozzy, who had Reilly along for today's

almost four-hour ride. Reese's sister slipped right into being part of the club whether Reese wanted her to or not. Headstrong and outspoken, Reilly easily became everyone's little sister. Even though she wasn't little at all.

No, she was a hot blonde. A younger, wilder version of Deacon's ol' lady. She began to insist on coming along for the club runs from the day she learned about them, even though women usually weren't included unless they were an ol' lady or a "regular," meaning a constant in someone's bed.

Reilly was neither of those.

She usually bounced around with who she rode with, usually whoever would take her. And what fool would say no to the opportunity of having a hot blonde's tits—and not small ones, either—pressed to their leather?

Even Shade had let her ride with him onc Sunday, to the surprise of everyone.

But on his sled in the wind, he didn't have to make conversation. All they had to do was enjoy the ride and the sense of freedom it brought. Every ride cinched their brotherhood even tighter.

After each official club run, they got the chance to eat, drink and be fucking merry, along with getting laid or a really damn good blowjob. Or whatever they were in the mood for, depending on a brother's taste.

As long as getting laid, head, or whatever, didn't involve Reilly, Tessa or Saylor. Those three ladies had "no trespassing" signs tacked to their foreheads by their president, sergeant at arms, Reese and even Rev.

He wondered what it would feel like to have Chelle's arms wrapped around him, her hands pressed to his gut, her tits to his back and her pussy hot against his ass.

A fantasy that would never happen.

No one broke away from the pack today to sneak off for a "sled screw," what they called getting laid on a sled.

He heard the women talking after a run one Sunday about how a sled's vibration either got them horny or got them off. He'd been so quiet, the sisterhood probably didn't even realize he was nearby and could hear them.

No matter what, their ol' men usually benefitted in one way or another. Either on the run or after. With their women either on their backs or on their knees.

The thought of Chelle soaking her panties while riding with him woke up his dick and finally freed him from the dark cloud hanging over him since the early morning nightmare.

Sometimes those memories lingered like a rotten fucking smell.

Funny how the ride itself hadn't helped clear his mind, it took thinking about Chelle to do so.

Whenever he got a chance yesterday, he'd sneak a peek at her. Whether she knew he was watching her or not, he didn't know.

Actually, he didn't care.

Truthfully, if she had turned around, caught him looking and invited him to fuck her right there on the plastic-covered couch, he wouldn't have said no.

He normally didn't jump on every opportunity offered, but he'd have a tough time resisting Chelle. He'd never been so drawn to a woman before. Never thought about a woman much past when his dick was inside her.

So, to think about Chelle like he was kind of worried him.

But something about her soothed his soul. Maybe that was what his brothers felt when they'd met their ol' ladies. When they found the women they wanted to stick.

Listening to Ozzy, Dutch and those who could remember the Originals, it seemed bikers normally weren't loyal to their other halves. Cheating was accepted, even expected, by the club members.

He hadn't seen that with Trip, Sig, Judge, Deacon and now, Cage. Those men kept their eyes on their prize and didn't dare let those eyes wander.

Would that change eventually? Shade had no fucking clue. He didn't know shit about MCs until accidentally becoming a part of the Fury.

He'd rolled into The Grove Inn almost two years ago. Ozzy spotted his sled and began to chat him up. Then Shade noticed his cut and asked about it.

After a few beers and no better place to land, he ended up wearing a prospect patch and finding himself living in a clean room, access to plenty of food, booze and weed, and with a job.

Shade saw it as his luck finally changing.

He went from no family to a fucking huge one. Loud and obnoxious? Sure. Loyal as all fuck? Abso-*fucking*-lutely.

Best part was they usually didn't dig. If he didn't want to talk about his past, he didn't. And so far, no one had picked up on him not being able to read or do complicated math.

If someone guessed, like he thought Easy had, it wasn't even mentioned.

Live and let live.

He was pretty fucking sure Easy picked up on his inability to read because whenever a customer walked into the office and Cassie wasn't around, Easy insisted he help that customer. When the local vet trained the two of them on the crematorium furnaces, Easy had always read instructions out loud, claiming it helped him learn faster.

Easy had quickly became a brother in truth.

He didn't make Shade feel stupid. He never fucking once made fun of him, either, even in jest.

In turn, Shade would do anything for Easy. And the man knew that.

As they turned onto County Line Road, he realized they weren't heading to Dino's Diner. No one told him what the plans were after the run today, and he hadn't asked. He should've known by the sweet butts showing up at The Barn early this morning before the ride.

Didn't matter to him where they ate afterward. He was planning to grab some grub, then hit Chelle's house for a few more hours of painting. There wasn't much left to do to finish up that first room. Rolling a quick second coat should do it unless Chelle wanted something else done.

If he got that out of the way today or tonight, then he could concentrate on work and hunting the Shirleys this week.

That reminded him to pull Judge and Trip aside for a quick update.

Cage led the formation off the hardtop onto the rutted, rough lane of the farm. Trip had been putting off having tons of driveway stone dropped because riding a sled over a thick layer of that shit sucked. The prez would rather have most of the long lane paved, but that cost a shit-ton of scratch.

Anyway, that project had been put aside and the money spent on buying Cage's modular home and getting it set up near Judge's house just on the other side of the tree line.

Trip kept going back and forth on whether the club should invest in a business that specialized in emergency housing like what was brought in for Cage at first. Or buying more modular homes, setting up a little neighborhood on one corner of the large farm and renting them out, almost like a trailer park but with permanent housing on foundations.

Shade ignored most of that talk because he didn't have a head for business. He only did what he was told or did what he knew needed done. He kept it simple and left the hard decisions to the ones in charge. That wasn't him and never would be.

He liked that just fine, too.

They rolled down the lane, breaking formation. Some of his brothers parking their sled near The Barn, some near the pavilion, and some tucking theirs away in the shed for the night. Shade left his near the back door of the bunkhouse so he could take a quick shower after he ate and before he headed over to Chelle's. He needed to rinse off the road dirt and the dead bugs.

He followed Sig—who had an arm draped loosely over Red's shoulders—around the corner and over to the pavilion where everyone was gathering. The sweet butts had set up a spread like a buffet and Ozzy was checking the pig on the spit.

Just the smell of it made Shade's mouth water. He never took good food, like Chelle's homemade chili yesterday, for granted.

Rev was lighting the fifty-five-gallon barrels scattered around the courtyard. Whip was propping open the double side doors to The Barn. Judge and Deacon were carrying a cold keg of beer outside and setting it in a blue plastic half-barrel full of ice.

Shade preferred when they came back to the farm to party, rather than go to Dino's. At the diner, they all had to sit at a bunch of tables pushed together in a back room. Where here, everyone was free to roam and do whatever the fuck they wanted.

Which was sex—and lots of it—drugs—for the most part in the form of pot—and loud rock and roll.

He also couldn't forget the drinking.

Today he wouldn't be drinking much, maybe a beer or two, before he hopped back on his sled and headed into town. He definitely would share a few bong hits, a few puffs off a joint or hits off someone's pipe before heading over to Chelle's, too.

He might not smoke hand-rolled tobacco like a lot of his brothers, but he never turned down weed. He relied on it to keep him sane when his past wanted to do nothing but spin him into insanity.

Sometimes when he began to unravel, he had to reel himself back in before he passed the point of no return.

Even with waking up to that memory, today would end up being a good day. With the run, his brotherhood and spending time with a soul-settling Chelle.

His gaze slid through the courtyard, over the two American Bulldogs who were wrestling in the grass, and landed on the pavilion where the sweet butts weren't the only ones waiting. Saylor and Tessa were helping Lizzy, Angel, Crystal, Billie, Brandy and Amber. At the same time, Daisy was trying to entertain Dyna with a stuffed teddy bear, the baby awake and aware in her stroller.

Cassie's daughter would only be around while everyone ate, then would be shuffled home once the sun set and everyone's morals and mouths began to get loose from beer, booze and sweet butts who lost their clothing. Not that they started out with much to begin with.

They were told to not let everything fly free when Cassie's girl was around. Even so, Judge would keep an eye on things and signal to his house mouse Saylor once it was time for Daisy to disappear.

The six-year-old usually gave Judge a huge helping of sass about having to leave, but it only took a few low spoken words from the big, bearded man to his future adopted daughter for that attitude to turn around.

He was the goddamn Daisy whisperer. Cassie would sit back with a grin on her face as she watched her ol' man and her "mini-me" interact.

Ry left the second week in August to start his freshman year in college. Judge had to be proud of his eighteen-year-old son, who announced he'd be back for Thanksgiving break. Plans were already in the works by the ol' ladies to have a huge Thanksgiving meal in The Barn. Shade had a feeling when Judge's son returned, he'd only have eyes for Saylor again. Unless he found some college girl to focus on, instead.

At that age, it was hard to focus on anything but pussy.

Shade had his first pussy at almost fifteen with a much older woman. He had no idea that was how sex should be for a heterosexual male until he was taught the ins and outs. But once he had a taste of it, he decided it was for him.

Now, he only did it in moderation. Unlike his brothers.

He didn't allow sex to control his life or thoughts because for too many years it had. Even when he didn't understand what it was, what it meant, or why it was happening.

Previously, it had been an activity only to be endured. Something he was forced to do and didn't have a say in the matter. If he resisted, things usually got worse. Unless resisting was expected and encouraged. He'd had two "owners" who got off on him fighting.

However, now he did have a say. A big one. So, when a sweet butt—or any woman—tried to push him to have sex with them, he usually dug in his heels. Nobody was making that decision for him anymore.

Nobody would ever do so again.

Just like someone touching his hair. In the past, it had been forced on him. He'd had no choice. His goddamn body was under his own control now. Nobody was stealing that from him again.

After getting a good buzz on, stuffing his gut, and managing to avoid the sweet butts' sticky fingers, he found Trip and Judge to tell them he needed a moment and a word.

That was all he had to say. Both knew what it was about and automatically headed inside The Barn with Judge's dog, Jury, on the man's heels. Without a word, they climbed their way to the second floor, ending up at the table where the exec committee made their decisions.

It was always just the three of them since the whole committee wasn't in on what Shade was doing. That was for their own protection. They all knew something was going on and probably could guess but the less they knew of the Clan Plan, the better. For now, anyway.

Shade studied the scarred, thick wood table as he sat. The same table the Originals used decades ago. The same table where Trip's father, Buck, sat as president and Judge's father, Ox, sat as sergeant at arms.

Both Trip and Judge were the second generation Fury, while Shade was a newcomer. A nobody. He didn't come from Fury blood. He didn't even come from any biker blood. Even so, he became as much a part of the Fury as the other two men sitting at the same table. That acceptance was one reason he didn't mind heading up the mountain to take out the fucking trash.

But he had his own trash to take out, too. That had been put on hold once he landed in Manning Grove and became a prospect. At first, he wasn't sure he'd stay because he'd never stayed anywhere for any length of time. It was easier to stay under the radar that way. But once here, he sat back, observed and discovered what his life had been missing.

Since the age of four.

He cleared his throat and picked his words carefully, telling them about the armed guard he handled during the week and the issue that happened Friday night with him almost getting caught.

Judge sat quietly and stroked his beard with one hand and Jury's head with the other as he waited until Shade was done speaking. No surprise, Trip's fingers twitched against the table because Shade was speaking so slowly.

Their prez didn't have a lot of patience, but he worked

hard on it. He did his best to be cool-headed and fair. Unlike the former Fury president.

Shade had heard the stories and if Trip had been anything like Buck, he probably would have shed that prospect cut and headed out back on his own. He'd lived with men who were cruel and over-controlling for a decade, he didn't need any more of that shit.

When he was done talking, Judge and Trip both sat back and considered Shade's words.

"You got a good count?" Trip asked, yanking his base-ball cap off, raking fingers through his hair and jerking it back into place.

Shade shook his head. "Tryin' to keep count of the men. Down to eleven now, if I'm right."

"Fuck. They gotta know somethin's happenin'," Trip said.

"Yeah. That's why I'm doin' this sit-down with you. Thinkin' we need to keep a closer eye on our women and kids. Expect the clan to strike back at any time."

"What's to stop them from bringin' in more?" Trip asked, his expression grim as he glanced at Judge. "Like from that Ohio clan. Hell, they could have branches of the Guardians of Freedom all over the fuckin' place."

"But are they all like the Shirleys?" Judge asked, tapping his index finger on the table and staring at the carved Fury logo in the center. "Are they all inbred hillbilly goat fuckers?"

Shade was pretty sure Sig started the "goat fucker" thing, but it had stuck with them all.

"Shirleys are a fuckin' cult-like clan," Trip reminded the enforcer.

"So's the Ohio branch," Judge answered. "Everythin' Red told us about them proved they are."

Trip sighed impatiently. "Sig still wants to do some damage out there on her behalf."

Judge leaned forward with a whole lot of unhappy pulling his lips downward. "Let's just worry about what's in our fuckin' backyard first. Let's squash what and who threatens us and our families. I got two kids. Wanna have another one. Got two women in my household to protect, too. Not to mention my sister and maybe even my aunt. That threat on that mountain needs to be extinguished. We already agreed on that. We need to get it done."

"Gonna be slow," Shade grumbled. Especially since he was the only one working on the Clan Plan.

Trip shrugged one shoulder. "Better to be slow and careful than rushed and reckless."

"Still thinkin' they're gonna strike back and soon," Shade warned. "Can't drag them all off the mountain and dispose of them cleanly. A couple I had to leave where they lay. They know someone's goin' in and takin' them out, that they aren't just wanderin' away or escapin' the cult. Truthfully, not sure why I ain't seein' more armed guards. They should know we ain't gonna just walk away once all the men are gone. Not when there are young boys who'll grow up to be a thorn in our fuckin' side. Or women used to produce more Shirleys. Can see them bringin' more men in from elsewhere. They rule that mountain, they ain't abandonin' it. That's their fuckin' kingdom."

Trip frowned. "Especially when the pigs let them do whatever the fuck they want up there. They're makin' their money with meth and shine. The more scratch they make the more weapons they can buy."

Jury groaned loudly as Judge rubbed her ears faster. "Gotta have a source to get their weapons illegally. They ain't walkin' into a gun shop and buyin' them. No legit gun dealer's sellin' them a weapon without an ID and background check."

"Sure they got a source somewhere," Trip muttered. "Or they're buyin' parts and makin' their own."

"Haven't seen that, but will keep an eye out," Shade told them.

He had found stashes of weapons and ammo but not a "workshop" where they were putting those weapons together. That didn't mean they weren't doing it in one of the cabins or homes. The Shirleys were whacked enough to let their kids help assemble them or even reload ammo.

"Lemme worry about protection down here," Judge grumbled. "Trust you to do whatya gotta do up there. You need help, let me know."

Shade nodded. Judge trusting him was a huge about-face from when Shade first showed up, when the big man decided his prospect name would be "Shady" because Judge didn't trust him. The night they worked together to get Autumn back changed everything. "We done for now?"

"We're done," Trip answered with a nod.

Shade rose to his feet. "Gonna head out."

Trip's eyebrows pulled together. "Ain't stickin' around for the party?"

"Got shit to do."

Judge's fingers combed through his long beard. "You ain't goin' up the mountain tonight, are you?"

"No. Switchin' days up there so it don't become a pattern."

The enforcer nodded. "Good idea."

"So, what or *who* do you have to do?" Trip ribbed him with a grin.

Shade wondered how much he should reveal. It wouldn't hurt to let his prez know why he was disappearing so they didn't worry. He didn't need his brothers heading up the mountain looking for him, thinking he got into trouble up there. "Got a side job."

"Job or piece?" Judge asked with one raised eyebrow.

Trip pushed his chair back and rose to his feet, too, his

grin growing into a big smile. "Gotta be gettin' pussy elsewhere since he hardly hits up the sweet butts."

"Yeah?" Judge asked. When he stood, so did Jury. The blocky-headed bulldog did a quick yawn, then nudged everyone in the nuts like she always did. By now, everyone was used to it. Not that anyone liked it.

"Ain't pussy. Just a small paintin' job to make a little extra scratch."

Trip's brow dropped low. "You hurtin' for scratch?"

"A little extra never fuckin' hurt."

Neither argued that and they didn't dig any deeper.

Thank fuck.

Chapter Seven

CHELLE CARRIED two bottles of cold water toward the front of the house and shook her head when she saw her girls peeking around the corner into the room where Shawn was rolling the last coat of paint.

She sighed loud enough for both of them to hear her and they quickly straightened, knowing they were busted. When they turned with wide eyes, they giggled.

Giggled.

God, she loved the sound of that. She just wanted her daughters to be happy and healthy.

However, their giggling had to do with ogling Shawn. A man too old for either of them. Or, at least, she figured he was. She still didn't know how old he was.

Doesn't matter, Chelle.

But—and that was a big *but*—their mother had been ogling the same man. So, there was that.

That should be weird, right?

Both her daughters were old enough to date, and did so, but she never expected to be interested in the same man as them.

Yes, definitely weird.

Doesn't matter, Chelle.

Unfortunately, her brain—and another important area —didn't agree.

"Madison and Josephine," she scolded as she approached them, hoping Shawn had no idea what was occurring in the foyer.

"Mom, he's hot," Maddie whispered.

"Yeah, like *really* hot," Josie agreed. "I was too focused on Pumpkin the other day to notice."

She bugged her eyes out at them and jabbed a finger toward the room. She mouthed, "He can hear you."

They both elbowed each other and giggled again.

Chelle rolled her eyes and heat crept into her cheeks.

"Mom's blushing!" Josie said way too loudly.

Chelle scowled at her. "Stop it," she hissed.

"C'mon, Mom, don't you think he's hot?" Josie asked. Again, in what seemed like a deafening volume.

She pinned her lips together in a flat line, refusing to answer.

"Mom, we know you don't date, but you need to get out there. It's not healthy for you not to have sex."

What?

"Yeah, you need your pipes cleaned out," was what her seventeen-year-old daughter actually said next.

"Girls, stop!" She grimaced when it came out as a yell. "And you better not know what that means, Josie!"

"Mom, I'm seventeen, not seven. I date, remember?"

"You better not be getting your pipes cleaned out," Chelle warned.

Maddie smothered a snort.

Chelle spun on her older daughter. "That's not funny. Your sister better not be having sex."

Maddie threw up her hands. "I have no idea if she's boning any boys."

Chelle's mouth dropped open, air rushed out and she

stared at her two girls. Both who were little girls not so long ago. With pigtails and everything. "I'm disowning you both before you give me a heart attack. Stop laughing! I'm being serious."

"*Mommmy*," Josie started and leaned into Chelle with a grin.

Chelle raised a hand. "No. None of this is funny. Just... go... elsewhere. Anywhere but here right now." Out of hearing distance of Shawn. "We need to get this room done." Though, Chelle wanted to disappear into the floor right now. Forget walking into that room.

He probably heard all of that, even with the radio on...

"Then can we go to Lycoming Mall? We're supposed to meet up with Cherise and Sammie to watch a movie and grab dinner at Applebee's."

At least she could call her brother to confirm her girls were with their cousins and not "boning" some random boys.

Madison was twenty and now technically an adult, but still... No matter how old she was, Chelle was allowed to worry. Like it or not, until she moved out on her own, Maddie had to follow Chelle's rules.

Ugh, she wanted to cry. When the hell did they grow up to the point where they were checking out the same man?

Or having sex?

Or having more sex than their mother?

The blood that had gathered in her face drained. She needed to schedule a sit-down with both of them again and have another discussion about safe sex. Just a reminder.

A precaution.

She also needed to remind them they could come to her about anything.

Even sex.

Oh God. Just not right now with Shawn on the other side of the wall.

"You both have school tomorrow."

"We'll be back before curfew," Josie assured her.

"You don't have any assignments pending?"

"Nope, all done," Maddie answered. "Josie?"

"No, I did all my homework during study hall on Friday."

"No tests to study for?" Chelle prodded. She sighed when both answered no. "Okay. Do you need money?"

Both girls got good grades and worked part-time, they deserved an evening of fun. At least they'd be with their cousins, who were within the same age range. Even better, weren't wild and crazy.

Her older brother Rick and his wife were pretty strict with their daughters. All four of the girls had grown up more like sisters than cousins. Especially after Brendan died. Rick had stepped in as their father figure.

Thankfully.

Neither girls answered the money question. Instead, they pasted hopeful looks on their faces, which meant they had their own money, but preferred not to spend it.

She sighed. "Fine. Go in my wallet and grab my Visa. I can't give you cash because I need to pay Shawn. Movies and dinner only. Got it? Anything else you pay for yourself."

Josie bounced on her toes, then gave Chelle a kiss on her cheek. "Thanks, Mom!"

"Thanks, Mom!" Maddie yelled as she rushed down the hallway toward the kitchen where Chelle's purse was.

"Take Maddie's car. It's more reliable," she yelled as they disappeared. She slapped a hand to her forehead. "Oh my God, who said having kids was a good idea?" She sighed again and walked into the room.

And froze just inside the doorway.

She bit back a nervous giggle that would've sounded like her daughters'.

Shawn stood in the center of the room with hands on

his hips and his dark brown, almost black, eyes on her. His long hair was still pulled back and he wore the same clothes he painted in yesterday. But then, so did she. No point in getting paint splatter on more clothing than necessary.

"Is there a problem?" Her question got caught in her throat at the way he was studying her.

She moved closer and held out one of the water bottles. When he took it from her, their fingers brushed and she swore she felt a shock.

He must have felt it, too, since he quickly jerked his hand away. She glanced down. Nothing in the room, or where they stood, would've created static.

"No problem," he finally answered, as he continued to stare at her while cracking open the lid on the now sweating bottle. "Just thirsty."

You're not the only one.

She cleared her throat, opened her water and hoped it cooled her molten insides.

She turned in a circle, pretending to study their progress, as she took a long sip, wishing it was vodka. When she was done, she said, "We should be done within the hour, right?"

"Yeah."

"I'll wait until tomorrow to uncover everything and move the furniture back."

"I'll do it before I leave."

She shook her head. "I'll get the girls to help. I just gave them money; they can earn it by helping me."

Chelle heard him make a noise in his throat and she turned her attention back to him.

"Good mom," was all he said.

"Are you asking if I am or stating I am?"

"Tellin'."

He didn't know her well enough to know if she was or wasn't, but she appreciated him saying it. "Thanks. I try."

There were plenty of times while raising two teenagers

where she questioned whether she was a good parent. But both girls still had all their fingers and toes, so she must have done something right.

"Once we're done, I'll get you paid."

"No rush," he mumbled, putting down his water and heading back to the wall he'd been working on. Before he picked up the roller from the paint tray, he turned to face her again. "Chelle." His voice was quiet.

She wiped a hand over her mouth and screwed the cap back on her water bottle. "Hmm?"

"Think I'm hot?" His voice also held a hint of amusement.

She knew the instant the blush hit her face. She turned away to hide it and pressed the water bottle to her cheek to cool it.

Oh my God, Chelle, you are not Josie's age. You're forty-one!

"Chelle."

Him saying her name the way he just said it sent not only her heart to flutter, but also the place between her legs that had been untouched for longer than she'd like to admit.

So much longer.

"Yes?" came out on a squeak.

When she glanced over her shoulder at him—because, *damn it*, she couldn't resist—she saw his lips quirk the slightest bit.

"That a question or the answer?"

She turned, not hiding her surprise. "You don't know you're hot?"

"Don't give a fuck about that."

That shouldn't be a shocker. After working beside him, she noticed he wasn't cocky or arrogant at all. Nor pushy or aggressive like she would've stereotyped bikers, even though she'd never known one personally before. Shawn seemed to be a more of a *roll-with-the-punches* type of guy.

"You don't seem to be vain." She added, "I think you're

too young," then grimaced. She should've kept that thought buried deep in her head. Evidence she'd been considering him as a *man* and not only someone helping her out for some extra cash.

"For who?"

She didn't even know if he was single. She should stop assuming everything about him and just encourage him to keep painting. How hot he was or his relationship status didn't matter.

Doesn't matter, Chelle, she reminded herself for the hundredth time.

"My girls are just obsessed with boys right now. Ignore whatever they say."

"Not a boy."

No, he wasn't. He was... *not* a boy. Far, far, *far* from a boy.

She mentally rolled her eyes at herself.

"They said you should be out datin' again. Takin' that means you don't got a man."

She let that last sentence swirl around her brain and wondered if she should blow it off or answer. She hated admitting she didn't have a husband because she was a widow.

She didn't need a man to be strong. She didn't need a man to be her backbone. She didn't need a man to support her financially. She might not be rich, but they were doing just fine. She'd raised her daughters on her own for all these years. Her daughters were doing well, even getting a college education. She was proud of them.

But still...

For some reason, she hated telling people her husband was dead.

Not because it hurt—even years later, it still did—but because it made her feel vulnerable. It was ridiculous, she knew, but she still couldn't shake that feeling.

She decided to ignore the question that wasn't quite a question and picked up her roller. If she concentrated on painting, then she wouldn't think about the man behind her who discovered she was single.

And wonder why it would matter to him.

Because it shouldn't.

The only thing that should matter was getting the room finished.

She released the breath she was holding as soon as she heard the sound of paint being rolled onto the wall across the room.

She was grateful he didn't keep pushing.

Because if he kept pushing, she'd push back. And she'd bet he'd like it about as much as she did.

AFTER THROWING out the plastic paint tray liners and the dirty roller covers in the garage, Chelle walked through the laundry room and into the kitchen to find Shawn leaning back against the counter with his legs crossed at the ankles and his arms crossed over his chest.

Probably waiting to be paid.

If he wasn't watching her, she might have stopped inside the doorway and let herself simply absorb what a beautiful man he was.

He might be a lot younger than her but he seemed to be an old soul.

She liked that about him.

Actually, there wasn't much about him she didn't like. She had enjoyed spending time with him, even if they hadn't had any deep conversations. Just his presence in the same room made her feel...

Whole.

Which was really strange and also a bit disturbing that a

man she just met made her feel that way. Because in truth, she hadn't felt completely whole in a long time.

When the Army representatives knocked on her door to "regretfully" inform her that Brendan had been killed, she thought she was going to die herself. Thought her heart had been so irrevocably broken it had stopped beating and would never start again.

For longer than she wanted to admit, she actually wished it.

She didn't think she could live without him. Her soulmate had been ripped from her and she didn't think she'd ever recover.

But the reality was, she had two other souls to take care of. Pieces of Brendan. It was her responsibility to make sure they survived the loss of their father. She needed to not only remain strong for them, but appear resilient, even if she was destroyed on the inside.

It was the most difficult thing she ever did in her life. She had taken a breath, patched up any cracks showing on the outside, and hoped it would be enough.

Her girls had been so young at the time they had a difficult time understanding that they'd never see their daddy again. While they were used to their father being gone a lot —every time he was deployed—he always came home on leave.

Always.

And then...

Never again.

He would never walk into their home again dressed in fatigues, put his rucksack down and hug them, tell them how much he loved and had missed them.

His voice had been silenced. His direct influence on his daughters gone. They'd never again feel his touch.

The next time they'd be near him would be when his remains laid in a flag-covered casket. She tried to remain on her feet while holding tightly to her little girls' hands.

The three of them jumped and Chelle's heart had beaten wildly with each explosive shot in the three-volley salute done by the Honor Guard.

After the ceremony, the tearful hugs and words of condolences from both people she knew and strangers alike, Rick had picked up both crying girls and took them away, leaving Chelle to say her final goodbye to her husband alone.

In truth, she wanted to climb into the hole, lay on the casket and let them cover her with dirt.

She hadn't had enough time with him.

Not nearly enough.

He was young and healthy and doing his duty to his country and family. This shouldn't have happened.

How could a good man die when evil continued to exist?

Life wasn't fair.

It could be downright cruel.

But there didn't seem to be anything cruel or evil about the man she approached. She went toe to toe with him and his nostrils flared ever so slightly as she slowly reached around him to grab her purse. It had been left knocked over and open on the counter after the girls had dug through it to find her credit card.

She remained right where she stood, her eyes locked on his darker ones, and blindly dug inside it for her wallet. After slipping it out of the zippered opening, she leaned in again as she returned the purse to the same spot, keeping her wallet in her now trembling hand.

She only dropped her gaze long enough to remove the cash and count it to make sure it was enough. Once she ensured it was, she held the bills between them, hoping he wouldn't notice how he affected her. Though, she was pretty sure she was looking at him like he was a glass of ice water and she was extremely parched.

Without looking at the money, he pulled it from her fingers with excruciating slowness. When he shifted forward, she held her breath, wondering if he was going to touch her.

The movement of air brushed along her skin, instead. Their chests were separated by only inches, his face even closer. So close, she could see the black flecks in his dark brown irises.

Her lips parted and her breathing shallowed as he reached behind himself, pulled out his chained wallet, unsnapped the flap and tucked the money inside with the quickness of a sloth. All without counting it.

She forced, "You don't want to count it first?" from her seized throat.

He shook his head, his eyes still holding hers and softly said, "Trust you," as he slipped his wallet back into his pocket.

Trust you.

He might as well have said, "I want to fuck you," because that was what her body heard.

Loud and clear, too.

A current ran through her, causing her nipples to pucker painfully in the sports bra she wore under Brendan's white button-down shirt. It was one of a few shirts she kept for working around the house, not for sentimental reasons. She had kept plenty of other items that held more meaning and memory.

Heat swirled in her belly as his eyelids drew low over his eyes, taking them from dark brown to black, especially with the way his pupils expanded.

Luckily, her pussy clenching hard jerked her free from her sexual stupor and brought her back to reality.

Good God, she needed to step back before she melted

from the scorching heat between them. Or she touched him inappropriately again. Without asking.

If she asked, would he...?

No, Chelle!

Where was the water bottle she used to spray Pumpkin with when he was a kitten and used to jump on the kitchen counters? Someone needed to squirt her with it.

Bad, pussy, bad!

She was losing it. She swallowed hard and forced herself to take a step back. Her fingers had soldered themselves to her wallet, so she loosened her grip and put it behind her on the table nearby, doing her best to gather herself.

She cleared her throat. "As soon as I get more money saved, we can do another room."

"Guess I'm done here, then."

She didn't want him to leave. Not yet.

If you were smart, Chelle, you'd let him leave before you do something stupid.

"Are you hungry?"

Like ask him to stay for leftovers.

He shook his head. "Stuffed myself earlier."

She wondered if he cooked for himself or someone cooked for him. Maybe he did have a girlfriend or wife.

She should just let him leave. "How about a beer instead of another bottle of water?" Of course, she should.

"You got beer?"

She smiled at his obvious teasing. "Of course I have beer. It's a local craft beer from a brewery in Williamsport, though."

"Beer's beer."

The talk of beer had cooled the smolder between them a smidgeon. She could breathe a little easier as she went to the fridge and opened it. "Don't let a master brewer hear you say that. It's an art."

"Yeah?"

She grabbed two bottles and shut the fridge door with her foot. "I watched a documentary on the process of making beer." She placed them on the counter and pulled out the bottle opener from her junk drawer. Even if they were twist tops she always used the opener to make it easier.

She jumped when the question, "Gonna make your own?" came from close behind her.

He grabbed one bottle, twisted it open and handed it to her, then opened the second one for himself.

"No, I'm just a nerd like that."

"Doubt you're a nerd."

"Don't bet on it. You'd lose." She lifted her bottle between them and when he lifted his in response, she tapped them together. "In celebration of a job well done."

His expression was unreadable, and he kept his eyes on hers as he raised the bottle to his lips. As he swallowed, Chelle watched his Adam's apple roll up and down his throat.

She wanted to lick him there.

Gah!

She took a long pull of her beer and broke his gaze.

"Chelle..."

"We make a good team," she said quickly.

He said nothing.

The temperature in the room spiked a few degrees again. "I need some air. Let's go sit out back." She rushed past him and unlocked the slider, shoving it open and taking a huge inhale to calm her nerves as she stepped outside.

She didn't bother to see if he was following but when she heard the slider close, her question was answered.

Since it was late enough for the sun to be down, she flipped the switch for the string of lights that hung from the outer edge of the overhang and met in the middle, like the top of a circus tent.

She loved the backyard area of her house. Over the

years she had done the work herself, or hired it out when she could, to get it to how she wanted it. Like installing the six-foot-high wooden privacy fence and the large patio made of stone pavers.

Once the girls learned to swim, she had a small above-ground pool installed for them and their friends to enjoy. Though, she got some enjoyment out of floating around on those hot, sweltering days, too. Or lounging on the patio in the shade, reading.

She had spent a lot of time out back, working on the landscaping, planting flowers, evergreens and butterfly bushes, and simply decorating the area with cute yard sale finds to make her happy.

And it did.

When the girls weren't home, it was a good place to enjoy the quiet. She had neighbors on both sides who kept to themselves, friendly but not overly nosy. And the neighbor directly behind her was elderly and didn't come outside too often.

So, her little haven was peaceful.

She settled into a thick-cushioned wicker chair and took another sip of beer, kicking up her feet on the matching ottoman in front of her and leaning back. Her sigh filled the silence.

She was bone-tired and tomorrow she was sure she'd be stiff and achy from all the taping and painting they did in the last two days, but it would be worth it. One room down, too many to go.

She wasn't in a rush since she wasn't moving anytime soon. Whether she'd stay in Manning Grove after she retired from her job, she didn't know but doubted she would since northern Pennsylvania could be very cold and snowy in the winter. It also depended on where her girls settled. She would love to be near her grandchildren.

She had a difficult time wrapping her head around her

babies raising their own. Hopefully neither would rush to make her a grandmother.

Again, that reminded her to have another discussion with them about safe sex. She already knew her girls would love every second of that conversation and she'd get plenty of eye rolls and sarcastic complaints.

Speaking of sex...

Shawn had taken the chair on the other side of the side table and after a few more minutes of silence, he asked, "You do all this?"

She stared out at the yard. "Yes."

"You swim?"

"Yes," she answered automatically, then twisted her head toward him at the odd question for someone who owned a pool. "Don't you?"

He didn't answer and also didn't look in her direction. Instead, he tipped the bottle to his lips. When he was done, he reached up and pulled the elastic band from his head, shook his long, curly hair out and let it fall around his shoulders and chest.

Holy hell.

He raked his fingers through the length a couple of times, released a long, low sigh and put his boots up on the ottoman in front of his own chair. Then he melted into it like every bone in his body no longer existed.

She smiled at how relaxed he looked. He had worked hard so he deserved to kick up his feet and have a beer. Or two.

"Beautiful," he said softly, still surveying the outside area.

She turned from his strong profile and let her gaze slide through the backyard to see it through his eyes. "Yes, it is."

"Not it. You."

She caught her bottom lip in between her teeth and

stared at him again. He was so quiet, she wished she could read his thoughts.

She didn't know the last time anyone had told her that, besides her girls while using her to practice on with hair or makeup.

Oh, and her hairdresser, Teddy. He always made a fuss about the natural color of her hair.

Other than that, no one had told her she was beautiful in a long, long time.

She blinked away the unexpected sting at the corner of her eyes. She should thank him but she was afraid her voice might crack.

After a few deep breaths, she said, "And, yes, I think you're hot," since she never answered him earlier.

He finally turned to her.

And grinned.

Holy hell, that grin made things flutter inside her.

"But..." *You're too young.*

"But?" The little lights hanging above them made his dark eyes sparkle like onyx.

Don't go there, Chelle. It doesn't matter that you think he's too young for you. Because he isn't for you, period. Too young, too old, too hot, too quiet... None of it matters.

She shook her head. "Nothing."

She wasn't surprised when he didn't push it. She had quickly learned that about him. He accepted anything she said at face value. If she wanted to tell him more, he was fine with it. If she didn't, he was fine with that, too.

She never met a man like that. The ones she knew pestered until they got an answer, even if it wasn't the one they wanted to hear. Her brother was like that. Brendan had been like that, too. They didn't know when to let a subject drop.

"Can I ask you a question?" Then, neither did she.

Instead of answering, one shoulder rose and fell. She

assumed that meant she could continue. She had also learned in the very short amount of time they'd spent together, if he didn't want to answer, he wouldn't.

"You speak very deliberately."

He lifted the bottle to his lips, drained the last of his beer and put the empty bottle down on the patio. All slow and deliberate, similar to how he spoke. "Not a question."

Okay, then. She'd follow up her inquiry with a very simple question. "Why?"

He stared at her for longer than she expected before he asked a question of his own. "It matter?"

She kept telling herself that anything and everything about him shouldn't. But that was a lie. "I'm curious." More than curious. It had been bugging her.

"Why?"

Yes, Chelle, why? "I'm a librarian. Words are my life." That was partially the truth.

"Books."

She shook her head. "No, not just books. Words in all forms. Stories, documentaries, lyrics, speeches. I love it all. Spoken, written, sung." She glanced over at him, and watched his profile as he continued to stare out through the yard. "So, of course, I'm going to notice when someone picks their words carefully." She paused, questioning her next question, but, *screw it*, she pushed on. "Do you have a stutter?"

"No."

She waited. Either he would expand on that answer or he wouldn't. She wouldn't force him. It could be he was embarrassed about whatever it was and she didn't want him to feel uncomfortable. But he also had to feel the natural rapport between the two of them, right?

She couldn't be imagining it.

He turned and stared at her for a long minute, during which she actually held her breath, and finally answered,

"Maybe I like to be careful with what I say. Once somethin's said, hard to take those words back."

While that was true, that wasn't the reason he spoke in the manner he did. If it wasn't a stutter, then it was something else. Possible head trauma in the past, or some sort of disability. Because in the last two days they'd spent together, he'd also mixed up words.

She'd caught it a couple of times when she was sure he wasn't aware of it. The couple of times he was, he quickly corrected himself. Every time it happened, it was when he spoke at a faster clip. Almost as if his brain misfired.

She wanted to dig deeper, but also didn't want him to clam up.

She enjoyed the easy companionship he provided. It was nice to have a conversation with an adult, even though he didn't speak a lot. She was around young children all day and her girls at home. Occasionally her brother or sister-in-law popped over, but they were both busy so neither stayed long. Now that the girls were older, they usually only checked in, unless it was a holiday, then the two families spent more time together.

And the staff at work... Well, she rarely had any kind of long conversations with any of them. She ate her lunch in her office or she stepped outside, if the weather was nice. But even after all these years, she really hadn't forged any close relationships. Like in high school, the school staff had their cliques.

All of that was probably why she spent a lot of time talking to herself. Or reading. Or listening to audiobooks and podcasts. Watching a classic movie by herself or a newer movie with her girls. Or just losing herself in music while cleaning or cooking.

The only time she felt lonely was when she thought of Brendan. Other than that, she was fine with her own company.

When he didn't say anything more on it, she finished her beer and stood. "I'll get you another."

He didn't get up to leave, or claim he didn't want another beer, so she headed inside and grabbed two more.

When she came back out, his arms were folded behind his head and his eyes were shut. But they opened when she stopped next to him.

He held out his hand for his beer but after tucking it between his thighs, he held out his hand again. She handed him hers and he twisted off the top for her. As he handed it back, he let his fingers slowly slide over hers, but didn't pull away completely.

Such a simple touch, such a complex reaction.

She didn't pull away, either, when he wrapped his hand tighter over hers.

His Adam's apple bobbed once. Twice. "Chelle?"

Her heart skipped a beat. "Yes." Honestly, no matter what he asked next, she was pretty damn sure she'd say that same answer.

And that could be reckless.

But he didn't ask anything. Nothing at all. He only took a few silent moments to stare up at her as she stared down at him while their hands remained connected.

Eventually his fingers twitched over hers. An unspoken message to accompany his words. "My brain sometimes hiccups. So, to hide it—when I'm forced to speak—I do it slowly. Like now. I choose my words carefully and think them through first so I don't fuck up. Sometimes you might hear me say the wrong word."

"Sometimes you catch it..." she began.

He tilted his head but didn't say anything more.

"Sometimes you don't," she finished. "Do you know why?"

"Got an idea."

He only had an idea? His issue hadn't been diagnosed by a professional? "Head trauma?"

"No."

She waited and when he didn't continue, she wanted to scream in frustration. He didn't have to tell her anything, but he told her enough for her to want more. She needed to know more.

She wanted to machine gun more questions at him. He couldn't just leave her hanging. That wasn't fair.

She squeezed her eyes shut.

Life isn't fair. You know that, Chelle.

She knew that only too well.

Her eyes popped open when he tugged on her hand holding the beer. Did he want her beer?

No.

That was *not* what he wanted.

He gently tugged again.

Was she going to give him what he wanted?

It wouldn't be smart to sit on his lap, so instead she perched on the arm of the chair, trying to keep most of her weight off it, just in case it wasn't strong enough to hold her. She kept her eyes locked on him even when he didn't release her hand and his other slipped under the oversized shirt, curled around her hip over her leggings and squeezed.

Holding her there, but not trapping her. Though, the slow back and forth slide of his thumb over the fabric at her hip might as well be a restraint. She couldn't pull away even if she tried.

She fought the urge to slip into his lap, what he originally wanted, and forced herself to remain where she was instead. To try to keep a grasp on reality.

Because right now, she really wanted to experience her fantasy. A night of her and Shawn connected in a more intimate way. No invading thoughts of kids, their difference in age, or what he belonged to.

Which was a motorcycle gang.

She had no idea what a group of bikers involved themselves in. Only what she'd generally read or seen in the news. Or the little she'd heard around town when it came to Shawn's MC specifically. Though after this weekend, she planned on doing some research.

However, what she'd heard about bikers involved violence, drugs, guns and run-ins with both law enforcement and other motorcycle clubs.

Even if he wanted her and she allowed herself to have him—even for a few hours—she didn't want any of that touching her daughters in any way.

She should break his touch and free herself from his spell. But the pull to hear more about him was even stronger than her self-preservation.

"Whatever it is, whatever causes these... hiccups. You haven't gotten professionally diagnosed with the cause. Am I wrong?"

"Not wrong."

"Why didn't your parents take you to see specialists?" She couldn't imagine not doing everything in her power to help her own child. Even if she couldn't afford it, she'd find a way.

"No reason to."

"I don't understand."

"It's simple."

He released the hand holding her beer and she placed the bottle on the ground next to her feet. She twisted toward him, so she could see his face better. "Tell me."

Chapter Eight

*T*ELL *ME.*

Not a demand, but a soft request. One he was surprised he considered answering.

He hadn't told anyone.

Like Easy, some might have guessed. But most didn't pay close enough attention to care.

Why he would discuss this with Chelle, he had no fucking clue.

But he was drawn to her in ways he'd never been drawn to a woman before. He didn't understand it, probably never would.

Truthfully, the reason why didn't make a difference.

She invited him into her house, first because of her cat and then due to needing help. He was done with both. He should leave.

Only he didn't want to. He liked her sitting close. He liked touching her even more.

He couldn't deny the connection between them. Seeing her response—the change in her eyes, her breathing, her body—she couldn't ignore it, either.

He had no idea when her girls would be home. But it would be a good idea if he was gone before they returned.

He just couldn't make himself remove his hand from her hip or stop wanting her to slide into his lap. To touch her more thoroughly. To release her hair from the sloppy loop at the top of her head and bury his face in it. To taste her skin, steal her breath, make her shudder with an orgasm.

To hear her say his name while that happened.

Not Shawn. Not Shade. But his real name. He wanted to give her that. A part of him he didn't give freely.

He was about to reveal a secret he hadn't shared with anyone else. But he wasn't sure how she would react to it. *For fuck's sake*, she was a librarian who loved words.

He fucking hated words.

Words screwed him up.

Words were a part of his life he still couldn't control. As much as he wanted to.

When he was young, one of his "daddies" tried to teach him. Eventually the man gave up in anger and frustration, calling Shade stupid and retarded.

Fucking *retarded*.

Slow and unable to learn.

Even though Shade wanted to learn. He tried.

He failed time and time again.

After that, no one else had ever been willing to help him. Not one person.

They wanted him for only one reason.

He didn't need to be smart for that. He only needed to be compliant. Willing to do whatever was needed so he wouldn't get that next fucking cut, that next burn, that next bruise, that next bloody lip. Those next damaging words.

Like being called a retard.

He cringed at the memory.

No. Not now.

He jumped when a soft, warm hand gently cupped his jaw. Chelle tilted his face back up toward hers. "Tell me."

Fuck. He only wanted to hold her.

To lose himself in her.

To forget what happened to him. Even if only for a little while.

They each had their own lives and neither of their lives would mesh.

To ask her for a quick fuck would be insulting. She was better than that.

She was smart. He wasn't.

She had a family. He only had a brotherhood of bikers.

They were so fucking different.

That didn't stop him from wanting her.

She seemed to want him, too, but his next words might change that.

Maybe it was for the best.

"Can't read."

The fingers cupping his jaw twitched and the muscles under his hand on her hip tensed. He released her so she could escape, put space between them.

But she didn't pull away. The only thing that moved were her lips, when she frowned and asked, "What?"

Was she going to make him repeat it?

"Why weren't you taught to read? Your school... your parents had to have known, right?"

"No parents. Was an orphan." That was the easiest way to describe his childhood.

"I'm sorry." Her brow furrowed. "Were you a foster child?"

No, he'd been bought and sold. The men had paid *for* him. They weren't paid to take care of him, like a foster family would be.

"Chelle," he said softly. He wouldn't get into this with her. Not here, not now.

Not with anyone. Even her.

He'd give her some secrets, but not all.

So far she hadn't pulled away, but if he even scratched the surface of why he couldn't read, she would be shocked and horrified and he didn't want to see her looking at him like that.

Not ever.

He didn't want her pitying him, either.

She removed her hand from his cheek and planted it solidly on his chest. "But—"

"Don't wanna talk about it, Chelle."

"But—"

He shifted sharply to get up, but the hand on his chest pushed him back into his seat.

"Hold on. Fine. You don't want to talk about it. I get it. But, Shawn..."

He clenched his teeth at that name. It didn't belong to him. Just like Chelle didn't belong to him, either.

"Don't you want to learn?"

Who the hell wouldn't want to know how to read? Not being able to read signs, directions, or documents, emails or texts even, had handicapped him. He had adapted as best as he could, but it still put him behind the eight ball. It made him look like a fucking idiot when he couldn't do something simple like read the color on a goddamn paint can lid. "Don't think it's possible."

"What do you mean? It's not impossible."

"Chelle."

"I can teach you," she insisted.

What the fuck? "No."

"Yes. I can teach you. My job involves my love for words. Sharing those words, expanding others' horizons, is what I do for a living. I want to share those words with you."

I want to share those words with you.

"Chelle..."

She lifted the hand not planted over his pounding heart to stop him. "We can barter."

He sucked in a breath and softly blew it back out. "Barter."

"Yes. I can teach you to read in exchange for painting the rest of my house. This way we both get what we need."

What he really needed was her. To be inside her. To take her mouth. To stop this conversation.

"Someone tried before. It didn't world."

"World?"

"Work," he spat out. *Goddamn it.* "Not a child. Don't wanna be treated like one." He regretted how harshly that came out, but, luckily, she took no offense.

"Plenty of adults don't know how to read, Shawn. It doesn't mean you can't learn. You just have to be willing."

"Chelle..."

"You can keep repeating my name until the cows come home but it doesn't change the fact I want to do this for you. And, in turn, I get what I need without having to wait until I can afford it. At the rate I can pay you to paint, it would take a long time to get my house finished. It's the perfect solution for both of us."

The perfect solution.

Not quite.

"Got a job." He spent his weekdays at the crematorium and a couple of nights a week hunting and tracking the Shirley Clan. She knew the first, he couldn't tell her about the second.

"I know. Only during the day during the week, though, right?" She shrugged. "We can paint on the weekends. I'll teach you to read after work. Unless..." Her lips pressed flat, making him want to run his thumb over them.

"Unless," he prodded.

"Unless there's somewhere you need to be after work."

She had no idea.

"I wouldn't want us spending all that time together and causing an issue with someone important in your life."

What the fuck was she talking about? Who was she worried about causing issues with? His brothers?

"You could always ask her and get back to me."

He frowned. "Her who?"

"The person who cooks for you. Why you weren't hungry tonight."

The sweet butts? She wasn't making any sense.

Finally, her guarded expression broke when she bugged out her eyes at him. "Your girlfriend... or wife... or whatever."

A slow grin grew across his face. She was digging, that was what she was doing.

He was used to being around women who were direct, not women who skirted around questions to get their answers. Any woman he knew would have just blurted out, "You fucking anyone?" and that would be that.

It was cute how she had gone about it.

What was also cute was the blush that shot from the V neckline of her baggy white shirt up her slender throat and into her cheeks. It made him want to release some of those buttons to see how far south it had spread.

"Don't got a regular."

Her brow dropped low and she gave her head a little shake. "A regular?"

"No woman," he explained.

He did *not* miss the flash of relief crossing her face before she quickly hid it. "Ah... Okay... Well... That means I wouldn't be taking you away from anyone... during our lessons... I mean." She rolled her lips under and the blush in her cheeks became even darker.

"Chelle..."

"Yes?"

"Know how fuckin' gorgeous you are?"

"Uh... I..." Her white teeth bit into her plump bottom lip and that was so fucking sexy. The sweet butts did it on purpose to tease the guys. Chelle did it without thinking about it.

"Know what? Like it that you don't. Gorgeous, genuine and humble. Can't fuckin' beat that."

"So..." She jutted out her hand. "Deal?"

He noticed the slight tremor of her extended hand. It wasn't nerves. She wasn't afraid of him. The tremble was caused by a rush of blood.

By her reaction to him.

She wanted him and she had no clue how much he wanted her. Even if she thought she knew, she'd be wrong.

His dick now pressed hard against the zipper of his jeans. He needed to adjust it. Or release it. He liked the second option best. He wasn't sure Chelle would.

She might not be afraid of him, but she might be afraid of what was about to happen.

Because it would happen.

If not tonight, then soon.

He wrapped his hand around hers and before she could shake it, he tugged on it. With a little gasp, her weight landed in his lap, her ass crushing his erection. He wanted to squeeze those soft cheeks, separate them, explore them. Any way she'd allow.

Their faces were only inches apart now. Her breathing ragged. Her eyes—light brown with a hint of gold—held a bit of surprise.

He kept his grasp on her loose, so she could pull away or, *hell*, even run away if she felt the need.

He would never do anything to her if she wasn't willing.

He'd lived that life. He'd never subject another person to the same.

In truth, that wasn't a life, it was only an existence.

But the woman in his lap was more than existing.

She was warm and soft and smelled good. Really fucking good. It wasn't perfume or soap or even paint he smelled.

He flared his nostrils and took his time inhaling, deeply filling his lungs with her.

Her mouth parted when she realized what he was doing. Picking up the unmistakable scent of her arousal. Which made him even harder.

A puff of air escaped her open lips when his dick flexed beneath her.

"Girls gone." He slid the glasses from her face and, without looking, set them on the little table next to his chair. "No man."

The man in the photo had to be out of the picture if her girls wanted her to date. And if she had another one, she would be saying it loudly and climbing out of his lap.

"Shawn." The name she thought was his caught in her throat and he followed the rolling movement as she swallowed.

He leaned in and slid his nose up along the length of her neck, breathing her in. He touched the soft, warm skin at the edge of her jaw with the very tip of his tongue and drew it back down. The urge to sink his teeth into her, suck on that delicate skin, was strong but the raging pulse under his tongue helped him keep control.

Her racing heart was either due to her being scared of where this was going, or because she was highly aroused.

The unmistakable sweet, but musky, scent said the second.

But he needed to hear it from her before he took it any further.

"Chelle..." The way he said her name made it clear what he was asking, even without saying the actual words.

The only word needed to be heard would be from her. When she said yes.

He slid his palm from her knee over the stretchy black

cotton that encased her thigh to the edge of where the heat radiated from her.

Where he wanted to bury himself deep, surround himself with that searing heat.

"We should keep this to our barter, right? I mean, it could get messy otherwise."

This. She meant the two of them.

Disappointment surged through him. She was right. "Could get really fuckin' messy."

But when the fuck was life neat?

"Messy could be worth it," was the last thing she said before grabbing his face and taking his mouth.

He figured that was a big fucking yes.

Her lips smashed against his and he waited for them to open, to invite him inside. He drew his tongue over the crease of her mouth, asking for entrance.

Her hands slid from his face into his hair and she gripped it tightly, opening her mouth with a groan. He met hers with one of his own.

His throbbing dick was caught crooked, but he ignored the discomfort, to explore her mouth. She tasted like beer, but then so did he. Her tongue tentatively touched his. Once, twice. Then they tussled.

With one hand on her ass, and the other on her jaw, he deepened the kiss, desperately wanting to flip her over, rip her leggings down and sink deep inside her.

In the place where he wanted to lose himself.

Maybe even find himself, too.

Find himself.

That thought made him break the kiss and pull back. They stared at each other and he wasn't sure who looked more surprised as they both tried to catch their breath.

"Fuck," he muttered, scraping a hand down his cheek. "Sorry, I—"

"No, it's…" She scrambled from his lap and he let her go.

He squeezed his eyes shut and tried to slow his barreling thoughts. He wouldn't be able to get the words out right if he didn't slow the fuck down. They would all come out a jumbled mess. Then he would sound like a bigger idiot than he was.

"My daughters will be home soon. It's better that we don't…"

He opened his eyes in time to see her snag her glasses from the table, shove them back on her face and grab her forgotten beer off the ground. She gripped the bottle so tightly, she appeared to be strangling it.

He unfolded himself from the chair and didn't give a fuck when she watched him adjust his dick in his jeans.

"So, do you want to get together on Tuesday for your first lesson?" She was a bit breathless, her words wispy.

He didn't want to push her. All he wanted to do was touch her.

And never stop.

He wouldn't be satisfied until he committed every fucking inch of her to memory.

Until he recognized her taste, her scent.

Until he heard her voice in his dreams.

Dreams to drown out the nightmares.

He needed to leave now.

To let her go.

Stick to their deal and come back Tuesday. He could spend more time with her then.

Only problem was, he wanted to spend more time with her now. Before she knew the hard truth. When she discovered she wouldn't be able to teach him. That he was incapable of learning something so simple. Which was to read and write words.

Words, which were her world. A world he didn't belong in. Most likely never would.

But these lessons and the painting were a good excuse to see her again.

He had that. Even if only for a little while.

But still... He wasn't ready for this night to end.

Not yet.

Chapter Nine

As CHELLE REACHED for the handle to the glass sliding door, the strings of lights went out, bathing them in darkness, causing her to pause and her skin to tingle. An arm snaked around her waist and the bottle was removed from her trembling fingers.

Everything on and in her began to pulse like the bass at a live rock concert while standing in front of one of the large speakers.

The elastic band was pulled from her hair and the second the strands fell loose, Shawn's nose was buried in them.

He said nothing, but the tightening of that solid arm and the press of his very solid erection into the small of her back said it all.

He didn't want to keep their relationship to only their deal. He wanted more.

He wanted her.

Her blood surged through her veins as he nuzzled her neck and then her ear.

Disappointment licked at her briefly when he pulled away, but only long enough to turn her. The arm securing her no longer pressed against her belly, it was replaced by the hard length of his cock.

With a finger under her chin, he tipped up her face and dropped his until his lips were only a whisper away from hers. "Say yes."

They didn't have a lot of time. Not before her girls came home. She was afraid of her daughters catching them in a compromising position.

She was also afraid of what would happen if she gave him that yes.

She wanted to. She did. But she hadn't said yes to anyone in a long time.

She had always been content with her own company. Unfortunately, every time she'd been on a date over the years, she compared the man she was with to Brendan.

Was it fair? No. And though she tried, she couldn't stop from doing it anyway.

Admittedly, Shawn was different from any man she'd dated before. This situation was also very different. It wasn't a date. Neither held any expectations, right?

That was why dating was difficult. Too many expectations to meet. Too much time spent analyzing everything the other person said, trying to uncover who they really were deep inside versus what they were showing on the surface.

None of that applied here.

No pressure existed, either.

They could just *be*.

Together.

For the moments they had.

Simple.

Uncomplicated.

But he needed to agree to that first. For her daughters' sake. No matter what, they always came first. Her wants and needs were a distant second.

Since he had never answered earlier, she asked, "Do we have a deal with the barter?"

"Yeah." It was more of a guttural grunt than an answer.

"No expectations beyond that?"

"None," he murmured without hesitation.

She hoped that was true. Because anything else beyond the barter could be messy, as she mentioned before.

Her life might be boring and predictable, but it was neat right now. Keeping it that way provided a steady home for her girls. They'd lived with enough turmoil right after their father was killed.

Afterward, she had struggled for a while to get their lives back in balance and, once she achieved it, she didn't want anything to upset it again. Once her girls were out on their own and settled, she'd have plenty of time to put herself first.

Even so, she could give herself this moment.

Just this one.

"Not here."

He closed the slight gap and his lips swept lightly across hers. Just a whisper of a kiss. He pulled away before she lost her head and encouraged him to take it deeper. They were standing right in front of double glass sliding doors leading into the kitchen.

That wouldn't be smart.

But then, how smart was it for her to say yes to this man. A quiet, mysterious man she only just met and hardly knew anything about.

Just because she felt some connection with him, didn't mean they should take the connection further. From an easy companionship while working together to intimacy.

Truth be told, she missed it, the intimacy with another being. The sharing of touch, words, and sexual desire. Of having another person turn her on by doing the simplest of actions.

No expectations, Chelle. Simply allow yourself a moment to forget everything and lose yourself in someone who desires you. The evidence of desire being hard to miss.

"Where?" he asked roughly when she didn't say anything further and didn't move, either.

Where?

Where could they go and remain undetected? To share a secret moment?

Not in the house. Not in her bedroom. Not in the garage since Maddie parked her car in there.

Maybe behind the shed that sat along the left side of the yard against the fence. They could duck behind it like a couple of teenagers. Out of direct view of the house and in a dark corner of her yard. They would hear the girls long before the girls would see them.

When she pulled away from him, she tugged on his hand and led him out from under the covered patio and over the grass.

"Chelle." Smooth gravel churning in warm, thick honey.

Was he having second thoughts?

No. He didn't hesitate as they approached the small metal shed that held her mower and gardening tools. When he realized where they were headed, he picked up the pace, now pulling her along.

As soon as they turned the corner, as soon as they were out of sight from the house, he spun her around and drove his fingers into her hair, smashing their lips together, sliding his tongue through her mouth.

A claim. That was what it seemed like.

Their lips moved, their tongues tangled and when they finally paused, they both had to suck in air.

His touch, his kiss, was electric.

She wanted more.

So much more.

Her heart thumped heavily as his fingertips traced her

face. Over her forehead, down her nose, over her lips. They curled around her throat, pausing directly over her wild pulse.

In the dark shadows of the night, she couldn't see his face clearly, couldn't see his expression or the intensity of his eyes.

She regretted that.

She wanted to experience him fully. Unfortunately, that wasn't going to happen.

Not tonight.

Maybe not ever.

Even so, she'd take what she could get. What he was willing to give.

While the September night was warm, she still shivered when he began to release the buttons of her shirt, starting from the top. He did it with excruciating slowness, his knuckles skimming along her heated skin until her shirt gaped open only enough to expose her bra.

His fingers hovered over her bare skin. They weren't touching her, but his energy was.

Holy shit, if he didn't touch her soon, she'd combust.

She blew out a breath and his gaze lifted from the top curves of her breasts to her face.

"Chelle."

Every time he said her name like that it sent a charge through her. Her nipples were painfully peaked and piercing her bra, just begging for his touch.

They didn't have all the time in the world, so she grabbed his T-shirt at the waist, quickly tugging it from his jeans. But before she could drag it any higher, he snagged her wrists and shoved her backward until she made contact with the shed, causing the metal siding to bow and the breath to rush from her lungs. He gathered both of her wrists in one hand and pinned them over her head against the shed, taking her mouth again.

Very, very thoroughly.

While he plundered her mouth, his free hand splayed over her chest, finally making contact, and... paused. She was sure he could feel her rapid heartbeat, maybe even hear it, too.

Finally, he slid his hand into her bra, cupping her left breast and pulling it free.

God, he was moving so slowly! His movements were as unhurried and deliberate as he spoke. He had to be doing it on purpose to drive her nuts. She wanted to scream at him to pinch her nipple, touch it, suck it. Anything. Anything!

He was torturing her by kneading her breast within his fingers but avoiding her rock hard nipple.

Please. Please!

He must have heard her begging him in her head because his thumb brushed over the very beaded tip. Once. Twice.

The third time her pussy clenched so hard, she gasped in his mouth.

He needed to fill her emptiness before she went totally mad.

He rolled the aching tip between his thumb and forefinger, forcing her whimper to get caught in his mouth. He did it again and then plucked it before moving to the other bra cup and freeing that breast, too.

Arching her back, she attempted to get closer to him. She ripped her mouth from his and panted, "Shawn..."

He stiffened at her saying his name.

Did she do something wrong?

It was quickly forgotten when he dropped his head and drew his tongue over one nipple as he played with the other. He switched again. Sucking, twisting. Tugging, pinching. All of it driving her to the brink.

She'd missed this... She didn't realize how much she needed it. Until now...

"Please," she begged in barely a whisper. He had to hurry.

Her belly was on fire, her breath caught in her throat and wetness trickled from between her legs, soaking her panties and the cotton of her leggings.

She had to get them off.

She needed to touch him. But that was impossible since he still held onto her wrists.

As if reading her mind again, he let go and she was suddenly free.

Before she could scramble to undress, he was tucking his fingers into the waistband of her leggings and jerking them, and her panties, down in one shot. He wasn't gentle about it but almost frantic.

She didn't care, she was relieved he was moving faster.

He rolled them down her legs and she kicked off her flip-flops so he could finish removing the leggings. Of course, he took his time rising. Running his fingers and his mouth up her legs and shoving the long shirt tails out of the way to press his nose into the apex of her thighs.

They didn't have time for that.

Did they?

No.

They needed to be quick about this. Quiet, too.

She only hoped her neighbors couldn't see them. But at this point, she didn't care if they did. The thought of being watched both thrilled and petrified her.

The tip of his tongue touched her *there*. Just barely, but enough to feel it and cause her lungs to empty.

Good lord, she wished they had time for that.

But they were outside behind a shed, surrounded by neighbors and in a time crunch, her daughters due home at any moment.

He probably realized that, too, as he continued to rise,

sucking each nipple deep into his mouth, his molars scraping the very tips.

When he finally stood tall, he reached behind himself, yanking out his wallet, and opening it with jerky motions. After he slipped a foil packet from it and tucked it between his teeth, he returned his large chained wallet to his rear pocket.

She wished there was enough light to see his eyes. She wished she could see him naked.

She bet his body was beautiful. Like the rest of him. His gorgeous hair, his striking features. His quiet soul.

The jingle from his belt buckle being unfastened sent a shockwave through her. This was happening.

Really happening.

The night was quiet, the only sound to be heard was the draw of his zipper and her ragged breathing.

His was just as rough as hers when he took the wrapper from between his teeth and tore it open. Slipping the condom out, he shoved the torn foil pack into his front pocket and his underwear down just enough to release his cock.

She wanted to taste the salty tang of the precum she was sure clung to the tip.

They didn't have time for that.

When his hands dropped to his cock, she snagged the condom from between his fingers, pushing them away.

"Let me." The husky words sounded foreign. Unlike her. She hadn't been this turned on in what seemed like a lifetime.

Only one other man made her this wet in anticipation. Only one other man had made her impatient for his touch. Only one other man had made her actually throb for him.

Now one more.

Shawn.

She stroked his cock twice first, causing his hips to jerk,

before holding the rolled condom to the tip. She took her time sliding it over his thick, throbbing length, which flexed under her fingers.

"Killin' me here," he growled.

She should find his impatience funny since he'd been the one driving her crazy with his leisurely pace. But she didn't laugh because he sounded way too serious.

He was suffering as much as she had been. Still was.

The only way to relieve their desperation was to welcome him inside her. To fill her emptiness.

Once the condom was secure, she reluctantly released him and, as soon as she did, she found herself sandwiched against the shed again. A denim-clad knee wedged between her thighs, nudging her legs wider, opening her up to him.

A trickle of arousal dampened the skin of her inner thigh. Was it because she hadn't had sex in a while, or was it because it was Shawn?

"Wasn't how I wanted you, Chelle."

How did he want her? Had he actually put thought into this? Had he had a plan? She wanted to ask that and more but doing so would involve too many words, ones she wasn't willing to say right now.

No more words were needed.

The cotton of his T-shirt skimmed over the puckered peaks of her nipples as he pinned her more securely against the shed.

He was taller than her, so she wasn't sure how this would work. She'd never had sex standing up.

Wasn't how I wanted you, Chelle.

No, it wasn't ideal, but this was how he was getting her. It would have to be enough. For both of them.

She opened her mouth to ask him how they were going to manage but her words became trapped when he crushed his lips against hers. Her question was answered when his hands gripped the backs of her thighs right below her ass cheeks and he hauled her up, holding her against the metal siding with his chest.

He ripped his mouth from hers. "Guide me."

Because his hands were full of her weight, she wedged her own between them and found his cock again.

He groaned, pressed his forehead to hers and shifted his hips, giving her the room to slide the thick crown between her slick folds until she found the spot. She expected him to thrust quickly and deeply, but like everything else he did, he took his damn time.

With one hand under his hair and wrapped around his neck, she used the other to hold onto his shoulder as he entered her inch by measured inch.

The urge to ride him with wild abandonment surged through her, but she remained still, enjoying that delicious stretch as he filled her.

When he finally hit the end of her, he paused.

She thought he was going to say something, so she waited, but he must have thought better of it. Instead, he adjusted his grip, his fingers digging into the flesh of her thighs. That little bit of discomfort was worth the whole bunch of pleasure when he began to move.

Her breath hissed out of her as he held her close, flexed his knees and drove himself up and into her over and over. The jingle of his belt buckle hitting the chain from his wallet joined his breath pumping from his lungs with each steady thrust.

Deliberate and unhurried. Just like everything else he did.

While slow and steady could be great, right now it wasn't what she needed or wanted.

Her nails drilled into the flesh at the back of his neck. "Fuck me."

Her demand caused his body to hiccup against her and he paused. Pulling his head back, he stared into her face.

His was unreadable due to the dark shadows hiding his eyes. "Want it to last."

While she appreciated that—and would love that, too—it wasn't feasible. Not while having sex against a shed in her backyard where anyone could discover them.

"It doesn't need to last, it only needs to be good."

She might not be able to read his eyes, but even in the dark she could see his crooked grin.

She returned it. "I prefer to be quick than caught, to be honest."

"Always good to be honest," he grumbled.

Her hand dropped from his neck to the small of his back, then slipped under his boxer briefs to grab a handful of his ass.

That was better.

She gave the muscular round cheek a squeeze. "So..."

"Know you like words, now ain't the time for them."

Well, then.

But he was right. The time to talk had passed, now was time to act. Talking could come later.

Except she had one more thing to say... "Fuck me."

With a little shake of his head, he got back to business. Each drive upward deeper and quicker than the last, until there was nowhere left for him to go, though it seemed as though he was trying to drill right through her.

As she clung tightly to him, she threw her head back, her skull hitting the thin metal sheeting and making an awful noise.

She didn't care.

She only cared about what he was doing.

And what he was doing was pushing her right to the edge.

Oh my God, yes.

He better not stop. He couldn't stop. Not now. He needed to keep going. She was almost there.

She'd never come this quickly. It couldn't be possible, could it?

Even in this unorthodox position in an unorthodox place?

His lips skimmed down her arched throat and he sucked at the hollow of her neck. His hot breath swept over her skin in ragged pants as he used his legs to power up and into her.

His hips hinged, his breathing huffed.

She was losing her damn mind.

He was stealing her cognizance. Making it impossible for her to think straight. To remember where they were.

She focused solely on the man who held her. The man burying himself deep inside her. The man about to make her come.

"Shawn," came out on a gasp. "I..."

His hips pistoned faster, knowing just what she needed. She encouraged his quicker pace with the grip on his ass.

He couldn't go any deeper but, for some reason, he wasn't deep enough. It was like she wanted to absorb him. Instead of two separate pieces, for them to become one.

Impossible.

Wasn't it?

"I'm coming," spilled from her.

He covered her mouth with his to swallow her cry as she surrendered to her orgasm. She squeezed her eyes shut as she shattered around him.

He didn't stop, not even the slightest pause, but now drove relentlessly into her, at an almost frantic pace, the shed's metal siding bending and creaking, making way too much noise with the intense pounding.

Just when she thought the orgasm was over, another one swept through her, surprising her.

Once he rode that out with her, he tensed, broke the kiss and shoved his face into her neck. With a long, low grunt against her damp skin, he tilted his hips one more time, driving deep, where he remained as he came, the root of his cock pulsing. Her name whispered along her skin, causing goosebumps. His warm breath did the same.

Neither moved, both frozen in time.

Aware they needed to separate. Neither wanting to do so.

Neither wanting to break that connection.

That base need to remain whole.

Whole.

Again, a weird and unexpected thought.

But it was true, she didn't realize how empty she'd been.

Until now.

Until Shawn.

Even though that couldn't be right. They didn't fit. Their lifestyles were completely different. Mismatched.

A sigh rushed from her, like releasing the air from a balloon, when he finally moved. Finally broke that connection.

The sense of loss rushing through her was startling.

He lowered her enough so her feet touched the ground and she could stand on her own, even though her legs felt like rubber.

He gripped her hips and brushed his lips over hers briefly. Then he stepped back, removed the condom and knotted it. She'd need to bury it deep within the trash so the girls wouldn't spot it.

Undeniable evidence of what their mother did behind the shed with a man she'd only known a few days.

He yanked up his underwear and jeans, tucking in his T-shirt and cinching up his belt. He bent over and picked up her leggings and panties, holding them out in front of her.

Her fingers curled around her clothes but he didn't let go. Not at first. With a gentle tug from her, he finally released them and she balled them against her chest. She jerked her head toward the bucket she used for weeding that sat on the ground next to the shed. "Just throw the condom in that bucket and I'll get rid of it." When there was no chance of the girls seeing her do so.

He gave a little nod and dropped it in the bucket, then turned to face her. He opened his mouth and she waited to see what words would escape but after a few seconds, the only thing that came out was, "Gotta go."

Even as the disappointment swept through her, she knew it was for the best.

"See you Tuesday at six," she said weakly, unsure if she should thank him for the orgasms.

Would that be weird?

That would be weird.

After another hesitation, but without a confirmation of him showing up Tuesday, he slipped silently into the dark.

The dampness between her thighs and the sound of her wooden gate latching closed a sudden wake-up call of what just happened.

Chapter Ten

CHELLE STEPPED out into the warm sun, squinting at the brightness. She paused to dig her sunglasses out of the small backpack that doubled as her purse when she worked.

It wouldn't be long before the winter swept into northern Pennsylvania, so she wanted to take advantage of the nice weather by walking over to the high school and eating her lunch on the bleachers at the football field. She had today's true-life murder mystery podcast cued up on her phone and her earbuds dangling around her neck.

After slipping her sunglasses on, she heard the double doors open behind her and a little girl chatting away at a quick clip.

With a glance over her shoulder, she noticed Cassie from Tioga Pet Crematorium with her daughter Daisy.

It was the middle of the school day, maybe Daisy was going home sick.

As soon as Cassie spotted Chelle, she smiled and gave a wave. "Hey, Mrs. Goodson!"

Daisy bolted from Cassie's side and ran up to come toe to toe with her and flopped her head back. "Hi, Mrs. Goodson! I'm ready for a new book!" Some of the children hadn't learned about personal space yet. Daisy was one of them.

Chelle took a step back and leaned over to get face to face with her instead. "You are? That's great. It looks like you're leaving right now, so come visit me when you get back. I'll pick one out for you." She straightened, squeezed Daisy's shoulder and turned toward Cassie. "Everything all right?"

Cassie waved a dismissing hand. "Yes, she's scheduled for a regular check-up. She won't be back today but she can get a book from you tomorrow."

"I want one now!" Daisy insisted.

One of Cassie's blonde eyebrows lifted in warning at her daughter's demand.

Daisy pouted and huffed in answer. Chelle waited for the accompanying foot stomp, but it didn't happen. Someone must be working with her on that.

The sass in that girl just oozed from her pores. She was grateful Maddie and Josie never acted like that. It would've made parenting on her own even more difficult.

"I'll find you a book this afternoon and put it aside for you for tomorrow. Is that a deal?"

Daisy smiled and gave her an exaggerated nod. "Deal!"

"All right, let's go, young lady," Cassie urged. "We don't want to be late for your appointment."

"Momma, am I gonna get shot?"

Shot?

Chelle rolled her lips under. *A* shot.

Cassie grimaced. "I don't know."

Cassie knew.

Chelle did her best to keep her expression blank.

"I don't want a shot."

"None of us do, Daisy, but sometimes they're necessary," Chelle said as the three of them walked toward the wide concrete sidewalk that ran in front of the elementary school. She noticed Cassie's SUV was parked at the curb.

That wasn't the only thing she noticed.

She caught herself before she stumbled.

Daisy broke away in a sloppy lope with her arms flailing and her cartoon-themed backpack swinging wildly, leaving a high-pitched squeal in her wake.

Cassie sighed loudly beside Chelle and quickened her pace. "She's going to be the death of me. And Judge wants another. I don't know if my sanity can take it."

Chelle smothered a nervous giggle as they got closer to the curb and the man she'd had two orgasms with last night. In the dark, behind the shed, with most of their clothes on.

Daisy had run up to him yelling, "Hey! Can I ride on your sled?" so loudly, they could hear her on an orbiting space station.

Sled?

"That's not a sled, honey, that's a motorcycle," Chelle corrected the six-year-old as she caught up to her. Shawn's dark sunglass-covered eyes met hers and held.

Even without seeing his almost black eyes, his quiet stare made her tingle in quite a few places of note. Which was not appropriate in front of a six-year-old, the girl's mother and a whole elementary school full of children.

After a few more intense moments, he dropped his gaze from Chelle to the blonde whirlwind standing next to him with a hand now planted on his denim-clad thigh.

Of course, if Cassie was a part of the same club as Shawn, then Daisy would know the members well. So, it shouldn't be weird that the girl was touching an adult male who was not related. If so, Cassie would be stepping in. Right?

Maybe they considered themselves family, just not in the traditional way.

Family or not, she wondered why he was there. Certainly not to see her?

"Not thinkin' your momma's gonna want you ridin' with me," he finally answered Daisy in his typical slow speech.

Cassie seconded that. "That's correct. Her momma does *not* want her on the back of your sled. Not because I don't trust you, Sh— *Shawn*," she grimaced, "but—"

"Who's Shawn?" Daisy interrupted with a scrunched-up face. "Shade's name is Shade, Momma! You're silly!"

Shade? That was a weird name. Chelle noticed the name matched the embroidered lettering on a rectangular patch sewn onto the front of his black leather vest. Another one said, "Manning Grove."

"Yes, your momma is very silly." Cassie peeled Daisy's hand from Shawn's thigh and tugged on it. "Okay, let's go."

Of course, Daisy dug in her heels. "Where's Saylor? Why didn't she pick me up?"

"She needed a break from all your questions."

Chelle turned her face away to hide her smothered laugh.

"She did not!" Daisy insisted. "Do I ask a lot of questions?"

When Chelle turned back, she realized the little girl had asked the man straddling the motorcycle.

"Yeah, baby girl, you do," Shade answered, his lips twitching.

Daisy laughed, not caring one iota that she did.

"Asking questions gives you answers to most of life's mysteries," Chelle told her. Not always, but it sounded good. She never wanted a child's curiosity to be dampened by being told not to ask questions. It was one way they learned.

"As long as you aren't demanding those answers and stomping your foot when you don't get them fast enough." Cassie tugged on her hand again. "C'mon, little miss curious, let's go."

"I wanna ride with Shade to the doctor's."

"We already had that discussion. He doesn't have your helmet with him, anyway. Judge told everyone they had to follow that rule no matter what. You don't want to get Shade," she shot a quick glance at Chelle, "in trouble, right?"

Daisy pursed her lips like she was actually debating the answer.

Cassie rolled her eyes and tugged again, finally getting the girl to move.

As they turned toward their SUV parked ahead of Shade's bike, Chelle asked, "Why are you here?"

"Escortin' them since her ol' man's busy." He said that as if it wasn't out of the ordinary.

"Why would she need an escort?" She wondered if that was typical in an MC. She needed to do more research when she got a chance.

When he didn't answer, she wondered what she was missing in that scenario.

Manning Grove was a safe family-oriented town. The police department was good. For the most part, the town's folk were friendly. Needing an escort made no sense. Even if Cassie and Daisy needed one, no matter the reason, why wouldn't they just ride in the same vehicle?

He muttered, "Gotta go."

Fine. He didn't want to answer and, truthfully, it wasn't any of her business, anyway.

She stepped back onto the curb. "See you Tuesday... *Shade*." She'd ask him about that nickname then.

If he was even willing to answer.

Shawn's head twisted toward Cassie, who was rounding the back of her SUV after strapping her daughter into the back seat. The tall, curvy blonde stopped dead and glanced over her shoulder to mouth to Shawn, "Tuesday?"

His jaw shifted sharply and he frowned.

With a sly smile, Cassie jumped into the driver's seat of her vehicle and started the engine.

"Gotta go," Shawn grumbled again and hit the starter on his motorcycle. When it rumbled to life, the loud exhaust vibrated through her center.

She wondered what it would feel like to ride a powerful motorcycle like his, even if she was only the passenger.

"Tuesday," was the last thing he said as he used his boot to shift the bike into gear, gave it some gas and then followed Cassie.

She'd have to ask him about that, too.

Because *asking questions gives you answers to most of life's mysteries.*

She couldn't deny she loved mysteries.

Shawn, aka Shade, was certainly one.

———

SHADE STRADDLED his quiet sled and stared at the house. Lights were on inside and, even though the night hadn't completely swallowed up the daylight yet, a porch light shone bright.

The house appeared welcoming. A great home, a great neighborhood, a great town for a woman raising two daughters.

He wondered if Chelle was alone inside waiting for him, or if her girls were home. If they weren't, he'd have a hard time concentrating on his first "lesson."

After fucking her against the shed Sunday night, he'd had a hard time concentrating on anything. He'd spent too much time remembering how her hot, wet pussy responded to him being inside her. It had fucking pulsed, even gripped him like a fist.

He'd used his own fist last night. Twice. But it wasn't the

same. No substitute existed for a warm, willing woman who made him hard as fuck.

Chelle did that.

Even thinking about her now, knowing they'd be spending time together and sitting close, woke up his dick.

But he wasn't here for that tonight. He was here for their deal. Their barter. Her attempt to teach him to read in exchange for his help with the painting. He was pretty fucking sure that deal would be quickly broken when she discovered he was impossible to teach.

After swinging a leg over his Night Train, he shrugged out of his cut. She knew now what and who he was, what and who he belonged to, but that didn't mean her girls did.

He also wasn't sure how she felt about it all.

He wouldn't mention it as long as she didn't. If it was an issue, he had no doubt, she'd bring it up.

Not that it would change anything.

His club was his family and that was fucking that. No woman would change that.

Jesus fuck, he was only here to learn to read. That was it.

He removed his black skullcap and face covering, and tucked them in the saddlebag next to his folded cut.

His stomach churned as he turned and stared at the house again. He scratched the back of his neck, then clamped a hand around it, twisting it back and forth.

He was only putting off the inevitable.

Her finding out how fucking stupid he was. How unteachable.

He pressed his lips together as the front door opened and she stepped outside onto the porch, calling out, "Are you just going to stand there? Or are you coming inside?"

He wanted to come inside Chelle. He wanted to mark her as his, like when Justice pissed on a bush to mark his territory.

The intense need to do just that had been eating at him.

While that thought was fucking crazy, it was too damn true.

He shook himself mentally before he sported a full-blown hard-on and strode from where his sled was parked along the side of her paved driveway, down her little flower-lined walkway and up the steps.

She didn't step back, she stayed right where she stood, only her face tipping up as he closed in. He didn't stop until he was only inches from her. Close enough to feel her breath softly escape her parted lips, see her pupils dilate and her nipples pucker under the thin, V-neck, long-sleeved tee she wore.

No buttons. No easy access.

But this white, almost transparent, shirt clung to her curves, emphasizing her tits and slightly narrower waist. She wasn't skinny, not even close.

Fuck no. That was one thing that turned him off to some of the sweet butts. A couple of them didn't have much substance, and he wasn't talking brain power. Because some of them lacked a bit of that, too.

He liked a woman with enough flesh to dig his fingers into. He wanted a woman whose body was as far from a man as it could get. Not hard, but soft.

He'd had sex with plenty of men and not by choice. Now he had a choice, he wanted generous tits, ass and pussy that made him forget his real name.

Chelle was all of that.

Even more.

She was the whole fucking package. Looks, personality and brains, too.

Even better, her presence settled him. He didn't know how, didn't know why.

It just did.

He used the back of his fingers to brush a few strands of her strawberry-blonde hair away from her eyes. "Where are your glasses?"

Her throat convulsed as she swallowed. When she licked her lips, he followed that movement, too. "I only wear contacts while I'm working. I haven't had a chance to remove them yet."

They stared at each other a few more moments and a flush covered her chest. He wondered if she was remembering what happened behind the shed, too.

She cleared her throat, but her words still came out huskily. "Come inside."

Yeah, he'd like to. He leaned forward until his mouth was to her ear. "Will you let me?"

He pulled back and saw the color tinging her chest had worked its way up into her cheeks. He didn't know many women who blushed as easily as Chelle.

It surprised him due to her age and lack of innocence. Chelle was no young virgin. She was a woman who knew what she wanted and hadn't hesitated to take it behind the shed.

With a hand curled around her hip—tonight she wore jeans—he turned her to escort her inside.

He reluctantly let her go to shut and lock the door behind them and then followed her to the back of the house and into her kitchen. The light fixture above the table in the eat-in kitchen was lit and on the table sat a couple of legal-sized pads of yellow paper, an open laptop, as well as pencils and some books.

She was prepared.

That meant she had thought about him in the time they'd spent apart. Had she spent just as much reliving those stolen moments behind the shed as she had his reading lesson?

Instead of going right to the table, Chelle veered off and went to the fridge instead. "Water?"

"Beer?"

She smiled. "Afterward, not during." She grabbed two bottles of water and brought them over to the table. "I could make coffee instead. I don't drink caffeine this late, but if you do..."

"Water's good."

She put the bottles down and pointed to one of the two chairs pushed together along the long side of the wood table. "Sit."

If they were going to be sitting that close to each other, he wouldn't be able to pay attention to her lesson. Instead, he'd be fighting the urge to touch and taste her. Maybe throw her on the table, spread her legs and eat her like a meal.

Fuck.

"Is something wrong? You just groaned like you're in pain."

Of course he fucking did. "I'm good."

He wasn't good.

He yanked a chair out and waited for her to settle in it before pulling out the other one and sinking his bones into it. "Gonna put on your glasses?"

"You have a thing with glasses?"

He grinned. "Just on you. If you're gonna act like my teacher, should look the part."

"I figured I looked like the librarian I am when wearing them, not a teacher. Tell me, what do I look like without them?" Amusement tipped up the corner of her lips.

Last night while he fisted his dick, he imagined those lips around it. "Hot as fuck with or without them."

"But you prefer the glasses."

"Prefer you spread naked on this table so I can see how pink and shiny your pussy is right before I devour it."

The air hissed from her.

"Girls here?" He should have asked that first before telling her his fantasy. Too late.

"I... uh... no." She swallowed and stared down into her lap for a moment. If she was as worked up as he was right now, she was probably trying to collect herself. "I picked tonight since they both work until after nine. I figured you'd be more comfortable without my daughters here. And maybe without them knowing you can't read. I wasn't sure if you wanted anyone else to know."

The reason he was here smacked him right in the face again. He should be grateful that she wanted to help him. Not act like a horny fucking asshole.

"Sorry."

She shook her head. "For what?"

"Tryin' to help and I'm bein' a dick." He normally didn't let shit like that fly from his mouth. He usually kept tight control on his thoughts and words. "Don't deserve that."

"I can't stop thinking about the other night, either," she whispered.

He twisted his head and stared at her. "We got time?"

Her hesitation gave him a little hope. Her next words shot that hope to hell. "Not if we want to get this first lesson done before Josie and Maddie get home."

Fuck.

He didn't know what he wanted more. To be inside Chelle or to have her try to teach him to read.

He wanted fucking both. He wanted both badly.

But she was right. They had to do these lessons when her daughters were gone. He didn't want anyone else knowing about his inability to read even the simplest sentence.

Even his own fucking name.

As if reading his mind, she said, "We'll start with your

name. The only problem is, your name has a lot of variations, so I'm not sure how it's spelled. Is it correct on your driver's license?"

Fuck, he had a fake driver's license. And the name Shawn certainly wasn't on it. He should clear up that misunderstanding. Especially since Daisy spouted out his road name in front of Chelle yesterday.

"Name ain't Shawn."

"Daisy called you Shade, the name I saw on your vest. That can't be your real name, right?"

"Cut."

"Cut?"

"My colors. The vest."

"Cut," she repeated, tasting it like a piece of hard candy. "Your *cut* said Shade."

"Road name."

"Do all bikers have road names?" She was as curious as Cassie's girl.

"Some do. Some don't. Personal choice." That choice was only given once you became a fully-patched member, but he wasn't getting into that with her right now. Most likely, not ever.

"If your name isn't Shawn, why did Cassie introduce you as that?"

He formed all the words in his head first before releasing them and only hoped he got them all right. "To keep the knowledge that the crematorium is owned by an MC limited. Afraid it'll scare off customers." So far, the business had made a fuckton of scratch but they weren't sure if it was because most people weren't aware the Fury owned it or if because people simply didn't care. They were the only business within a two hour radius from Manning Grove that provided home euthanasia plus cremation.

It also helped that Cassie kicked ass when dealing with customers, especially when they were wrecked emotionally because they had to put their pet down. Like Chelle had to do with her cat.

But it was smart business to not flaunt it was MC owned. They didn't hide it about Crazy Pete's but the bar wasn't considered a biker bar exclusively. Anyone was welcome as long as they didn't make trouble.

The town's folk didn't care the MC owned The Grove Inn, either, since it had been a rat trap before Trip bought the motel. The town approved of all of the renovations. It went from an eyesore and sketchy to a decent place to stay for tourists, visiting family and business folks alike.

"Makes sense, but why Shawn?"

Yeah, she asked as many fucking questions as Daisy. Only her questions weren't a demand and not yelled at an ear-piercing level.

He shrugged. "Guessin' 'cause it's close to Shade and she don't know my real name."

"Which is?"

"Julian."

Shade felt her stare rather than saw it. If she had a reaction to his real first name, he missed it because he was too busy picking at the label on his water bottle. She was starting to ask too many fucking questions and his spine was getting tight.

"Does anybody call you that?"

"No."

"And none of the other guys in your club know your real name?"

"The other *guys* in my club are my brothers. Know of only one who knows. Judge ran my sheet when I first became a prospect."

He waited for her to ask what a sheet was but she surprised him when she skipped right over it. His rap sheet was pretty damn clean because he'd always stayed off the grid. Without a real ID and an unknown social security number, law enforcement had a difficult time identifying him when he did get caught. But once his prints were in the system, those minor charges began to build on the fake name he gave the pigs the first time. The same name he gave Judge. Julian Jones.

In truth, he should've used a fake first name, too. But his real first name was easy to remember. He just didn't know how to spell it. Or even sign it.

Anyway, the name he used whenever he got arrested didn't matter now. He had no plans on getting caught ever again. He hated being physically restrained and hated being contained in a small box even more. He'd already done that for too many fucking years of his life. He was done with that shit. He'd kill anyone who forced that on him again.

"Who's Judge?"

Jesus fuck, more questions. "Owns Justice Bail Bonds and is our sergeant at arms."

"What's that?"

"The man who enforces the club's rules." He needed to end this line of questioning. If she didn't stop digging, he would walk the fuck out and end their deal. "Feelin' like a quiz, teach, instead of a lesson. Am I here so you can learn about an MC, or to teach a dumb fuck like me to read?"

That had her sitting back in her chair abruptly with her light brown eyes narrowed. "You're not a *dumb fuck.*"

"You'll see."

"Not being able to read doesn't make you dumb."

"Not bein' able to learn does."

"Someone already tried to teach you outside of school?"

They were definitely not going there. "Chelle, too many fuckin' questions. Heard what you said to Daisy about questions. I ain't a mystery to be solved."

She twisted in her chair, her denim-covered knee making contact with his. "Sorry. I didn't mean to pry, but I wanted to teach you to spell your name first. I figured that would be important. I'll stick to the curriculum, instead."

Shade closed his eyes, now feeling like a rude dick since she was only trying to help. He just wanted to keep them from falling down a rabbit hole where she tried to find out every detail of his fucking life by asking a million questions.

"I'll try not to ask any personal questions from here on out. I only have one more."

He opened his eyes and met hers. She wasn't pissed, she wasn't upset, but he could read the disappointment. Seeing that was like a kick in the nuts.

Instead of apologizing to her, even though he wanted to, he said, "Runnin' outta time."

"You're right. Sorry for wasting time."

"Fuck, Chelle," he groaned. *Fuck him*, he caused that flat tone in her voice. It wasn't only disappointment, it was hurt. Now he really felt like a piece of shit.

He snagged one of her hands she had curled in her lap and pulled it to his lips, brushing them over her knuckles. "You don't have to do this. I can paint everything you want done and you can just pay me whenever you get the scratch."

She shook her head but didn't pull her hand from his. "No, that's not fair and I want to do this. So... Let's get started. I've never taught an adult to read before, so please bear with me. I'll do the best I can. I have access to resources that will help guide me and also you. I can also ask some of the teachers for guidance, too, if we run into any issues. I brought home a few lesson books and read through the introductions—"

"Did your homework," he interrupted.

"Yes, I was trying to be prepared. But first, do you know the alphabet?"

They were back to business. If he had a chance, he'd

make up for being an asshole later. *If* she wanted that. He hoped to fuck she did.

"Yeah. Alphabet and numbers." He wasn't as bad with numbers like he was with letters. He could do some basic math. But even that he tried to avoid since he was afraid he'd get it wrong.

One "daddy" managed to teach him to count up to ten along with the alphabet, but then got frustrated when he even struggled with those. At first, the man insisted Shade was doing it on purpose just to be difficult. Then he gave up and called him stupid. And worse.

After giving up, that owner told him he'd only be good for one thing... To be someone's pet. That Shade should be collared and leashed like a dog. Not to be petted, coddled and loved, but taught obedience.

Used as his owner saw fit.

His next owner removed the locked leather collar but didn't treat him any better and also didn't give a fuck whether Shade was smart or stupid.

His previous owner was right. He was only good for one thing. The reason he was purchased, or traded, and why he was sold once an owner got bored with him, or he got too old.

No. Not now.

He forced himself back to the room when Chelle asked, "You just don't know how to string them together to write and read, correct?"

"Yeah. Can't put them together."

She scratched her forehead. "I'm not sure how you graduated high school without being able to take tests and do school assignments."

That was because he never spent even one day in a school.

Luckily, she didn't wait for that answer. She was now consciously trying not to dig.

His chest loosened and he finally released the grip on her hand that had tightened when he was yanked briefly into his past. She hadn't complained but he didn't want to hurt her, especially during those moments he was dragged backward and sometimes lost track of the present.

She squeezed his forearm and shot him a little smile. "Okay, let's begin..."

Chapter Eleven

TEN LEFT.

Ten, if his count was correct.

Ten, as long as they didn't bring in any more males into the Shirley compound.

If they were smart, that was what they'd do, if they hadn't already. No one claimed the Shirleys were smart. If they were, they never would've grabbed Dyna after being warned not to fuck with the Fury.

With his boots propped up on the stone ledge circling the center fireplace, he stared sightlessly at the cold gray ashes at the very bottom of the hearth. The night was too warm to start a fire. Not that he planned on being in The Barn long anyway.

Church was currently deserted. Not only a rare occurrence, but why he didn't bother to head out to the pavilion to numb himself before hitting his mattress.

Even the bunkhouse had been quiet when he'd walked down the corridor. The prospects would be doing their late shifts at Crazy Pete's and maybe something was going on at the bar tonight, drawing the rest of his brothers.

If there was, he hadn't been told about it. Not that he

would've gone. He tended to avoid Crazy Pete's and preferred to stick close to the bunkhouse when he drank. Because most of the time he drank until his brain was numb and riding his sled in that condition would be fucking stupid.

He didn't need to catch a DUI, or wreck his Night Train, which cost him a small fortune, and he definitely didn't need to break his brain worse than it already was, by splitting his melon open on unforgiving pavement.

He flicked the ashes off the joint he was smoking and tucked it between his lips once more. With a deep inhale, he held the hit as long as he could, the burn filling his lungs.

He released it when his body began to fight for oxygen and watched the white stream shoot toward the ceiling, eventually the smoke particles scattering and disappearing.

He lifted the half-empty bottle of Jack from where it had been propped on his thigh and tipped it to lips, the whiskey causing a different type of burn to settle in his gut.

After two long pulls on the bottle, he set it down on the wide wood-plank floor next to the bus bench, and scrubbed his face with his hands.

He ran the last two hours over in his mind again. What he'd done, what he'd seen. What he might have missed.

He was disappointed he didn't have the chance to grab another Shirley tonight. Even though the urge to draw blood was there, the right opportunity hadn't been. It hadn't been safe enough to remain undetected. To sneak in, to sneak out, leaving one less Shirley on the Earth.

Tonight, too many armed hillbillies were set up around the main compound's perimeter. The clan only had ten men left—that he knew of—and half of those had been guarding the first clearing.

Shade figured they'd upped their security since their men were either being found bled-out in the woods or simply gone.

They were now fully aware that they were being hunted.

Shade was pretty fucking sure they also knew by who.

That made the Fury vulnerable. Like he warned Trip and Judge, backlash was inevitable. When and where? He didn't fucking know.

But it was one reason he'd insisted on following Cassie to Daisy's school the other day. Why he'd also waited outside the pediatrician's office until they were done so he could tail them home.

The club didn't have enough men to put one on every woman and child, and it would be smart if Trip would work harder on bringing in more prospects just for that reason alone.

One problem with any new prospects would be knowing if they were reliable and trustworthy. The club had no initial way to test their loyalty. It would also be more mouths to feed and house while trying to figure out if they were a good fit.

Only one room in the bunkhouse was set up for prospects and it included three bunkbeds to house six recruits. While there were two empty private rooms with bathrooms available right now, no one got those until that room was earned by being patched in. The two prospects they had now, Tater Tot and Possum, were only recently recruited and it would be a long while before their membership would be voted on. They were also both young as fuck.

A little dumb, too.

But they were extra hands at Crazy Pete's and extra eyes when the club needed them. The Fury just needed more. He'd leave that shit to the exec committee and just continue to do what he was told.

He was good with that.

What didn't sit well with him was what Chelle discovered Tuesday night during his lesson.

They had sat at her kitchen table as she did her best to

teach him to read using books and a computer program for kids.

Fucking *young* kids.

Almost two hours later, after frustration from her, frustration from him, he was ready to give up and walk out. She had a lot of fucking patience but, by the end, her patience had been thoroughly tested.

They got nowhere.

Just what he feared. It wasn't that he didn't want to learn, but his brain was broken.

Finally, he thanked her for trying and told her to contact him when she had more scratch for painting. Before he could get up, she had latched onto his arm and yanked him back into his seat.

He could see the wheels turning in her head as she pursed her lips and searched his face.

When she only stared at him for the longest time, it started to freak him out. "What?"

"I think I know why you're struggling."

At least one of them did.

He wasn't sure if he should be relieved or scared at that announcement. Or a little of both.

She pulled up a website on her laptop, pointed some things out to him, asked him some questions and after he answered, she got quiet.

Again, he could see her mental wheels turning. Her chewing on her bottom lip didn't help the burn in his gut.

He knew his brain wasn't normal, so he expected her to tell him something he already knew.

She continued to stare at him until he shifted in his seat and prodded, "Gonna share or keep to yourself?"

He fought a grimace when she gently corrected him because he'd missed the word "it." He should be grateful she wanted to help him enough to point out his mistake so he could correct it.

But before he had a chance to repeat his question correctly, she said, "I think you're dyslexic."

Dyslexic. "I'm what?"

"Dyslexic," she repeated.

He had no fucking clue what that was. "That another name for a retard?"

Any color in her cheeks drained away and her brown eyes went wide. "What?" she whispered. "Did someone call you that?"

If she only knew what he'd been called... If that one particular word made her react like that, he couldn't imagine how she'd be bothered by the rest.

"Don't use that word." Color rushed back into her cheeks and it wasn't because of embarrassment or sexual desire. Her expression dripped with pure anger. "You aren't... You're not... *that.* You just see things differently and have a hard time visualizing words and letters while on paper or in your head. That's probably why you speak so slowly and mess up or omit words when you don't."

That he already knew. He tended to screw up more when he didn't think his words through carefully or he rushed to answer. Or sometimes when his adrenaline was kicked up a few notches and he had a hard time focusing.

"Dyslexia makes learning to read more difficult but not impossible. It just takes work. A lot more work."

She chewed on her bottom lip again and he wanted to stop her by taking her mouth. But she was distracted. Clearly turning over this new discovery in her head. Maybe even reconsidering if it was worth her trying to help him.

He wouldn't blame her if she bailed. Then he'd just go on with life like he had been for the past thirty years.

"I don't know enough about it. I'll talk to some teachers and see what they can recommend. Books, programs... whatever." She groaned and slapped a hand to her forehead. She was back to being pissed about something. He just didn't know what. "I should know way more about it than I do."

She was angry at herself, not him, this time. "Chelle…"

"I'm a fucking librarian!" she shouted. "Encouraging children to read is a huge part of what I do."

He made sure to take his time and get all the words out correctly because he wanted to make sure what he said was crystal fucking clear. "Chelle, ain't your fault. You can back out. Don't gotta do this."

This wasn't life or death. With all the shit he'd dealt with in his life, not being able to read was a minor problem. He'd survive it like he already had all these years.

The cords in her neck became tight and her eyes held a scary determination. Maybe the intensity should worry him, but instead it turned him on.

"No, I'm doing this. *You're* doing this. You might never read perfectly or as easily as others, but you're going to read, damn it. You're missing out on so much…" She fisted her hands in her lap and squeezed her eyes shut. When she opened them they held a shine. A fucking total turnaround from seconds earlier. "I don't know what I would do if I couldn't lose myself in a good book. You should be able to experience that, too."

"Basics would be good. Doubt I'm gonna be sittin' around readin' a book, Chelle. I can wait 'til the movie comes out," he semi-joked.

She sniffled and blinked quickly.

She was about to cry. Actually shed tears for him.

His chest ached from him knowing she was this affected by his problem. He didn't want her upset over him. *Hell*, he didn't want her upset over anything. Not on his watch. "Chelle."

She sniffled again, rubbed her eyes, then flapped a hand around. "Sorry. I didn't mean to fall apart like that."

He had a feeling it took a lot for her to fall apart. That

as a single mother she had been forced to be strong for so long, she didn't know how not to be. She was afraid to show any kind of crack in her shield. A shield she probably originally picked up for her daughters.

To show them strength. To protect them.

Like a mother who'd do anything for her children would.

He leaned closer, drove his fingers into her loose hair and pulled her face to his. "You're a good woman, Chelle."

When she opened her mouth to respond, he stopped her by taking it. Sweeping his tongue through, tasting her, then deepening the kiss.

He'd gotten a hard-on in record time, especially when she climbed into his lap and encouraged him to kiss her more. She also encouraged him to touch her tits. He didn't find it a struggle to oblige her on any of that.

But before he could drag her outside and back behind the shed for a repeat of Sunday night, her youngest girl texted her to say she was leaving work and was on her way home. Apparently, something Chelle insisted on with both her girls.

That simple message cooled shit off quickly since Josie only worked fifteen minutes away. While Chelle was quickly putting away the evidence of their lesson, he headed out with the promise she'd let him know once she had a new plan in place to tackle this new problem. His dyslexia.

He had seen the raw determination in her eyes before he left, so he had no doubt she would.

With another long drag on the joint, he filled his lungs once again.

Since coming to Manning Grove, he'd been around a lot of strong women. Stella, Red, Cassie, Reese, Jemma... Every Fury ol' lady wore that badge of honor. Even Reilly, Tessa and Saylor had backbones made of steel. *Hell*, the sweet butts were tough, too. So, he recognized it in Chelle.

The strength.

She didn't need to announce it. One could clearly see it. Recognize it. Feel it.

Whatever had happened in her past made her stronger. Whatever reason the man in the picture was no longer a part of her life, but still meant enough to her to keep his photo on her mantel. Whatever reason she never mentioned the girls' father if he was one and the same.

She drew on that strength. Kept moving forward. Never let the bad cripple her.

He did the same. The bad, the horrible, the unthinkable... Everything that tried to drive him to defeat, drove him to be a survivor instead.

They failed to break him.

Everyone in the BFMC were survivors in one way or another. That was one reason he fit in so well. If they knew what happened to him, they wouldn't look at him any differently.

Whatever they did to survive became the building blocks to who each of them was now. What shaped their past, shaped them now and would shape their future.

No one had to talk about it. It was just there. Lurking beneath the surface.

The door separating the bunkhouse from church opened and a flash of red caught his attention.

If anyone knew about being a survivor, it was Autumn.

Not only was he surprised Red was in The Barn this late at night, but more that she was in there at all. She usually only came into this part of the building when Sig was with her or when she and the ol' ladies were hanging out. To see her alone made him wonder what the fuck was going on.

She immediately spotted him on the other side of the fireplace and headed in his direction.

"Couldn't sleep?" he asked her as she settled on the old school bus bench next to him and curled her PJ-covered legs beneath her. She leaned into him, shocking the shit out of him.

He resisted putting his arm around her even though she seemed to need comforting. Something clearly bugged her. He didn't know what and the fuck if he was going to ask because she wasn't his woman. But she *was* family, so if she wanted to share, he'd listen.

"Haven't tried yet," she answered softly. "You?"

He shook his head.

It was well known she had trouble sleeping. But then, that was to be expected. Some nightmares could feel only too real.

One way to avoid them was by not sleeping. The other method was what he was currently doing.

He took one more long drag on the joint, then flicked the roach into the open fireplace. Without dislodging Red, he grabbed the Jack from the floor, untwisted the top and let the whiskey slide down his throat, warming his insides.

He tipped the bottle toward her, but she shook her head.

He wondered where the fuck Sig was and why she wasn't with him. The VP had a bad temper and if he saw his ol' lady cuddled against Shade, he'd probably lose it.

But if this was what Red needed, he'd risk Sig's wrath.

Sig was a man who didn't hide he was broken and had found the perfect woman, someone who understood. Not surprising, he was never letting her go.

The VP didn't have to worry about Shade making the moves on his ol' lady. It wasn't like that, never would be. He respected both her and Sig too much to try to steal her away. And she loved Sig too much to even consider it.

Their connection was so fucking strong it affected all of them. Every single one of them recognized it and only wished they could find the same.

That other half of their soul. Their missing piece.

While Trip had Stella, Deacon had Reese, Judge had

Cassie, and now Cage had Jemma, he wasn't sure their relationships were as vital as Sig and Red's. They all feared if something happened to either Sig or Red, the other would cease to exist.

Like they only lived for each other. Because of each other.

That was some intense shit.

"If you ever need to talk, Shade, I'm here. I'd understand."

His heart seized in his chest and he quickly drew a blank mask over his face. "Don't know what you're talkin' about."

"You think I don't recognize it?"

His pulse began to race, causing a ringing in his ears. She was quickly destroying the numbing effect of the booze and pot and was unaware she was doing so.

"I see it, Shade. You can hide it from the others, but you can't hide it from me. Everyone in this club is haunted in one way or another, but your ghosts are similar to mine. I get it. I understand being unable to sleep because you're afraid when you do, you'll be taken back there, to that darkness."

Everything she said was true. She didn't need a confirmation from him.

"Tell me I'm wrong."

She wanted it, anyway. "Not wrong."

She tipped her head toward the bottle of Jack Daniel's perched on his thigh. "You're self-medicating."

Jesus fucking Christ. He did his best not to tense against her but was finding it impossible. They didn't talk about this shit. None of them. If they recognized it, they kept their fucking mouths shut. As long as whatever it was didn't hurt anyone, no one said a fucking word.

Like Easy keeping quiet about Shade's inability to read.

But here she was, calling him out. He didn't like it, not one bit. He fought fire with fire. "So does Sig."

That shot didn't even phase her. "Yes, he does. Sig needs what he needs to get him from one day to the next. Unfortunately, a big part of what he needs is no longer available to him."

"'Cause of you."

"Because of me," she echoed. "I feel guilty about that."

Fuck. Sig had given up what he needed, what kept his sanity somewhat level, for her. So, her guilt wasn't unexpected. "You shouldn't." Her ol' man was trying other ways to fill that need. Some helped, some didn't. That was how much the man loved her. How much he lived for her.

"Maybe. But I do. I sometimes think I should let him have that."

Yeah, her guilt was so fucking thick, he could almost taste it. "But you don't."

"I don't because if I did, the guilt would eat at him. I think it would make what haunts him worse. It might even destroy him."

"He wants to be loyal to you."

"Yes. Even if it hurts him."

"Even if it hurts him if he's not."

"It'll hurt both of us if he's not," she whispered.

And there was the problem. They were damned if Sig did, damned if he didn't.

The sadness in her voice pained him. This was not a woman who let herself wallow. She had spent over a year in a dark place some might not have survived and once she found the light, she embraced it and usually didn't let anything dim it.

"He loves you. Would do anythin' for you." Sig would die for her, but Shade saw no point in mentioning that. Red knew her ol' man would give his life up in a heartbeat for her.

"I feel the same." She leaned her head against his bicep and sighed. "I wish life was easier for all of us."

She wasn't the only one.

"Anyway, I just wanted to tell you I'm here if you need me. If you need to talk." She lifted her head from his arm and tipped her face up to his. "I don't know where you disappear to at night, Sig won't tell me, but I can guess."

Fuck. "Autumn..."

"Just be careful, please. That's all I ask. Because if I ask you to stop, I know that request will go ignored."

He wanted to explain but couldn't. The plan with the Shirley Clan wasn't to be discussed. Not with anyone. Not even one of their victims.

"I told him I didn't want anyone going back up there. Not ever. Then what happened with Dyna... You guys weren't given that choice..."

Just like that, in a blink of an eye, Red vanished. Physically she still sat right next to him. But her eyes went distant, her expression empty and she disappeared inside her head.

She was gone. To wherever she went.

Unfortunately, he had an idea where.

It still happened to her a lot. Probably more often than she or Sig would like. Something else in a long list of things no one talked about. They were all used to it and Sig usually knew how to draw her back.

Most times she snapped out of it on her own, like when the door from the bunkhouse opened again and who he expected to walk through it did. The man's eyes landed immediately on his ol' lady. As he approached, Shade saw Sig's teeth were clenched tightly and a muscle was jumping in his cheek.

Like his brother Trip, Sig's temper was easily ignited. Seeing his woman with another man, no matter how innocent, could light that fuse without a match.

Sig knew whose heart Red belonged to. The VP also knew it wasn't like that between Shade and Autumn.

Sig was also aware the woman had a way about her that

drew Shade. She wasn't as loud as some of the other ol' ladies but she was more of a quiet strength. One Sig drew from. One Shade drew from, too, just not in the same way as the VP.

But that didn't mean Sig liked it. His demeanor clearly said he didn't.

Sig had claimed his woman. And no one would threaten that claim, real or imagined.

Red gave Shade a soft smile and unfolded herself from the bench. Her gaze dropped briefly to the wide black leather band that circled his left wrist as she said, "If you need me, I'm here. Please remember that."

As Sig approached, his body tight, Red turned to face him. "Couldn't find you," he growled.

"I came down to grab something from the kitchen and heard a noise in here. I thought everyone was at Crazy Pete's, so I came to see what it was."

Sig's brown eyes sliced from his ol' lady to Shade. "Shoulda came and got me." His words were for Red, but his low snarl was for Shade.

Red wrapped an arm around Sig's waist and patted his chest. "I'm not a prisoner, remember?"

The anger quickly drained from Sig's face and concern replaced it. "Shit's still not settled with the Shirleys. Don't need you wanderin' down here without me knowin'."

While that might be part of the reason, that wasn't everything. But Red had a way of making her man see reason. That way was also pretty damn effective.

"I'm sorry for making you worry. I was only keeping Shade company for a few minutes. I'm allowed to do that since he's family," she reminded him with a pointed look.

Sig tipped his head down to her, opened his mouth, then snapped it shut. He blew air out of his nostrils and gave her a little nod.

Crisis averted.

He didn't fault Sig for being possessive of Red. He lost her once, he wasn't losing her again, whether that threat came from inside the club or outside. But he should also realize, every fucking one of his brothers knew the two of them were meant to be together and would never fuck with that.

One day Sig might realize it, today was not that day.

Tomorrow probably wouldn't be, either.

It took a long time to mentally reprogram and the three people currently in The Barn knew that better than anyone.

Sig dropped an arm around Red's shoulders, gave Shade a chin lift and turned his woman back toward the door.

He wouldn't mention it now in front of Sig, but when he got a chance, he'd tell Red he appreciated her offer. He'd never take her up on it, but it was nice to know it was there.

"Goodnight, Shade," she called over her shoulder as Sig steered her out of church.

"'Night, Red, Sig," he called back.

Sig's answering grunt as the door closed made Shade grin.

He lost that grin when he glanced down at his left wrist again. He untied the leather cord that secured the wide leather strip and unwrapped the wristband. He ran his thumb over the thin raised line.

Red had no reason to worry about him.

No reason at all.

Chapter Twelve

JULIAN DOVE under the bed and quickly shimmied on his belly all the way to the wall. As the heavy footsteps came down the hallway and his name was being bellowed, he curled into himself, trying to become as small as possible.

It wouldn't work. It never did.

He was always found. Always.

But if he could put it off even for a few minutes...

Just a few...

The door opened so violently, it slammed into the springy thing at the bottom of the wall and made it twang loudly, causing Julian to jump and bite back a whimper.

His heart was now in his throat, making it difficult for him to swallow. Making it difficult for him to breathe.

The boots came closer. If he opened his eyes, he was sure they'd be next to the bed.

Fury shifted the air around him, the violent energy finding its way all the way down to the floor and under the bed.

When would this end?

When?

A large hand snagged his ankle, squeezed it painfully and used it to drag him out.

Julian balled himself up tighter, except for his hand that shot out to grab the leg of the bed nearest the wall.

He wasn't strong enough to hold on for long. Not yet. One day he would be.

One day soon...

But not today.

A sharp yank on his ankle ripped his fingers from the metal, scraping his palm. Causing pain. But that pain was nothing close to what would come next.

His head cracked against the bottom of the bed frame as he was dragged on his belly from his hiding spot.

He hoped he wasn't only punished this time. He hoped this "daddy" killed him.

He was tired of the pain.

So tired of the torture.

Just... tired.

He wished he could close his eyes and never open them again.

Never see the rage on this daddy's face or any future daddies when he didn't want to submit.

He never wanted to submit.

Only, sometimes he was tired and it was just easier.

But he hated it all, every second.

They thought by telling him he was a "good boy," he'd comply.

They thought by giving him treats and sweets when he'd been a "good boy," he'd do what they said without a fight.

They thought by promising him gifts, like a new toy or a game, he'd willingly do the things they wanted.

They thought wrong.

As soon as he was out from under the bed, that hand grabbed the back of his waistband and hauled him into the air. His pants dug into his stomach and made it hurt as he hung helplessly, the blood rushing to his head.

"I'm sorry," he whispered, trying not to cry. Some daddies liked when he cried, this one didn't.

Sometimes pretending he was a "good boy" helped.

Sometimes saying he was sorry and promising he wouldn't do it again, lessened the anger.

Sometimes acting like he didn't mind what was to come next stopped the lesson on how to be a "good boy."

But not today.

He squeezed his eyes shut when he saw the blur heading in his direction.

He didn't try to avoid it. He welcomed it.

He hoped that fist knocked him out so he wouldn't remember what would happen afterward.

He got his wish...

Shade opened his eyes once he removed the hand covering them and stared up at the dark ceiling, remembering that particular night. The night when Julian woke up and found himself locked in a closet. *The* closet. Where he ended up when he wasn't a "good boy."

He was naked and curled up on a towel so what was leaking from him wouldn't get on the floor.

Julian reached around and clenched his teeth when he touched himself there. It hurt so badly, he wanted to cry. But if he cried, he might be heard. So, he bit the inside of his cheek instead. That sometimes helped.

The only thing good that came out of hiding under the bed was he'd been knocked out before he got his punishment.

Julian held his hand in front of his face since he couldn't lift his head. The warm wetness on his fingertips was pink. A mix of this daddy's "magic juice" and blood.

The last time this happened, he couldn't use the bucket

in the corner for days without it hurting. That meant he'd have to eat as little as possible so he wouldn't need to use the bucket.

If he stopped eating all together, maybe he'd starve.

And if he starved...

Fucking motherfucker.

Julian had never been allowed to starve. He'd been worth too much.

Shade squeezed his eyes shut again. If that memory haunted him now while he was awake, it would only get worse if he went to sleep. It would suck him in like a whirlpool and drag him under until he was unable to escape.

As long as he was awake, he could free himself.

But that didn't mean the memory of that night, or even another one, wouldn't continue to swirl around in his head.

At least, he could do something about it if he remained awake.

He could go back out into The Barn, burn another joint and drink the rest of that bottle of Jack. Finish what he'd started before Red had interrupted him.

Or he could evict that memory from his head by replacing it with something else.

Someone else.

He rolled onto his side, grabbed his phone off the little table next to his bed and flopped onto his back again. He held the phone above his head and when he hit the side button the bright glow from the screen lit up his face and made him squint.

He stared at the phone's icons, his finger itching to press the one screaming his name.

Do it.

He shouldn't bug her.

Just do it.

Not when he was in this dark headspace.

Just fuckin' do it.

She might not understand that headspace and he wouldn't be able to explain.

Fuck it. She could say no.

He opened his text app and tapped the microphone symbol. He spoke slowly and clearly into it, turning his words into text. *Girls asleep?*

It was late. She might be asleep herself. Especially since she worked tomorrow.

She might be busy with her girls.

Or had turned off her phone.

He dropped his head back onto his pillow, stared sightlessly up at the ceiling again, dragging his fingers along the raised scar that started at the bottom of his left pec and ended at his waist. A habit when he wasn't wearing a shirt. Just like when he rubbed his thumb back and forth over the scar on his left wrist. Two unwelcome reminders of his past.

Like the long hair spread over his pillow, the short wiry hairs nestling his dick were still damp from his shower. He brushed his fingers over his dick that had thickened at the thought of meeting up with Chelle. Of being inside her like the other night.

Of her clenching around his dick and soaking it when she came.

His phone binged and he held his phone above his face again, looking at the screen and giving the order, "Read my text messages."

The computer-like voice read Chelle's answering text. *Yes. You're not.* The voice paused before asking, "Do you want to reply?"

"Yes," he answered the program. *No. Can't sleep. Can you get out?*

The next text message came a lot quicker than the last. *And go where?*

To meet me, he dictated. His dick was getting harder by the second at the thought of her being willing.

Where? came her next text.

He blew out a breath. He had no fucking clue where. There was no fucking way he was bringing her back to the bunkhouse and he couldn't go to her house if her girls were home.

This was probably what it was like for teenagers trying to get laid. What the fuck did they do?

Fuck in a vehicle, right?

He had caught Saylor and Ry one night when he'd come back to the farm around three a.m. They'd been in the backseat of Ry's cage parked in the tree line edging one of the fields.

His sled's high beam had bounced off the rear reflectors on the vehicle and he investigated, worried it might be the Shirleys staking out the farm.

It wasn't.

What it was, was trouble.

Trouble for the two eighteen-year-olds with both Judge and Rev.

Not only that, if Rev killed Ry, Judge would kill Rev. Then it would be the Originals all over again.

Shade decided Ry getting his rocks off wasn't worth the club imploding, so he'd approached. Once he did, he wished he hadn't and decided right then and there, if the club fell apart because of two horny teenagers, then so fucking be it.

But Ry managed to leave for college in one piece. And Saylor was... Saylor.

Neither Judge or Rev ever discovered the kids were humping like rabbits while everyone else was passed out or sleeping.

Shade wished that was something he could forget, too.

You there? came the flat female voice from his phone. *Name the time and place.*

Now, he answered. But where? *At the crematorium.*

Address? she asked. *You came to the house for Pumpkin, I didn't come to you. Remember?*

How could he forget? But, *for fuck's sake*, he didn't know the address.

Before he could come up with another location or admit he didn't know the address where he fucking worked, another text from her came through. *Never mind. I Googled it.*

Of course she did.

He rolled out of bed, pulled the first T-shirt he could find over his head and searched for his jeans. *In ten?*

He found his jeans and was yanking them up when his phone dinged again and the voice said, *That won't give me time to shave. Just an FYI.*

His answer? *Don't give a fuck about hairy legs.*

I wasn't talking about my legs.

He snorted and snagged his wristband off the table before hitting the button on his phone and trying not to chuckle when he answered, *Don't give a fuck about that, either.* He quickly covered the scar on his wrist with the wide leather.

See you in ten, the computer voice read.

He might have to convince her to use voice messages instead of texts. He'd rather hear her voice announcing her pussy wasn't clean shaven instead of a damn computer.

Or, *hell*, he could just call her. A primitive method that worked well way before text messages.

He shook his head. No matter how they exchanged messages, the fact was he was as hard as a goddamn rock now. He'd zipped up his jeans just in time. He double-checked to make sure he replaced the wrap in his wallet after using the last one behind the shed, then shoved in a second one, just in case.

As he reached for his cut hanging on the back of the door, he paused and stared at it. He probably shouldn't wear it. He would need to take it off before getting into her cage, anyway.

Fuck, he didn't know what she drove.

If she drove one of those Smart Cars, they were screwed because they wouldn't have enough room *to* screw.

They could always use the back of the crematorium van, but that was kind of...

No.

He did have the key to the crematorium. But if they fucked in there, he'd never be able to concentrate while at work again. He'd always be thinking about bending Chelle over the desk. Or having her against the wall.

Or having her straddle his lap in Cassie's leather office chair.

Yeah, no.

They could head over to The Grove Inn. Maybe Ozzy had an empty room. The only problem with that was, once he got Chelle in a bed, he might not let her back out. At least not until morning. Maybe not even then.

If he could work out a whole night with her, if she could come up with an excuse to give her girls for why she was gone all night, he'd consider that for a future fuck. But not tonight.

Tonight he'd take what he could get.

Even if it was a quickie in a fucking cage behind a pet crematorium.

———

"THANK FUCK," Shade muttered as Chelle turned off the lights to her mom mobile. He never thought he'd be so fucking excited to see a station wagon in his life.

But here he was. He had a raging hard-on and was about to get laid in one.

A first.

The passenger side window powered down and she dipped her head so she could see him sitting on his sled as she called out, "Here?"

"Yeah."

She glanced around the back lot of the crematorium. He had parked his sled in front of the rear loading dock, and she'd pulled into the spot on his left. "Um... I'm not sure I can do it here."

"Gonna forget where you are in a few."

A little snort-laugh bubbled from her. "You promise?"

He grinned. "Promise."

"Then hurry up," she demanded, now wearing a wide smile.

She began to roll the window back up but he stopped her with, "Put a coupla windows down. Otherwise, they're gonna steam up."

"Are you talking from experience?" she teased.

"Nope."

"Then how do you know?"

"Saw it recently. Up close and personal." Too up close and way too fucking personal.

"Oh." All the windows powered down at once and the engine went quiet.

He swung a leg over his sled, shrugged out of his cut, and draped it over the seat. He had decided to wear it because it felt weird riding his sled without it. His colors were an important part of him now.

He stepped up to the station wagon, what he guessed might be a Subaru, but wasn't sure, and began to work out the *how-tos* in his head. Luckily, this vehicle had more space than Ry's, which was a tiny sedan.

Ry had been sitting in the back seat with Saylor on his lap, riding him like a naked rodeo queen. Shade figured Chelle could do something similar.

But tonight he really wanted to get his mouth on her

first. He was dying to get a good taste of her, something he could remember later. When he needed a good memory to rub out one of the bad ones.

Or he just needed to rub one out.

The driver's door opened, Chelle climbed out and immediately opened the rear driver's side door. When he didn't move, she looked over the roof of the car and said, "Get in."

Get in.

Damn.

He liked this woman.

He didn't waste another second and climbed into the back seat. Once both doors were shut, he asked, "You had sex in a cage before?"

Her perfectly shaped eyebrows pinned together. "Car."

She probably thought he'd fucked up the word for a vehicle. "We call anything other than a sled a cage." He sighed and formed his words carefully again. "We call any vehicle other than a bike a cage."

"Oh. Then, yes. I lost my virginity in a rusty Ford Pinto wagon behind a Taco Bell." She shook her head. "Man, that was a long time ago."

"Worth it?"

"No. It... Well, it sucked. It was painful and awkward and the boy just wanted to get off. Which he did in less than a minute, thankfully. Worse, the car had vinyl seats, it was summer and sweltering hot. I thought I left all of my skin behind on that damn back seat." She turned and faced him. "It took me a long time before I wanted to try it again."

"This ain't gonna suck. Glad you didn't give up sex 'cause of one selfish asshole."

"It wasn't only one selfish asshole, there were a few. Then I met..." She sighed and shook her head again.

"You met..." he prodded. *Until you met the man in the picture. The one who claimed you by puttin' a ring on your finger after you vowed to be his wife 'til death. The man whose children you carried inside you 'cause you loved him that much.*

"Another time," she said softly. "Now isn't it." Her warm, slender fingers cupped his cheek and her thumb brushed over his lips. "Now I want to concentrate on you. On why we're sitting in the back seat of my Subaru Outback at the rear of a place where you turned Pumpkin into ashes."

He opened his lips and touched the tip of his tongue to the pad of her thumb. "Yeah, puttin' it like that, this is a shitty decision."

"Life's full of shitty decisions. What's another one? And, anyway, since you texted me, I've been only getting wetter and wetter in anticipation. So, we're doing this."

We're doing this.

Yeah, he liked this woman.

Not only because she liked sex, but because she was honest. Genuine. Down to Earth.

"Since you texted me back, been hard as a fuckin' rock." He could be honest, too.

The hand on his cheek dropped to his lap and she pressed it to the evidence. He covered her hand with his and, lifting his hips a little, encouraged her to stroke him over his jeans.

Yeah, he liked this woman.

She unashamedly liked sex and didn't play games by acting hard to get. She wanted his dick and wasn't shy about it.

But tonight, she was getting his mouth first. He'd figure out a way.

He wrapped her fingers around his balls and squeezed. When she kneaded them gently on her own, his breath hitched.

He said the next slowly and carefully, so he didn't fuck it

up because he wanted her to know it wasn't an option. "Want you to ride my face."

Right before he turned fifteen, he was trained on how to please a woman with his mouth by an older woman who was very experienced in training boys. Being trained by her was nothing like the ten years spent with his ever-changing male owners. It was completely different.

Once Julian discovered his desire for women—their softness, their motherly instinct, their gentle touches—he remained in the woman's possession. For the most part willingly.

Even though she was firm with him, she'd been nothing but kind. Her training methods weren't harsh or painful. The more he tried to please her, the more she spoiled him. For a couple of years, he lived like a prince after a decade of living like a pauper.

She never once called him stupid or retarded. But she also never tried to educate him. Except to pleasure her.

Then once he turned seventeen, grew more body hair and his voice deepened, he was again too old.

But instead of being sold, he was set free.

The only reason he had a good idea of his age was because it was always a selling point when he'd go back on the block to be sold or traded. Every bidder, buyer, or trader was looking for a specific age range. For some that range was narrow, others much wider. Though, sometimes the broker lied about his age. But Julian did his best to keep track.

One thing he never forgot during those years was his birthday because when he needed to escape inside his head, he'd close his eyes and remember the ice cream cake his mother had given him on his fourth birthday. The last birthday he ever celebrated.

None of his owners wanted to make a deal out of his

birthday, even if they knew it, because it meant he'd gotten another year older.

No. Not now.

"Are you okay?"

No. "Yeah."

"You disappeared. Are you having second thoughts?"

"About you? Fuck no." He slid her hand from around his balls back up his hard shaft. "Proof of how much I want you. Was just tryin' to figure out the best way to give you my mouth in this fuckin' car."

"It would be easier in a bed."

He only grunted because he couldn't argue that.

"But who doesn't like a challenge?" she asked lightly with a shrug.

Yeah, he really, really liked this fucking woman.

"Can you answer a question for me first?"

Christ. Yeah, he liked her, but not all of her damn questions. Having sex in a cage shouldn't take a lot of conversation. Only an exchange of bodily fluids and orgasms. That was it.

He should say no, but he had a difficult time telling her that. For that reason, he sucked it up. "If you gotta."

"I do." She climbed onto his lap, straddling it, and studied his face carefully when she asked, "Why do you want me?"

Her hot, soft pussy was now pressed against his hard-on and she felt the need to ask that? "What d'you mean?" He sank his fingers into the round curves of her ass, realizing she wore thin leggings like the first time he fucked her.

"Shawn..." She raised a *hold-on* finger between them. "You never told me the other night what you want me to call you. Now I know your name isn't Shawn, it feels weird calling you that. Do you prefer Julian or Shade?"

Never Julian. "Shade." Because that was who he was

now. He was Julian in a past life. The one he no longer lived. "That the question?"

If what to call him was her question, it was an easy one and he could now move on to burying his face between her thighs. With his mouth busy, he couldn't answer any more fucking questions.

"No. Am I like... robbing the cradle here?"

Fuck, he hated even the slightest trace of insecurity in her voice. "No."

"The reason I ask is... I turned forty-one two months ago. How old are you?"

"Not forty-one. Agreed to one question. You asked more than one."

"You're not going to tell me?"

Again, insecurity colored her question and he needed to make things clear with her so he wouldn't hear it again.

"Age ain't nothin' but a number, beautiful." He didn't give a fuck how old she was. He didn't give a fuck she had two daughters who were practically adults. He gave a fuck about her. End of discussion.

"Sometimes that number matters."

"Not to me." Most of his life, he'd been with people older than him. Whether by force or by choice.

The only exceptions had been in the last couple of years with sweet butts, but he avoided tangling with them as much as possible. Mostly because they were nosy and needled him to get naked. They'd get pissy when he'd refuse to answer questions or do anything more than yank down his jeans only enough for them to blow him or let him blow his load inside them.

Since they only served one purpose for him—the whole reason they wanted to be a sweet butt—he would like it better if they left him the fuck alone. He never approached them, they approached him.

But those weren't the only reasons he avoided the club girls.

After he discovered he liked women, he quickly learned he didn't prefer younger ones. They always seemed to be too loud, too pushy, too everything. Everything Shade tried to avoid. What might be a turn-on for his brothers, wasn't for him.

"Wouldn't give a fuck if you were fifty-one, Chelle."

"I'd have a problem if my girls dated someone too old."

"You ain't too old, beautiful. You're just right. Don't see a number, see you. Your girls ain't done cooking yet. So, yeah, they don't need someone who's too old shapin' their lives, someone who ain't their smart momma. You're the only one they should listen to right now for guidance, not a man who wants to mold them to his wishes." Or needs. Or to fill his sexual desires or perversions.

She frowned. "Are you talking about grooming?"

Fuck, he went too far. He should've just shut her up with a fucking kiss. "Somethin' like that."

"What do you know about grooming?"

The real question was: what didn't he know about it?

Christ. "Nothin'. Just sayin'. No more questions. Not tonight. I'm hard for *you*, Chelle, that's all you gotta know."

The halogen security lights along the roof of the building illuminating the rear parking area caused shadows in her station wagon. Even with the pockets of darkness, he could see her chewing on her bottom lip.

The age thing was going to bother her. He could lie about his age or he could just tell her the truth and hope she didn't order him out of her car, leaving him with an unrelieved hard-on.

He forced a breath out through his nostrils, reached up and thumbed her lip free from between her teeth. "Promised I'd make you forget where we are. Now need a promise from you."

Her throat visibly rolled as she swallowed hard. "Okay."

"If I tell you, it ain't gonna change a thing."

She nodded but didn't answer.

That wasn't good enough. "Need to hear it, Chelle."

"Okay," she said softly.

That had to be good enough. "Turned thirty a few weeks ago."

She didn't say anything for the longest time, but she didn't have to. He saw it in her face. The conflict. The struggle. What he feared.

"We're just fuckin', Chelle, that's it. Nobody gotta know shit if it bothers you. Your girls don't gotta know. My brothers don't gotta know. Nobody. You teach me to read. I help you paint. The other shit is for us, between us. Our business, no one else's. I want you. Wanna eat you out 'til you beg me to fuck you, then gonna fuck you 'til you beg me to stop. In that time between, you're gonna come and gonna come hard. And I'm gonna love every goddamn minute of it. 'Cause I wanna please you and me pleasin' you is gonna get me off. You got that?"

He didn't know how many words he fucked up in that long spiel, but he didn't give a fuck and as long as she got where he was going, that was all that mattered.

She breathed out a shaky, "Yes."

She got where he was going. *Thank fuck.* "Good."

"Let me tell you something, too. You saying that... All of that... With as slowly and deliberately as you speak... That was..." A shuddered breath slipped from between her lips.

"What?"

"That was like foreplay. If I haven't soaked your jeans yet, I will soon."

"Fuck yeah," he whispered.

Too many questions or not, he could fall for this fucking woman.

He'd never done it before, never thought he would, but Chelle could be the one to prove him wrong.

"I never thought I'd be a cougar."

"You're the right kinda pussy for me and I'm about to make that kitty purr."

Her fingers gripped his chin. "I've always been a romantic at heart but let me tell you, what you're saying is a lot more effective than sappy poetry."

"We done talkin' yet?" Because he was so done talking.

When she took his mouth, he got his answer.

Chapter Thirteen

Chelle loved to kiss and she spent a lot of time doing it. Too much time for him. If she didn't stop claiming his mouth, he would blow his load in his jeans. Especially since she kept grinding herself against his dick at the same time. Not gently, either. Like she was trying to get off and getting close to doing just that.

That was certainly not fucking helping, but he also hated to discourage it. Problem was, if he lost his shit in his jeans, it would make a goddamn mess and also make for an uncomfortable ride home.

So, yeah, as much as he appreciated her lips on his, their tongues sparring and her soft groans and whimpers filling his mouth, it needed to stop...

Right fucking now.

He twisted his head enough to break the vacuum seal she had on his mouth, dug his fingers into her hips to stop her rocking against him and pressed his forehead to hers in an attempt to settle his shit.

At this point, he wasn't sure if he'd keep his load in his nuts for the time it would take to make her come with his mouth. But, *fuck it*, tonight that goal was at the top of his list and he would just have to risk it.

"Clothes off," he ordered.

"All of them?" Her husky, breathless voice made his dick twang like a door stopper.

Fuck. "Up to you, beautiful."

A soft hiss escaped her at his nickname for her. She liked it. That meant he'd use it more often.

She quickly scrambled off his lap and flopped onto the seat next to him, kicking off her flip-flops and shimmying out of her leggings. Shade did notice no panties. No wonder she was worried about soaking his jeans.

She didn't stop there. She yanked her top over her head, and he realized whatever she was wearing had a built-in bra.

Fucking genius.

Only problem with that was, now he wanted to spend a good deal of time sucking her tits and he was sure they were running out of time.

He needed to prioritize.

She balled up her clothes and tucked them behind the seat. "The seats fold down."

Now she told him, after he already had a plan. If it didn't work, he'd use that info to resituate.

"You're still dressed," she remarked on the obvious.

She was not. The woman was totally naked perched on the back seat of her car.

"Yeah," he breathed, taking her in.

He wasn't lying when he called her beautiful. She was more than beautiful but he wasn't sure there was a name for it.

Oh yeah, he was. It was Chelle.

His mouth began to water as he picked up the scent of her arousal. "Lift up," he ordered. As soon as she did, he shifted until he was lying on his back, stretched out as much as possible. Which wasn't enough. The back seat was kind of cramped, forcing him to bend his knees enough to fit. It could still work.

After that, they would do the naked rodeo queen thing.

But first…

He brushed a few hairs out of his face that had escaped the knot he wore when he rode his sled and reached out a hand. "Climb on." As she began to move, he stopped her. "No, face the other way."

He knew the exact moment she understood his plan. Her lips rolled under and she didn't even hesitate.

Yeah, he liked this fucking woman.

With just a few awkward adjustments, with her wet pussy hovering right over his mouth, she began to lower herself. He stopped her again. "Not yet."

Her scent filled his nostrils and her thighs began to quake as she straddled his head.

Fuck yeah. He tested his theory by sliding a finger between her slick, plump folds.

Fucking soaked.

Dripping even.

She wanted him as much as he wanted her.

When he slid his finger through her again, a little noise escaped the back of her throat, which made the pressure in his balls almost unbearable.

"Do you want me to…" Her fingers fiddled with his belt buckle. He stopped her with a hand on hers before she got too far.

"No." *Christ*, her giving him head while he ate her pussy would be his undoing. "'Nother time."

She might have shivered at the last part.

If she was willing for another time, he was, too. But that wasn't now, that was later.

Right now, he pulled on her hips, bringing her down just far enough for the tip of his tongue to replace his finger.

When her sweet tang touched his taste buds, he closed his eyes and savored it for a moment.

"Shade?" His name quivered just like her legs.

"*Fuck*, beautiful. Just appreciatin' everythin' that's you." How the fuck that came out correctly, he had no fucking clue, because his brain was scrambled right now.

His throbbing dick wasn't making it any easier to think, either.

"Lemme have you," was the last thing he said before he pulled her hips even lower. *Now* they were done talking. His mouth was full with something better than words.

With his fingers splayed in a V, he separated her and gave her the attention he'd been dying to.

No joke, it was the best thing he'd eaten in a long damn time. If they had the time, he'd make it a full course meal, but he had to settle for a snack.

Didn't mean a snack couldn't be satisfying.

With his other hand on her hip, he adjusted her position some more and when his lips sealed around her clit, her body went electric, arched and she ground herself against his mouth.

Fuck. Yeah.

He'd find a way to do this again because they were doing it in a fucking bed next time, where he could spread her wide and take his damn time. Turn her into a boneless mess.

Until she was unable to move.

Unable to ask questions.

Unable to even think.

He fucked her with his tongue, nibbled along her labia and sucked her clit hard. Then started all over again, causing her to jerk against him each time.

"Shade." It was a warning. One that only encouraged him to suck harder, lick faster and tongue her deeper, but not stop. *Hell no.*

Yeah, he wouldn't forget her taste, which was now burned into his brain. He would dream about it. Her scent, her noises, the way her fingers clutched his calves as she tried to hold herself up, tried not to frantically ride his face until he was forced to take his very last breath.

Dying like that might be worth it.

She shook and shuddered, her moans filling the wagon's interior. Filling his ears. Filling his muddled brain.

"I... *Oh, God...*"

He didn't let up; they had a clear destination and were almost there. He wanted her to come in his mouth, scream his name, shred his jeans with her fingernails because her orgasm was that intense.

Clamping down on her clit, he slipped one finger inside her, gathering her own wetness, then found that puckered spot, the one most women ignored and he pressed on it. He didn't go any further than circling, testing and teasing.

That was all it took.

He fought to stay with her when she shot up, slammed her palms on the roof of the cage and slammed herself back down onto his face with a wail so loud it had to be heard a block away through the open windows.

Fuck yeah.

He gave her a few seconds to let the last of the ripples ebb away before lifting her off him, swinging his legs around until he sat up and she collapsed like a rag doll against the rear passenger side door.

Yeah, he was good with his fucking mouth.

Not wasting a second, he yanked his wallet from his back pocket, dug out a wrap and tossed it at her. With trembling fingers, she tore it open and held it until he had his belt buckle undone and his jeans shoved down far enough to free his steel-rod of a dick.

He plucked the latex disc from her fingers, rolled it down

his length, thinking only one thing... He needed to be inside her. Now.

"That's it?"

That's it?

It took him a couple of heartbeats for him to understand her question. Then it hit him. *Fuck.*

Enough light from outside the Subaru lit the interior so he would need to keep his shirt on, even though he really wanted to have Chelle's naked body against him.

He wanted to feel her soft skin against his.

But he wasn't ready to give her answers for her endless questions.

At least, not yet.

And definitely not right now.

The way he sat, he could shuck his jeans and still not reveal some secrets he was unwilling to share. However, it was still risky.

"Gonna take too long to get my boots off. Can't wait, beautiful. Need you now."

He finished securing the wrap and spread his knees as much as he could with his thighs hobbled by his jeans.

It would have to do.

He held out his hand. "Beautiful, get on."

He expected some pushback, but, surprisingly, none came. Instead, she planted one hand on his shoulder, put the other in his, and he helped her to straddle his lap again.

Yep, naked rodeo queen. Amazing what he could learn from two eighteen-year-olds.

"I want to see you naked," she said. "It's only fair."

It wasn't a whine like the sweet butts did when he kept his clothes on, but, instead, a demand.

He liked that.

Only from her, though.

He might even be willing to explore that bossiness a little

more and maybe even test the waters. Waters he hadn't tested since he'd been freed.

Yeah, they'd need to fuck again when they had a lot more time.

Not only for possible exploration but because when, and if, she finally saw him naked, the answers to her questions wouldn't be short. He'd also have to decide beforehand how many of her questions he'd answer and how much of what he answered would be truth.

But there was one truth he had no problem telling her. "You look better naked than me."

She rose up, grabbed his dick—which he liked—and tucked the tip where it needed to be—which he liked even more. "I doubt that," she whispered.

Then the time for conversation was over again.

As she lowered herself and welcomed him inside her, he whispered, "Fuck. Yes. Beautiful." Not only his new name for her, but because what he was seeing and feeling was just that. Beautiful.

All of it.

All of her.

Tight, wet, silky heat.

Surrounding him. Drawing him in.

What he would give to not have that layer of latex between them...

What he would give to leave something of him inside her after he came...

The only good thing about wearing a wrap was that it might prevent him from coming in less than ten seconds.

Because, *fuck*, if he allowed himself that, it just might happen, especially as he watched her face go soft as she leisurely slid down his length. Her lips parted, her eyes slowly closed, and her head fell forward, hiding the pure ecstasy on her face as he filled her. Once she was seated, she stayed there.

He waited. Not wanting to move, not even wanting to breathe. Because, if he was being honest, she could sit there forever. The two of them connected.

She didn't even have to move an inch and he'd still be A-fucking-okay with it.

When she lifted her face to his again, she said nothing. Only stared, her hooded eyes dark.

His heart thumped when she reached behind him and released the knot, letting his hair tumble loosely around his shoulders.

He hated anyone touching it and would even go as far as breaking someone's wrist before allowing it. His strong craving for Chelle to touch it, for it to brush along her skin, overrode his usual instinct to protect himself. She would never use it as a weapon against him or a way to control him.

Her fingers drove into the length above his ears and he quickly reminded himself that this was different. She was different. Especially when she used it to urge him to drop his head.

"Please," she whispered.

She didn't have to ask.

She directed him to one pointed nipple and he drew it deep into his mouth, sucking hard and flicking the pebbled tip with his tongue. Her back arched and she began to slowly ride his dick, rising to the very top and burying herself to the root.

Her tits were worth worshipping.

Her mouth a fucking treasure.

Her pussy as close to Heaven as he'd ever get. Because if there was one, those pearly gates would remain locked the day he approached them.

When the fingers gripping his hair tightened, the sharp pull on his scalp made him pause. Until her mouth pressed to his ear. "Kiss me."

Another demand, not an ask.

He reluctantly released her puckered nipple, shiny and wet from his attention.

"Kiss me." The order whispered across his lips as she ground in a circle against him, driving him so deep there was nowhere left to go.

He plundered her mouth while cupping both tits. He squeezed and kneaded, loving the weight of them in his palms, the soft flesh within his fingers, the brush of the hard points against the pads of his thumbs.

A vision filled his head of her naked, on her back, her strawberry-blonde hair spread around her head like a fan, while she pushed her tits together as he tweaked the tips and he fucked the soft, pale mounds. Not letting up until he was ready to come, and when he was, finishing in her mouth.

She would accept all of him, his whole length with each thrust, and every drop of his cum when he spilled it at the back of her throat. By then she'd be so wet and on the verge of her own orgasm, when they'd flip around, she'd ride his face again until she exploded inside his mouth and he licked her clean. He'd savor every last drop of her in exchange of her savoring every last drop of him.

He forced himself from the fantasy he was determined to make a reality and concentrated on tonight. His future plans needed to wait.

He had her here and now. It might be in a fucking Subaru station wagon, but it was better than not having her at all.

She'd only come once. Once wasn't enough.

Not for him, not for her.

Not tonight.

Chelle changed her rhythm when she began to rock back and forth, frantically grinding her clit into him, her whimpers filling his mouth. Their tongues stopped tangling, their lips stopped moving, but they remained connected, now only sharing their breath, which was ragged and quick.

His fingertips dug deeper into the soft flesh of her tits. When she released his hair, she wrapped her arms around his neck, drove forward one more time, holding him close.

What came next was unmistakable.

She twisted her head, pressed her cheek to his and cried, "I'm coming."

That announcement was unnecessary. The proof came when she clamped tightly around his dick, each intense ripple driving him closer to his own final destination.

A few seconds later he reached it, grabbing her hips as his lifted. Her arms tightened around his neck and her breath swept over his ear as a groan rushed up from the very depth of his soul.

"I feel you," she whispered.

No surprise. He had felt that to his toes.

When his dick stopped pulsing, he collapsed back into the seat and rode the high of his orgasm while it lasted.

Luckily, Chelle wasn't in a rush to move. She kept a tight grip on him, her tits smashed against his heaving chest, her cheek still cemented to his.

What happened next caught him off guard.

Something broke open inside him, a warmth or a glow, like the rays of the sun radiating from his center and beaming outward, chasing away some of the darkness. The lingering darkness that had swallowed him whole so long ago and he could never quite shake, no matter what he did.

His hands automatically slid up her ribcage and around to her back until his arms wrapped tightly around her, too. He wished they could stay like that, and he could hold onto that warmth forever.

They couldn't. He couldn't.

But in those fleeting moments, he saw what could be.

How he could be.

He had wanted to meet her tonight to push out bad memories and replace it with one that was good.

This ended up being so much fucking more.

For fuck's sake, it gave him hope.

He wasn't sure he could—or should—hang onto that hope. But even a flash of it was more than he ever expected.

What was even stranger was that this happened during sex, something he had hated and was forced to do against his will for so many years.

When he was on the edge of fifteen, he began to enjoy it and even seek it out once he learned it could be pleasurable, and not punishment, with the right person.

Having sex with Chelle was more than simply getting off, it was on a whole other level.

It hit him why. It was that connection. One he'd never had with anyone before.

He hadn't been seeking it, but it managed to find him.

He wasn't sure if Chelle felt it, too. Or if he was imagining it.

No matter what, he wouldn't mention it. He'd keep that crazy shit to himself. Because that was what it was. Crazy thoughts from a fucked-up brain.

He needed to pull out before his dick softened even more and the wrap leaked.

With his nose buried in her hair, he took one more long inhale, capturing her scent, then loosened his hold so she could lean back. He held the bottom of the wrap as she lifted herself enough to free him but she didn't move off his lap.

"It's late. I have to get up early tomorrow." She sounded disappointed.

"Yeah." They both had to work tomorrow. He'd find himself back in this rear parking lot again in a few hours.

"Can we do this again? Soon?"

Fuck yeah, they could. "Not here."

She laughed softly. "No, not here. I suggest a bed next time? And maybe less clothes?"

"Likin' your suggestion." The bed, not the clothes part. "Club owns a motel. Could go there."

Her brow furrowed. "They do?"

He assumed everyone in town knew who owned and ran The Grove Inn. "Yeah."

"Or we could use my bed when the girls aren't home."

"If we're in your bed, don't wanna race." Which would happen in her house if they were going to keep it from her girls.

"Rush," she corrected him.

Shit. "That, too." They wouldn't be able to take their time if there was a threat of her daughters coming home. Catching them. Discovering that their mother was fucking a biker eleven years younger than her.

Not only a biker, but one who couldn't read and had done too many things in his life he couldn't talk about.

With a soft, but satisfied, sigh, she finally moved to sit next to him, grabbed her leggings and top from behind the seat and began to tug them on.

He slipped off the full wrap, knotted it and, like last time, had nowhere to dispose of it.

He wondered what Ry had done with his in the same situation. At least, Shade hoped to fuck the kid wore one with Saylor. Judge's son had a solid future ahead of him and he didn't need to be fucking that up just to get himself off.

Either way, wasn't Shade's problem.

His problem was in his hand. He grabbed an empty plastic shopping bag tucked in the back seat pocket and threw it in that for now.

As he yanked his jeans back into place and secured them and his belt, Chelle said, "I've been researching dyslexia and gathering some material we can use for your next reading lesson. I also talked to some teachers and they gave me some pointers. It's doable, Shade. It might not be quick, but you should be able to learn to read. We just need to go about it an unorthodox way. There are plenty of lesson plans and programs out there, I just want to pick an effective one for you."

For fuck's sake, there went his orgasm high. "Chelle, you don't gotta do this. It's a lotta work."

She smiled. "So is all the painting you're going to do."

He brushed his thumb over her lower lip. "Right. We'll do some this weekend."

"And I'll get a lesson together for Tuesday. One night a week won't be enough, though. I'll make a schedule."

She would make a fucking schedule.

"Fuckin' you once a week won't be enough, either. So, fit that in, too."

Christ, painting, reading lessons, fucking Chelle...

He needed to head up the mountain at least once a week, too.

Another problem might be, if he was gone from the farm more often, questions about his whereabouts could be raised. He might have to give Trip a heads up. But then, of fucking course, that would lead to more questions.

And questions would lead to more answers he didn't want to give.

Fuck.

Chapter Fourteen

THE LESSONS WERE SLOW, torturous and frustrating as all fuck. Only bearable because he got to spend time with Chelle.

Painting sucked ass. Only bearable because he got to spend time with Chelle.

And her girls.

A couple of times in the past two weeks, one or both of her daughters joined them. Basically making more of a mess than actually helping. It was worth it, though. He got to listen to the three of them chatter away. Joking, laughing, talking about boys, school and their jobs. He got to watch them interact, their love and the closeness they shared unmistakable and real.

Even better, more talking between them meant less talking for Shade.

But within all the words they shared with each other, they only talked about what was happening in their lives currently or in the near future.

They never talked about the past.

Never mentioned the man in the picture.

Chelle never mentioned her husband. The girls never mentioned their father.

He wasn't sure if that was normal for them, or if they didn't want to talk about him in front of Shade.

Maybe the reason the man was no longer in the picture was because he was abusive and a complete dick, and they were happy to be rid of him. But if that was true, it made no sense why Chelle would keep her wedding picture on the mantel.

And only that one.

He wanted to ask. He fought asking every fucking night they spent together at her kitchen table and every weekend he was there to paint.

He didn't ask because it wasn't his fucking business. If she wanted to talk about him, she would and Shade would simply listen.

Not only were the reading lessons frustrating, so were the last two weeks since they hadn't had the opportunity to fuck again.

Shade had even pulled Ozzy aside and asked about using one of the rooms.

Oz had given him a knowing look, a grin and a, "Fuck yeah, brother, whenever you need it."

Chelle also decided they weren't fucking again until they could do it in a bed. And not until Shade was fully naked.

He was good with the first, not so good with the second. But he'd figure it out when the time came.

Only they hadn't had the time to do it in a bed and her requirement meant a quickie behind the shed was out. Which sucked because he needed to be inside Chelle again soon.

Most of the time he sat next to her with a raging hard-on, dying to sweep the books and the laptop to the floor and take her right there on the kitchen table.

It had come close a couple of times.

After his lessons, he'd gone back to the farm, did what Red called a little self-medicating and then, a little self-help.

But, *for fuck's sake*, that was getting old.

Instead of painting this afternoon after the club run, he hoped they'd hit the motel instead.

Chelle's girls were spending the day with their cousins and some friends, so they probably wouldn't even know their mother wasn't home. If they came home early, they were more than old enough to take care of themselves and at least wouldn't catch him with his pants down and his dick in their mother.

He might not talk a shitload, but he had a hard time not staring at Chelle like she was his favorite meal. So, he figured the girls had a feeling about the two of them.

On the weekends, while they painted, or even during dinner afterward, he caught the nudges and whispers between the sisters whenever they noticed Chelle and Shade "accidentally" brushing against each other, whether it was their fingers, shoulders or even their hips.

Even more telling was the flush in Chelle's cheeks, the sparkle in her brown eyes, or the way her nipples responded when he was close.

Or her ragged breathing when he was even closer.

Even so, he was pretty damn sure they would approve of their mother getting laid. Maybe even encourage it. That meant they wouldn't be upset if they caught him with his dick in their mother.

However, Chelle would.

So, they did their best to keep the fact to themselves that they were climbing the walls to climb each other. Shade was fucking fine with that since he wanted the woman to be able to live with getting dick from a biker eleven years younger than her.

While they kept that secret from Josie and Maddie, he'd

given his prez the lowdown on him helping out a single mother with painting for some extra scratch.

That was exactly how he worded it, too, and then shut the fuck up since there was nothing else to say.

Trip had stared at him for way too fucking long without saying a word.

When Trip finally spoke—right before Shade walked away thinking they were done—he surprised the shit out of Shade by saying, "Invite her on the run Sunday."

That was the last thing he expected to come from the Fury president's mouth. The man never encouraged anyone to bring females along on a run, especially women who weren't ol' ladies. He tolerated Reilly on the runs because Reilly was Reilly. And while she wasn't claimed by anyone, she had forced them to accept her as part of the club. The fact was it was easier and less aggravating to cave to Reilly than fight her, since she had the same stubborn blood as her sister, Reese.

But Chelle wasn't Reilly. *Thank fuck.* She also wasn't an ol' lady or even Shade's regular. And they were keeping what was between them on the D.L.

"Ain't like that."

"Gonna get cold soon, so when it *is* like that, she'll have to wait 'til spring to get a good handle on our club."

It was more like Trip wanted to get a good handle on Chelle. Shade wasn't sure he liked that.

"Ain't like that," he repeated under his breath. But when his president gave an order, he needed to listen. Right now, Shade was thinking it was only a suggestion and didn't want it turning into an order if he could help it.

"She can't have that big of a fuckin' house for all the time you've been gone the last coupla weeks."

Fuck, Trip had noticed. Or someone else had noticed Shade had been missing a lot and mentioned it to Trip.

"Been up the mountain, too."

"Know when you go up the mountain, since you give Judge the heads up." Trip tilted his head. "Also know you ain't into the sweet butts and never saw you touch one of the hang-arounds. Pretty sure you're into pussy like the rest of us. A man can only go so long before he's gotta sink his dick into something attached to long hair, sweet curves and a skilled mouth. A fist ain't gonna cut it on the regular. Unless you got yourself a Fleshlight..."

Trip let that hang and so did Shade. Even if he had a latex pocket pussy—or even ten—that was no one's fucking business.

"She know about the club?"

Jesus fuck. "Yeah."

"She got a problem with it?"

He had no fucking clue. But if she did, he doubted she'd let him around her girls or to sit at her kitchen table twice a week. Or make him dinner on the days they painted.

He really fucking doubted she'd be letting him inside her.

"Don't think so." But she also didn't know much about the club and bringing her along on a run might change that.

"Then she shouldn't have a problem sittin' her ass on the back of your sled. And I'm fuckin' sure you won't have a problem with havin' her tits smashed into your back, her warm pussy grindin' against your ass and her arms wrapped around your waist on our Sunday ride. Also don't gotta say it, but your Night Train's got a rumble that will make her cream her fuckin' jeans. Hell, Stella comes almost every time we fuckin' ride and I don't got a Night Train."

His chest began to tighten. "Ain't like that, Trip."

"Then why'd you ask Oz about a room?"

Fuckin' Ozzy.

"My guess, it wasn't even a split second after you asked him, he sent out a fuckin' group text to everyone, includin' the women, askin' who you're bangin'."

Goddamn Ozzy!

"Also musta forgot we got security cameras along with those security spotlights that not only light up the rear of the crematorium but lit up a Subaru station wagon and its occupants a coupla weeks back."

Fuck! Even though his heart had seized, blood still rushed to his brain at that news.

"So..." Trip took a couple steps closer to him, caught his gaze and leaned in until the bill of Trip's pulled-low baseball cap was only inches from Shade's forehead. "My guess is I'll see her on Sunday. This time with fuckin' clothes on."

"Trip..."

The prez leaned back and raised a palm. "Look, you ain't Deacon or Easy, or some of the others, who bounce from hole to hole. Or in Deke's case, used to bounce, 'cause I'm pretty fuckin' sure he'd like to keep both his testicles. If you stuck your dick in anything and everything with tits, I'd respect that. What I'm thinkin' is if you're sinkin' your dick in the same wet spot over and over, she's somethin' to you. What? Don't fuckin' know. But do know I look forward to findin' out." He paused and added, much more firmly, "On Sunday."

Shade's jaw got tight. "Guessin' that's an order."

"Thought it was pretty fuckin' clear it was."

"If she says no?"

"Guessin' the ol' ladies would love to meet her. They're pretty fuckin' convincin' even if you're not."

Fuck, he wasn't going to let Trip unleash the Fury sisterhood on Chelle. "She got kids, prez."

Trip tapped his finger to his temple and cocked an eyebrow. "Figured that when you mentioned single mother. She don't got a babysitter, we'll get it covered."

Shade unclenched his jaws enough to say, "They don't need a sitter."

Trip gave him a single nod. "Even better." Then he turned on his boot and walked away.

Apparently, the Fury prez was done talking.

Fuck.

He had called Chelle later that night when they were both in their own beds. He didn't want to wait until the last minute in case she needed to find an excuse to be gone most of the day and, if it was up to Shade, most of the night.

He expected her to balk at coming along on the run. She didn't. In fact, she was surprised and even a little eager. But she also reminded him about what he said that night in the Subaru regarding keeping things between the two of them.

What he didn't want to tell her was that what happened in that Subaru also happened to be caught on camera. He was pretty fucking sure that her knowing some of his brothers saw her naked while riding his face, and then his dick, would embarrass her.

Then she'd definitely not want to join them on the run.

Maybe she'd even tell him to fuck off.

Instead, he used the excuse of Ozzy running his big fucking mouth to his prez as the reason for the invite. He also reminded her of the interaction between him and Chelle in front of the school with Cassie and Daisy.

Those reasons were good enough for her, *thank fuck*. But then, she wasn't the arguing type like some of the other ol' ladies. Like Reese.

Especially Reese.

Some men, like Deacon, were into that. They get off on the fight and fire.

With that said, if any of his brothers—and he wasn't sure who all knew about or saw the recording—mentioned the action in the Subaru in front of Chelle, things would get ugly. Especially since his brothers liked to bust each other's balls, as well as tease the women.

That right there was the reason he was waiting for

Chelle outside The Barn instead of hanging inside with everyone else while they gathered for their Sunday run.

There was no fucking way she was walking into church on her own.

There was also no fucking way she was talking to any of his brothers without Shade by her side listening to every fucking word.

Maybe one day he'd tell her the story about the video and they could laugh about it.

Today was not that fucking day.

Tomorrow wasn't, either.

And once he could read half-decently, her house was done being painted, and she got shot of his ass, maybe he wouldn't have to tell her at all.

Ignorance could be fucking bliss.

This was the perfect case for that saying.

So, as long as his brothers kept their fucking mouths shut about the unintentional porn Chelle and Shade headlined in, he'd be good.

So would they.

That very same Subaru made its way down the farm lane to where he halted his pacing, turned and waited, while twisting his hand back and forth along the back of his neck.

He'd already smoked part of a fatty not even a half hour earlier, but his nerves were still on edge.

He had really wanted to keep the shit with him and Chelle just between the two of them. He didn't want her worried about their age difference and today there would be a whole shitload of people doing a bunch of math in their fucking heads. Especially if they figured out how old Chelle's kids were.

Cassie already knew Chelle, but she certainly wasn't one to judge. Luckily, the ol' ladies weren't a bunch of catty bitches. The sisterhood all got along and supported each other like a family should. Reese was the oldest of the bunch, but Chelle was still about five or six years older than Deacon's ol' lady. As long as Shade didn't give a fuck about Chelle's age, nobody else should, either.

He pointed away from the line of sleds parked in front of The Barn and she followed his direction, steering her car to the right of the building and the opposite side to the courtyard and parked. Her cage would be safer there since after the run everyone would be coming back to the farm to party.

When she climbed out of her Subaru wearing jeans that hugged her curves, some kind of heeled boots, a snug long-sleeved, thermal-like V-neck shirt that emphasized just how big her tits were—and how hard her nipples were—he was close to shoving her back into the rear seat and fucking her all over again.

This time everyone could watch full-color, 3D action with sound effects.

Fuck.

She had a denim jacket in her hand, was wearing her glasses and had her long strawberry-blonde hair pulled back from her face.

He wanted to grip that ponytail while she sucked him off until he came down her throat. He was putting that on the to-do list for later.

Her eyes followed his hand as he reached down and straightened his dick.

Her lips parted, color shot up into her cheeks, and her brown eyes heated.

Yeah, he really, really fucking liked this woman.

He might have a difficult time making it through the whole ride. Some of his brothers dropped out of formation for a quick sled screw or head job in a private spot and then caught up later, but they'd have a lot of eyeballs on them today, so he'd do his best to stick to his original plan.

"C'mere," he murmured needlessly as she approached.

As soon as she was close enough, his hand shot out, curled around the back of her neck and yanked her to him. Their bodies crashed together at the same time their lips did. He took her mouth hungrily.

He quickly lost track of time but, at the back of his mind, knew if he didn't stop kissing her, they would be definitely skipping the run and Trip might not be happy with that. A run was the one time they were all together at once, even if it was on their sleds in the wind.

Their group rides were considered important because it was the perfect bonding time for the brotherhood. A solid brotherhood made for a solid club which helped prevent a clusterfuck like what happened with the Originals.

Like church meetings, the club runs were required. A brother better have a damn good excuse not to be on one. Sticking his dick in Chelle wouldn't be one, though Shade would disagree.

He reluctantly broke the kiss but didn't pull away.

"You must be happy to see me," she teased, tilting her hips just enough to brush against his erection. Her doing that didn't help the pressure in his balls.

"Always happy to see you, beautiful."

A rough clearing of a throat had her stepping back and him dropping his hand from her neck.

"Gonna bring her in and introduce her?"

If it was up to Shade? No.

He turned to face his prez who stood with his hands on his hips and his ball cap tugged low as he stared at the two of them from the corner of The Barn. With his dark sunglasses and his hat, his eyes were hidden, but Shade had no fucking doubt Trip was sizing Chelle up.

It wouldn't bother Shade as much if he didn't know Trip saw her naked. Or at least some of her. Shade hadn't seen the video and he'd been assured it had been deleted.

He hoped to fuck it was.

With his eyes still on Trip, Shade blindly held out his hand and didn't move until her fingers interlaced with his. He gave them a slight squeeze and pulled her into his side.

"Chelle, Trip. Blood Fury president."

Trip jerked up his chin. "Good meetin' ya. Heard you're a teacher."

"Librarian," she corrected.

One dark eyebrow raised above Trip's sunglasses. "Librarian. School Daisy goes to."

"Yes."

"School my boys will go to."

"Oh, you have children?"

"Workin' on it," Trip muttered. He jerked his head toward the front barn door. "C'mon. Everyone's dyin' to meet you."

Chapter Fifteen

SHE WAS TRYING NOT to be nervous, but she was quaking a little on the inside. Especially after Shade muttered a curse under his breath and his fingers tightened around hers. That made Chelle squeeze his tighter.

The last thing she expected was for him to hold her hand. It seemed to be him claiming her, but hopefully it was more of an attempt to reassure her, instead.

They had originally decided to keep their sexual attraction, along with the rest, between them, but here she was, about to meet his "family." Him being tense about it only made it worse for her.

She took a deep, bolstering breath as they followed the club's president into what looked like a huge barn. Once she stepped inside the door, she realized that if it had been a real barn in the past, it was far from one now.

First, it was noisy with music blaring and people talking, laughing and shouting.

The interior reminded her of some sort of country-western bar, with a round center fireplace, wide wood-planked floors, a bar, pool tables and more. But instead of a room full of patrons wearing cowboy boots and hats, it was all leather, denim and smoke.

One thing that stood out was the men all wearing their vests declaring them members of the Blood Fury MC.

Trip peeled off from them and headed over to a tattooed woman with black hair and blue stripes. The way she was dressed, along with her physical appearance, made her look like some kind of rock star. When the club's president dropped his arm around her shoulders, she lifted her face to him and he dropped a kiss on her lips.

"Is that his wife?" Chelle whispered. She didn't know why she was whispering, since it was so loud in that huge space, no one would hear her anyway.

"Ol' lady."

She hadn't done too much digging yet on MCs and needed to do more, but one thing she had learned so far was the meaning of "ol' lady."

"I assume that's who he plans to have kids with."

"Yeah, if he wants to keep breathin', it'd be smart if he only knocked up Stella."

"That would be smart, I guess," she murmured, taking in the whole atmosphere of what he called "The Barn" in his invitation. He'd explained it was their clubhouse, the base for their MC.

"How many of you are there?"

"Dunno. Thirteen, maybe? A couple prospects. Some ol' ladies and..." He stopped speaking.

"And?" she prodded.

"And some other women."

Some other women.

"Like girlfriends?"

His gaze circled the interior of the barn and came back to her. "Not girlfriends."

She remembered reading something about women, similar to groupies, who liked to hang around biker clubs.

She'd also read that the ol' ladies, children and the "other women" were considered property of a club and, as such, were under the club's protection. She found that a bit curious but also... archaic.

However, she'd been so busy with learning everything she could about dyslexia and getting together appropriate lesson plans, she hadn't had time to dig any deeper. She could ask Shade a bunch of questions, but he always got tense when she asked too many, and she wasn't sure if he'd answer them anyway.

Sometimes he acted like he never heard her question.

Though, that was a typical trait with every male she'd ever known. From her grandfather—who did it to Chelle's grandmother until she died suddenly and then he regretted ignoring her every day for the rest of his own life—to her own husband and brother, and even her coworkers.

He tugged her hand, began to make rounds, and kind of grunted introductions to the women, who were all genuine smiles, curious looks, but super friendly, to the men wearing cuts.

She was surprised she knew some of them.

She had seen Judge, of course, a couple of times when he picked up Daisy from school. He was hard to forget. But she was finally introduced officially Shade-style, which went something like his introduction to Trip. "Judge, Chelle." That was it.

Then she recognized four more, who also recognized her. Rev, Whip, Cage and Rook, all the mechanics at the garage in town where she took her Subaru. She had no idea they were part of the Blood Fury MC. They seemed just as shocked with her walking into their clubhouse with Shade as she was seeing them.

Before Shade could introduce her to anyone else, they heard a shriek that made everyone freeze.

"Mrs. Goodson!"

Chelle's heart stopped. Completely arrested in her chest at what she saw. *Who* she saw.

What was she doing here? "Angel?" It couldn't be.

What was Maddie's closest childhood friend doing here?

And dressed the way she was. She wore clothes, but barely.

Her dark hair was pulled in two pigtails jutting out from the sides of her head. She wore the tiniest powder pink shirt, like one Chelle expected to fit a toddler, clearly no bra, and her flat belly was completely exposed, as was her navel, which was decorated with a dangly piercing. The turquoise shorts she wore were no bigger than the panties Chelle would wear during her time of the month. Angel had finished the outfit with turquoise and white striped knee-high socks and neon pink and white sneakers. The only thing missing were pompoms and she could be out on a football field doing a cheer.

However, if Angel did a split, Chelle was certain a couple of her female parts would be flapping in the breeze.

"Oh my God!" Angel squealed, running over and body slamming into Chelle, almost plowing her over. She was saved from toppling backward when Angel wrapped her arms around her.

And, of course, Shade grabbing her arm with a firm grip and a loud, "What the fuck?"

"I haven't seen you in so long!" came the piercing exclamation.

Chelle winced. "Um..." *Holy shit.*

"What are you doing here, Mrs. Goodson?"

She was beginning to ask herself the same thing.

It didn't help that she was having a hard time breathing with Angel trying to squeeze her insides out like a tube of toothpaste. "Please... don't call me that... here. You can call me Chelle."

Angel leaned back but didn't release her completely. "I

almost didn't recognize you! With your glasses and jeans and cute ponytail and everything! And because you're," she swept a hand through the air, indicating The Barn, "here." She frowned and asked again, not so enthusiastically this time, "What are you doing here?"

Her blue eyes landed on Shade for a few seconds, then sliced back to Chelle. Angel dropped her arms, stepped back and put some space between them. "You're here with Shade?" That sounded like an accusation more than a question.

"I... uh..."

"Yeah, she's fuckin' here with me. Got a problem with that?"

Angel blinked. "You're together?"

"No... We..."

"Gonna ask again, Angel, you got a problem with that?"

Shade's growl had Chelle turning toward him and staring. But he only had eyes for Angel and his eyes were saying a lot. None of it good.

Angel's throat undulated and she stared at Shade as a forced "no" slipped from between her tight lips.

Chelle grabbed his forearm and squeezed. "Shade was nice enough to ask if I'd like to go along today on the run. I've never been on a motorcycle before, so I thought I'd check that off my bucket list."

"You're going on the run?"

That question had a sharp edge and caused the muscles under Chelle's fingers to turn to stone.

"Aren't you?" Chelle asked, confused.

Oh shit.

It hit her then why Angel was at the clubhouse dressed the way she was but not included on the ride. Angel was one of those "other women."

The other women Shade didn't want to put a name to.

The name Chelle had read about briefly. Actually, there

had been a few names she had skimmed over. None of them great. The best one being a "club girl." The worst being...

Ooooh shit.

Did she have sex with a man who had sex with one of her daughter's childhood friends?

Oh... shit.

Heat hit her cheeks, her mouth opened and she turned wide eyes to Shade.

As soon as he saw her reaction his face got hard and he spun on Angel. "Go find somethin' or someone to do."

Chelle dug her nails into his forearm. "No! No... It's okay. It's fine. This is just all... new to me." She grimaced. "Seriously, it's fine." She turned to Angel and gave her a smile, hoping it wasn't too lopsided. "It's really good to see you, Angel." Chelle just wished she hadn't seen so much of her.

It took the girl a few seconds, but her anger at finding out Chelle was not only with Shade, but going on the club run with him, mysteriously disappeared.

After a quick frown at Shade, Angel plastered on a smile Chelle could tell was fake, bounced on her toes which made her very perky unrestrained boobs bob freely and said, "Well..." Her fake smile turned into an exaggerated pout and she pressed a hand between those very pointy boobs, making her nipples practically punch out of the thin, skin-hugging fabric. Was that all for Shade's benefit? "*Aww*... I miss Maddie. I haven't talked to her in like... *forever*."

Chelle swallowed the automatic response of, "You should give her a call." Because if Angel talked to Maddie, the cat would be out of the bag about her and Shade.

Or at least about being here today on the run.

Then she'd have to live through a double daughter inquisition on why she was on this motorcycle ride with Shade and why they hadn't been told about it.

Then they'd pester her about... Well, about everything.

Her girls were experts at digging up the truth. They both also had good imaginations. The longer Chelle held out, the wilder her daughters' stories would get until she was forced to tell them the details.

Plus, the last thing she wanted Josie and Maddie to know was that their mother got nailed behind the shed in their backyard or on the rear seat of the Subaru, where they also sometimes sat, by a man eleven years her junior.

She grimaced.

"How she know your girl?"

She snapped out of her musings and realized Angel had wandered away. She had draped herself over the young mechanic, Whip, where he sat at the bar on a stool, while she whispered something into his ear and straddled his thigh.

Or... rode it.

Whip had his hand down the back of her shorts and was...

She spun toward Shade.

"Sorry, what?" Her face felt touched by the heat of a thousand suns.

Shade glanced over where she had, frowned and grabbed her hand, pulling her along.

"How she know your girl?"

She had no idea where Shade was taking her, but followed anyway. "Maddie and her were really close when they were younger. I figured they just drifted apart like some girls do. But Angel was also one of my students. Her and Maddie were in the same grade level all the way through graduation."

"It bother you?"

"I wasn't expecting to see someone my daughter's age here." She wasn't expecting to see people she *knew* here. Now she would look at everyone in town in a whole new light. She would wonder who else had a "secret" life.

"She's legal. All of them are."

Them. She assumed he meant the "other women." Because all the ol' ladies she had been introduced to—but not given time to have a deep discussion with, which might have been by design—seemed to be at least in their mid- to late-twenties. And those were the younger ones. Reese seemed to be the oldest and Chelle guessed the lawyer was a few years younger than her.

"I... I didn't mean it that way. I guess it's hard to look at Maddie and see her as an adult. I'll always be her mother and think of her as my little girl. Seeing Angel... Knowing..." She sighed. "It just opened my eyes, is all. Reality just smacked me upside the head. Maddie's twenty and in college. She's not a little girl anymore, as much as I hate to admit it."

"Still hard," he mumbled, heading toward a steel door at the back of the barn area.

"Yes, eye-opening for sure. Where are we going?"

"Show you the bunkhouse. Maybe it'll get your mind off Angel and all that shit. Got about twenty or so before we hit the road."

"The club has a bunkhouse? Is that where you live?"

"Yeah."

With a barn and a bunkhouse, this place really did remind her of a ranch. Though, she seriously doubted any of them knew how to rope cattle, wore silver belt buckles the size of platters or line-danced. "Do you all live here?"

"Some in the bunkhouse. Majority on the property. Trip and Stella live in the farmhouse you drove past."

Interesting. She wondered if it was normal for most MCs to have their members live on the same property. Another question she should research.

"The bunkhouse is beyond this door?" she asked as he opened it.

"Yeah."

"Am I going to see your room?"

"Yeah. Bathroom to the left if you need it before the—" He stopped walking suddenly and since Chelle was busy looking to the left at the door he indicated, she slammed right into him.

She caught her breath after losing it and, with a hand to the small of his back, stepped around him.

And realized why he had stopped.

Oh.

Oh shit.

"This shit happens on the regular. You ain't good with walkin' by them, we'll go elsewhere."

"I..." The air she had sucked in, after it had been knocked out of her when running into him, went rushing back out again.

A barrel-chested man stood with his back pressed against the wall in the long corridor, not even a dozen or so feet from them. The profile of his salt-and-pepper-bearded face was tipped downward and his fingers fisted handfuls of long, platinum blonde hair belonging to the woman on her knees in front of him.

Whoever it was didn't seem to care he now had an audience as was evidenced by his continued thrusting into the woman's mouth.

If the woman cared about being watched, it was hard to tell since the man was holding her in place by that grip on her hair while he fucked her face.

What she was witnessing was the actual definition of a face-fuck, if someone did a Google search.

Chelle, still stuck in place, couldn't tear her eyes from the scene before them, even though her brain was screaming that she shouldn't be watching.

"That's it, girl, swallow it whole. That's a good girl. Open that throat, take it deep. That's it. Like a pro."

Why did that gruff voice sound familiar?

The fine hairs on the back of her neck prickled.

"'Bout to give you your present for bein' a good girl," came the low, gravelly grumble. With one more deep thrust, the man's loud grunt filled the corridor and Chelle didn't need Google to tell her what happened next.

Why wasn't Shade getting her out of there? Why was he okay with standing there watching this?

More importantly, why was she?

As shocking as it was to see someone getting head right out in the open, where anyone could watch, it also affected her in a way she hadn't been expecting.

She was all for adults doing whatever they were into as long as it was consensual. And children weren't around.

She'd never been a voyeur before, but...

But then, she'd never really had the opportunity to explore that.

She guessed it was no different than watching porn. Except this was in person.

When he was *finished*, the man's head tilted back against the wall and he patted the top of the woman's head. "Thanks, baby girl."

The blonde pulled her head back, the man's still-hard cock now out flapping in the breeze, and she used her hand to wipe the saliva—and whatever else—clinging to her lips. "Anytime, Dutch."

Wait.

That disturbing prickle crawled from the back of her neck down her spine.

Wait. Wait. Wait.

Dutch?

Oh shit!

She hadn't recognized him at first because the lighting in the hallway was dim and he wore a leather head-covering like Shade did when he rode his "sled."

A skullcap was what he'd called it when she asked him

why he didn't wear a helmet. Why he thought a skullcap was sufficient instead of a helmet, Chelle didn't know, but that was not the current issue. No, the current dilemma was, Chelle knew the man who just...

Who just...

The woman used Dutch's cut to haul herself to her feet. Chelle realized right then and there, she wasn't even sure she could call the platinum blonde a woman. She might be as old as Angel, if that.

She turned, a grin on her face, which was quickly lost when her light blue eyes went wide.

Really, really wide. So did Chelle's.

Oh shit. "What is going on?" Chelle whispered, now thinking the moment she stepped into the MC's clubhouse she actually stepped into another dimension instead.

Maybe going on this run with Shade wasn't such a great idea.

Beside her, Shade asked, "Know Dutch?" sounding a bit amused.

Unfortunately, she did. "Uh... yes."

Chelle wasn't finding any of this amusing, especially since Dutch owned the garage where she took her Subaru. And while she wasn't expecting to see him here, especially with his jeans open and his saliva-covered cock out, she *really* wasn't expecting to see him getting a blowjob by another one of her former students.

Chelle remembered Crystal sitting cross-legged on a carpet square in a half-circle as she read to the children during story-time. At the time, the girl had light brown hair, not platinum blonde, and had always been quiet, polite and pleasant.

Now Chelle just watched her give head to a man who was old enough to be her grandfather.

"Holy shit!" Crystal yelled as she recognized Chelle. But instead of running up and giving her a squeeze, happy to see her like Angel had been at first, the girl's face went pale when she repeated, "Holy shit." This time in a pained whisper.

Chelle seconded that feeling.

"Well, this is awkward," Crystal announced with a grimace, wiping her mouth again, probably to make sure no evidence of the happy ending was left behind. A very different ending than ones she experienced during Chelle's story-time. "What are you doing here, Mrs. Goodson?"

"I'm... Uh..." She lifted a hand toward Shade, then let it flop back to her side, at a loss on what to say after that unexpected performance.

"Showin' her around before the run," Shade answered, then muttered, "Seein' more shit than she expected."

"She's with you?" Crystal asked him, her eyes wide again.

Chelle thought they were about to have a repeat of what happened with Angel until Dutch asked, "How's that Subaru runnin'?" while casually tucking his cock back into his jeans and zipping them shut.

Yes, Chelle was seeing much more today than she expected.

She would also have to find a new garage because she doubted she'd ever be able to look Dutch in the eye again while he explained a needed repair on her Subaru. Or while he played Santa in the town's Christmas parade.

Ugh! Her girls had sat on Santa's lap and had told him they were a good girl when he asked.

Chelle might have to call a real estate agent, put her house up for sale and move.

She turned to Shade, whispering, "Am I awake?"

"Bet you wished you weren't," he answered, now not so amused. He tugged her hand to continue down the corridor.

As they walked past Dutch and Crystal, Chelle managed

to ask, "How are you, Crystal?" in a lame attempt to be polite.

"A fuckin' pro," Dutch answered for her with a crooked grin. "Bet you're due for an oil change soon."

Yep, she was putting her house up for sale and never coming back to Manning Grove, not even to visit her brother.

Shade shook his head and kept her moving, but not even after another dozen feet, slammed to a halt again. This time Chelle managed not to run into him. And the sight that made him stop wasn't anything like the previous one. Thank goodness. She wasn't sure she could take much more.

What made him stop this time was another blonde coming through the back door at the end of the long hallway.

Of course, Chelle recognized her, too, because that was just the way the day was going.

The newcomer, Reilly, also worked at Dutch's garage, but in the office.

Did everyone in town have a connection to this club? Had she been living under a rock?

Shade's terse, "Where were you at?" got not only Reilly's attention, but Chelle's, too.

The young woman shot Shade a frown. "Out back."

"No shit. Doin' what?"

"Since when do I answer to you?" Reilly asked just as sharply.

"Doin' what, Reilly?" he repeated, his tone leaving no room for anything but an answer.

Just then, the back door opened again and a man, somewhere in his early thirties, with dark hair, a just as dark beard and wearing a Fury cut came through it.

The man spotted them, jerked up his chin at Shade and kept walking right past them, not even registering the uncomfortable stand-off between Reilly and Shade.

"Doin' what, Reilly?" Shade asked again, but much slower than normal. And his normal was normally slow. "Doin' somethin' stupid?"

Reilly's green eyes narrowed. "No. And it's none of your business."

"Wanna be a part of this club, it's our business."

Chelle wasn't sure what the hell was going on.

Reilly shot daggers at Shade, who didn't even flinch. After a few moments, the blonde rolled her eyes and sighed dramatically. "I was out sharing a bowl with Dodge."

"That all you were sharin'?"

"Yes," she hissed, finally moving toward them.

When she got within arm's reach, Shade's hand snaked out and grabbed her bicep. "Don't be the reason someone's colors get stripped. Wanna be part of this, you gotta play by the rules."

She jerked her arm out of his grip. "It's not my rule."

"No, but it's the club's. Which means, if someone touches you, shit's gonna get ugly for that brother."

"I know what it means."

"Then gotta do your part discouragin' anyone with two eyeballs and a dick from doin' somethin' stupid. Ain't a game, Reilly."

"I know," she hissed.

Chelle couldn't tell if Reilly was now upset or even angrier. Either way, the other woman rushed away, heading toward The Barn.

"What was that about?" Chelle whispered once Shade pulled her into a nearby room and secured the door behind them.

"She's hot and unclaimed and anyone wantin' a taste is playin' with fire. Don't wanna see any of my brothers get born."

"I think you mean burned."

Shade squeezed his eyes shut. "Fuck. Burned."

The situation with Reilly had been enough to mess with his head and screw up his words. Reilly might believe he was being harsh, but Chelle, as a mother, saw it for what it was. Concern. "You care about your brothers."

His eyes opened slowly. "Yeah."

"You also care about her." Reilly might not see it as such because she was young, but what happened between them in the hallway was now clear to Chelle.

"She's family, too."

Chelle pressed her lips together at his answer and nodded. She turned in a circle, taking in the small room she now stood in. "*Everyone* from Dutch's garage is here today."

"Yeah."

"I had no idea they were all a part of your club."

He frowned. "Why would you?"

She shrugged. While she was sure it wasn't a secret, no one would know unless the men were seen around town wearing the club's colors. Every time she had been at Dutch's, the guys had worn typical mechanic's coveralls over their clothes.

"Since Reilly isn't allowed to be touched by any of your brothers—without serious consequences, anyway—then I assume she's not the same as Crystal or Angel?"

"Nope. Reilly's Reilly."

Well, that was as clear as mud. "What does that mean?"

"She makes her own way. And thinks she can do whatever the fuck she wants."

"So, some women in the club who are part of your 'other women' label don't have to get on their knees." She turned and focused her attention on him where he leaned back against the closed door with arms crossed over his chest. He didn't look happy with her conclusion.

"Chelle, nobody's gotta get on their knees. There are big doors on this fuckin' barn, any of them could walk outta them at any time. If one of them decides to suck Dutch's dick, it's because she wants to."

"She could say no?"

He didn't answer. Chelle didn't like that silence.

"She can't say no," she concluded.

"She can say no to bein' a sweet butt. That's where the line's drawn."

A sweet butt. Now she remembered that as one of the terms she skimmed over. Not quite as unpleasant as patch whore, but not much better, either.

"Basically, to remain a part of the club, a sweet butt," she wasn't comfortable with that name at all, "has to be willing to do whatever with whomever." Probably whenever and wherever, too. Like in a hallway when the building was full of people.

"She can say no to takin' abuse, 'cause that shit ain't tolerated here. The guys are aware of what each sweet butt likes and don't like. They respect that. They're in the mood for somethin' specific one night, they pick the girl who's into the same. She ain't into it, they don't force her. Doin' what they're only willin' to do keeps the sweet butts loyal to the club and keeps them comin' back."

Chelle wasn't sure what to think about that information. She would definitely do more research on MCs as soon as she got a chance.

"Now, that's more fuckin' shit than I shoulda told you. But I get you hadta hear it. It settle your mind?"

Did it? Chelle wasn't certain. Maybe if she didn't know Angel and Crystal. But she knew them since they wore pigtails, and not for the reason Angel wore pigtails today.

"Chelle." He pushed off the door, stepped close to cup her cheek, making her look up at him. "They didn't wanna be here, they wouldn't be. Like you. You're here 'cause you wanna be. Or did 'til you got some shockers. They know what they're gettin' into before they get into it. And, remember, the doors swing both fuckin' ways."

He had spoken very slowly, like he normally did when he wanted to get every word correct. Because on this point every word was important and he wanted Chelle to understand.

She did and she didn't.

While she never would judge a woman's sexual wants or needs, she had a hard time wrapping her head around why a woman would just service a bunch of men whenever they wanted it. Unless...

"They don't get paid, right?" If so, that would be prostitution, which was illegal in Pennsylvania.

"Nope. Again, they're doin' it 'cause they wanna, Chelle. That's it."

He now sounded like he was done talking about this. But Chelle wasn't done. Not yet.

"I assume you've taken advantage of their... willingness?"

"Ain't gonna lie—"

She quickly shook her head and raised a hand between them to stop him. "That's all you had to say."

His dark brows pinned together. "That gonna be a problem 'tween us?"

"Have you... Since we..." She swallowed, trying to loosen her tight throat, thinking about why Crystal and Angel were there in the clubhouse and what that meant for Shade.

And those were only two women of an unknown number. Chelle could only guess there were more. With the way things were going today, she might even meet the rest when she least expected it.

Even though they weren't dating, or even serious, the thought of Shade being with those available women bothered her. While it shouldn't, the truth was, it did. So much so, it caused a burn in her gut.

She hadn't felt this type of jealously since...

Never.

What she was feeling was the same way the day had been going, strange and unexpected.

Tucking a thumb under her chin, Shade lifted her face again and held her gaze. "Listen, beautiful, gonna get one thing straight, then we're done talkin' about it. Yeah?"

She wasn't sure she could agree with that, so she didn't.

He continued, anyway, without it. "Not into that. They don't do shit for me."

Really? They were young and nubile. Perky and willing. Chelle assumed most guys would be panting after that. Especially when those girls were at their beck and call. "Why?"

"Prefer a woman like you."

"Older."

"Nothin' to do with age." He tapped her temple gently. "Has to do with up here." He pressed his hand to her heart. "Here." He dropped his hand to squeeze her hip. "Here." He slipped his hand down, cupping her pussy over her jeans. "And here."

She pressed her hand over his, keeping him there. "Why there?"

"'Cause that's mine. No one else's. Know you didn't fuck any of my brothers the night before. An hour before. Hell, fifteen minutes before. You save that for me."

Her breath had hitched, her nipples had pebbled and her pussy had twinged at his rough claim.

"Unless I'm wrong?"

"You're not wrong," she whispered.

"That also means for the time that's mine..." He removed her hand from the V of her legs and moved it to his. "This is yours. No one else's. When you're ready to move on, I'll move on. Not before. Yeah?"

This time she agreed. She wasn't young, nubile or even perky but she *was* willing. And his declaration that he was solely hers as long as she wanted him made lava flow through her, only at a much quicker pace. "Yes."

He tilted his head and stared down at her. But his dark eyes had gone hot and his cock now hard under her palm. "Done with this tour?"

"I think I've seen enough for now."

He grinned. "Yeah. Everyone's seen enough once they've seen Dutch's dick."

"I'll have to find a new garage. I'm not sure I can face him again after that."

Shade snorted softly. "No lie, you spend enough time 'round here, you'll see his dick more than his face."

"Wonderful," she said dryly.

"Not so much for us."

"I mean, for an older guy, Dutch *is* kind of hot. If you're into his type."

Shade's eyebrows rose. "You into his type?"

"Not particularly." A rough and gruff Santa-type might not be for her but she was sure plenty of other women were into it.

"Watchin' that get you wet?"

Heat shot into her cheeks.

He grinned, dropped his head and, "Yeah, watchin' that got you hot," whispered over her parted lips.

"*Ain't gonna lie,*" she echoed him, making the corner of his eyes crinkle. "A little, until I realized who they were." She side-eyed his neatly made bed. "We don't have time, do we?"

"Not time to fuck, but—"

Before he could get the rest out, she dropped to her

knees and did something she'd been wanting to do since the night in the Subaru. She figured it was only fair since he had given her great head, she'd return the favor.

He certainly didn't turn that favor down.

Chapter Sixteen

Right outside of town, Shade gave the signal that indicated to his brothers behind him he was breaking formation. When someone veered off, they usually closed up rank to keep the pack tight.

As soon as he hooked a left to head to the west end of town, hollers and horns were heard behind them in an obnoxious send-off.

Fuckers.

Chelle propped her chin-strap on his shoulder and, with her face shield raised, yelled, "Is that normal?"

"No." Today was Bust Shade's Balls Day.

"Where are we going?"

He caught her question before the wind whipped it away. Instead of answering, he reached back, squeezed her thigh and decided to leave his hand where it belonged, now that they weren't in view of his brothers.

He hadn't told her about his plan, but figured, after the quickie blowjob in his room earlier, she wouldn't be opposed to it.

That had been the first time he had her mouth on him

and he hoped like fuck it wasn't the last. Dutch had said Crystal sucked him like a pro, but Shade disagreed.

Chelle was so much fucking better.

He had slipped her glasses from her face, tucked them into the neckline of his shirt and, gripping her ponytail with one hand and the side of her face with the other, he forced himself to keep his eyes open and watch her give his dick a spit-shine.

It was the hottest fucking thing ever and it took everything he had not to pull free from her greedy mouth, rip down her jeans and throw her onto his bed to finish them both off.

He managed not to, but the whole fucking ride he'd been thinking about his plan and his erection had been raging. He'd never thought their runs were too long until today.

And that was even after he'd emptied his load down her throat earlier. With a warning first, of course. But she ignored the warning and, knowing she was about to accept all of him, made him come even harder.

Yeah, he really fucking liked this woman.

He might even more than like her.

But he'd take what she'd give him, because he'd been dead serious when he'd told her he was hers as long as she wanted him. When she no longer did, he'd walk away and chalk up his time with Chelle as one of the better chapters in his fucked-up life story.

Five minutes later, pulling into the parking lot of The Grove Inn, his balls were screaming, his dick throbbing with its own heartbeat and the keycard Ozzy slipped to him before the run was burning a hole in his back pocket.

The refurbed '70s-style motel had the office in the center, the manager's apartment above the office, ten rooms to the left and another ten to the right. He did a tight loop and then crab-walked his sled backward into the spot in front of the last room on the right with the numbers two and zero nailed to the dark blue door.

After slipping him the keycard, The Great Oz had also bumped his shoulder and said number nineteen was empty so they could go hog wild and not have any pigs in uniform called for a disturbance.

The motel manager also cocked an eyebrow at him and shot him a knowing look, which Shade read as the man had seen the video of him and Chelle in the Subaru.

Fucking great.

While Chelle did a pitstop before they left for the four-hour-long ride, Shade grabbed Easy and pulled him aside.

Before he could even ask the brother who all had seen the video, Easy smacked him on the back, crowing, "Fuck, brother, you got yourself a fuckin' MILF. That hair, that *fuckin' body*, those glasses. She teachin' you things? In *and* out of bed? Bet she uses a ruler to do it, too. Yeah?"

They hadn't even had a chance to fuck in a bed yet, but he wasn't telling Easy that.

He locked gazes with the brother who was closest to him. "Assumin' you saw the video."

Easy's face gave the truth before his mouth spit out the lie. "What video?"

"Trip said it was deleted. That true?"

Easy took a step back and raised both palms. "Not sure what video you're talkin' about." Then he grinned like the asshole he was. "Dude—"

"Don't need to hear about it. Just need to hear it was deleted."

"Yeah. Trip zapped it himself."

Thank fuck. "Who all saw it?"

Easy pursed his lips and his eyes shifted to the side.

Fuck. "Should I ask who didn't fuckin' see it, instead?"

"Yeah, that list is a fuck of a lot shorter."

"Christ," he muttered.

"Your technique got a solid seven. Chelle's mom-bod got a fifteen on a scale of ten. She rocks it."

"Brother," he growled.

Easy laughed and wacked him on the back again. "Brother, it's gone, and everyone's probably forgotten it by now. You rarely tap pussy, so thanks to the video we no longer wonder whether you eat hot dogs or tacos or, hell, even sausage-stuffed tacos. Also proved when you hunt snatch, you go after the good shit."

Even though Easy was like blood to him and had kept his secret of being unable to read, right at that moment Shade wanted to shove his fist down his throat to shut him the fuck up. He was close to doing that when Chelle joined them and he had to swallow his irritation. It chapped his ass that Easy, as well as some, if not all, of his brothers had seen his woman naked.

Thank fuck she didn't know.

They also all knew Chelle was about to lose her clothes again, this time in a real bed.

He helped her off his Night Train, then swung his own leg over while she removed her helmet.

"I would ask why we're here, but I'm pretty sure I can guess," she teased as she straightened her ponytail.

"Normally we eat after the run and I plan on eatin'... just not food."

He took the helmet from her and hooked it over the handlebar.

"I'll have you know, I'm shaking," she whispered, holding her hand out, palm side down. She wasn't lying, it had a visible tremble to it.

He grabbed it and pressed his lips to the center of her palm. "Hopin' that's from anticipation."

"What else would it be from?" She approached the door and glanced over her shoulder at him. "You have the key?"

The way she looked right now, with her flushed face and

the sparkle in her eyes, he could stare at her all fucking day. He took a quick snapshot of her like that in his mind so he could remember it at another time.

He slipped the keycard from his back pocket and handed it to her since she was blocking the door.

"How long do we have the room for?" She slipped the card into the slot, the light turned green and she opened the door.

"The rooms ain't rented by the hour, beautiful. Got as long as you want."

"All night?"

He stopped in the doorway and watched her move around the room, turning on the lights to inspect it. It had taken a while for Ozzy and a local Amish construction crew to refurbish all the rooms, but it was now finished and The Grove Inn was like a whole new motel.

It was also no longer rented to the dregs of the Earth. Business people and families regularly rented rooms now. The motel turned a good profit and Trip had been smart to buy the failing business.

"What about your girls?"

"They won't be home until later and, anyway, they're both old enough to stay home alone. I just need to be home early enough tomorrow morning to get ready for work and to make sure Josie gets up and goes to school on time."

"You fuckin' serious?"

Her eyebrows pinned together. "You don't want to?"

He quickly went to her after shutting and locking the door behind him. When they were toe to toe, he grabbed her hands and pulled them to his chest. "Beautiful, ain't nothin' I want more than to nail you to the mattress all fuckin' night."

She laughed. "*Sooo* much better than sappy romantic poetry."

Good, because he was far from sappy or romantic, and

didn't know one damn line of poetry and hopefully never would. "What excuse you gonna tell your girls?"

"That's what I need to figure out." When she chewed on her bottom lip, the memory of her on her knees sucking him off smacked him right in the face.

He needed her spread naked on the bed and soon.

She pulled away and drifted around the room again. "I'll tell them a coworker was rushed to the hospital and asked if I could babysit her children overnight."

"You good with lyin' to them like that?"

She spun around and bugged her eyes out at him. "What am I supposed to tell them? A sexy biker is nailing your mother to the mattress in a motel?"

"Not sure I'd word it like that," he said with a snort.

"Well, either I'm going to tell them the truth or I'm going to lie. I'd rather the lie in this case because I don't feel like dodging one thousand and one questions about the truth. That's a conversation I'd rather not have with my daughters."

"Whatever you're good with," he finally said.

Chelle wandered over to the nightstand where a plastic bowl sat full of what looked like wraps. She picked up a foil packet and held it up. "Is this normal? Maybe they're edible and are a substitute for the mints left on the pillow?"

"Ozzy's an asshole."

"Why?" She tossed the wrap back into the bowl. "He's looking out for you by making sure you practice safe sex."

"Trust me. He's an asshole." Proven when he texted everyone after Shade asked him about a room. Not that the level of his assholiness hadn't been proven many times before that.

"Well, I think it's sweet and he has a lofty goal for you if he thinks we're using all of these tonight."

Shade grinned. "Who said we ain't?"

Chelle scooped her cupped hands into the bowl of

wraps and then let the packets rain back into the bowl. "You might die if you try."

She might be worth dying for. Though, he kept that shit to himself. Especially when she stalked her way back over to him, a determined look in her eyes that made his dick twitch.

She stopped in front of him, tilted her head to the side and announced, "First thing first. I'm only getting naked if you do."

He lifted one eyebrow. "That right?"

"Yes," she whispered, "that's right."

"Drive a hard bargain, woman."

She pressed her hand to his erection. "Well, something is certainly hard."

He pulled her hand back up to his chest. "Chelle, wanna be naked with you, but..."

He sucked in a deep breath. If he wanted shit to be real with Chelle, he needed to be real with her. At least with what she'd see on the outside. The rest... *Hell*, he'd hide that shit as long as he could. Forever, if possible.

Her fingers flexed within his and she frowned. "What?"

The last time he was completely naked with a woman was when he was seventeen. When he didn't have a choice.

That woman knew about his past since she had bought Julian from a broker. She had complained about the permanent damage done to him from his previous owner and the broker had knocked down his price.

Deb had always reminded him she'd gotten a bargain.

His name coming from Chelle on a whisper snapped him back to the motel room.

If he was going to do this, he just needed to get it done and over with.

He also needed to know now, instead of later, if what he was about to reveal bothered her enough she wouldn't want to stay the night.

Could be his plan would end before it even started.

The fingers he held against his chest clutched at his shirt when she whispered, "What?"

His chest expanded and contracted once... twice... "Not gonna tell you. Just gonna show you."

"What?" she whispered again, the color draining from her face.

He released her hand and backed away, shrugging out of his cut and draping it over the back of the upholstered chair in the corner by the door. He sat on the edge of the seat, removed the large Buck knife strapped to his calf—ignoring the little noise she made when she saw it—and unlaced his boots. Once his feet were bare, he rose and went to the bed to remove the bedspread and blanket, throwing them into a corner.

He returned to where she stood watching him with big eyes.

He cupped her face and pressed his lips to hers before pulling back just slightly. "Want you naked first, beautiful."

"You promise not to back out?" Her question had a shake to it.

He put that shake there when he hadn't meant to. He caused it and it might get worse before it got better.

He forced himself to nod, anyway. "Promise."

Without taking her eyes off him, she slipped out of her denim jacket and tossed it over his cut. Then sat on the end of the bed to remove her boots and socks, like he had, and got back to her feet.

Now they both stood in the middle of the room, only wearing jeans and their shirts.

She grabbed his hand and pressed it flat to her belly, shifted it up over one tit so the hard bead of her nipple pressed into his palm, then guided it back down to her waist.

He stepped closer, grabbed the bottom of her shirt, and ordered, "Grab your glasses." As soon as she had them off and folded up, he tugged her shirt over her head, tossing it onto the seat of the chair. Her soft flesh was overflowing from her bra, and he tugged both cups down enough to free her nipples.

He sucked one, then the other, as he reached around and unhooked the back, letting the bra fall to the floor. Cupping both tits, he tested their weight and went back to sucking her nipples, giving each some attention. While still worshipping her tits, he unfastened her jeans and shoved them down to her hips where she took over and shimmied them off, along with her panties.

Once they hit the floor, he stepped back and saw how soaked the crotch of her panties were.

"Since your room," she whispered her answer to his unspoken question.

Hours. She'd been wet and wanting him for hours. *Jesus.*

"My sled get you off?"

She nodded and color bloomed up her chest. "Once."

"That it?"

She nodded again.

"Next time make it twice. Let your hair down."

"You first," came her soft demand.

He slipped the leather skullcap from his head and tossed it with their clothes, then removed the elastic band, pushing the long strands away from his eyes once it fell around his face.

He didn't want anything blocking his view.

"Fuckin' beautiful," he whispered as he touched her everywhere with his eyes. "Want you to come on my tongue before I come deep in your pussy."

He could see the pulse in her neck jumping as she reached behind her head, her heavy tits pulling high as she did so. She slowly pulled the hair band from her ponytail along with a few bobby pins he hadn't noticed. Her hair wasn't quite as long as his, but it was still long enough to reach the creamy skin of her shoulders.

She dropped the items in her hand to the floor and cupped her own tits, circling both nipples with the pads of her thumbs before brushing them over the tips. Her eyelids became heavy and her lips parted.

And, *for fuck's sake*, did he want to fuck her that very fucking second.

If she was any other fuck, he'd just unzip, turn her away from him, plant her palms on the mattress and fuck her from behind.

But she wasn't.

Not even close.

And the deal was, if she got naked, so did he.

He just didn't look forward to seeing her reaction when he did. He also didn't look forward to her endless questions.

"Need another promise, beautiful."

"It's unfair to ask me now. I did my part."

"Know it and I could stare at you forever, but need this from you now and promise I'll explain at another time. Just not now, not today. Tonight's just for us and by askin' questions, it'll no longer be only the two of us. It'll bring other people into this room who I don't want to share you with. Need you to not ask questions and, if you do, don't get bent when I don't answer."

If he had fucked up any of his words, she didn't correct him and he knew why when she whispered, "You're scaring me."

Her heart was probably trying to escape her chest the same as his was. "Not tryin' to scare you, just prepare you."

"Shade," she breathed.

"Gotta hear the promise, beautiful. Askin' you to give me that."

"Okay, I promise, but I apologize in advance if I break

that promise. Because of that, I also promise not to get mad if you ignore my questions because I couldn't help myself."

He only nodded because he was done talking. The time was here. He just needed to get it done.

He wanted to touch Chelle and for her to touch him. He wanted to feel her silky hair, her warm fingers, her soft skin against him. To experience her fully. Unlike behind the shed, unlike in the Subaru. To do that, he needed to shed his armor first, which were his clothes.

"Sit on the bed," he forced up his closing throat.

"So it's more like a striptease?" Her attempt at lightening the mood didn't mask the worry on her face. And that was what it was. A deep-rooted concern. Not curiosity.

She perched on the end of the bed naked, waiting for him to be the same.

He ripped his shirt over his head and threw it behind him toward the chair, unsure if it even made it that far. He quickly unbuckled his belt, unfastened his jeans and shoved them down his legs. He stepped out of the pool of denim and glanced up at Chelle when he heard her suck in a sharp breath.

She was no longer sitting. Fuck no. She was on the move.

When she reached him, she said nothing.

Though, even if she had, he might not have heard it over the pounding in his ears.

It took everything in him to remain in place when she tentatively reached out and touched the top of the long, raised scar that started right below his left pec and stopped below his navel.

When she stepped back, she looked almost relieved. But it wasn't the scar on his torso he'd been worried about her seeing. That was nothing. That was a war wound compared to the others.

The others he received when he was tied down while on his belly and gagged to muffle the screams.

Sometimes his hands were restrained at the small of his back. Sometimes to the headboard. And if he wasn't a good boy, sometimes his ankles were tied to the footboard.

He squeezed his eyes shut for a second.

No. Not now.

He should just get dressed and end this between them. Before she saw everything. Before she looked at him differently. Before he saw the horror on her face.

As he turned to grab his clothes, what he heard made him go solid.

He glanced at her and saw her eyes filled with what he was trying to avoid and her hand clamped over her mouth, smothering the whimper.

The instant she realized her own reaction, she dropped her hand and tried to hide it all.

She couldn't.

It was too late.

"How can I not ask questions?" She also couldn't hide the anguish in her voice.

"'Cause I need you not to." He needed her not to fall apart. Because if she did, he might. And if he did, then he was done. He would disappear into the dark and have a hard time escaping it. Right now, he was teetering on the edge of that pit.

She blinked a few times, the shine in her eyes apparent. She grabbed his arm and turned him around and he heard another sharp inhale. His name came out on the exhale.

"Gonna give you five minutes on this, then we're done. Either you wanna stay or wanna go afterward. Gonna be your decision."

"What I'm seeing doesn't define you."

Yeah, it does. More than you know.

Chapter Seventeen

She touched every scar on his back. Every fucking one.

Shade didn't know if she was counting them, something he'd never done because he didn't care to know.

She started at the top and worked her way down.

"These look like cigar or cigarette burns," she whispered, more to herself than to him.

It wasn't a question but, even if it was, he wouldn't answer that they were both.

"I don't know what this is." She brushed her fingers lightly over one and then another along his rib cage. He knew what she was touching. They were different from the circular scars because they were done with a hot Bic lighter.

Because of his countless scars, he never had the club's colors tattooed onto his back. The ink wouldn't hide them and he didn't want to explain to the tattoo artist what they were or how he'd gotten them. It wasn't only one or two, there were so many, it would only be human nature to ask.

Having the Fury's colors inked permanently onto his back was not a requirement, *thank fuck*. If it had been, he might've moved on. The only requirement the executive committee made for displaying their colors was for them to wear their cuts when representing the club.

Over the years, once Deb freed him, he'd had his arms tattooed, but only on the skin exposed when he wore a tank top, which boiled down to only his arms. Everywhere else he was tattoo-free and planned on remaining that way.

The closer Chelle got to the small of his back, the tenser he became. Every muscle locked, his jaw clenched and his fingers curled tightly into his palms.

While the circular scars continued down the back of his legs and finished at his feet, they skipped over his ass, since that was Daddy David's favorite part of him. He didn't want to ruin the "perfect sweet peach" he paid for.

However, the motherfucker had done something else to Julian one night in a fit of rage that ruined him in future buyers' eyes. While the burns were bad enough to bring down his value, this was worse since most owners didn't want the skin of their sex slave marred in any way. Unless they planned on snuffing the child once they were done with him or her.

From what he had seen over that decade, he knew that was what happened to damaged goods. Sold cheap and disposable.

But most wanted their boys to be young and their skin to be perfect, especially if they were used for commercial purposes. Films, photos or to add to their stable as an investment to make scratch.

But what Julian did one night had pushed David to lose his shit and lash out in a way Julian never expected. In a way most people wouldn't expect. At least, normal people.

Chelle traced each letter in the word "MINE" that had been carved into the small of his back with the same knife Julian had come close to killing David with. It wasn't only the claim that had been cut slowly and deliberately into his skin, under it was an arrow that ended at the top of his ass crack.

That permanent claim had been his punishment after the struggle over the knife. That struggle also almost filleted his gut wide open. When he failed at slicing David's throat, Julian had tried to plunge the knife into his own chest to end it all.

Even at fourteen, he hadn't been strong enough to follow through once David got a hand on the knife. When they fought over the blade, it sliced Julian open.

Unfortunately, not deep enough for him to die. But enough to leave a permanent reminder after a "doctor" showed up at the house to stitch Julian closed.

After he was bandaged and the bleeding had stopped, David was still furious at not only Julian, but at himself for trusting Julian.

It had taken a year, but Julian had managed to convince David he was trustworthy and enjoyed everything David did to him and would willingly do things in return. It was only then that the man allowed Julian to move more freely about the house and actually moved him into his bedroom, where Julian continued to pretend to be compliant.

Every night Julian laid in that bed with David next to him while he worked on his escape plan as the cum seeped from him. When Julian was finally trusted enough to have access to the kitchen, he hid a butcher knife under his clothes and then under the mattress. Finally, when David was sleeping, Julian tried to slice the motherfucker's throat.

He only managed to nick the skin before David woke up and they began to struggle over the blade. The price Julian paid after it was all over was the long, thick scar along his stomach and David's claim carved above his ass.

Once he was healed, David traded Julian back to the broker at a loss.

And where Deb bought him at a bargain.

"I don't understand," Chelle whispered, covering the word with her palm. "You didn't ask for this, right?"

What child would?

"You don't need to answer that. If you had, you wouldn't want to hide it." She traced the arrow with her fingertip and finished in the crack of his ass at the end of the point. The spot David had claimed as his was obvious to anyone seeing the scar.

Shade breathed a little easier when she didn't continue down his legs to touch every scar there, too, but instead tugged him toward the bed.

"Chelle."

She shook her head. "No, you're not naked yet and we had a deal."

When she guided him over to the side of the bed, he took that to mean she wasn't disgusted enough with what she saw to bring their time together to an end.

"Can't get more naked than I am."

When she sat on the edge of the bed, he stepped between her thighs, his dick beginning to wake up again after deflating while she examined his scars. He wrapped his left hand around the root and tugged to help it along. It didn't take much since she watched his hand slide back and forth along his dick until he was hard again.

"Yes, you can," she finally answered, tipping her head toward his dick.

He dropped his gaze downward and stopped pumping.

Fuck. She was right. He hadn't bared everything yet.

Since he already revealed so much, he might as well do the rest.

He released his erection since he was about to lose it again anyway and held his hand out to her. Keeping her eyes locked on his, her fingers worked to untie and unwrap the black leather cuff he wore around his left wrist. To reveal what was left behind after the first time he'd wanted to die. His first failed attempt.

She set the leather cuff aside and slowly dropped her gaze to his wrist which she now held in a loose grip. What she saw didn't surprise her.

"Already knew what was under it," he murmured.

"I had a feeling on why you were keeping it covered after seeing the rest."

Her eyes closed and she swept a thumb lightly back and forth over the scar that wasn't as thick or as noticeable as the scar on his stomach but was still visible enough to cause questions since it crossed the inside of his wrist.

He didn't know then but knew now, Julian had cut himself in the wrong direction. He should've sliced along the vein instead of across it, then maybe he couldn't have been saved. But he'd only been eight at the time and only had a shard of the dinner plate he had broken so he could end his suffering.

That particular daddy never gave him anything breakable again. From then on, Julian ate from paper plates, drank from paper cups and had to use his fingers instead of utensils.

"Are you embarrassed?"

The soft question brought Shade back to the room and the beautiful, naked woman before him. He could be spending time on her, instead, they were wasting it on him. "Just no one's business."

"Including mine."

He couldn't deny that, so he said nothing.

Maybe one day he'd tell her, rip himself open and spill his guts, but today had been for them. He meant it when he said this time was for the two of them and no one else.

Simply revealing his scars had brought the monsters he wanted to forget to the present. They didn't deserve one more second of his life.

Not fucking one.

"Your scars aren't from falling while climbing a tree or skinning a knee, Shade. They—at least the ones on your back and legs—were deliberate and not self-inflicted, which I assume this one on your wrist was."

Shade couldn't do this. Julian couldn't, either.

"Chelle, I want you, but don't want this. Promised to get naked, I did. You promised not to ask questions, and, yeah, you ain't askin' questions, but you keep talkin' about it, tryin' to get me to do the same. I get why, but can't do this right now. Brought you here to do you. Now you've seen everything, still wanna do me?"

Now you've seen everything, still wanna do me?

She stared up at the man standing before her. Totally naked and completely vulnerable after exposing every scar on his body from a life hard-lived.

He didn't want her to ask him about it, but she struggled not to. It was difficult not to demand answers. To not be outraged.

She had to swallow her questions and quell her wrath at whoever did this to him and respect his need to keep his secrets.

For now, at least.

Receiving those injuries had been painful. She was also sure the memories hurt almost as much. When he was ready to spill his secrets, she'd be ready to listen.

But for now, he was right, this time was for the two of them. No one else.

Not for anger. Not for shame. Not for anything other than sharing the connection they had with each other.

An unexpected connection neither of them could ignore.

He had lost his erection while she explored his body and lost it again when she had revealed the scar on his wrist.

The leather wrist cuff wasn't for him to look cool or badass but to hide the evidence of a decision he'd been driven to make. She had no idea how old he'd been when he'd attempted to end his suffering, but the scar was faint and, since he was only thirty, he had to have been very young at the time.

Way too young.

The thought of him being forced to make that desperate decision hurt her heart more than the burn scars or the scar that claimed him as someone's property.

Maybe someone else needed to claim him, someone he was willing to accept. Someone he chose. Someone who wanted him for who he was, not what he was or had been.

He was not an object to own, instead a broken but beautiful soul. She had recognized it the first time he walked through her front door.

So, yes, she still wanted him. Beside Brendan, no one else ever existed who she wanted more.

She could tell him that or she could show him.

Or, better yet, both.

From her seated position, she rose to her knees until they were face to face. This time when she touched him, it wasn't to follow the path of scars. It was to touch *him*.

She started with his long hair, made up of varying shades of brown that fit his darker complexion as it curtained his face and ended past his shoulders. It was beautiful and unique just like the rest of him. She combed her fingers through the wild curls, marveling on just how soft and springy they were.

The tips of his small dark nipples were hard, so she leaned into him, sucking on one and then the other as she continued to gently stroke his hair over his warm chest.

She wanted him to feel loved, appreciated and not used.

Cupping his face, she drew him closer, lightly brushing their lips together, running her nose along his, and then going back to his mouth to dip her tongue inside and taste him fully.

Shade was as opposite to Brendan as he could get. The long hair, the dark beard, the tattoos...

Being in the service, Brendan had to be "squared away" with a high and tight haircut and his face smoothly shaven. He never had a desire to get ink. Or if he did, her husband never shared that with Chelle.

Shade was a biker who appeared to live loose and easy, while Brendan lived by the strict rules of the Army.

She found that she didn't prefer one type of man over the other. She appreciated how each lived their lives in a way that made them happy.

At least, she hoped Shade was now happy after dealing with whatever he had in his past.

She also hoped to make Shade happy tonight.

Deepening the kiss, he took control of it, sweeping his tongue through her mouth. The man knew how to kiss. The way he took her mouth, as if he owned it, stole her breath.

She never realized that kissing could be such a turn-on.

Wrapped around his cock, his hand was stroking the hard length once again. Another surprising turn-on that made her insides warm and her pussy wet.

She grasped the back of his neck, under the fall of his hair, pushing her aching breasts into his chest. With her other arm around his waist, she pressed her palm to the raised lettering at the small of his back.

She whispered, "Mine," against his lips. Sucking in a breath, he inhaled her claim.

She continued lower until her fingers brushed over his ass, his hip, then followed the angled line of lean muscle to where he stroked. With her hand over his, she murmured, "Also mine."

She removed his hand from his cock and raised it to her breast. "Yours." After a heartbeat, she guided it to her pussy where she cupped his fingers in the crux of her thighs. "Also yours." She was so wet that his middle finger slipped easily inside her. As he worked her gently, she vowed, "As long as you'll have me, I'm yours."

She didn't expect him to move as quickly as he did.

He surged forward, taking her with him, until she was flat on her back and he was settled between her legs, kissing her frantically, with his hard, silky length pressed to her inner thigh.

His kissing slowed and, after it completely stopped, he rose to his hands and knees, caging her in but breaking their connection and leaving her bereft by the loss of his touch. Chelle shivered with the intensity of his dark eyes and the seriousness of his expression.

Beginning at her mouth, he touched her with nothing but his breath.

Inhaling each other for a breath or two.

He moved lower, each exhale sliding over her skin. Causing goosebumps and making her nipples ache with need.

He explored her by simply inhaling, exhaling. Warm streams of air feathering across her skin. An invisible, ghostly touch.

It shouldn't be enough.

Surprisingly, it was.

The energy flowed between them, alive like a separate being.

As he worked his way lower, she let her eyelids drift shut, amazed at how something so simple could turn her on, make her wetter, drive her closer to orgasm.

He ended his exploration where he said he wanted to put his mouth.

Still, he didn't. His mouth remained close but didn't make contact.

He hovered right there. Close, but yet, not close enough.

Every cell in her body ached for him, called to him.

Her need for him was off the charts.

She'd never experienced anything like this, not once.

When a powerful shudder swept through her, her pussy began to throb, and a groan escaped. Her fingers tightly clutched the sheet so she wouldn't lose her mind and scream for him to fuck her.

He was driving her to the brink.

Of her sanity.

Of her control.

Of an orgasm.

Just like that, she climaxed, surprising her that she came so easily.

With nothing more than his phantom touch.

Before it was even over, his mouth was on her. His fingers and tongue spreading her open, his lips closing around her clit.

He devoured her.

She was his last meal and he was going to savor every damn bite, then lick the plate clean.

Within a matter of moments, her hips were bucking off the bed, but he stayed with her, riding those waves until they were gone.

Then *he* was gone.

Her eyes opened so she could watch the muscles bunch and stretch under his skin as he reached for a condom in the bowl. She had never thought of male appendages as being attractive before, but his was. His cock was beautiful, like the rest of him.

After ripping the packet open and rolling the condom down his length, he wasted no time coming back to her.

Ending up, once again, on his hands and knees, staring down at her, not saying a word.

Nothing needed to be said. His eyes spoke volumes.

He settled his narrow hips between her thighs, then used his knee to nudge her left one higher up the bed. He anchored his knee into the mattress, holding her there, open and ready.

"Put me where you want me."

The low, gravelly command sent a shiver through her. She reached down and slid the head of his cock through her slick folds, back and forth until it caught.

Right where she wanted him.

She expected him to plunge into her, he didn't. Instead, he dropped to his elbows, buried his hands in her hair and sealed his mouth to hers.

His cock nudged her open, slowly sliding inside her little by little.

Yes whispered through her mind when he paused long enough for her to appreciate that satisfying stretch and fullness.

That sense of connection.

But when he began to move...

His hips...

Yes.

Oh, yes.

His hips rolled slowly, but powered deep with each thrust. All the way from rim to root.

Then back out from root to rim.

Holy shit. The gliding movement of his hips was like nothing she'd experienced before. Fast enough to be satisfying but slow enough to drive her mad.

Sliding her hands down his back and over the scars now burned into her memory, she hesitated over one...

Mine.

She stole that claim from whomever had made it and took him for her own.

You are mine.

And I'm yours.

Not just for tonight, but for as long as you're willing.

She gripped his ass, her fingertips digging into the muscles that flexed with each thrust.

Suddenly, it became clear.

He wasn't fucking her.

He was making love to her.

Nothing like the quickie behind the shed.

Nothing like their time in the car.

While she had enjoyed every second of those stolen moments, this was a whole different realm.

It was caring and gentle and... *amazing.*

Definitely unexpected.

But then, this man was different than anyone she'd ever met before.

And he'd only revealed a sliver of himself so far.

She had so much more to discover.

———

CRYING.

Not loud. Muffled. Like it came from a faraway distance.

A woman?

Mommy?

Shade's eyes flashed open and he flopped to his back, his heart thumping heavily.

This was not his room. He had no idea where the fuck he was.

He jackknifed up to a seated position and glanced around.

The motel.

He scrubbed his hands down his face with a groan. He'd

fallen asleep. A memory of his mother crying must have woken him up.

With a twist of his head, he glanced at the empty spot beside him. Had Chelle left? She had no way to get home unless someone had come to pick her up. Would she have left without telling him?

That didn't make sense.

After they'd eaten pizza, after she'd texted her girls with her made-up excuse for not coming home, after they'd had sex a second time... They'd both drifted off to sleep.

He heard it again.

Soft crying. Not far away at all.

Fuck. It wasn't a nightmare that woke him. It was reality.

He bolted out of bed and nabbed his boxer briefs from the pile of discarded clothes, slipping them on and going to the bathroom door.

He tilted his head and listened for a second, his hand hovering over the door knob.

Chelle was crying.

What the fuck.

He squeezed his eyes shut and simply breathed for a few seconds. After his fingers made contact with the metal door-knob, he still hesitated, trying to keep his heart in his chest. His stomach churned as he slowly turned the knob.

The bathroom was pitch black and he flipped the switch to see Chelle wearing his T-shirt, sitting on the linoleum floor in the corner against the tub, her face buried in her arms, which were crossed over her knees.

He quickly took the two steps to her and fell to his knees, putting one hand on her back. "Chelle." His voice cracked on her name.

She sniffled but didn't raise her head.

He cleared his throat and tried again. "Chelle," he said louder, but still not more than a whisper. "What the fuck, Chelle?"

Hearing her cry was cracking his chest wide open.

"What's the mad?" *Fuck, fuck, fuck.* He screwed that up. "Matter." He wedged his hand under her chin to tip her face up.

Her eyes and nose were shiny and red, and tears flowed freely down her cheeks. She sniffled again.

"Are you hurt?" He didn't see any blood or bruising or... *fuck...* anything. He couldn't imagine this woman would cry over a stubbed toe. Curse, yes. Cry, no.

She nodded slightly.

"Where?"

She pressed a hand over her heart. "I hurt for you."

His own heart seized, and his mind raced. What the fuck was she talking about?

"I don't even know the details but my heart breaks for you."

If she knew the details it would only be worse. So much fucking worse. Especially since she was a mother and would put herself in the place of his own mother that day at the mall. That day at the auction. The last day she ever saw her son before he was ripped away from her forever.

"Don't need to cry for me," he said slowly, trying to get the words right. He thumbed away a falling tear.

Julian had stopped crying for himself and the helplessness of his circumstances when he was five. It took him almost a year to figure out crying didn't change a fucking thing. It was only a waste of energy and showed weakness.

"How can I not? I don't know who did this to you and when. I'm picturing all kinds of scenarios in my head. And none of them... *All* of them..."

She sat up, cupped his face and looked right at him. *Hell,* right through him. Not like he was invisible, but like he wasn't. She was trying to see inside him, right to his very soul. Her bottom lip trembled and a couple more tears spilled over from her beautiful brown eyes.

Every tear she shed was like a stab to his heart.

"At least tell me whoever did this to you went to jail, paid for what they did."

None of them went to jail, or if they did, it wasn't because of what they did to him. Whether they ended up behind bars after Julian was gone, he had no fucking clue.

"You're not even going to tell me that?"

Hearing the raw pain in her voice was more torture than what any of his "daddies" and "uncles" had put him through. Julian had learned to block out the physical pain, but Shade couldn't block Chelle's genuine concern or the hurt she felt because of him keeping his past to himself.

"Don't know the answer, Chelle." It was sort of true, sort of not, since he hadn't found everyone on his list yet. But the one who left the visible reminders, the scars that made her cry, was dead. That motherfucker had been first on his list. Shade was still working his way backward. All the way to that day in the mall parking lot. If he could find them all to give them what they deserved, he would. Every single fucking one of them.

Prison wasn't good enough for monsters who ate little boys to satisfy their perverse hunger.

But he couldn't share that with Chelle. Not now, not ever. Just like he'd never be able to tell her about what he did for the club up on Hillbilly Hill.

He had worried about how she would look at him after seeing his scars. The woman ended up crying over him with only his external ones. The ones she couldn't see were so much worse. But if she knew about the rest... A decade of being a child sex slave or even with what he was doing with the Shirleys...

He rose to his feet and held out his hand. Without hesitation, she gripped it tightly and he helped her to stand. Without another word, he escorted her out of the bathroom and back to bed. Once he had her back under the covers, he tucked her into the curve of his body and held her close like he had earlier when they had fallen asleep.

He doubted either of them would do the same this time.

She pulled away and rolled until their faces were just inches apart. Her arms wrapped around him instead of the other way around.

With a hand to the back of his head, she pressed his face into her neck and squeezed him tightly. While he couldn't see it and she tried to hide it, he knew she continued to cry. As she did so, the hand not holding his head stroked up and down his bare back.

Since she was the one upset, he should be comforting her, not the other way around. Tonight would be the first time in the last twenty-six years he received comfort from anyone.

It took him awhile, but when he finally let his muscles loosen and he breathed a bit easier, he realized he'd forgotten what that felt like.

Chapter Eighteen

Now that it was October, the leaves were beginning to drop and the greenery dying off for winter. Time was running out before his cover on the mountain would get sparse. Once late fall and winter came, he'd be too easy to spot. That meant he would have to finish the job come spring.

He didn't want to do that, but he might not have a choice.

His concern was, during the winter they'd bring in more men from somewhere else. That somewhere else being wherever Shirleys sprouted from when they weren't breeding their own on the mountain.

He'd been trying to keep track of their numbers, but it was difficult since they were never all together at the same time. Most likely on purpose. His best guess was only eight men remained. And eight men could still wreak havoc on their club if they had a mind to. On that, Shade was pretty fucking sure they were planning something because their survival depended on fighting back and stopping whoever was taking out their menfolk.

Shade spotted a few older male teens who could easily

step into the missing men's spots. Some might not be more than fourteen or so but by Shirley standards that was old enough to take a female and start breeding babies, even if the woman or teenage girl was related. Most likely, they *would* be related. The Shirley family tree looked like a straight trunk with barely a branch to be seen.

The past few weeks, he continued to go to Chelle's on the weekends to paint. He also went over to her house the nights the girls were working late to continue with his lessons. Even better, a couple of times during the week they met at the motel. No lessons, no painting. Just them and that bowl of wraps.

He could read a few simple words now, which was more than he ever expected, but it was still difficult. He often got the letters turned around and had a hard time visualizing the words, whether in his head or on paper. Trying to read a short sentence could be excruciating and frustrating. While he'd wanted to give up many times, Chelle refused to let him quit.

She was determined to get him to the point where he could at least read at a basic level. But all Shade wanted to do was be able to read the names on his list. He'd been working backwards, starting with David. Before he left David's house, he forced the fucker to tell him the name of the man he bought Julian from and had him write the name, along with his own, on a scrap of paper. When he was done with "Daddy David," Shade drew a line through his name. Just like the line he made across David's throat. The same one Julian tried to draw all those years ago when he was fourteen and failed.

That night, Shade didn't fail. He got the info he needed and made sure David would never hurt a child, or anyone, again.

He saved the next name, who turned out to be a broker, to memory. After finding that broker and getting him to write down three more names on his list of men who had owned Julian—names he remembered only too well—he sliced that motherfucker's throat, too.

A different type of monster, but a monster all the same. A man who bought and sold, sometimes even traded, children didn't deserve to breathe.

After that Shade was stuck. He had three names he couldn't read. It hit him later he should have recorded the broker saying those names with his phone. But then, a voice memo could end up used as evidence.

In this situation, the less evidence the better.

Even so, Shade wasn't in a rush. He had been willing to take his time to find each and every one of them. Even if it took him the rest of his life.

The only problem with not taking care of that business sooner than later, Shade knew none of those fuckers stopped their perverse habit of buying children to satisfy their desires. None of them would ever change. The sooner Shade got to them, the sooner they'd be done doing the shit they did to kids like Julian. The only good child molester was a dead one.

He couldn't think too hard on all the other ones out there Shade didn't know firsthand. He was sure there were plenty more deviants in the world. As long as there was a supply of children, there'd always be a sick demand.

And it wasn't just children bought and sold, as evidenced by his mother being the original target. Julian, at the time, ended up being an unexpected bonus.

He was only missing one owner yet. The man who bought him at the first auction when he was four. The motherfucker who owned Shade until he was six years old and became "too old" for him.

A six-year-old was too old for the sick motherfucker to fuck.

A six-year-old like Daisy.

That right there was one reason why he watched closely over Cassie and Daisy whenever he could. His excuse was to protect them from being snagged by the Shirleys, so no one questioned why he did it.

But if someone snatched Daisy, that motherfucker would have more than only Judge to deal with. And Judge would lose his fucking mind.

Hell, the whole club would.

But for now, he needed to get out of his head and concentrate on tonight's mission before he did something stupid and got caught.

Before the night was over, he hoped the Shirleys' number would be down to seven because tonight he was taking another one. He just needed to find the one he was looking for.

He had skirted the main compound by coming from the west, hoping like fuck he didn't step on a goddamn land-mine or booby trap. He had picked his way carefully through brush and around trees to go directly up to one of the smaller clearings, one more remote because it was higher up the mountain. An old camper had been parked there so long ago, it was now mostly hidden by weeds.

In a past scouting trip, Shade noticed signs of someone living in it, which surprised him since it appeared abandoned. One night he'd watched a Shirley bend his wife, or aunt, or sister—whatever the fuck she was—over a broken picnic table that sat right outside the door of the rusty camper. The woman, who couldn't be much more than eighteen, if that, wasn't fighting so Shade assumed she was willing. In fact, the female was vocally encouraging him. Really fucking loudly, too. Otherwise, Shade would've stepped in. But since he wasn't taking out any of the Shirley women unless in self-defense, he needed to get that fucker alone. Living remotely and away from any of the other Shirley residences made the man a perfect target. Shade just needed to time it right, so he wasn't spotted and the Shirley was caught off guard.

He was so high up the mountain tonight Shade couldn't risk dragging the body back down to where the van was parked.

While his preference would be to go in, slice throats and leave the bodies where they fell, he had to change up the pattern to keep them guessing. Whether by having them disappear completely by reducing the bodies to ashes at the crematorium or leaving the corpse behind and making it look like an accident. Or even dragging the body to a spot where it could start decomposing or the coyotes or bears, or whatever other meat eaters roamed the woods, could find it and enjoy a good meal.

"Circle of life" and all that fucking happy crap.

He paused at the edge of the overgrown clearing. The Shirleys loved to breed, they just hated to weed. He moved from one cover to the next, trying to get as close as possible, listening for signs of life inside the broken door of the dumpy camper.

Shade wouldn't even let Jury or Justice live in a rust trap like that.

He needed to stop worrying about shitty dwellings, discarded garbage, overgrown weeds and Shirley women getting fucked from behind, and find his damn target so he could get the fuck out of there before morning light.

Since it was late Friday night, he'd like to get at least a couple hours of sleep before heading over to Chelle's to paint.

A scampering noise came from behind him, along with the breaking of branches and twigs under feet.

Whatever it was wasn't trying to be stealthy and was moving quickly. He hoped to fuck it wasn't a hungry coyote.

He adjusted his grip on his knife and spun to face whatever it was head-on, and as he did so, realized it wasn't an animal coming for him at all. At least one with four legs.

No, this little animal had two legs and was almost on him.

Before his brain could process what the fuck was happening, since the last thing he expected to see was a young boy, the aluminum baseball bat made contact with his leg, collapsing it at the knee and knocking him to the fucking ground.

What the fuck!

He rolled onto his belly and tried to get up so he could grab the kid or bat or both, but before he could, the kid howled like a banshee and took another wild swing, making contact with his head and scrambling his brain worse than normal.

Luckily, he was able to dodge a direct impact, but the extreme agony that followed knocked all the oxygen from his lungs and prevented him from rising again.

He groaned when he tried to roll over to prevent another strike.

He couldn't do it.

Shade blinked, trying to get the blood out of his eyes and clear his blurry vision, so he could protect himself.

Instead of finishing the job—which the kid could've easily done with Shade on the ground and unable to move quickly—the boy began to run. Not in the direction of the camper but away from it. "Mom! Mom!"

"Mommy! Mommy!"

No. Not now.

For fuck's sake, he couldn't think straight. He needed to stay in the present and not get sucked into the past. He needed to stay conscious and get the fuck out of there.

Shade pulled in a slow breath, filling his depleted lungs. Trying to clear his double vision. Trying to think past the unbearable pain.

But all he could see was spots. Worse, blood poured from the wound on the side of his head. His fucking leg might even be broken.

Fuck!

He needed to move, otherwise he was going to die on Hillbilly Hill and that was one hill he didn't want to die on.

Gritting his teeth, he pulled himself in the direction of the van. It would take him days to get there dragging himself through the mud, leaves and over rocks. If he even remained conscious for that long.

His thoughts wavered as he continued to pull himself along, driven by the thought of never seeing or touching Chelle again. Never inhaling her scent, never hearing her husky laughter, or her moans as he fucked her...

He didn't know how long or how far he crawled but once he found a hole near a tree where he could hide in the dark, he did his best to cover himself with loose brush.

If the Shirleys found him, he was dead. To prevent that, he needed his brothers to find him first.

Thank fuck Judge insisted he put an app on his phone so he could be located if something happened. A fuck-up just like this. It was one thing the enforcer insisted on before agreeing to Shade going up the mountain alone.

He could no longer see shit between the dark of the night, the blood in his eyes and his spinning head, so using his fingers, he felt his way down his possibly broken leg—hissing when a bolt of pain as hot as white lightning shot through him—until he located his cell phone in the side pocket in his cargo pants. He only hoped it hadn't been destroyed.

After working it out of his pocket, he brought it to his face but couldn't focus on it. He couldn't even see the screen through his fucked-up vision.

He tilted the screen downward and hit the side button, grateful when the phone lit up. He concentrated as hard as he could to see if he could identify his contacts app. Once he thought he found it, he pressed it, then hit whatever contact he could find.

He didn't have a lot of numbers in his phone. Mainly his brothers and Chelle.

Fuck. He hoped he didn't dial Chelle by mistake.

He barely got it to his ear in time to hear, "Yo, brother. Whassup?"

"Need..."

"Yo, Shade! What the fuck is—"

"Help."

He hoped to fuck he said it out loud and not only in his head. Because the night was closing in on him in a hurry. The little vision he had narrowed until there was nothing left.

Nothing but darkness, stillness and silence.

———

BRIGHT LIGHTS.

Loud beeping.

The distant murmur of voices.

Nothing but more darkness, stillness and silence.

———

BRIGHT LIGHTS.

Loud beeping.

The murmur of voices. Not so distant.

The sharp smell of antiseptic burning his nostrils.

Shade blinked.

Blinked again.

He did a mental inventory of his body.

He didn't hurt but floated on a fluffy cloud instead. That

might have to do with the needle stuck in his hand and hooked to an IV.

He blinked again as things became slightly clearer.

He was in a hospital. He glanced down and saw he was wearing some sort of shitty ill-fitting gown, but at least his scars weren't exposed. *Thank fuck.*

He gingerly turned his head toward the person or persons who had been speaking by the door and now approached his bed.

"Welcome back." Trip. "Had us fuckin' worried for too fuckin' long."

Right.

"App did its job, thank fuck." Judge.

"If you hadn't had coverage, you woulda been fucked." And Sig.

"He's still fucked but at least he's breathin'," Trip said.

"Yeah, but they got him on the good shit," Sig added with a wicked grin, lifting some button thingy from where it lay on the bed and sliding it under his hand.

"Not for long. They were waitin' for him to wake up before they kick his ass out for not havin' insurance," his prez said.

Fuck. The hospital bill was going to hurt worse than his fucking injuries.

"You get knocked so fuckin' silly you can't speak?" Trip asked with a raised eyebrow.

Before he could answer, Judge chimed in, "Need to discuss what happened up there but not here. Once you're back at the farm and there ain't any extra ears."

"What excuse d'you make?" His question was nothing more than a croak. He was thirsty as fuck, too.

Sig poured him a plastic cup full of ice water and Shade sipped at it, his stomach doing a little roll.

"Told them you wrecked your sled," Judge answered.

"No road rash," Shade said.

"Yeah, well, if you want some we can give you some," Trip responded. "They didn't dig any further than what we told them. What you tell your woman's gonna be up to you. Just not the truth, yeah?"

Shade closed his eyes for a second. *Fuck*, he would have to make up a story for her that didn't involve wrecking his sled. Especially since she'd see his sled had no damage and would easily figure out he was lying to her. And there was no way he was going to let his brothers smash up his Night Train to make it look like an accident.

"She know?"

"Yeah, Cassie called her," Judge answered. "She's on her way over now. So figure out a believable story before her ass gets here."

"So..." Trip started, his hands on his hips under his cut. "Got a bunch of stitches holdin' in your brains. Luckily, no skull fracture, but got a concussion. They couldn't find any breaks in your leg but said you got somethin' called a bone bruise, which is worse than it sounds. All that shit means you're gonna be off your sled for a coupla weeks between the two injuries. They're gonna release you with a brace and pain meds. Supposed to keep weight off that leg, keep it elevated and iced, and not do anythin' stupid 'til you're feelin' better."

He couldn't ride his sled? How the fuck was he going to get around? "Only got my sled."

He wasn't telling them anything they didn't know. Most of the guys had some sort of backup transportation they used in bad weather. Shade was one of the few who didn't and had to catch a ride with someone else when needed. But he rode his sled as much as he could, even in winter.

"The van?" He could drive that back and forth to work. Hopefully, one of them found it where he'd left it. If not, someone would need to go get it. But that was a conversation that had to wait until they were sure no "extra ears" were around.

"Ain't goin' anywhere 'til you're feelin' better. Doc wants you off your feet. No weight on that leg so it heals faster. Thought I made that clear."

"Not likin' this," Shade muttered.

"Ain't for you to like. Your prez is givin' you an order," Judge reminded him.

"The longer you're down and out," Trip continued, "the harder it is on the rest of us, so you're gonna only be down for the time needed 'til you can get back up and stay there. Got it?"

Sig rapped a knuckle on the little wheeled table next to his bed. "Will assign you a sweet butt to wait on you hand and foot to make sure you don't do nothin' stupid." He shot Shade a cocky grin. "Or you can do somethin' stupid, just while horizontal. Let 'er do the work."

"Don't need that," he told his VP.

Judge shot him a look that clearly told him to stop back-talking the club's officers.

"Don't want a sweet butt up my ass twenty-four seven," he muttered anyway. Last thing he wanted was one of the sweet butts being all up in his business and he definitely didn't want one riding his dick. He was Chelle's until she was tired of him and that meant he wasn't dipping his dick into anyone but her.

Judge spoke next. "Ain't got another choice. Jemma's too busy to be your personal nurse between workin' long hours and raisin' Dyna."

"She's welcome to come check on him whenever she wants, but I'm taking care of him."

Everyone's head spun toward the door. Chelle's hair was a mess, her face make-up free and she wore yoga pants under an oversized sweatshirt.

To Shade, she never looked more fucking beautiful.

"He'll need bedrest," Trip told her. "For at least a few days anyway, but even after that he still needs to keep off that leg for a coupla weeks."

"He can do that at my house," Chelle said firmly.

"Your girls," Shade reminded her as she moved closer to the bed, nudging Sig out of the way. Her daughters didn't have any clue that they'd been spending more time together other than on the weekends when they were painting.

"They'll want to help," she told him matter-of-factly.

"Chelle, they don't know."

She shrugged. "They still don't have to know. I'll have your brothers set you up in my spare bedroom." She glanced around the room, her gaze landing on each one of them.

"They're gonna wonder why you're takin' care of me."

"And I'm going to tell them the truth: because I want to. I'll also tell them the sooner you're healed up, the sooner we can get back to painting."

"Paintin'," Sig said on a snort.

Christ, she had an answer for everything. She walked into that room and took control. That was hot as fuck.

"If I had to choose, Chelle's a lot better nurse than," Sig swallowed what he was going to say and finished with, "one of the prospects."

That was for fucking sure. Better than even one of the sweet butts. But he couldn't put her out like that. "Chelle—"

"Now that I see you're alive and acting stubborn as hell, I'll head back home to get things set up. Bring him over to my house." She gave Trip a look. "My house. If you don't bring him there, I'm coming to find him. This isn't negotiable. Did you hear me?"

Shade wasn't the only one being stubborn in that room.

Judge turned away and Trip dropped his head. When the Fury prez lifted it again, his eyes were crinkled at the corners and he was struggling to keep a straight face. "Yeah, woman, we hear you." He finally smirked. "Gonna go out and update everyone."

"Everyone who?" Shade asked.

"Everyone," Trip repeated, but more slowly. "Everybody wanted to be here who could be. Includin' Mashed Potatoes and Pus Sack."

Sig hooted. "Kinda likin' those names better than the ones I picked."

Chelle frowned. "Are those road names?"

"Nah," Trip answered with a grin.

"Tater Tot and Possum are our prospects. Trip just likes to bust their balls," Judge explained.

"Wait. They got balls?" Trip asked. "Pretty sure they both got vages. Big bushy ones."

With that, Trip walked out. Judge followed him with a deep chuckle and a shake of his head.

Both Shade and Chelle turned their attention to Sig who still stood there watching the two of them.

"Wanna give us a minute?" Shade asked him, annoyed the VP was eyeballing Chelle.

Though, it seemed more out of curiosity than anything else. Sig wouldn't do Autumn wrong even by simply eyeing up another woman. He only had eyes for her and normally used them to keep a close watch on her, too.

"Will give you more than one." He headed toward the door, but before he stepped out, he glanced back over his shoulder. "Got yourself a fuckin' MILF there, brother. Good for you." Then the asshole winked at Chelle.

He was probably just getting him back for the night Red curled up with Shade on the bus bench.

Chelle stared at the now closed door for a second then slowly turned back to Shade, her cheeks still a bit pink. "I'm a MILF?"

"Haven't looked in the mirror?"

"I never thought of myself like that."

"Wear that badge proudly, beautiful. You earned it."

She sat on the edge of the bed and grabbed his hand without the IV, bringing it to her lips.

"Chelle..."

"I was really scared for you," she whispered. Her confession came out shakily and he could see her emotions starting to bubble to the surface. "I think my heart stopped when Cassie called me, but I'm grateful she did."

He gripped her hand tighter and pulled it to his chest. "Chelle, don't gotta take care of me. Don't wanna put that on you."

"I don't want anyone else taking care of you but me." The shake was quickly gone from her voice and her emotions hidden.

"Chelle—"

"I don't want to argue about it."

Well, fuck. "You got work."

"I have the rest of the weekend and the girls will help. Between the three of us, we got you covered until next week. By then you should feel a little better and I have a set of crutches from when Maddie broke her leg when she was fifteen. You can use those once you're allowed to be up and about since you're supposed to keep your weight off your leg. And like Trip said, no riding your motorcycle. Between my vehicle and the girls' we got you covered to haul you around, if needed, or I'm sure one of your brothers can in a pinch. Hopefully, it'll only be a couple of weeks."

"Heard all that?"

"Yes, I was waiting for you to finish your business with your brothers before I came in. And then I—"

"Heard about the sweet butt."

She tipped her head. *Fuck,* she heard about the sweet butt. No wonder why she was insisting on taking care of him. "If that's the only reason you're doin' this..."

"It isn't. Now, I'm done talking about it. Make sure they

bring you to my house." She leaned in, brushed her lips across his, then pressed their foreheads together lightly. "I'm just glad you're okay." She squeezed his hand. "I can't wait to hear how this happened."

Shit.

She sat up and her brown eyes locked with his. "By the time you get to my house, you should've had time to make up a good story."

Chapter Nineteen

SHADE'S FINGERTIPS skimmed over the closed laptop Chelle had tucked next to his hip on the bed. She told him to use it to watch movies or to work on some reading lessons, if and when he felt up to it.

Right now, he didn't feel up to shit. His stitched-up head throbbed like a motherfucker, his eyes were sensitive to light and he was still in a fog. Had to be the pain meds. They were probably the only thing making his injuries bearable.

It wasn't like he wasn't used to pain. He'd lived a third of his life with a lot of it. However, a baseball bat to the head was a first and the doctor told him the bone bruise was much more serious than it sounded. His knee and surrounding area looked ugly as fuck. All shades of purple and swollen.

Once he was discharged, Easy and Rook had brought him from the hospital directly to Chelle's house like she ordered.

Both of them wore smartass smirks as she bossed them around on where to put him and the shit Easy had picked up from his room in the bunkhouse. Things he needed. Unlike his cut. Shade didn't think it was smart to have it there with him, but Chelle waved that concern away. According to her, it was time to let the girls in on who he was. At least with his being a part of the Blood Fury MC. She said they weren't stupid and they might see him around town wearing it, anyway.

As for him fucking their mother, he figured Chelle wanted to still keep that on the D.L. since she directed Easy and Rook to set him up in a spare bedroom on the opposite end of the house from the master bedroom. Though he hadn't seen it yet, Chelle said her room took up the whole floor over the garage and it was her favorite space in her house besides her backyard.

While he'd prefer to be in her bed, he'd respect whatever decision she made in regard to her daughters. She was raising them right and he wouldn't be the one to fuck that up.

By the time he'd been discharged and transported to Chelle's late Saturday afternoon, both girls were already gone. He had no clue if they were at work or where, not that it mattered. Chelle had already given them the heads up he'd be staying with them for at least a week, most likely two. He could only imagine how that conversation went since they tended to ask as many questions as their mother.

Those apples didn't fall far from that curvy tree.

He leaned his head back on the pillows and closed his eyes, running what happened last night through his mind again.

He had fucked up, plain and simple. He should've been paying the fuck attention on that mountain but, instead, let his brain fill up with shit that shouldn't have mattered in the middle of dealing with the Shirleys.

That clan was fucking crazy and dangerous, and even desperate, now that their men were getting picked off at a good clip.

Shade hadn't gotten a chance to give Trip and Judge an

update on what happened, but he had a feeling they'd want to hear about it sooner than later. He just had to decide if he would admit it was a young Shirley spawn who took him out. His ass might get ridden long and hard for that one.

Maybe he'd skirt around the facts and just say it was a Shirley male. No one needed to know it was a pint-sized one.

In the meantime, while he was on Trip-ordered recuperation, someone else might need to take over their Clan Plan until Shade was back on his feet and before the mountain no longer provided cover due to the oncoming winter.

He'd need to mention that, too, and see what they thought. If anyone was going to take his place, even temporarily, Shade expected it to be Rook. Rook wouldn't think twice about taking out one or more of those Shirleys, especially after they kidnapped his niece.

Yeah, Rook would be a good choice and he'd also keep his fucking mouth shut about it since he was trying to keep his ass out of the joint.

The front door slammed shut and he expected to hear Chelle call out to him to let him know she was home from her grocery store run. But the only thing he heard was the sound of heavy boots moving quickly through the first floor. That didn't sound like Chelle or her daughters.

For fuck's sake, he hated lying in that bed as vulnerable as a goddamn baby.

His fingers curled around the handle of the knife he had tucked under a knitted throw near his elevated left leg. Chelle had tossed the blanket at him before she left since he was only wearing a T-shirt and a pair of snug boxer briefs. He wouldn't be able to wear jeans for a while. At least, not until the swelling went down on his leg and he no longer needed the brace.

She suggested he toss the throw over his lap if her girls came into the room until she had a chance to pick him up some loose shorts and sweatpants. He wasn't sure if she was more worried about them seeing his junk or about him keeping his scars a secret.

Either way, he hadn't worn shorts since before "Daddy David" left his mark. He didn't even own a fucking pair. But that didn't fucking matter, what mattered was the sound of boots stomping up the stairs.

At this point, he wasn't covering up his lap or legs in case he needed to protect himself from whoever was in the house.

His phone was in reach but calling anyone would do no good. It would take too long for anyone to get to the house, so he was on his own with a fucked-up leg and a beat-to-fuck brain.

Fuck.

"Chelle?" a man called out.

Shade could hear him moving toward her bedroom.

"Maddie?"

At least it was someone Chelle knew, but Shade still didn't like not knowing who the fuck he was. Chelle hadn't mentioned a man in her life, especially one who had a fucking key. It would've been nice if she would've shared that fact instead of leaving him in her house like a goddamn sitting duck.

"Josie!" the deep voice yelled. Shade heard a muttered, "Where the hell is everyone?" The footsteps paused right outside his door. "Answer your damn phone, Chelle," came the irritated mutter. "I'm at your house. Call me back ASAP."

His fingers tightened around his hidden knife as a tall, broad-shouldered man with reddish-brown hair appeared in the doorway and froze. His eyebrows shot up as he took in Shade lying on the bed.

"What the hell?" the stranger muttered and shook his head. "I was wondering why Chelle needed Maddie's crutches from storage. Guess they're for you since it looks like you got the short end of someone's stick."

Yeah, an aluminum stick wielded by a damn inbred snot monkey.

The man wasn't done yet. Fuck no, he was just getting started. "Not sure who you are. Not sure where you came from. Don't even care. Just want to know why the hell you're in my sister's house." What apparently was Chelle's brother scanned Shade from injured head down to bare toes again, then his angry gaze landed on Shade's cut which was tossed over a backpack on a chair by the bed. The one Easy packed full with Shade's things.

The brother lingered on the Fury colors a little too long. "Also want to know why the hell you're in my sister's bed."

"Ain't her bed." With his brain being both scrambled and foggy, along with his rapid heartbeat, he decided it was best to keep talking to a minimum. Otherwise, he was afraid he'd screw up everything he attempted to say and sound like a fucking idiot.

"Pretty sure she owns that damn bed." The man opened his mouth to continue but snapped it shut when the phone in his hand rang. He scowled at it, swiped his finger across the screen and put it to his ear. "Yeah, too late, sis. I'm standing here looking right at him." His dark gaze shot back to Shade when he paused. "Yeah, I won't kill him if you don't want me to." Shade could hear Chelle through the speaker talking really fast and very loudly. "I hear you. I promise I won't hurt him too badly, then."

He ended the call while Chelle was still talking. Shade guessed she wouldn't be too happy about that.

"How do you know my sister? And why are you laid up in her bed?"

"Coulda asked her that before you hung up on her."

The man tilted his head and took a step into the room. "I'm asking you."

Chelle's brother had some size on him. He was both heavier and taller than Shade, who was in no condition to go head to head with him, anyway. Even with a knife. The second he got out of bed, he'd probably collapse into a helpless heap.

Instead, Shade spoke slowly and picked his words carefully. "You know your sister better than me and even *I* know Chelle don't do what Chelle don't wanna do."

"You just said a whole lot of nothing. Try again."

"Here's the short answer, then. We're friends."

Chelle's brother continued to stare at him, not bothering to hide his suspicion. Shade appreciated the man was protective of his sister, but this whole thing was annoying as fuck. Especially with the headache he had.

"What's your name?"

Since his name was visible on his cut, there was no reason not to tell him. "Shade."

"Shade? What kind of name is that? I'm sure if she mentioned the name Shade I'd remember it."

"Sure she don't tell you everythin'."

That made the man's expression darken. "If she was seeing someone, she'd share that with me."

"Think so?"

"Yes, unless she's hiding him for some reason. Like," he tilted his head toward Shade's cut, "if she was embarrassed."

Shade did his best to keep every muscle from locking tight since it would only make his head throb more. "Nothin' to be embarrassed about. Just friends."

"Yeah... I'm not thinking that's quite it. She's never had a half-naked man hanging around her house before."

"That you know of."

"The girls would tell me if some *shady* man was hanging around their mother and trying to take advantage of her."

"Maybe they ain't like you and don't think I'm shady."

"Then I'd be disappointed in their judgement. We raised them better than that."

Shade frowned. "We?"

Chelle's brother scratched his chin and pursed his lips, then smiled. Not a friendly one, either. "You'd know that if you were *friends.*"

"Maybe we don't spend a lot of time talkin'." Shade then raised an eyebrow and also smiled. His wasn't friendly, either.

Shade could see the man's blood pressure rising when his eyes narrowed, and his grip tightened on his cell phone to the point he was white-knuckling it.

The man jerked his chin toward Shade's lap. "Think what you're wearing is appropriate around my nieces?"

At their ages, Shade was pretty fucking sure they knew what a dick looked like and how they had been conceived. "Chelle gave me a throw to use for when the girls are around."

"How about when she's around?"

"Don't think she minds seein' me like this. Think she prefers it." He ran the hand not wrapped around the hidden knife over his dick to make a point.

The man's jaw shifted. "Does she now."

"She ain't complained yet."

The man's nostrils flared. "She *ain't* complained yet," he repeated slowly. "Thought you said you were *just friends.*"

"Might be a little more."

"How much more?"

"Gonna have to ask Chelle that. If she wants to tell you, she can tell you. 'Til then—"

He swallowed the rest of that when Josie yelled, "O... M... G!" from the doorway, making Shade wince. "Are you okay, Shade?"

Chelle's two daughters rushed up to the agitated man standing in the middle of the spare bedroom to give him a quick hug while Shade tugged the corner of the throw over his lap.

"Hi, Uncle Rick," Josie greeted.

"Hey, Uncle Rick. What are you doing here?" Maddie asked, her eyebrows pinched together. She seemed to pick up on the tension between Shade and the asshole... *Rick.*

"Your mother said she needed your crutches. She didn't say why, but now I see why for myself. You know him?"

"Yes, that's Shade," Josie answered her uncle, like a banged-up biker laid up in their spare bedroom was an everyday occurrence. "He's been helping out Mom."

"I'll just bet he has," Rick muttered.

Maddie's eyes, which were just like her mother's, sliced from Rick to Shade. She bugged those eyes out at Shade in an unspoken message, then quickly turned her attention back toward her uncle. "Shade was in an accident and needs to borrow them."

"Why's he here?"

Maddie's mouth opened and her eyes sliced back to Shade for a second. "Because..." She grimaced.

"Because they're good friends and that's what good friends do for each other," Josie answered quickly.

One point to Josie.

"And we wanted to help, too," Maddie added.

Rick frowned. "How long has your mother been friends with him?"

"Months," Josie lied, earning herself another point.

"Then why didn't I know about him?"

Maddie wrapped an arm around her uncle's waist and patted his chest. "Because she knew you'd be overprotective like you're being right now. I'm sure she appreciates you caring so much, but not so much you scare away her friends." Maddie was working on a few points herself.

"He's been hanging around the house?"

"He's been helping Mom paint," Josie chirped.

Rick's frown deepened and he stared at Shade for a little too long. Shade was going to keep his mouth shut so he didn't say anything he shouldn't in front of Chelle's daughters.

"It's fine, Uncle Rick," Maddie assured him.

Clearly Rick didn't believe that. "I'm going downstairs to wait for your mother," he grumbled. "Why don't you girls come with me. I don't like you two being alone in here with... him."

Maddie laughed. "It's *fine*, Uncle Rick," she insisted, very much sounding like her mother when Chelle got bossy. "He's harmless."

If she only fucking knew how harmless he wasn't. Unfortunately right now, in the condition he was in, it was too damn true.

"I'm not liking this," Rick muttered as he left the room and stomped back down the stairs.

The girls turned their attention from the empty doorway back to Shade. Their smiles quickly faded.

"Are you okay?" Josie asked, both looking and sounding concerned as she took in his injuries. She cringed and hissed when she studied the side of his head closely and then his leg. She then perched on one side of the bed and Maddie sat on the other.

Shade wasn't sure Rick would like that.

Rick could fuck right off.

"He gonna give your mom shit?"

"Probably," Maddie said with a laugh. "He's very protective of us. But he's really a big teddy bear. All rough on the outside with a gooey soft center."

"He's lookin' out for you girls."

"Yep. Ever since Dad died," Josie said.

Shade stared at Chelle's youngest. *Ever since Dad died.*

No wonder why their father hadn't been around. Or was never mentioned.

"Good he stepped in," Shade mumbled, now wondering how long ago Chelle lost her husband and the girls lost their father. The man in the picture.

"How did this happen?" Maddie asked.

Shade gave them the same story he gave Chelle. "Got jumped outside a bar in Williamsport."

If Chelle didn't believe it, she didn't say so. She also didn't ask why he was at a bar in Williamsport when the club owned Crazy Pete's in town. Most likely, she recognized it as bullshit. He was just relieved she didn't push for the truth. At least, not yet.

But then, she'd been keeping the info about her dead husband to herself, too. While it sucked that the girls no longer had a father, it didn't suck for Shade to know that there wasn't an ex-husband around to make things messy between him and Chelle.

Rick was bad enough.

"Cops get them?" Josie asked.

"Them?"

"Yes, there had to be more than one, right? To take down someone like you?"

What the fuck was Josie talking about? "Like me?"

She waved a hand toward his cut. "You belong to that motorcycle gang right outside of town, don't you?"

"Club," he corrected her. "Ain't a gang."

"Either way, how cool!" She popped off the bed and ran her fingers over the patches on the back of his cut. "Can I try it on?"

Say fucking what? "No."

Josie gave him an exaggerated pout. "Why?"

"One of the rules of a club. No one wears your colors but you."

"Your club has rules?" she asked in awe.

"Yeah."

"Cool." She returned to the bed to sit on the edge again.

"I've seen your club riding through town and also at Dino's. I didn't realize you rode with them."

Probably because he usually wore sunglasses, a skullcap and sometimes a bandana over his face. His hair was always pulled up, too.

"Some of them are really hot," Josie continued. She wrinkled her nose. "Not Dutch, though, he's old enough to be my grandpa. But I should've guessed you were one of them with that badass bike of yours. When you're better, can you take me for a ride?"

"Anyway," Maddie started, ignoring her younger sister. "Why did Mom put you in this room?"

He frowned. "Where was she gonna put me?"

Maddie shrugged. "In her room."

Oh fuck. Where the fuck was Chelle? "Your mom back yet?"

"No. Why are you in here instead of her room?" Maddie asked again. *Again* sounding just like Chelle when the woman was determined to get an answer.

He muttered something he seemed to be saying a lot of lately. "Ain't like that."

Fuck! Chelle needed to get her ass home and deal with her girls' questions.

"We know she has the hots for you," Josie said with her voice lowered.

"And we know you have the hots for her," Maddie added, her smile getting larger.

He didn't like that smile, either, and he hoped to fuck Rick wasn't standing outside the door eavesdropping. He seriously didn't want to have to stab the fucker in self-defense right in front of his nieces if he went after Shade.

"We can tell," Maddie said matter-of-factly.

"She's never looked so... I don't know... happy... no, *dreamy*... no, *satisfied* before." Josie leaned in. "Not ever. The only thing different in her life recently besides losing Pumpkin is *you*."

"Both of you have been hiding whatever has been going on between you," Maddie accused him.

What the fuck. "Your mom home yet?"

Maddie ignored his question. "All those nights she's suddenly been 'busy' when she's always been a homebody? *Please*. And when she finally comes home she has a look of bliss on her face, is wearing a smile like she has a dirty secret, and smells like she just showered. And I *know* she's not going to the gym."

He swore his heart had left his fucking chest and was now pounding in his head directly under his stitches. "How d'you know?" he asked Maddie, not sure he wanted to hear the answer.

"Because I followed her one day. I saw *exactly* where she went. She was going to do cardio but not the type you get from using a treadmill. The type you get when you go horizontal," Maddie said, wiggling her eyebrows. "And, funny, how the motorcycle parked in front of the same room that she went in to," she put a finger to her lips and rolled her eyes toward the ceiling, "looked *exactly* like yours." Her gaze swung down and held his.

Neither of them blinked for what seemed like forever. Finally, he broke. "No shit."

"No shit," Maddie echoed.

"You're giving Mom the business, aren't you?" Josie asked with an excited look in her eyes.

Jesus fuck. "Your mom home yet?"

Maddie ignored his question. "Well, whatever you're doing keep it up. I haven't seen her this happy—or *satisfied*—in a long time."

"Ain't like that," he said weakly.

"Mmm hmm," Maddie murmured.

"She's been helpin' me."

"I bet," Josie chimed in.

"Look. She's been helpin' me. Ain't lyin' about that. That's all it is."

"*Riiiight*," Josie drew out. She winked at him. "*Helping*. In a motel."

"We didn't want anyone to know——"

"That you two are having sex," Maddie finished.

No, that he couldn't fucking read. And, yeah, that him and Chelle were having sex. He wasn't admitting either one of those things to them.

Both girls got to their feet.

"We're going to tell Mom it's okay if you stay in her room. We don't mind. We're both old enough to deal with her having a man sleep over."

"We've been wishing she'd find someone for a long time."

"She's been lonely since Dad died."

"Right? I keep telling her to get on one of those dating apps."

His gaze ping-ponged back and forth between the sisters. This was not a conversation he wanted to be a part of. "It ain't like that," he mumbled again.

Both ignored him again.

"She acts like we can't hear how often she uses her vibrator."

"I know, right? It's about time she gets the real thing."

"I mean, we're both having sex more than her."

Oh fuck. "Your mom home yet?" he just about shouted.

Both froze, tilted their heads and listened.

"*Ooo*. I think she is. I hear Uncle Rick and he sounds pissed," Josie said.

Fuck.

Maddie nudged her. "Let's go save Mom and grab the crutches so we can move Shade into her room."

"It ain't——" he started one more time.

They were gone.

Thank fuck.

Chelle could deal with her girls. Once she was done dealing with her brother.

He told her it wasn't a good idea for him to stay with her. The last twenty minutes proved it.

Once he talked to Chelle, he would have his brothers come get him.

Chapter Twenty

SHADE'S BROTHERS did not come get him. Of course, Chelle wouldn't hear of it.

Instead, after Chelle got rid of Rick, Maddie brought up her crutches, adjusted them to his height and all three Goodsons moved his ass right into the master bedroom and into Chelle's bed.

He stopped saying, "It ain't like that," when Chelle came into the spare bedroom before the girls did and told him about the conversation she had with them.

The whole time she was getting him up to speed, he wondered if they also told her about how they were having more sex than their mother. Shade wasn't fucking bringing it up, but maybe she should know.

But, *for fuck's sake*, that wasn't his business. Just like it wasn't his business on how she dealt with her brother, who slammed the front door hard enough when he left that the windows rattled.

Yep, that wasn't his fucking business, either, and if she wanted to tell Shade about it, that would be up to her.

Though, he really wanted to punch that motherfucker in the face for disrespecting his sister by slamming her front door and storming out. Especially with the girls in the house.

Not that Shade was going to complain about being moved, but he was happy to see Chelle's bedroom was the shit. As in good shit. It was large with a high ceiling and a huge master bathroom he'd be able to move around in easier on crutches. Her bed was huge, too, compared to the one in the spare bedroom. That kind of sucked since he couldn't fuck her in it right away. He'd put that on a to-do list along with all the ways he was going to do her in that big bed.

She had loads of over-stuffed pillows which she propped behind his head and under his leg, along with a decent-sized TV on the wall with all the streaming apps. The room even had French doors leading out to a tiny balcony over-looking the backyard.

She announced it was her favorite room in the house and he could see why. With the way she had it decorated he knew instantly she'd done it herself. He didn't know shit about decorations or color palettes, or even furniture, but the second he hobbled into the room, he felt like she'd wrapped her arms around him.

He didn't think he'd ever want to leave it. Especially after she brought him up dinner on a tray and sat with him while he ate.

He tried to concentrate on the food, but it was difficult with her sitting next to him, looking as hot as fuck as she did in a pair of snug yoga pants and a sweatshirt which fell off one shoulder. It sucked not being able to mess up her hair and put a flush in her face like always happened after fucking her at The Grove Inn.

"You okay with this?" he asked around a bite of chicken stuffed with ham and cheese. It was fucking awesome. In the weeks he'd known her, she hadn't made one bad meal. The woman could satisfy him in both the kitchen and in the bedroom.

"If I wasn't, I wouldn't have moved you in here."

"Figured you didn't want your girls to know." He forked the last green bean into his mouth.

"I didn't, but..."

He swallowed and stabbed another piece of chicken. "But they're fuckin' smart and figured it out."

"Apparently, I raised spies."

Shade grinned and scooped up a forkful of the best mashed potatoes he'd ever eaten. "They like that their mother's gettin' dick."

"Not just any dick. Your dick."

"Even better."

"They actually high-fived me downstairs and had the gall to tell me I won't have to buy so many batteries anymore." The corners of her lips twitched.

Shade tried not to snort mashed potatoes through his nose. "Hopefully, they didn't share that 'til after your brother left."

Chelle sighed and scrubbed a hand over her eyes. "I'll work on Rick."

"Why? He don't have to like it. He don't have to like me, either."

She bugged her eyes at him just like Maddie had earlier. "He's my brother."

"So?"

Her mouth dropped open. "So? So, I rely on him."

"For what? Your girls are practically grown."

"He's still family and he cares."

"While that's fuckin' great, he shouldn't be gettin' involved with who you wanna fuck."

She opened her mouth, snapped it shut and, after a few more seconds, finally said, "He worries about me and the girls."

"Stop makin' excuses for him, Chelle."

"If it wasn't for him..." She glanced away.

He put the tray aside now that his stomach was full and grabbed her hand, pulling it into his lap. "If it wasn't for him, what?"

She closed her eyes and whispered, "He was my glue."

Her glue. There was only one reason to need glue. "Why were you broken?"

When she didn't answer, he studied her profile.

Yeah, it was still painful. It was why she didn't talk about her husband. It made him think the man didn't die that long ago. That it was still fresh.

Though, the girls didn't act like it. It seemed strange that they would take the loss of their father a lot easier than Chelle would take the loss of the man she had those children with.

He whispered, "Tell me about him," giving her fingers a squeeze.

Her head snapped back to him and she frowned. "Who?"

He took his time and formed his next words carefully. "The man in the picture on your mantel. The man who slid a ring on your finger. The man whose children you carried inside you. The man you loved. The man who ended up breakin' you so your brother needed to be the glue that kept you together."

"He didn't mean to break me." She closed her eyes and he actually felt her pain in his own chest. He only wished he could take all that pain from her instead of her feeling it, too.

"Never mind, Chelle, don't gotta tell me."

Her eyes opened and he could see the shine in them. He didn't want to cause her to cry. Not now, not ever.

If just thinking about him hurt her this badly, talking

about him would only be worse. That was why she never mentioned him.

"I think I need to explain because then you might understand why Rick is so," she sighed, "Rick. Why he's so protective. Why we ended up here, in Manning Grove."

He cupped her jaw and swept a thumb over her cheek. "Don't owe me shit, Chelle."

"The girls avoid talking about their father because they know how I get. It still hurts. Even after fourteen years."

Fourteen? *Damn*, fourteen fucking years and his loss still affected her this much.

"It's not fair to them. I tell them they can talk about him and what they remember, which isn't a lot since Josie was only three and Maddie six. But while it might not be much, it's at least something. I know they discuss him when I'm not around and they've gone through some old pictures I have stored in a shoebox in the attic. But they don't want to hurt me or see me upset. And that's not fair to them."

"You loved their father. They see that, Chelle. They love you, too."

Her throat rolled up and back down. "I only wish they had more time with him. He was gone a lot. The hardest part is they hardly knew him and that hurts more than anything."

"Why was he gone?" From what Shade remembered, his father had hardly ever been around, either. He hoped to fuck it wasn't for a similar reason. Because if it was...

"We got married after Brendan enlisted in the Army and right before he was shipped off to boot camp. Shortly after that, he was shipped overseas. We knew it was a possibility, but..." She shook her head. "Both pregnancies happened when he was home on leave. Eventually he ended up in Afghanistan as part of what was known as Operation Enduring Freedom. There's another name for it now, not that it matters." She shook her head. "None of it matters now."

Maybe that part didn't matter but the rest did.

"Anyway, I need to talk more about their father to them. But..." Her eyebrows knitted together. "We were so young when we got married. We weren't even dating that long, but we had an instant connection. From the moment we met, he felt like my soulmate and he thought the same. But, really, how well could I know him in that short amount of time?"

"Enough to fall in love with him. Enough to marry him, Chelle, and have his babies." He pressed a hand over her heart. "You knew in here. Sometimes you just know."

She tilted her head, stared at him and slowly repeated, "Sometimes you just know."

Fuck.

But before he could wrap his heavily medicated brain around that, she continued, brushing that moment off as if it was nothing. When it was a lot more than nothing. A whole lot fucking more.

"Truthfully, I'm not sure if I would have survived without Rick. He and his wife were why I moved here from Virginia. I was falling apart and I..." She inhaled an audible breath. "He stepped in as a father figure for the girls. Our daughters are more like sisters than cousins. He never complained once and I... I owe him a lot."

Thank fuck he was there for her back then, like family should be, but this was fourteen years later. Maybe she was falling apart back then, but now she was a strong, independent woman who lived her own life. She didn't need her brother's opinion on who she could and couldn't sleep with. "Thinks you're embarrassed about bein' with me. About acceptin' me in your bed. In your life."

"He said that?"

"Said you kept me a secret 'cause you're embarrassed."

She frowned. "That's not true. We both agreed to keep

this between us. It had nothing to do with me being embarrassed. You know that and I told him that, too."

She gave him a little truth, now he was about to lay some on her. "Chelle, you're a goddamn librarian at a school and I can't even fuckin' read." She opened her mouth to argue and he raised his palm to stop her. He wasn't done. "Don't have any kinda education. My job's reducin' people's pets to ashes. A fuckin' monkey could do that. Also live in a fuckin' bunkhouse that's part of a barn. I don't own shit but my sled. Got no family 'cept a bunch of bikers. Ain't gonna blame you if you don't want no one to know you're fuckin' me."

"None of that matters to me, Shade. And he wouldn't be happy with anyone I'm dating."

"Beautiful..." He blew out a frustrated breath. "This ain't datin'. He knows that, knows what this is. Anyway, wouldn't even know how to date if that's what you wanted."

"What does that mean?"

He shrugged. "Never dated."

"You just fuck women and move on." It wasn't a question, but a statement dripping with disappointment.

She might not like it, but it was fucking true. "Yeah, Chelle, I just fuck women and move on." He didn't know anything else. He'd never wanted to know anything else.

Not until now.

Her fingers flexed in his. "I didn't mean it like that."

"Yeah, you did."

"You told me you were mine until I'm tired of you. What if I never get tired of you?"

Eventually she was going to get tired of the secrets, the shit he couldn't tell her, his nightmares, his lies. All of it. That was a fact. "Like that you think that, Chelle, but..."

"Unless you get tired of me first. I'm so much older than you."

"Eleven years ain't nothin', beautiful."

"Eleven years is something, Shade."

"Not to me."

"You say that now..."

He'd say that forever. But he didn't know about forever. Or even if forever was possible. He didn't want to promise her something he might not be able to deliver. So, he kept that to himself.

He didn't want to be responsible for the type of pain she still felt fourteen years later after losing her husband because she loved that deeply.

But her loving that intensely didn't surprise him. Not at fucking all.

He wanted that from her. He really fucking did. But he was mired in too much shit. And until he shook off some of that shit...

Unfortunately, he'd never be able to scrape it all off and that could end up being an issue.

But that was one more thing he couldn't tell her so, instead, he shot her a smile.

"Beautiful, you're a MILF, remember? And I don't see your age, I see you."

"While that's sweet—"

"Ain't sweet, it's the truth."

A soft tap on the door, and Josie's voice coming through it, interrupted them. "Mom? Maddie asked me to bring this up."

Shade reluctantly released Chelle's hand so she could slip off the bed and go over to the door. She opened it only far enough for Josie to pass a small plate through.

"Thank you. I'm sure he'll appreciate the gesture."

"He okay?" her youngest asked.

"As good as he can be for now."

"Can I visit him later?"

Chelle glanced over her shoulder at him. He nodded.

"Yes, later. I'll let you know when. I'll be down shortly to help clean up the kitchen."

"We got it, Mom."

Yeah, Chelle was raising her girls right. Hearing them interact with her always pulled at something deep inside him. Something he had missed for most of his life. He didn't remember a lot about his mother, but he did know she loved him. Unfortunately, those few good memories hadn't been enough to hang onto during the bad.

He only hoped his mom would have been with him like Chelle was with her girls. Though, imagining that made her being torn away from him even harder.

He was goddamn robbed.

He closed his eyes and just breathed, pushing down the fury and renewed drive for revenge beginning to bubble up from his gut.

No. Not now.

When the bed shifted, he opened his eyes just as Chelle was putting the plate on the tray next to him and saying, "Maddie made Oreo pie just for you."

His blood ran cold.

Oreo pie.

He stared at the recognizable and still intact dark brown and white cookies that made up the outer edge of the slice. More crumbled Oreos topped what looked like a layer of chocolate pudding and whipped cream.

His stomach rolled.

"Chelle," he barely managed to get out.

"What? You look green. Is it the meds? The pain?"

Oh fuck. "Grab me a can. Somethin'."

"A can?"

"Gonna puke." *Jesus,* she needed to hurry the fuck up.

She bolted from the bed into her bathroom and was back in a flash, shoving a shopping bag-lined trash can into his chest. Luckily, she was just in time.

With a groan, he leaned forward, jamming the can between his thighs. As everything he had eaten not even ten minutes earlier surged up, she rubbed his back and held his hair out of the way.

Just like a fucking mom probably would.

He kept puking until his stomach ached and felt hollow.

When he was done heaving, when there was nothing left in his gut, a wet washcloth appeared in front of his face. He wiped his mouth and muttered, "Musta been the meds."

She pulled the can from between his legs and removed the bag. "I'll get you some ginger ale to settle your stomach. And another bag. I'll leave the can within reach, just in case."

Just in case... The only thing making him sick to his stomach was...

"Chelle... Take the pie." He kept his eyes averted from the plate, but he knew it was there. He could smell it, even over the puke. A smell he'd never forget. He swallowed the saliva flooding his mouth again. "Tell Maddie..."

She grabbed the plate and quickly dumped the piece of pie into the bag and showed him the clean plate. "I'll tell her you loved it, but now need to rest."

"Yeah."

She left with the tray and the tied-off garbage bag in her hands.

This was exactly why he couldn't promise forever.

He never knew what the fuck would happen next.

This time all it took was a goddamn slice of pie made with cookies that one of his owners used as a reward. When he did what he was told. When he didn't fight. When that particular "daddy" thought Julian had been a good boy.

When his "uncles" and "daddies" used bribes like TV time, music, video games, and even treats like Oreos, he tried not to be good. He always chose to be bad.

And when others wanted him to fight, he always tried to seem willing instead.

They robbed him of his mother, he wanted to rob them of as much pleasure as he could.

So, fuck no, Julian wouldn't do shit simply to watch TV. Or to play video games.

Or even eat a fucking Oreo cookie.

What they wanted, he didn't.

All Julian wanted was his mother.

And to be free.

———

"ARE you ready for your sponge bath?" Chelle teased as she entered her bedroom and closed the door behind her.

A low chuckle came from Shade as she approached. "Didn't know a sponge bath was a choice or woulda started demandin' them a week ago."

"Well, since I assisted you in the shower earlier, a sponge bath isn't necessary."

"Shoulda let me decide that."

She skirted her king-sized bed and put the book she'd been reading down on the nightstand.

He flipped the covers back for her and after kicking off her pink fuzzy slippers and shrugging out of her pink fuzzy robe, she climbed in next to him.

He grabbed the remote next to his hip and turned off the TV. He had to be crawling out of his skin to get out of this bed and room. He still had a week to go before he was allowed to put weight on his leg. He got around her master suite without a problem using the crutches. And occasionally he worked his way downstairs. But for someone who was used to doing what he wanted, when he wanted, and a lot of that "doing" was in the wind on his motorcycle, being stuck in her house had to feel like jail.

Quite a few of his brothers had stopped in and that was when he'd make his way carefully down the stairs. He didn't want them in her room. He acted like the master bedroom was their private domain and didn't want to share it with any of them.

Some of the Fury ladies—the sisterhood he called them —had also stopped by. All were super nice and friendly, and wanted to help out where they could.

Being a nurse, Jemma, Judge's sister and Cage's "ol' lady," visited every couple of days to check to see if his stitches were starting to dissolve, and to check for signs of infection and make sure the bone bruise was healing properly. Chelle was relieved when she said everything looked as it should, but mostly due to the fact Shade had followed the doctor's orders.

Chelle had a feeling he only did so because his president had forced him to.

Either way, he was slowly getting better. He no longer had any symptoms of his concussion. His healing scalp was starting to itch and he was still forced to wear the leg brace by Jemma's orders.

He probably hated being stuck in her bed most of the day, but she didn't find it any kind of hardship. She loved walking into her room and seeing him in her bed. He certainly was a sight that made her warm all over.

Selfish? Yes. But she got over that feeling quickly whenever he'd wrap himself around her possessively every night. Come morning, she'd wake up to his erection tucked in the crease of her ass. Also every morning, she helped relieve that erection in one way or another.

She grinned and her nipples were already pebbling at this morning's memory.

"What?" he asked, shooting her a suspicious look.

"I was just thinking about this morning."

"Yeah," he breathed. "Been thinkin' 'bout how you used

your mouth on me before you left. Think you sucked what brain cells I have left outta my dick this mornin'."

She rolled her eyes, but remembering the taste of him on her tongue made her pussy twinge.

Every morning she also made sure he had everything he needed before she left for work and, if the girls were home or came home before she did, they always checked on him, too.

One hard and fast rule she made was he wasn't to go up and down the steps when no one was home. She did not want to walk in the door at the end of the day and see him lying in a heap at the bottom of the steps.

She hoped he followed that rule but didn't ask since she didn't want to be a nag. She also didn't want to sound like an overprotective, hovering mother, even though that was difficult not to do. It was only instinct even though he was too old to be one of her offspring.

Thank goodness because that would be even more awkward.

Eleven years difference between them was bad enough. It might not bother him, but sometimes it bothered her. If what she had with him was only sex, it wouldn't bother her as much, but at some point they both realized what was between them was *way* more than sex.

They just hadn't discussed how much more and what that might mean.

Chelle wasn't in any rush to see where things went. She couldn't have any more children—and had no desire to do so, anyway—and she had no reason to get remarried any time soon, if ever.

The girls hinted several times when Shade wasn't in earshot that they liked having him around. He was "cool" and his "brothers" were all "hot." Chelle agreed, but, unlike her daughters, she tried not to stare at them and giggle when they visited.

Somehow—Chelle hadn't gotten a straight answer how —Maddie figured out Shade couldn't read and approached him when Chelle wasn't home to ask him about it. Then she began to help him with his reading lessons.

The day Chelle walked in to find the two of them sitting in her bed against the headboard with the laptop between them along with other lesson material, she just about broke out into tears at what type of woman Maddie was turning into. She never once made fun of an adult man unable to read, but instead wanted to help him overcome his problem. It made her heart swell.

Any other woman coming home to find her twenty-year-old daughter in bed with her thirty-year-old... whatever he was to her... would probably seep suspicion, jealousy and anger. But Chelle immediately saw it for what it was, especially since neither looked guilty or even tried to hide what they were doing.

After that, Chelle had pulled Maddie aside and told her not to mention his dyslexia and inability to read—or read well at this point, since he was now reading some simple words and sentences—to anyone unless Shade gave the okay. Not even to her sister. Chelle would leave it up to Shade when to tell Josie, if at all.

Josie ended up discovering the truth when she confronted Maddie about her spending time with Shade in their mother's room with the door shut. They actually had gotten into a bad fight about it when Josie assumed Maddie was trying to steal Shade from behind Chelle's back.

Unfortunately, Chelle hadn't been home at the time, so poor Shade waded in, finally forced to admit the truth of what they were really doing. Of course, after that, Josie wanted to help him, too.

So now the poor man had three bossy women as instructors but seemed to be taking it in stride.

Chelle noticed that about him. He seemed to adapt to whatever situation he was in at the time, like a chameleon.

"You can turn the TV back on if you want, I'm going to read another chapter or two before bed."

"Would rather stare at you."

She turned her head to stare back at him. "That's creepy," she teased, but, truthfully, she could stare at him for hours and not get bored. His hair and dark features... His body, even with the scars... Everything about him turned her on.

She didn't think she'd ever get tired of having sex with him, either. She'd never been with anyone as good as him and he wasn't even that old. Even so, his skills were off the charts... like he'd had training on how to please a woman. *And* he'd paid attention in that class.

Cunnilingus 101.

French Kissing 102.

Advanced Love Making 301.

She wondered if any such classes even existed. If so, a lot of men needed to sign up, that was for damn sure. If Shade had taken one, he should have graduated at the top of his class. Definitely magna *cum* laude.

She rolled her lips under at that crazy thought.

He raised a dark eyebrow. "What?"

"Nothing," she chirped innocently and grabbed her book from the nightstand, opening it to the spot where her bookmark was tucked. Before she could begin reading, he yanked it from her hands.

"What the fuck is this?" He scowled at the dust cover for the book she had borrowed from the town's library.

"Can you read the title?" While his reading had improved and the book had a simple title, the subtitle was long and so was the author's and co-author's information. He wasn't at the point where he could read the rest just yet. At least without taking the time to try to break down and visualize each word. For him, reading would always be a slow process.

"Says *No...* something. But know what the fuck the piece is on the front."

The large title was *No Angel.* And it had a picture of a biker at the top.

"Not piece, picture," she corrected him.

His jaw shifted tightly, and he raised the book between them. "What-fuckin-ever, Chelle, what the hell is this?"

She took a deep breath. He was getting pissed and she didn't know why, so she needed to keep her cool as much as she could. "It's a book about the Hells Angels. You didn't want me asking questions about your MC, so I decided to do a little research of my own." Not only with this book and others, but online, too.

"What the fuck? Why?"

"Why not? I find it fascinating and I love learning about new things. This book is a true story about the first federal agent who ever infiltrated the outlaw club. He was a part of the inner circle for twenty-one months. *Twenty-one,* Shade, without getting himself killed. Or, at least, I don't think he did, I'm not done reading it yet. Can you imagine?"

He stared at her for the longest time like he didn't know who she was, then suddenly snapped out of whatever zone he'd been in. "Chelle, the Fury ain't like the Hells Angels."

"But they're a motorcycle club, too. Wouldn't they be similar?"

He inhaled a breath so deeply, his chest slowly expanded like an overfilled balloon under his tank top. The sleeveless shirt was the minimum he wore around the house so the girls wouldn't see his scars and ask questions. As he released that inhale, he talked slowly and carefully like he did when he wanted to make sure all his words were correct and every word was heard. Which automatically made her brace.

"They're an outlaw club. We ain't. I mean," he shook his

head, "the Fury used to be when the Originals were around. They probably did the same type of shit the Angels did, or do, but we ain't like that now."

"Oh. I—"

"Christ, Chelle, don't read this fuckin' book." He tossed it across the room where it landed with a thump on the carpet.

With a gaped mouth, she watched it slide another foot before coming to a rest. "But I'm almost halfway through—"

"No. Just stop. We ain't them. Never will be them. Every fuckin' MC is different."

"Since you've never read it, how do you know what's in it?"

"Don't need to read it to know." He gritted his teeth and stared at his lap for a moment. After what seemed like a few more calming breaths, he faced her again. "Beautiful, listen, you got questions, ask."

Ask? "You basically told me to not ask questions about your life, which also includes your club."

"Yeah, got that. But don't fuckin' read that." He jerked his chin toward the book. "If you really need to fuckin' know, then ask. I might not be able to answer every question —'cause you know how to ask a shitload—but will answer what I can."

"You'll answer what you can," she repeated, not bothering to hide her disappointment. That statement pretty much meant he wouldn't answer anything.

"Yeah."

"So, basically, everything about your life will remain a secret."

"We all got secrets, Chelle. All of us. Even you. But club business remains club business, it's nobody else's business. That's one of the fuckin' rules and I ain't breakin' any rules 'cause I don't want my colors stripped."

His colors stripped? She dug deep into her newly-found, but still limited, MC knowledge. "I read on a website about a brother having his colors stripped."

Shade groaned and scraped a hand over the black wiry hairs of his beard.

He said he'd answer what he could, so... "You lose everything when that happens."

"Yeah."

"And depending on why they're stripped that could be... deadly." Or bad enough to the point where the offender wished he was dead.

"Yeah."

"I don't want you to lose everything, so I won't push if you can't answer."

He twisted his head to look at her. Relief. That was what was in his face.

"All I'm askin', beautiful." He grabbed her hand and lifted it. His gaze remained locked with hers as he pressed it to his lips.

His mouth parted and he tucked one of her fingers inside and sucked it while his tongue swirled around it. He could distract her from a topic he didn't want to discuss way too easily, *damn it.*

Her lips parted and she released a ragged breath. It didn't take much for him to make her wet and wanting. A look, a word, a touch and she melted.

They hadn't had intercourse for the last week. They'd done other things but not that. She had wanted to make sure he was on the road to recovery before they did. When Jemma stopped by earlier, her opinion was that he was.

That meant it was time to take things back to where they were. Maybe not completely yet, but close.

She'd gone for years without sex. Since she started having it with Shade she struggled if it was only a few days. That was how good he was.

He always made her want more. More of him, more of what he could do to her, more of... everything.

And here he was in her bed right now. At least for another week. No reason to go to sleep wanting a man who wanted her and who conveniently slept by her side. Especially when his almost black eyes told her clearly what he wanted.

More than her mouth on him, like this morning. More than his fingers inside her, like last night. More than his lips on her breasts.

So much more.

His voice was thick when he asked, "Girls here?"

"Yes, they're watching a movie downstairs with some friends." When she left them, the five girls were cuddled up on the couch together under blankets, passing around large bowls of popcorn and containers of Ben & Jerry's, engrossed in the latest Jason Momoa movie.

He pressed her hand to his boxer briefs and slid her palm along his erection. It pulsed beneath her fingers, causing everything on her to pulse, as well.

When she sank her teeth into her bottom lip, he pulled her lip free and brushed his thumb across it. "How quiet can you be?"

That question sent a shiver of anticipation through her. "Are you okay for that?"

"Jemma said not to put weight on my leg yet. That's it."

She curled her fingers around his hard-on, gave it a stroke downward and cupped his balls. They were hot and soft and this morning she had her mouth all over them while his fingers dug into her hair, encouraging her.

Her, "Well, pressing your knee into the bed can't be good for that," came out a bit breathless.

He pursed his lips and only stared at her.

"Oooh." She smiled slyly. "You want *me* to do the work."

"My tongue's gonna do the work when you sit on my

face. Then my dick's gonna do the work when you sit on it after you come all over my beard."

She raised a *wait-a-minute* finger as she slipped from the bed. "I'm going to lock the door."

"That'd be good."

On her way back to the bed, she tugged her panties off from under the vintage-style nightgown she bought just to wear for him. The baby doll design was antique white with eyelet lace around the edges and made her breasts look like they were twenty years younger. The nightgown covered the important bits but still made her feel sexy as hell and Shade loved it.

The first time she came out of the master bathroom wearing it, he'd instantly gotten hard. Unfortunately, it had only been the second night after "being jumped at a bar," so they couldn't do anything about it since he was still dealing with the effects of a concussion at the time.

But right now, his brain wasn't rattled and his cock was hard, so she didn't bother going back to her side of the bed, she climbed on and right onto his lap instead. His cotton-covered cock flexed against her bare pussy.

He needed to get rid of those boxer briefs. Like now.

"You got wraps?" he growled, his fingers digging into her hips.

She didn't. They hadn't needed them until now. Though, even now they really didn't need them, did they?

She rolled her lips under and tried her best to feign innocence. "Did I forget to mention I got my tubes tied after Josie?"

He tipped his head up from studying her cleavage to look her directly in the eye. "Yeah, you kinda forgot to mention that."

"*Welllll*, after having Josie, I didn't want to raise a third baby by myself while Brendan was serving overseas, so we decided to stop at two." They had wanted to wait until after his time served to start a family, but that plan got shot to hell. Every time Brendan came home, they spent so much time having sex, they sometimes forgot to use a condom. The only regret she had when it came to those two unplanned pregnancies was the girls never getting to know their father before he got killed in action.

Shade's, "For fuck's sake, Chelle, all this time..." drew her back to the bed.

"Pregnancy isn't the only reason to use condoms," she reminded him.

"No shit. But been dyin' to fuck you without one."

He was? "You were?"

He shot her a look.

"Haven't you always used one, though?" *Please say yes.*

"Yeah, beautiful, always used a wrap."

"Well, then... What are we waiting for?"

Chapter Twenty-One

JULIAN STARED at the cracked sugar cone on the hot blacktop surrounded by a muddy-looking puddle of what used to be chocolate and vanilla swirled ice cream. His heart thundered in his chest because he knew what came next, and worse, he could do nothing about it.

Every time he ended up standing in that parking lot, the same event happened over and over. He knew how it ended but he couldn't change it, no matter how hard he tried.

They'd end up in that big room in a big house in a crowd of strange men. The men Julian couldn't stop from touching and poking at his mommy as she stood naked on a raised platform at the front of the room.

Like livestock.

No matter how much he fought it, he couldn't stop himself from turning around and seeing his mommy standing behind their minivan encouraging him to hurry up.

He couldn't stop himself from crying over losing his ice cream. That ice cream cone he bugged her to buy him. When he glanced over his shoulder, the ice cream was gone, the pavement bare. Like it never existed.

His head spun back to his mommy.

She was gone, too. Like she never existed.

He screamed for her and began to run toward the black van parked in the spot next to theirs. He had to warn her. He had to stop those men.

He needed to make sure he didn't get caught so he could tell the police about the stranger danger.

He sucked in air as he ran and yelled, *"Stranger danger!"* as loud as he could. His lungs burned and his throat hurt like when he got sick. Hot tears slid down his cheeks.

He swiped them away, rubbed at his eyes and yelled, *"Stranger danger!"* again. Why wasn't anyone helping them?

When Julian slipped between the two vans, he spotted his mommy. And those two men.

He could see the whites of his mommy's eyes and she looked really, really scared.

He needed to be brave. He needed to save his mommy.

It was all up to him. Nobody was coming to help them. Nobody cared.

He needed to be a brave boy. She told Julian after the last time his daddy left that he was the man of the house now.

She had been on her knees in front of him, grabbing onto his shirt, the one with the Kool-Aid stain that she wanted to throw away. *"You're the man of the house now, Julian."*

He didn't understand. *"Where did Daddy go? Isn't he coming back?"*

His mommy had begun to cry even harder, but he didn't like when she cried. *"He went home."*

Home? *"Daddy lives here."*

She shook her head, not bothering to wipe her tears away, so Julian did it for her by pressing his hands to her cheeks. *"No, he only came to visit. He has another home, another family, somewhere else."*

He didn't understand that, either. *"He's not coming back to visit?"*

She shook her head again. Her loud sob made his tummy hurt. *"He doesn't want his other family to know about you. About us."*

He began to cry just like his mommy. After tugging him into her arms and squeezing him until he couldn't breathe, she whispered into his ear, *"You're the man of the house now, Julian, so you need to be brave. For Mommy."*

He needed to be brave for Mommy. He promised her he would. His mommy also told him keeping promises was important.

So, he needed to save her from the bad men even though he knew what was coming next. What always happened next.

He had to at least try this time. Maybe this time he'd be able to do it. To change what happened next.

She wasn't tied up yet. She was struggling, screaming his name, encouraging him to run.

He couldn't run. He couldn't leave her. He needed to save her.

You're the man of the house now, Julian.

As she fought the men trying to tie her up, her hand reached out for him. He rushed to the side of the van and reached out, too.

The tips of their fingers touched and she grasped for his hand, trying to get a better grip, but their fingers kept slipping. A syringe appeared in one of the man's hands and he was about to jab Mommy with it. An arm snaked around his waist and jerked him away. He desperately tried to keep his hand connected with hers, because if they didn't...

If they didn't, they'd be separated forever. They'd never see each other again.

Except for in that big room in a big house full of strange men.

After that? He wouldn't be able to see her at all.

So, he couldn't let her hand go. He couldn't.

"Mommy!" He used all his strength to break free of the man to lunge for her hand. But all he grabbed was air. "Mommy, no!"

The van was gone. The men were gone.

His mommy was gone.

And soon, so was Julian.

Never to exist again.

Gulping air into his searing lungs, Shade jackknifed up, confused. He blinked the burn from his eyes and swiped at the beaded sweat on his brow, his chest pumping and his panting rapid and ragged.

Why now? Why this fucking nightmare now?

He knew why.

"Mom?" he heard through the closed bedroom door.

What the fuck was going on?

He twisted his head to see a pale Chelle, also sitting up and staring at him with wide eyes full of confusion and shock, seeing him for the freak he was.

The freak they created.

He closed his eyes again and tried to slow both his breathing and his heartbeat.

Fuck. Fuck. Fuck!

"Mom? Is everything okay?" came again through the door.

"Yes, Josie. It's..." She turned her attention from the door back to Shade. After a slight hesitation, she called out, "Everything is fine." She tried to make it sound believable, but Shade saw the truth in her face.

Everything wasn't fine. Not for her. Not for him.

He should have warned her. Because *this* was what the fuck happened when he didn't drink and smoke himself into oblivion at night so he could sleep without remembering.

He'd gone almost two weeks without one fucking drink

due to his meds and he only smoked a bowl out on the balcony when Chelle and the girls weren't home. *For fuck's sake*, at night before bed, somebody was always home.

"But I heard Shade yelling for his mom."

"It was just a bad dream. Go back to bed."

"Mom?" A slight pause, then, "Are *you* okay?"

"Yes, baby, I'm okay. Thanks for checking on us. We're fine."

Another hesitation, a little longer this time. He could hear the reluctance in Josie's voice when she announced, "Okay, we're going back to bed."

We're going back to bed. That meant Maddie was out there, too. He had woken both her daughters and made them worry about their mother.

Shade waited a few pounding heartbeats for them to move away from the door before he muttered, "Sorry you gotta lie to them." He swung his legs off the bed, grabbed the crutches propped against the nightstand next to his side of the bed and pulled himself to a stand.

Two more fucking days. Two more and he could stop using the crutches and brace and get back to normal.

Right. Normal.

When the fuck had his life ever been normal?

He clenched his jaw and yanked open the nightstand drawer, grabbing the pipe, lighter and tin of bud Easy had refilled for him the other day. He didn't bother to watch Chelle's reaction at seeing it stored in her bedroom.

He made his way to the French doors, unlocked them and awkwardly made his way through them, then shut himself outside. He sighed when the bedroom light turned on inside and cast a glow through the door over the seat he settled in. He propped the crutches against the wood railing and his foot on the only other chair on the tiny balcony. He dumped his shit in his lap so he could fill his metal pipe.

Fuck it. Chelle most likely wouldn't approve of him

smoking, but the balcony was private and unless the girls recognized the smell, they'd never know. Though, he was pretty sure Chelle's daughters knew what pot smelled like. While they hadn't come out and directly confessed, they'd both hinted to him they'd tried it at least once. Maybe more. But without numbing his brain, he wouldn't get through the next few minutes, the next hour, or the rest of the night.

He was packing the pot tightly in the bowl with his finger when the door opened and Chelle came out wearing her robe and slippers since the mid-October night was cool.

He didn't bother to look at her, but had no choice when she lifted his bare foot from the seat of the chair, settled in its place and tucked his foot back on her lap, her warm hands holding it there to prevent him from pulling away.

He didn't bother to fight her, instead took his time to finish prepping the pipe before lifting it to his lips and lighting it. He pulled a long drag deep into his lungs, held it until his body screamed for air, then blew it up and away from Chelle.

He waited for her to bitch and when she didn't, he took another long, deep hit, the smoke filling his lungs and slowly settling his rushing pulse.

He had the strange need to apologize to her. For what, he wasn't sure.

No, he knew. He had a long fucking list of shit.

Starting with getting involved in her life and finishing with the reason they were both sitting in silence out on the balcony in the middle of the night while he got baked.

But if he started rattling off apologies and the reasons for them, once he was through, the shock on her face would be worse than the expression she wore after he woke them up because of his nightmare.

He had no idea what he'd said in his sleep.

But his face had been wet and his throat raw once he

became aware of his surroundings. Every muscle in his body had been locked tight, too.

He hoped to fuck he hadn't grabbed for her hand, thinking she was the mother he needed to save. Because that would be fucked.

More than fucked.

He flicked the Zippo again, lifted the pipe to his lips and held the flame to the bowl. He closed his eyes as the smoke once again filled him and began to push out the tension.

Not all of it, but most.

Because Chelle sitting quietly next to him, simply waiting, still made him somewhat tense.

He wanted her. He wanted to keep her. He wanted to fucking claim her for his very own.

But he wasn't sure that was possible.

Not now. Not yet.

Maybe not ever.

And if he couldn't, those sick motherfuckers got to screw him all over again against his will.

They would once again manage to take from him what was his.

His mother.

His childhood.

His body.

His sanity.

Chelle.

Fuck them. They couldn't have her. None of them could fucking have her.

She was his.

He was keeping her. He only had to find a way how.

"Will you tell me now?"

He stared out into the night. All the neighbors' windows were dark. They seemed to be the only ones awake. Like it was only the two of them who existed right now. No one else. "Chelle, you don't wanna know."

"If I didn't, I wouldn't ask."

If he told her what she wanted to know, it would no longer be just the two of them. They would be inviting unwelcomed guests. Monsters he didn't want to share her with.

"You said you were an orphan. Start there. How did your parents die?"

He didn't even know if his parents were dead. Once he was freed, he'd done his best to find his mother, but without being able to read, he couldn't search as thoroughly as he wanted to. He hoped once he got through the list in his wallet, he might get closer to finding her. Then maybe one day, he'd succeed.

He finished the bowl and before he could pack another one, she plucked the pipe and lighter from his fingers. But by then, the pot had done its job, anyway.

"Talk to me," she pleaded in a broken whisper.

Being stoned made it easier to tell his story. He had no idea if his words were right or wrong, she didn't stop him to correct him if they weren't.

She only listened.

He didn't tell her everything, but started with what happened that day at the mall when he was four. He told her about the auction and then glossed over the worst memories. He revealed enough so she got a good idea of what happened to him during those ten years, but not every fucking detail.

Not about the first time with a man at four, not about the last time at fourteen, either.

He explained about the Oreos.

He explained how he got the scars, but not why.

He told her bits and pieces about Deb. She didn't need to know what kind of training he'd gone through to learn how to please a woman.

He shared only the stuff she would absolutely need to

know. The rest he left hazy or skipped. She was smart enough to fill in some of the blanks if she wanted to. If she could stomach it.

Hell, pockets of time existed that were complete black holes. Incidents that his brain blocked so he wouldn't remember. Not if he wanted to be able to continue to function. As a human. As a man.

When he was done, when he couldn't talk anymore, she stood up, dropped to her knees before him and laid her head in his lap. He burrowed his hands into her hair, her silky strands snaking around his fingers.

She cried, but was quiet about it. Just as she had said nothing while he got stoned and then while he talked, he stayed quiet while she shed tears for him.

No, not for him.

For Julian.

For a stolen kid. For a little boy lost.

He had never shared any of what happened with anyone. No one. Not even Deb when she asked. But Deb knew his life had been rough and damaging before she bought him and that past was the main reason she let him walk away once he turned seventeen.

Even though he had nowhere to walk to. Nowhere to go. Since he belonged nowhere and to no one.

It took him eleven years from the day Deb released him to find somewhere he belonged. To find his family.

It took him almost two years after that to find Chelle.

He wasn't sure he could hold onto her, but he wanted to fucking try.

The fist gripping his tank top at his gut tightened. "You call me beautiful. But it's you who is beautiful, Shade. Anyone who survived what you did... Even though you won't tell me everything you went through, everything that happened to you... Those bastards who tried to break you, failed. You were too strong for them to do so. They failed and you didn't. Despite what they did, you grew up and grew into a beautiful soul, Shade, instead of something ugly like them."

"No." She was so wrong. His soul was tainted and damaged, it wasn't beautiful or whole.

She lifted her head and held his eyes. "Yes, I see it, even if you don't."

"You don't know me." It wasn't only his past that could come between them but what he'd done recently and what he still needed to do.

Because he wasn't done.

He would need to keep those secrets from her, too.

An invisible hand squeezed his throat.

Secrets would always exist between them. Always. He fucking hated that.

"I know you skipped over a lot, but I now know enough. Thank you for trusting me enough to share it." She rose higher onto her knees and pressed her lips gently to his. When she pulled back, she said, "You didn't mention your father. I would've thought he would have turned over every stone trying to find you and your mother."

A real father would have. But he might not have even known they had gone missing since he abandoned him and his mother for his "real" family. "Don't know where he is. Don't give a shit, either."

He hoped that was the end of that discussion, but he shouldn't be surprised that with Chelle, it wasn't.

"Do you have the same last name as your father?"

"Don't know. He left when I was four."

"Do you remember him?"

"Barely." Shade no longer remembered what the man looked or sounded like.

"Did he live with you?"

"No." He didn't realize it at the time, but his father had

never lived with them. He only "visited" his mother. Even that stopped the day Julian became "the man of the house."

"Could he have been married?"

Her question had him tipping his head down and studying her. She was disturbingly smart. Much smarter than him. If he thought too long and hard about it, he'd convince himself he wasn't good enough for her. Not even close. But she was old enough and wise enough to make that decision for herself. And after that nightmare and what he just revealed, she hadn't kicked his ass out. Not yet.

"Yeah, think he was married to someone else."

"After he left, he never came back to visit?"

Not after that day. The day his mother cried about giving his father an ultimatum. At the time, Julian didn't understand what that meant, but Shade knew now. His mother tried to force his father's hand to leave his wife, and whatever kids he had with her, to be with her and Julian. "Don't think so."

"I'm sorry."

He frowned. "For what?"

"For everything," she said softly.

He ran a thumb across the soft skin over her cheekbone. "Ain't nothin' you did."

"Doesn't mean I can't be sorry about it."

"No reason to be." It wouldn't change a damn thing.

"How can I not feel for a little boy who lost his father, then his mother, and then his childhood?"

"Got a big heart, beautiful."

She shook her head. "I'm a mother. I can't even imagine..." Her face twisted like she was about to cry again.

Chelle putting herself in his mother's situation was one of the reasons he didn't want to tell her. He had been right. It had to be difficult to be a mother and not wonder what it would be like if the same happened to her daughters that happened to him.

"Don't gotta. Your girls are grown and safe."

"Are they? What's to stop someone from grabbing either one of them and auctioning them off just like your mother? Enslaving them or forcing them into prostitution. Or... whatever those bastards do." She rose to her feet and turned to look out over her dark backyard with one hand on her hip and the other pressed to her forehead.

Fuck. "Chelle..." He grabbed the crutches and pulled himself to his feet, hobbling the one step needed to close the gap between them. He pressed his chest into her back and his face against the side of her neck. "This is why I didn't wanna tell you."

She turned and tucked her head under his chin and wrapped her arms around his waist. "No, I'm glad you did. I needed to know. I'm sorry. I shouldn't let my imagination run wild." She laughed awkwardly. "I might need a hit of that pot now. My mind is racing and I don't think I'll be able to sleep until it stops."

"You took the lighter and the pipe from me."

She glanced over to where those items sat on her abandoned chair. "I... couldn't."

"Ever smoke before?"

"When I was a teenager. A few times with friends."

"Did you like it?"

"I don't remember."

"If you need it, it's there. It's good shit."

She laughed softly. "What kind of mother would I be if I smoked pot while my daughters were down the hallway?"

"One who might worry all night about her girls being kidnapped and not be able to sleep."

She sighed. "Maybe it would've been better if you told me in the light of day."

"Too late now. Grab it."

She moved away from him, grabbed the stuff off her seat and brought it back to him.

He took it from her fingers, lit what remained in the bowl and pulled a small amount of smoke into his mouth, then he sealed his mouth over hers and while they shared a kiss, she inhaled his hit.

They continued kissing until the smoke escaped her nostrils, then he gave her two more hits by sealing their lips together and sharing kisses. He decided that was enough for now and waited to see how the pot affected her.

It wasn't long before she melted against him with her arms looped around his neck and her face pressed to his chest. He held her there for a little longer.

He figured she could stand like that forever, but it wasn't as easy for him with the crutches, so he finally was forced to ask, "Think you can sleep now?"

She nodded slowly against his chest, pulling a smile from him.

"You want, I can go to the spare bedroom."

She pulled back and frowned. "Why?"

"Still want me sleepin' next to you?" He wanted to be sure. He needed to be sure what happened to him, even though it was so long ago, didn't change anything between them.

She actually appeared insulted. "Why wouldn't I?"

He lost track of how long he stared at her. It could've been seconds, minutes or even an hour. Eventually he said, "Beautiful, if I could pick you up and carry you to bed, would do that right fuckin' now."

She combed her fingernails down his bearded cheek. "How about if I help you back to bed and we pretend that you did the whole caveman routine."

"Not the same."

She rolled her lips under for a second. "I'm not sure even if you were fully healed if you could throw me over your shoulder and take me to bed like a Neanderthal."

"Wanna bet?"

She shook her head. "No need. I'll go willingly."

They both went willingly.

It wasn't only the premium Kush that put them to sleep, it was her getting on top of him and taking her time to make love to him. Sweetly and slowly.

And that's what it was. Her love.

Now that he had it, he didn't know what to do with it.

He'd do his best to figure it out.

CHELLE PULLED a breath in through her nose and stretched with a groan. Normally when she woke up stiff and sore, she didn't enjoy the feeling. But this was a welcome discomfort from a very enjoyable reason. She smiled, sighed out all the air from her lungs and rolled to her side. Her eyes popped open and she quickly lost that smile.

Shade's side of the bed was empty.

Her heart shot into her throat and she sat up, glancing around her bedroom.

His crutches were still propped by the bed, the curtains over the French doors remained closed, the bathroom was dark and the door open.

She closed her eyes, blinked them open once more and glanced at the empty, wrinkled sheets next to her.

Nope, still gone.

It was Saturday and last night, while still draped over his chest and catching their breath from sex, she had discussed getting back to painting this weekend since he was finally allowed to ditch the crutches and brace.

Oh yes, he'd ditched the brace all right. He'd left it on the nightstand next to his side of the bed. She twisted her head to where he'd kept his backpack and cut for the last two weeks. Of course. Those were gone, too.

She closed her eyes again, pressing the heels of her palms against them, stemming the sting.

She was sure there was an explanation.

He wouldn't just leave, would he?

Without a word?

Just... leave?

Just like that? Without saying goodbye or letting her know where he was going? Or telling her that he was moving back into his room on the farm?

Nothing?

That wasn't Shade. He wasn't like that.

Or maybe he was.

Maybe he was right when two nights ago he stated, "You don't know me."

Maybe she didn't know him as well as she thought.

He had revealed some of his secrets, but not all. She had no idea how many he really had.

It could be so many, he'd lost track of them all himself.

Maybe it was her age.

Maybe it was her having two grown daughters.

Maybe it was Rick's dislike of him and the idea of someone like him being in Chelle's life.

Maybe it was all of it.

Maybe it was none of it.

She had no idea because he left without a damn word.

Anger quickly bubbled up and replaced the deep-seated hurt.

He'd used her. That was what he did. She was an easy mark desperate for love and attention. Thrilled that a man eleven years her junior would even want her or find her sexy. He was gorgeous, great in bed and could get any woman he wanted.

Why would a man like that want her? An older widow and single mother.

She fought the sting in her nose and eyes.

Well, fuck him. Fuck him for making her fall in love with him.

Fuck him for breaking her heart like this. Pretending to care for her as much as she cared for him.

Fuck. Him.

She grabbed her phone off the charger, turned it on and while it booted up, she sat on her bed and seethed.

Because anger was easier than heartache.

When her home screen appeared, a message popped up. She knew who it was from before she even saw the name.

She read the simple message—made up of only two damn words—ten times to make sure she wasn't imagining it. After the tenth time she still wasn't sure if she should be heartbroken or angry. Or both.

Love you.

"Love you," she whispered.

He loved her? Why would he text her that instead of telling her in person? Where the hell did he go?

She double-checked her texts to make sure that was the only one from him. It was.

She checked her voicemail to make sure he didn't leave her one. He hadn't.

She tried calling him and the call went right to his voicemail.

She tried texting him and received no response.

He had stayed in her house, in her bed, for the two weeks Trip had forced him to. The minute he was done with that sentence he left.

Those two words weren't good enough, he couldn't just send them in a text and then disappear.

She wanted an explanation.

She pressed her phone against her forehead.

She wanted to tell him she loved him, too.

But she wasn't going to send it in a text nor would she leave it in a voicemail. If he wanted to hear it, he would need to hear it in person.

For that, he would need to come home.

Chapter Twenty-Two

A POUNDING on her front door made her heart skip a beat and the spoon she was stirring the tomato sauce with slip from her fingers. Chelle helplessly watched it sink to the bottom of the pot and disappear.

"Shit."

A second round of pounding made her jump and her eyes turn from the bubbling sauce toward the front of the house.

Neither girls were home but should be back in time for dinner.

Chelle swallowed her heart back into her chest and turned down the burners on the stove before wiping her hands on the nearby dish towel and facing the direction of the door.

Another round of knocking. Short, loud, not to be ignored.

The last time she'd heard knocking like that, the people on the other side had delivered bad news.

Really, really bad news.

News that changed her life. Her daughters' lives.

She swallowed hard again, took a deep breath, straightened her spine and marched out of the kitchen and down the hallway to the front door.

She flipped on the porch light and put her eye to the peephole.

The shaky confidence she clung to fled when she saw who stood on her porch.

She unlocked the door, swung it open and stared at the two men on her doorstep. She remembered both of their names because both men were hard to forget.

She also remembered the last time two men in uniform knocked on her door. These two men wore uniforms, too. Only theirs were black leather vests with club colors.

A brotherhood of a different kind.

A brotherhood all the same.

She hoped to hell they weren't about to deliver the same type of bad news. Her pulse began to rush again as her heart pounded as hard as they had knocked.

Please don't be dead.

Please don't be dead.

Please, God, don't let Shade be dead.

She pressed her steepled fingers to her mouth and stepped back, giving Shade's brothers room to enter the foyer. Once they both stepped inside, the house seemed so much smaller.

Daisy's future father was a huge, bearded man who could easily scare the shit out of anyone with his appearance alone. His cousin Deacon, though not quite as large, wasn't any less intimidating. Not with his Viking looks and his serious expression.

Both sets of dark eyes were glued to her.

"He here?" Judge asked.

The blood drained from her face and her knees wobbled slightly, so she locked them in place.

Her lips parted but it seemed like her, "No," took forever

to travel from her tight chest into her throat and out of her mouth.

Whatever crossed both of their faces was quickly hidden. Not fast enough.

She'd seen it.

Their worry. Their confusion.

It didn't help when they glanced at each other before looking back at her.

"We figured he was here. That he was takin' a couple extra days off his feet and to," Deacon raised one eyebrow, "to—"

Judge made a sharp noise at the back of his throat.

Deacon finished with a weak, "heal."

"You don't know where he is?"

Judge shook his head, his short hair hidden by a gray knit beanie. "Ain't answerin' his calls or texts. His voicemail's now full."

"His bike?" she asked optimistically.

Two of his brothers had dropped it off early Friday morning in anticipation of him being able to ride again. When she checked her garage Saturday morning, it was gone. His Harley was so loud, she had no idea how he rode it away without it waking her up.

Unless he didn't ride it away for that reason.

"Sled's gone," Deacon confirmed.

"It's not here, either," she murmured.

"He didn't show up for the club run yesterday or for work this mornin'. Yesterday could kinda understand, but this mornin'?" Judge shook his head. "He woulda called Cassie to let her know."

She turned, went to the stairs and sat down on the fourth step. "Why would he just disappear like that?" She glanced up at Judge. "Have you checked all the places he normally went?" She tilted her head. "Like that bar in Williamsport?"

A muscle jumped in the big man's cheek. It took him a few heartbeats before he admitted, "Yeah, we checked that bar in Williamsport."

"You guys have a fight or somethin'?" Deacon asked, drawing her attention.

"No." After the nightmare Thursday night and their talk out on the balcony, he seemed to be okay. Friday night, she had sat out on the balcony with him as he got stoned again before they went back in, had sex and fell asleep.

No tension at all had existed between them. The sex had been great, he seemed relaxed and nothing seemed off. She had no idea why he just up and left without telling her that he was leaving.

Maybe she should show them his last text to prove she wasn't lying and that things had been good between them. That this was just as much a mystery to her as it was to them.

But she wasn't ready to share that text yet. It was his private message to her. He might not want them to know how he felt about her. Shade had his secrets and his feelings for her might be another one.

Even though he didn't let anyone know why he left or where he went, his two word admission wouldn't help them find him, anyway.

"He's been hurt badly once. At least, once that *I* know of. How do you know he's not hurt again... or dead?"

Both men glanced at each other again.

That made her fear of Shade lying somewhere injured or dead—and no one knew where—turn to anger. "I don't know what he'd been doing or had done to get injured like that. But whatever it was..." Her fingers curled into her palms and she pressed her fists into the tops of her thighs. "The getting jumped behind a bar in Williamsport story was bullshit. I don't like that he had to lie about what happened."

"Ain't for you to like," Judge muttered under his breath.

She bugged out her eyes at the man who wore the sergeant at arms patch. Wearing a pained expression, Deacon stepped between them with his palms raised. "We get it. You're worried."

"Well, you're worried, too, if you're here!" She failed at controlling the sharp rise in her voice. But his brothers not having a clue where Shade could be was making her start to unravel.

When the Army had shown up at her door all those years ago, they knew exactly where Brendan was. They knew exactly what happened. She had closure. Things weren't just left in the air, making her wonder. Making her worry for him.

She closed her eyes.

Making her daughters worry, too. In truth, Josie and Maddie now knew Shade better than they knew their own father.

Shade and the girls had actually gotten close. It had warmed her heart to see that, but now it broke her heart to think they would feel his loss, too.

She lost the love of her life before.

She couldn't lose another man she loved.

She couldn't.

She barely survived the first time.

If it hadn't been for her daughters being so young back then...

"Don't I deserve to know the truth about where and why he was injured? Why he spent two weeks laid up in my bed? He couldn't tell me because he didn't want his colors stripped. But that's bullshit. Maybe between us we can figure out where he is and whether he needs help. You can tell me the truth. For his sake."

Judge's scowl was dark. "That's club business, Chelle. Gotta understand, we don't share shit like that."

Her brow dropped low. "Even with your ol' ladies?"

Judge's head jerked back and his nostrils flared as his dark eyes narrowed on her. "You ain't his ol' lady."

She must have looked as wounded as she felt from Judge's words because Deacon grimaced and quickly assured her, "Not even with our ol' ladies."

When he realized he had cut her deep, Judge's next words were softer and not so harsh. "It's just the way it is, Chelle. If you can't accept that, maybe Shade ain't for you."

While those words hurt, too, she appreciated the truth.

With Shade's past, and also with his MC, he would always have secrets. If she couldn't accept certain things being kept from her, she needed to move on.

She planted her elbows on her thighs and dropped her head into her hands, digging her fingers into her hair.

She didn't want to move on. She wanted to accept him as he was. Dark past, secrets, his brotherhood, all of it. Everything that made him who he was.

He didn't keep things from her to hurt her, he kept them to himself because he had no choice. To keep his family, to keep his brotherhood, maybe even to keep his sanity.

For at least a decade he'd had no one to love him, to care for him, to nurture him, to treat him with dignity and respect. To see him as a human being and not a perverse play thing, a toy, a sexual outlet. Someone whose only worth was being a slave. A piece of property to be owned by another person.

His childhood and his will had been taken from him. So much had been stolen from him.

These men before her, his club, they cared. They gave him what he'd been missing in his life.

A home. A family. Support and loyalty.

She wanted to be that for him, too.

The only problem was, none of them could give him that if he was gone.

And where he went and whether he'd ever be back was a mystery.

A mystery only time would solve.

———

SHADE GLANCED at the names on his list. The faded paper that held them had been folded into fourths, the edges of the folds now almost worn through.

He could decipher the letters and sound out the names now. He might not be able to do it quickly, but he could do it.

Thanks to Chelle.

Thanks to Josie and Maddie.

Thanks to their patience and understanding.

Almost every name had been written in a different hand-writing. Some shakier than others, depending at what point during Shade's visit he had the man write down the next name. Which actually was the one prior since Shade had been working backward from fourteen years old to four.

Every name on his list now had a line drawn through it. Except for one. The last person he needed to visit.

But it would.

There wasn't much he wanted in life.

Chelle.

His brotherhood.

Revenge.

He needed to deal with that last want before he'd allow himself to have the first one. His gut instinct told him he'd be forever restless if he didn't deal with his thirst for revenge first.

But it would soon be over.

He had one name to go. The original broker. The man who had invited a bunch of strange men into a big room in a big house. The man who ran that original auction where his mother stood naked on a wood platform while those strange men touched her and made her cry.

The room where Julian stood at the back with another man and watched his mother be sold. The room where he last saw her.

The room where he was forced to stand on that box and had his clothes cut from him until he was naked, too. The room where strange men also touched him.

The room in the house which was owned by the broker who sold him to the highest bidder.

The highest bidder whose name was now crossed off Shade's list.

A straight line had been drawn through his name, similar to the straight line drawn across his throat, directly below the man's bouncing Adam's apple.

That man would not be buying any more little boys, abusing any more stolen toddlers, and he would not be the start of any child's decade-long torturous nightmare.

No, he wouldn't be doing any of those things anymore.

Shade was disappointed, but not surprised, to find his first "daddy's" tastes hadn't changed much over the last couple of decades. In fact, the little boy Shade found in his old "room" was maybe about three.

Shade wasn't good at judging ages on children but whether the boy was three, four or even seventeen, it didn't matter. The "daddy" didn't deserve to take another breath. Shade only hoped he saved the boy from a lifetime of nightmares. Or at least, less of them.

He also hoped the boy had someone to go home to and someone to love him no matter what. At least, once the pigs found him after Shade left an anonymous tip on the missing and exploited children hotline an hour after he made sure no evidence was left behind. No evidence of Shade's existence, but plenty of evidence on why the man's throat was cut.

Not too many people would care about the man's loss. At first they might, but in the end, when the man's secret life came out, no one would even bother to pretend. Only pedophiles liked other pedophiles and sometimes not even then. Ones who thought being attracted to a twelve-year-old was acceptable, but four-year-olds? To them, that was sick.

That irony had not been lost on Shade, even when he was a boy named Julian.

Shade tucked the list back into his wallet and kept to the shadows as he moved along the side of the house and into the backyard. It was a big house in a gated community with a guard posted at the entrance. The neighborhood probably had its own security, too. Rent-a-cops who were most likely paid off to look the other way during the "invitation-only" parties and ignore the complaints about the amount of vehicles parked on the neighborhood streets. Because even though the parties were exclusive, they were highly attended. And nosy neighbors tended to notice.

Parties where the "caterers" delivered women and children in vans instead of food. Where the delivery vans pulled into the large garage and the garage doors closed behind them before those deliveries were unloaded.

The garage where the guests pulled in their own fancy vehicles and had their "party favors" loaded for them before leaving.

Yeah, Shade bet nothing had changed in the last twenty-six years. Though he doubted this was the same big house from back then. He was sure the broker moved every year or so.

But whether in this neighborhood or the last, or the one before that, the same cycle continued year after year. New location, new names, new faces, new perverted clientele.

The money too great, the opportunities too easy.

And plenty of women and children to choose from.

A light coming from one of the large rear windows

made him go solid. He figured the property had motion-activated security cameras and spotlights so he needed to be careful. He didn't care if he got caught on camera, that was a given, he only cared that he wasn't recognized.

He'd watched the house for the last two days. He'd memorized the pattern of the occupant. The broker was a creature of habit.

Not good for him, but good for Shade.

The kitchen went dark and another window lit up at the other end of the house. The man was settling in with a bourbon and his nightly television.

But not for long.

Chapter Twenty-Three

As soon as Shade had sent that text to Chelle, he had shut off his phone, tucked it into his sled's saddlebag and left his Night Train in the car rental company's parking lot. He left his phone behind mostly because he didn't want Judge tracking his location. He knew the enforcer would do just that once Shade didn't show up for work that following Monday.

But he also didn't want to be distracted by texts and voice messages. He was pretty fucking sure his phone was full of them. They would just need to wait.

Now he'd been gone for twelve days. It had taken less than two weeks to track down the men on his list and exact revenge for ten years' worth of abuse. Twelve days seemed a flash in time in comparison and the men on his list died easy deaths when they should've suffered like their victims had.

But at least they wouldn't create any more victims. That was the most important part. The world would be slightly better without sick fucks like them. However, the men on his list were only a tiny fraction of those types of motherfuckers who existed.

Everyday people lived in their bubble, unaware of the

dark underbelly of the world. Unless it directly affected them. Shade thought back on how many times he could've been saved but people didn't want to "get involved." It wasn't "their business" and turned away.

Yeah.

The saying was "see something, say something," not "see something, turn a blind eye." But, again, unless that "something" touched their lives directly, most people couldn't give a fuck.

Shade gave a fuck.

He gave a huge fuck.

Which was why he now had the broker tied to a kitchen chair waiting to take his last breath. The last person on his list, the one who had paid the men to snatch his mother and him in a mall parking lot twenty-six years ago before turning around and selling them for a profit.

The man had already pissed his pants at the sight of Shade's knife. He'd also denied knowing who Shade was, which shouldn't surprise him. "Sam Miller," one of a multitude of names the man probably used, most likely couldn't remember all the souls who passed through his hands.

Or he didn't care.

Or both.

But after a little bit of poking at the guy's memory, Miller final remembered a boy named Julian and his mother, Cecelia. Though, Miller didn't remember their actual names because he never asked, he only remembered the circumstances surrounding them coming into his possession.

Because as it turned out, it wasn't random.

Not random at fucking all.

Shade pressed the sharp tip of his Bowie knife against the pad of his index finger, keeping his eyes glued to the ten-inch blade as he slowly turned it. The overhead light caught the flat side of the blade twice with each revolution, and he made sure that reflection would hit Miller directly in the eyes.

A reminder to the asshole of what was to come.

"He didn't say anything about a kid. I swear!"

"Only my mother."

From the corner of his eye, Shade noticed Miller also watching the rotating blade.

The man's Adam's apple lifted to the top of his throat and dropped back down. "Yeah, you weren't a part of the deal," he insisted.

The deal. "What was the deal?"

"To grab the woman. That's it."

Shade tilted his head and studied the knife. The blade had a fresh edge to it since he'd sharpened it only last night. "That's it?"

"He wanted a percentage once she sold."

"Like on consignment?" Shade lifted his gaze from the blade and stared at Miller. When he didn't get an answer fast enough, he repeated, "On consignment?"

"Yes... Sort of."

"He say why he wanted my mother to disappear?"

Miller shook his head. "The less I know the better."

Right. "He say what to do with her son? A four-year-old boy?"

"He didn't. Again, he didn't even mention him..." Miller paled even more, if possible. "You."

"He know you had her son, too, before the auction? He get a cut of what you sold me for?"

That question hung in the air between them for way too long.

"Missed your fuckin' answer." He took a step closer to the chair and Miller jerked against his restraints, the whites of his eyes growing larger.

Shade barely caught the answering, "No."

Sounded like his sperm donor had his mother snatched

but didn't give a fuck what happened to his son. He didn't give a fuck that his mother's disappearance would leave a four-year-old boy without any parents. An orphan for the state to deal with. Because there was no way the bastard was claiming him as blood.

Nah. Why the fuck would he want to do that? Claiming a child born to his side piece would ruin his life.

"So, you were a greedy motherfucker and kept all the scratch you scored for me for yourself?"

No answer, of fucking course.

"And he never asked about me when you gave him his cut from my mother?"

Miller shook his head and his Adam's apple made the slow journey up his throat again but stuck there for a few seconds before dropping like a rock. "Look, I'll pay you. The amount I got for you. What I got for your mother. Then we can forget this whole thing. Okay?"

Right. Simply forget. Easy.

Shade rounded the chair and stopped behind it. The man's flesh broke out in goosebumps. Everywhere.

The reason Shade could see almost every inch of him was because he had cut off the broker's clothes before he finished securing the asshole to the chair. He doubted Miller was as humiliated by that act as his mother had been. Or Julian had been.

Fuck no, Miller didn't have a soul. Why the fuck would he be embarrassed?

If a career of selling women and children to the highest bidder didn't bother him, then nothing would.

"How about this... I'll make you a trade. Most boys who are... *compromised*—"

"Molested," Shade corrected him. "Tortured. Abused. Raped would fit, too."

"...End up liking the same *things* as what was done to them. They follow the same pattern. You probably like boys, right? I've got one for you. Innocent, untouched. Still old enough to be trained. You could be his first. You could teach him the same lessons you were taught. I bet you'd like that."

Before leaving a house, he always searched for any victims. He'd start at the top of the residence and work his way down to the lowest level, usually the basement.

"What do you get in exchange for this untouched meat?" Shade asked slowly, pretending to be interested. Trying to remain as calm as he could, even though the blood was surging through his veins and his fingers had tightened on his knife to the point of pain.

"All you have to do is let me go."

That would never happen. "Lemme get this straight... I get the boy, I let you go, and you just find a new boy to sell."

"No!" burst from Miller. Then he said more quietly, "No. I'll never do this again. I swear. You take him for yourself and I'll forget all about him, all about you, all about this business. I'll walk away from it all."

Yeah, right.

"Seriously, no one has touched him yet. Just think of how tight he is. And he'll probably fight if you're into that."

He'll probably fight.

Shade's stomach churned. The urge to puke was strong, but he swallowed down the saliva pooling in his mouth. He tamped down the panic attack he teetered on and let the anger flow through him instead. "Oh yeah? How old?"

"Twelve."

Shade sucked in air through his mouth, trying to settle the bile rising in his gut. "Where's his mother? Got her, too?"

Miller shook his head. "She's gone. They were homeless, living in their car. Got her cleaned up and sold her for a pretty penny."

Jesus fuck. He was clenching his teeth so hard he wouldn't be surprised if he cracked all his fucking molars.

"If you'd rather have a woman, I can get you one. I can get whatever you're into. Boys, girls, women... All you have to do is let me go."

Yeah, he wasn't picking from that fucking menu. "Why didn't the boy sell at the same time as the mother?"

Miller gave him a crooked smile, appearing relieved that Shade was actually considering the trade. Yeah, he was taking the fucking boy all right, but not for the reason the bastard thought.

"He was too old for that crowd. He also fought my guys and got some bruises. No one wants marks on their purchase unless they put them there themselves."

Christ. A twelve-year-old was too old for that crowd. Twelve. The age Julian was when he was sold to David. But "Daddy David" was done buying tweens.

"I was hoping once those bruises healed someone would buy him cheap. The longer my product doesn't sell, the more they cost me to keep them clean and fed."

His product. "Wanna know where his mother went and who bought her."

Miller's expression closed up when his hope to be released disappeared. "I don't know."

Shade came around to stand in front of Miller. He lifted his chin and looked down his nose at the motherfucker. "You fuckin' know."

Miller shrugged as much as his restraints allowed. "Even if I did, it's too late."

Shade frowned. "Why?"

Miller pressed his lips together.

In return, Shade pressed the tip of his blade to the hollow of Miller's throat. "Why?"

"There's an agent who buys women..."

"What kinda agent?"

"He buys them for a filmmaker."

"Porn?" If so, he could still find her and get her son

back to her. Reunite them. Save her from that life. Save them both.

Again, Miller didn't answer. *Fuck him*, he didn't have a choice.

Shade rounded the chair again, fisting the Bowie knife, and this time, when he stopped behind Miller, he drew the sharp tip of the blade along the top of the man's back in the shape of a large rectangle. Not deep enough to draw blood, but enough to score lines no deeper than a scratch.

"What are you doing?" Miller asked in a panic, the flesh on his back quivering.

He *should* be scared.

"What kind of fuckin' film?" Shade asked. "You don't answer, gonna flay pieces of flesh from your body 'til you do."

Miller shuddered. "Then you won't get the boy."

The asshole thought he had the power to negotiate. He didn't. "I'll get the boy."

"Let me go and I'll tell you everything you want to know."

"Like who bought my mother?"

"I don't know who bought your mother!" Miller exploded. "That was over twenty-five years ago. I don't keep fucking records! I have no fucking clue what happened to her."

Shade drew the rectangle again on the man's back, following the same lines, this time putting more pressure to it. Blood began to well in the slices.

"Jesus Christ!" Miller screamed, wriggling in the chair as much as he could. It wasn't much because Shade had him tied down as securely as he could. He hadn't left much wiggle room for the fucker.

Shade started at one corner of the rectangle, used the tip of his knife to work the corner of skin up and began to saw the layer of flesh away from the muscle underneath.

"Holy fuck! I don't know!" Miller screamed. "I swear I don't know who bought your mother. If I knew, I'd tell you. Just don't... Don't cut me anymore!"

Shade paused. He believed him. He'd need to find his mother himself. But now she wasn't the only mother he'd need to find. "What kind of filmmaker bought the boy's mother?"

When Miller was slow in answering, Shade pulled up the flap of flesh again and began to saw more away from his body.

"Stop!" Miller shrieked. "Just stop. I'll tell you..." His head flopped forward and he panted loudly. "I'll tell you. Just... Just... stop. Please..."

"Ain't heard the answer yet," Shade warned and yanked on the loose corner of flesh.

"I... *Fuck*! The kind she doesn't recover from."

Shade let the slippery chunk of bloody flesh slide from his fingers. "What the fuck does that mean?"

When he took out the trash, he normally did it in a calm manner and felt nothing. Numb. Dead inside. The same way he'd felt for many years of his youth. He would draw inward to deal with what was happening around him, to him. But what Miller just said made his heart thump. And if his heart was beating, he wasn't dead inside. He was very much alive.

What Miller revealed also made him remember bits and pieces of discussions Julian heard whenever he was sold or traded back to a broker. Discussions, and even jokes, about what happened to the women who weren't "pretty enough" or had become drug addicts. Or the kids who got too old or were considered untrainable.

Jesus Christ. Shade struggled to pull in his next breath.

A fucking snuff film.

The world was full of sick motherfuckers. Sick, sick

motherfuckers. Both the people making snuff films and the people who jerked off to them. Goddamn sick.

"You sold her to that agent?"

"He was the highest bidder."

"What was his name?"

"They don't use their real name. Every time they show up, they use a different one to stay anonymous."

"How do the winnin' bidders pay?"

"Cash. It's all in cash. Occasionally in gold. There's never any paperwork. No traceable payments, no receipts, no real names. It's cash and carry."

Cash and carry.

For a human life.

"My mother. Was she sold to a filmmaker, too?"

"I told you, I don't remember who bought your mother. How stupid are you?"

How stupid are you?

Do you have brain damage?

Are you retarded?

Your mother must've taken drugs when she was pregnant with you.

He bit the inside of his cheek until he tasted blood.

No. Not now.

He ignored the oozing flap of skin hanging from Miller's back, grabbed a handful of his hair and yanked the man's head back until it couldn't go any further, then he pulled some more until the broker's throat was stretched tight. Instead of his throat, Shade placed the blade along the man's receding hairline. "How 'bout I scalp you instead?"

"I swear I don't remember!" Miller screamed, his face red and tears leaking from the corners of his eyes, piss dripping off his lap and puddling on the seat of the chair. It smelled like he might have even shit himself.

Shade leaned forward, stared directly down into Miller's wide blue eyes and whispered, "Think harder," letting the sharp edge of the blade bite into his tanned skin at the top of his forehead.

Tanned because he probably sat around the pool out back during the day. The pool that came along with the big house in this exclusive gated community. Bought with the souls of women and children.

Fucking motherfucker.

"Don't! Please... *Please...*"

"How many women and children have you sold who you've forgotten?" Shade nudged the blade deeper into the man's skin, causing a few droplets of deep red blood to roll down his temples and into his thinning gray hair.

"I... I don't know. I don't know!"

"Guess."

"I don't know... Maybe... Maybe... a hundred?"

No, that wasn't right. "Wrong answer."

"Maybe five hundred. I didn't count!"

Shade removed the blade from his now bleeding hairline, leaned down and put his mouth closer to Miller's ear. He murmured slowly, "Don't think that's the right answer, either."

His grip tightened on the broker's hair and his hand holding the knife moved in a blur.

He wasn't wasting any more time on this motherfucker. Not a goddamn second more.

A wet gurgle was heard before the man's neck gaped open. Shade loosened his fingers and Miller's head remained tilted back. His eyes became unfocused and the remaining air in his lungs hissed and bubbled from his throat.

Blood began to roll down Miller's naked chest and over his lap, down his thighs and drip onto the cream-colored ceramic tile under the chair.

Shade stepped over to the kitchen sink, scrubbed his

knife clean, dried it on a dishtowel and tucked it back into the sheath strapped to his calf.

He left his latex gloves on when he washed the blood off his hands. He'd dispose of them elsewhere. Most likely burn them along with his completed list.

Then he did what he always did before leaving one of these fuckers' houses.

He jogged up the stairs, found the attic and from there worked his way down, checking every room, every closet, every possible location a child or an adult could be hidden or kept captive.

For a newer, luxury home, the stairs down to the basement shouldn't creak the way they did. As he took each noisy step down to the level below the earth, the temp dropped at least a degree or two.

The basement walls and floor were made of concrete, reminding Shade of a burial vault. The smell of bleach assaulted his nostrils. The eerie quiet invaded his brain. And his heart was doing its best to escape his chest.

He blinked as his world began to close in on itself. He fought it. The darkness. The memories.

The dank smell of dark basements came flooding back.

No. Not now.

In a house like this, the basement shouldn't be musty or dank. It should be well-lit and finished off into a rec room.

Or a man cave.

A room the whole family could enjoy.

Not turned into a dungeon.

He paused on the last of the squeaky steps and took a deep breath so he wouldn't turn and bolt back up them. With clenched jaws, Shade forced himself to turn his head.

To see.

To see past his memories. To see the present.

What he saw weren't actual cells. Not made of concrete

and bars found in prison or jail. Nothing permanent like that.

No, they were cages. Ten of them that could be easily relocated to the next big house with a big room that could hold a lot of strange men with pockets full of cash.

The portable cages were made of thick black wire. Holding pens. Not for animals for which they were designed. But for humans.

Women. Children. Maybe even men.

All were empty.

But one.

The one at the very end. In the darkest corner of the basement. Farthest from any kind of window that might allow even the smallest amount of light to shine in, might give the tiniest amount of hope.

In the cage were two things.

A boy. And a bucket.

A fucking boy. And a fucking bucket.

Shade's nostrils flared at the stench rising from the bucket, recognizable over the smell of the bleach, and he hadn't even approached the cage yet.

No, he was still stuck on the last step.

His heart thundered and his brain screamed at him to fucking run.

He remembered these cages. And other cages similar to these.

The wire boxes Julian had been placed inside until it was his turn to stand on that wood platform at the front of the big room full of strangers who wanted to inspect him. Who touched him in the front, lifting and prodding, who made him bend over so they could inspect him in the rear, who opened his mouth, who made him lift his arms to see if he was beginning to grow hair in his pits. Or hair on his balls or hair anywhere but his head. The men who made him speak to see if his voice was changing yet. Because those were signs of him getting older.

Too old.

They'd turn him and check for bruises and scars. For any identifiable markings, like a brand or a tattoo.

When they were done, they'd nod and smile at him, as if they expected him to smile back. Some even asked Julian if he'd like them to be his next "daddy."

No. The answer was always no.

His answer would make that smile disappear and a hard expression replace it. One Julian had quickly learned to recognize. The unspoken message that said, "I'll teach you to behave. To be a good boy. I'll train you right."

They always thought they'd be the one. The one to tame him. The one to make him pliable. The one to break him.

They never were. None of them succeeded. They all failed.

Every. Single. Fucking. One.

No. Not now.

Shade forced himself to step onto the basement's concrete floor and move between the two rows of cages. He didn't look left or right, he focused on the cage at the end.

The one containing the boy with the bruises. The child wearing nothing but stained underwear and filthy tube socks, the formerly white cotton soles now almost black.

The boy whose face was dirty except for two clean streaks down his cheeks. From when he was scared.

Only, he didn't seem scared now.

His eyes followed Shade's path and when Shade stopped in front of the boy's cage, they stared at each other.

"Who are you?" The kid's voice was raw like he'd spent too much time screaming or crying. Most likely both.

Yeah, he was past the stage of fear. That ship had sailed. He was now angry. Pissed. The look in his dark eyes hard. Maybe even deadly.

Shade didn't blame him.

"I was you once."

The boy with the shaggy brown hair frowned up at him unable to hide his confusion. Shade didn't blame him for that, either.

Shade had to look questionable. He was dressed in all black. His hair was pulled up and covered with a beanie so he wouldn't shed strands of DNA, his hands were covered in latex gloves so he wouldn't leave identifiable prints. His boots were a generic brand purchased at a Walmart in Tennessee, the size and tread pattern not unique in any way.

Though Shade took precautions, Miller's house was full of strangers' DNA with all the men, women and children coming through it. His would just be one of hundreds identified, if at all.

"What are you going to do with me?"

Yeah, it hurt for the kid to talk. That made Shade's throat hurt, too, from the memory. "Set you free."

The boy's brow furrowed. "You're going to set me free? Just like that?" He tried to rise but even at twelve he was too tall to stand straight in the cage, so he crouched back down. The cages weren't tall, so their human occupants had to hunch over or sit. It made it harder to fight when it was your time to be shackled and removed from it.

If you managed to struggle too much, there were electric prods—the same kind used on cattle—that were used to help convince you to comply.

"Just like that," Shade answered.

He pulled out the key ring he'd found in Miller's pocket and had tucked into his own. One by one he flipped through the keys and tried them in the padlock. The fifth key opened it.

The boy's anger was gone and uncertainty was slowly creeping into his face. "Where's my mom?"

"I don't know." It was sort of the truth and better than no answer at all.

"Do you think she's here somewhere?"

The hope in his voice squeezed Shade's heart to the point of almost crushing it. "No."

"Are you here to help me?" More hope, this time guarded. Like he still was very unsure of Shade's motives.

The kid was smart not to trust anyone at this point.

"That's not why I'm here, kid, but I'm gonna help you."

"Why are you here?"

Shade dropped the padlock onto the floor and yanked open the cage door. If the boy jumped him, he'd need to subdue him. Shade hoped to fuck he didn't try anything; the boy already had enough bruises. An ugly one across his cheekbone, a dark purple handprint circling his left bicep and one encircling each wrist. Maybe Shade should think about tracking down and killing Miller's goons, too.

No, he needed to get back to Manning Grove. He'd done what he'd set out to do. It was done. Over.

If he was going to track down and deliver karma to anyone else, it would be his father, even though Shade didn't know his name, didn't know anything about him. Julian had his mother's last name and had no idea if she had taken his father's as her own but doubted she did since they weren't married.

He hardly even remembered what the man looked like twenty-six years ago. Now, he had to be in his fifties.

No matter what, one day Shade would find him. Then he'd get the truth from the bastard on why he'd thrown his family to the wolves.

Shade already knew the answer, but he wanted to hear it from the asshole who made his mother a side piece and couldn't bother to raise him.

His father couldn't risk losing everything he had and the family he loved. So, he got rid of the family he apparently didn't want. Julian and his mother had become an inconvenience. A risk to his "real" family once his mother had enough and began to make demands.

But right now, finding his father wasn't a priority. The boy before him was.

His father was a dead man walking. The boy before him was the future.

So was Chelle. And his club.

The kid's repeated, "Why are you here?" louder and more demanding this time, snapped Shade's attention back to him.

"Gonna show you."

The kid didn't move from the far corner of the cage. "Why?" That one worded question was full of insecurity.

"So you know the job you'll think you need to do when you're older is already done. I did it already so you don't have to. It's done."

It was done.

The boy frowned and Shade realized he had a split lip, too. Fucking assholes. "I don't understand."

"You will, kid. Come out of the cage." Shade stepped back and gave him some space. "Not gonna hurt you."

The kid still didn't move.

Right. So they needed to get to know each other a little better first before the boy somewhat trusted him. "Miller said you're twelve. That true? Asshole's like him are known to lie about that shit."

"Yeah."

"You got a name?"

"Do you?"

Even in this crazy, unknown situation that could make most children break, this kid still had fire. Like it was him against the whole fucking world. It made Shade want to smile, but he was not in a smiling mood. "Yeah, it's Shade."

"What kind of name is that?"

"One I picked."

"I don't understand."

"You will. What's yours?"

Shade could see the conflict on his face. He wanted to trust Shade because he realized he might not have a choice. But he also was not quick to trust anyone right now. Not while sitting in a cage, talking to a stranger in a house where the owner wanted to sell him to the highest bidder.

That could cause a shitload of distrust toward anyone standing in that same house.

Even so, Shade needed him to come out of the cage and didn't want to force him. He'd rather the boy came out on his own, even if it took a bit of time. By allowing him the choice to leave the cage on his own, it would prove to him his choice hadn't been completely taken away. That he still held onto that power.

Unfortunately, Shade wanted to get the fuck out of this house as soon as he could. He wanted to be long gone before Miller was found in his kitchen bled out.

"Listen, I can call you Kid, but prefer to call you by your name. Sure it's better than Kid."

"Judah."

The name was said so softly, Shade thought he misheard. "What?"

"Judah. I hate it. I prefer Jude."

"Then gonna call you what you prefer. Got any family other than your mother, Jude?"

He shook his head. "Not that I know of."

For fuck's sake, what was he going to do with this kid, then? "Not one fuckin' person?"

"If we did and they didn't help my mom and me when we were homeless, then they're dead to me, anyway."

The anger was back. Jude's spine had snapped straight, his eyes turned hard. His mouth thinned to nothing but a slash.

"At your age, you can't survive out there on your own. You'll end up on the street workin' johns or slingin' drugs, or back in one of these sick motherfucker's hands. Ain't gonna let that happen."

"Then what am I supposed to do?" Tears, whether from the anger or from the perceived hopelessness of his situation, filled Jude's eyes. They didn't spill over but remained contained. Barely. "I've got nowhere to go. No one besides my mom."

Christ. Truth was, the kid didn't even have his mom. "Yeah, you do."

"Are you going to help me find my mom?"

The hope was back. But just for a fleeting moment. It was dashed when Shade answered, "Not sure that's possible."

"Then why would I go with you? You could be like him."

"Ain't like him. Was like you."

Jude stared at Shade, still blinking back those welling tears. "Was that what you meant when you said 'I was you once?' Were you taken like I was? Like my mom and I were?"

"Yeah, kid. Spent ten years being bought and sold. Ten years being a fuckin' slave to these sick motherfuckers. That ain't happenin' to you."

Fuck. The tears were no longer being held in check. The reality of his situation along with his mother's was hitting Jude hard because of what Shade just said.

"I want to find my mom."

Yeah, me too, kid. "Will see what I can do. But we can't find her if you stay in that cage. Need to get out of there and come with me."

Jude roughly wiped at his cheeks and winced when he touched the bruise. "But I don't know you."

Jude was starting to mentally break down. To fall apart.

Shade needed to get him out of that house before that happened. They needed to get a few states away before they stopped and he could let Jude melt down and cry himself empty. Then maybe he'd sleep. The dark circles under those leaking eyes were proof he hadn't had any.

"Can drop you off outside a pig pen... a police station if you'd rather. Just know, with no family they're gonna put you in the state's hands and into foster care. You want that?"

Jude shook his head and sniffled. "No." His answer was thick with tears. "I want my mom."

"Wish I could give you that, kid. Can't." *Fuck.*

"Tell me the truth. Is she gone... for good?"

His goddamn chest was cracking wide open. He knew what the boy was feeling. He'd felt it, too. When endless layers of hopelessness had piled on, weighing him down, drowning him in despair.

This was only the beginning for this kid.

Once he got somewhere safe and some undisturbed rest, Jude might have a better outlook. But with what the kid just went through, and what he still would go through, that better outlook might not come so easily.

Not for a long time.

"Can't say for sure, Jude. But my guess? Yeah. I get you don't know me, but I'm the best chance you got. Need you to come out now. Got somethin' to show you, then we gotta split. 'Cause if we don't split soon, we both might end up at the police station. Then neither of us will be able to make our own choices. They'll be made for us."

And that would fucking suck.

Jude got to his feet, staying hunched over so he didn't hit his head and made his way to the opening.

"Need help?" Shade asked him, noticing the kid's legs seemed a bit wobbly.

"No."

"All right, then. We gotta go." Shade turned and headed

back toward the steps, assuming Jude was behind him. There was no other way to get out of the basement besides the stairs, so he'd have to follow eventually.

"Gonna get you clothes and sneakers and whatever else you need once we get outta Georgia."

"We're in Georgia?"

Shade glanced over his shoulder. Jude had stripped off his sagging, dirty socks and was following him barefooted. "Yeah, where were you livin' in your car?"

"Mississippi. Mom thought we had family there. She was wrong."

When Shade hit the top of the steps, he cracked open the door and listened for a few moments to make sure they weren't walking into any surprises.

The house was silent. *Thank fuck.*

The basement door opened into the large kitchen. So even if he hadn't wanted to show Jude what happened to the broker, he wouldn't have missed the dead body on their way out.

From where they stood, Jude got a good eyeful of a gaping neck and a naked body washed in blood.

Something the boy would never forget.

"When I said I wanted to show you this, it was 'cause I wanted you to know the job was done already. He's done. He paid for what he did to me. What he did to you. What he did to our mothers. You got that?"

Jude's eyes were wide as he stared at Miller, but he nodded.

"No reason to ever look back. Only look forward from here on out."

The boy was quiet and neither of them moved for about a minute.

But a clock was ticking in Shade's head. They had to move and soon, but he also knew the boy needed to process what he was seeing.

Still staring at Miller, Jude asked, "Will you go to jail for killing him?"

Shade stared down at the boy, who was taller than expected now that he wasn't crouching in a cage. "Not as long as you don't say shit. We keep this secret between the two of us."

Jude nodded and pressed his lips together. Then his eyes narrowed on the dead man. He began to walk toward the chair, catching Shade off guard.

"Hey, don't step in the blood. Gonna leave trackable footprints."

Jude acted like he didn't hear Shade and kept going, but he did stop just outside the pool of congealing blood.

It fucking shocked the shit out of Shade when the boy loudly snorted a hocker into his throat and then spit it onto Miller's slack face. Then he calmly walked back to Shade, his expression eerily blank.

"You know you splattered your DNA on that asshole."

Jude turned dark eyes up to Shade and shrugged. "I'm twelve. He was going to sell me to some butt-fucker. Nobody will care he's dead once they figure out what he's been doing. I'm sure they're going to find a whole bunch of questionable DNA in this house."

Shade's eyebrows shot up. "You sure you're only twelve?"

Jude raised his chin. "I'm twelve, not stupid."

Yeah, Shade remembered being twelve, the age he began to plot his escape from hell. "Let's go, kid."

"Where are we going?"

"Home."

Chapter Twenty-Four

SHADE ROLLED his sled around to the rear of the farmhouse. He'd given his prez the heads up he was on his way.

Trip stood on the porch waiting, his hands on his hips, his black baseball cap pulled low, but his head tilted as he watched Shade shut down his Night Train.

Shade yanked the skull bandana down his face and tucked his sunglasses into the pocket of the leather jacket he wore under his cut. He debated whether to wear his colors, wondering if he'd be allowed to keep them after disappearing without a word for two weeks.

Trip didn't look happy.

Shade wasn't surprised.

He was also surprised it was only Trip waiting on his porch. He expected it to be the whole executive committee.

"Should I get off?"

Shade turned his head to the boy who still held on to him. "Yeah."

Jude got off the Harley and Shade waited for him to remove the helmet and hand it to him. Shade dismounted and tucked the brain bucket he bought for Jude back in Georgia under his arm.

He would need to leave the helmet here for now. As long as Trip agreed to that.

Trip's eyes slid from Shade, landed on Jude and stayed there as he and the boy climbed the porch steps.

Shade jerked his chin toward the boy next to him. "This is Jude."

Trip didn't say a fucking word, so Shade continued. "Jude, this is my prez, Trip." He hoped to fuck Trip didn't say otherwise.

He had already given Jude the rundown on the MC. How it was set up, what he should expect and some things he might not expect, too.

Jude had listened and asked questions, both curious and anxious, but sad, too. The kid had cried every fucking night in each motel room they stayed in. Every fucking night. That meant every night Shade would have to find a hidden spot and smoke a bowl before they settled in bed so he could handle it.

The kid needed to cry, so Shade let him cry. It was just difficult to bear because he remembered how long he cried every night himself.

Only he was four at the time and it took a lot longer for Julian to comprehend what was happening and why it was happening.

Trip finally jutted a hand out and Jude stared at it for a second with uncertainty before shaking it. "Jude," Trip greeted.

Shade could see the club president brimming with questions, especially when he stared at the discoloration on Jude's cheek.

Jude shuffled from foot to foot.

Shade was surprised he wasn't doing the same. He scratched at his beard, trying to keep his shit together. "Stel here?"

Trip's dark eyes sliced to him. "Yeah."

Shade spoke slowly so he didn't fuck up his words with the way his pulse was rushing. "Think she could keep him company inside while we stay out here?"

Shade needed to explain himself but didn't want to do it in front of Jude. He'd already gone over the story with the kid a couple of times to make sure he understood it and why they needed it.

After a few seconds of silence, Trip nodded and went to the back door to yell inside for Stella. She appeared in the doorway in less than a minute, quickly masking her surprise at seeing a twelve-year-old boy she'd never seen before on her back porch.

Trip turned back to Shade before saying anything to his ol' lady. "He your son?"

"Yeah."

He didn't miss Stella's eyes go wide then narrowing after doing a bit of figuring in her head. It didn't help that Jude seemed tall for twelve.

"Stel, this is Shade's son, Jude," Trip announced. "Take him inside, yeah? Shade and I need to have a chat."

Stella forced her mouth into a smile as she held the door open for Jude. "C'mon in, Jude. It's a lot warmer in here."

Jude glanced at Shade and he gave the boy a slight nod. "Go with Stella. We won't be long."

"We'll come in when we're done," Trip assured the boy.

They waited until not only the screen door closed but also the main door. The whole time Trip's eyes were glued on Shade with his hands back on his hips. Once they heard the final click, Trip asked with his voice low, "How old is he?"

"Twelve."

Trip's eyebrows got lost under his ball cap. "Had him pretty young, then."

"Yeah."

"His mother?"

"Dead. Why I disappeared. Needed to go deal with that mess. Introduce myself to my kid. Get him to know me a bit before bringing him home."

He hated lying to his president, but it was his secret to keep. It was also Jude's. He asked Jude what story he wanted to go with long before they crossed the border into Pennsylvania.

They both figured it was easier to say Shade was his father instead of brother or uncle, so he'd automatically be the boy's guardian, no questions asked. Or at least, Shade hoped so.

He never wanted to be a father, never thought that was for him. But he'd watched Cage with Dyna. Judge with Daisy and Ry. Chelle with her girls.

He also knew how badly Trip wanted to have babies with Stella.

That would come. When Stella was ready.

Just like kids would come when Sig and Red were ready. Maybe even Deacon and Reese. But Shade couldn't see Reese with a baby on her hip. She was currently hyper-focused on her career.

Trip's next question snapped Shade back to the porch. "Where'd he get the bruise?"

"Evil stepdad. Asshole didn't want him once the mother was gone. Decided to call me. Told me to come get him or the state would." The lie slipped too easily off Shade's tongue.

However, Trip wasn't buying it. One thing Trip wasn't, was stupid. "Good thing he called you, then."

"Yeah. Good thing."

"Hopin' he got what was comin' to him for strikin' a kid."

"He did."

Trip nodded before glancing over his shoulder at the door through which Stella and Jude had disappeared. "Don't really look much like you."

"Takes after his mom."

Trip's dark gaze sliced back to Shade's and held it. "No badge-wearin' assholes are gonna show up here lookin' for him, right?"

"He's got no one but me." And that lie might end up actually being true. Shade hoped it wasn't, he hoped Jude had family out there who would want him. But what kind of family let a woman and her son live out of a fucking car with winter coming?

Blood who wasn't real family. They were only forced to be when necessary.

Like Shade's own father.

Trip glanced past Shade toward The Barn. Then his dark brown eyes moved to the left to where the pavilion stood, then even farther left, just past the tree line where Judge and Cassie's house had been built. In that direction, but out of view, was also the modular home where Cage, Jemma and their baby girl lived.

"You positive on that? Don't need the feds showin' up accusin' you of kidnappin'. Or worse."

"Hear you, prez."

Trip's gaze snapped back to him. "Won't be happy if the feds raid the place lookin' for an underaged boy."

Shade forced out a painful, "Ain't like that."

Trip rubbed at the dark wiry hairs on his chin. "Said that about Chelle, too. Have a feelin' you were also wrong in that case."

"He's mine," Shade said firmly.

"DNA test gonna prove it?"

Shade's mouth got tight. He needed to hold strong with his story. For Jude. So he didn't answer. And that was answer enough.

After a few uncomfortable moments, Trip finally nodded his head. "Just tell me havin' him here ain't gonna bring any heat."

Shade couldn't promise that, so he didn't. Instead, he made sure the words he said next also held what he couldn't say. He only hoped Trip would pick up on everything unsaid. "I'm all he's got."

Trip muttered a curse under his breath, ripped his ball cap off his head, raked his fingers through his hair and jammed it back on. He planted his hands on his hips again and dropped his gaze to his boots, his jaw working.

Shade didn't realize he was holding his breath until Trip said, "That ain't right."

He shot the club president a confused look.

Trip cleared up that confusion. "You ain't all he's got. He's got us."

Oh thank fucking fuck.

Shade's chest loosened a sliver and he could breathe slightly easier.

"Can't have him stayin' in the bunkhouse."

Shade expected that. "Yeah, know it."

"What're you gonna do? We can get you a modular like we did Cage. Set it up on the lot next to his place. Keep you two close." Trip always wanted everyone close. Preferably on the farm. He hated the fact Ozzy, Dodge and Dutch lived elsewhere. Also that Deacon spent most weeknights in Mansfield with Reese. The prez didn't like it, but he lived with it.

"Yeah, maybe..."

"What other choice you got?" Trip frowned. "Unless you're plannin' on buyin' out your membership? Leavin' us?"

Fuck no, not after Trip just welcomed Jude among them as family. "No. Ain't leavin'."

Trip didn't hide his relief. "Yeah. I mean, we're all family. Bein' a single dad's gonna be tough, but you got all of us to help."

"Not sure about that."

Trip's eyebrows pinched together. "About what?"

"About where we're gonna settle. Gotta talk to Chelle." He had also talked to Jude about Chelle and what she meant for their future, if she'd have them.

A smile spread slowly across the prez's face. "If she ever talks to you again."

"Yeah."

"Had her worried."

"Didn't mean to."

"Shoulda told her where you were goin' or where you were after you got there. Or maybe answered your fuckin' phone when we called you or when she did."

"Couldn't find my phone."

"Right. Guess you found it once you hit the town limits since you texted me not even fifteen minutes out."

Yep, Trip was far from stupid.

"Didn't mean to leave without a word," Shade lied.

"Yeah you did."

The cool late October air flooded Shade's lungs with a sharp inhale.

"Look, we all got our shit. Every fuckin' single one of us. Got that you had to deal with some of yours. But next time you do, clue us in first. 'Specially after what happened up on Hillbilly Hill. We all went searchin' for you again, thinkin' you stopped breathin' up there and thinkin' we'd have to escalate the Clan Plan."

"Didn't mean to make anyone worry."

Trip ignored that and kept rolling. "Rook and Easy have been goin' up doin' some recon, lookin' for some signs of you. Or what was left of you. You might wish they found you dead once they find out they did all that fuckin' work for nothin'." Trip surprised Shade when he laughed. "Just so you know, you also drove Judge fuckin' nuts with him not bein' able to track your ass. Figurin' that's why your phone got *lost*. Also didn't help that Cassie was worried the whole time, too. So, he had to deal with her stressin' over you, which got him even more worked up. Don't be surprised if the giant ain't so gentle on your ass 'cause of that. Might wanna have your kid with you the next time you see him. This way he don't use the club hangin' in The Barn on you like he did Cage."

One side of Shade's mouth pulled up. "Got it."

"Now my balls are fuckin' turnin' blue." He tilted his head toward the door. "We done talkin' out here?"

"Yeah."

"Figure out your shit and lemme know what your plan is either way. Figurin' you haven't talked to Chelle yet."

"Headin' there next."

"Yeah, well, hide your crazy-assed knives so she don't grab one and cut off your nuts before you get to explain."

"Made a whole bunch of people unhappy," he muttered.

"All except one," Trip pulled open the screen door, "that kid inside."

Trip pushed open the custom-made wood door and Shade followed him into the kitchen where Stella was leaning back against the counter talking softly to Jude who sat at the table Trip's grandfather built by hand.

In that instant, Shade could imagine Trip's sons sitting at that same table just like Jude was.

By the look in Stella's eyes, Shade had a feeling Stella could see it, too. Because the warm look she gave Trip said a lot. So much so, Shade kind of felt bad for what he needed to ask next of the couple.

If they agreed, they would have to hold off going upstairs and working on making those babies. If they even made it that far.

Shade had a feeling they did a lot more than eat on that sturdy table.

"You good?" he asked Jude. After he got an answering nod, he turned to Trip's ol' lady. "Askin' if you can watch him for a little while, while I go deal with Chelle."

Stella glanced at Jude. "Are you hungry?"

"I could eat," Jude answered with a grin.

Stella turned back to Shade. "He could eat."

"Not surprisin'," Shade muttered. The boy was a bottomless pit. Shade had been going broke feeding him on the trip from Georgia to Pennsylvania. Grief had not made him lose his damn appetite.

He also dropped a wad of scratch when he bought Jude a prepaid cell phone, some clothes and a pair of sneakers. Shit he'd probably outgrow quickly as much as he ate.

Stella clapped her hands together once and announced, "Trip will make his famous pancakes."

"With bacon?" Jude asked, his eyes lighting up.

"Fuck yeah, with bacon. Who eats pancakes without bacon?" Trip said. "Nobody I know."

"Hopefully you got a whole pound of bacon," Shade warned.

"Amish dropped off a whole shitload yesterday. Snagged a couple pounds outta the bunkhouse cooler before it disappeared."

"There you go. Fresh from the pig," Shade told Jude. "You eat and I'll be back as soon as I can."

"Where you going?"

"To figure out where we're goin'."

Jude nodded, remembering their discussion about Chelle. "Good luck."

"Gonna need it, kid."

As he turned to leave, Stella called out, "Might want to wear a cup, Shade."

He shook his head and walked out the door, hoping to fuck he didn't. He'd find out soon enough.

———

THAT COULDN'T BE RIGHT. Chelle's eyes must be deceiving her. She'd wanted to see what she thought she was seeing so badly she now imagined it.

Like a mirage.

That was all it was. She was conjuring up that bike in her driveway. The man sitting on the seat sideways, the kickstand down, his ankles crossed and his arms folded over his leather-clad chest was only an illusion. She was only dreaming his head was tipped down, hiding his profile with his long, loose, curly hair.

Her pulse rushed.

Yes, she had to be seeing things.

Because there was no way the man in her driveway, the one who disappeared for two weeks without a word, would simply show up without warning.

The man who left her alone in her bed with only a text that said "Love you," to keep her company.

The man who made her sick to her stomach with worry thinking he was lying somewhere dead. Alone. Somewhere where his brothers—who kept searching for him, because they also worried—couldn't find him.

Yes, she had to be imagining him in her driveway.

Just to be sure, she smashed her foot on her Subaru's accelerator, making the tires chirp as she swung her station wagon like a mad woman into her driveway. She slammed on the brakes next to the motorcycle that kept showing up in her dreams.

She didn't even take the time to park her car in the garage. She barely took the time to shut off the engine, or even make sure it was in Park, before she kicked the driver's door open and bolted from the seat.

He barely got to his feet in time before she hit him.

Not with a stinging smack across his face, since he deserved that for disappearing for two whole weeks. No, she hit him full force with her body instead, almost knocking him backwards with the impact.

Her hand clamped around the back of his neck, the other drove roughly into his curls at the back of his head, fisting his hair tightly. Then she hit him with her mouth.

He accepted her tongue, her whimper and then the sob that rushed up from the bottom of her gut.

She didn't let go. Not of his mouth, not of his neck, not of his hair, for the longest time. Not that he fought to be free. Instead, he clutched her ass with both hands and lifted her against him until she was practically on her toes.

The deep, gaping hole in her chest began to fill. With warmth and relief, and so much more.

She had the urge to hit him, to weep, to laugh and then hit him again.

She did none of that. She only kept kissing him and holding on because she was afraid this was all a fantasy.

That he wasn't really here. Or if she let go, he'd disappear.

That was when she realized *why* he'd left without warning. He didn't tell her because she never would've let him go. Wherever he went, whatever he did, she would've tried to convince him not to go there, not to do what he felt needed to be done.

The hard truth was, that wasn't her decision. It was his alone.

Hopefully, whatever the reason why he left was done and he was back for good.

She reluctantly released his mouth when he pulled back slightly. Only enough so they could both breathe.

She tipped her head back a little more, hoping the thought that popped into her head was wrong. "Wait. You're not here to say goodbye, are you?"

"Not unless you want me to."

It had been only two weeks and she couldn't believe how much she'd missed his voice. Gravel coated in honey. *God,* she'd missed him desperately.

So, no, him leaving was not what she wanted. "I can assure you, if I wanted that, I wouldn't have greeted you the way I did."

"Just sayin', better not be greetin' other men like that. Crushin' your tits into their chest, your mouth doin' its magic and then slippin' them the tongue. Givin' them a hard-on like I got now."

She raised her eyebrows and feigned shock. "Oh, I might have to apologize to the dishwasher repairman."

"Not funny, Chelle," he growled.

"Neither was you disappearing like that."

He pressed his forehead to hers and breathed, "Yeah." A couple pounding beats of her heart later he added softly, "Didn't mean to worry you."

"But you did. I expect you won't do it again. My heart can't take it." She pressed her face into his neck and clung to him tightly, her hands fisting in the thermal shirt he wore under the two layers of black leather. A jacket and his cut. "I thought I was never getting a chance to say goodbye."

"It wasn't a goodbye."

"But I didn't know that. Don't make me live through that ever again. Please. If you plan to just up and leave one day, please say goodbye first. It'll hurt, but I would need to see you one last time."

"Not sayin' goodbye, Chelle. Ain't ever sayin' goodbye. Leavin' you would be like carving away a piece of me."

She wanted to believe that. But after the last time... "You left without a word." She didn't bother to hide the hurt in her accusation. His disappearance had upset her, and he needed to know just how much.

"Sent you a text."

"That said nothing."

"Said a lot."

"Not enough, Shade. It wasn't enough."

"It was everythin'."

It might have been everything to him, but he didn't tell her in person and those two words, as much as they meant to her, didn't make up for the worry and fear of finding out he loved her and then him simply disappearing like he didn't.

She needed to explain. "I never got to say goodbye to Brendan. You have to understand that was the hardest part for me. It still is. If I had one more minute with him... Even for the chance to say goodbye... You left without a goodbye after texting me you loved me."

He sucked in a breath. "Chelle..."

"You never got to say goodbye to your mother, either, did you?"

With flared nostrils, he stared over her head instead of answering. His reaction was her answer.

"So, you know how that feels. You were only four when you were ripped from her. Only a year older than Josie was when she lost her father. At least my girls had me. My brothers' family. You had no one. I'm still amazed you survived."

"Almost didn't."

True. He almost didn't.

Her fingers circled his left wrist over the wide leather band and she lifted it to her lips. "Sometimes you just need to be free of the pain. I'm not sorry you survived, but I am sorry to do so, you had to continue to suffer. I want to say living was worth it, but only you can determine that."

He pulled his wrist from her fingers and cupped her face. She tilted her head and rubbed her cheek against his warm palm.

"Took a long time for it to be worth it."

"When you were freed at seventeen?"

He shook his head. "At twenty-eight."

"What happened when you were twenty-eight?"

"Found my family."

"Your club."

"And now you. Sorry I couldn't explain, but it's best you don't know."

She released a long sigh. "That worries me."

"Best you don't know," he repeated.

"I'm always going to wonder."

"Chelle." Her name came out as warning.

He didn't want her to push, so she wouldn't. She pressed her palm to his chest instead. "Okay. So, give me a good reason why I should forgive you for leaving the way you did?"

"Don't gotta forgive me, beautiful. But know it's done and over. At least what I set out to do. Needed to finish a previous chapter before startin' a new one."

She pinned her eyebrows together. "A new one... With me?"

"With you, the girls..." An uneasy look crossed his face. "Problem is, wasn't expectin' to discover some shit that I did about my father. Might have to deal with that later."

She frowned. "But not now."

He shook his head. "Not now. Got somethin' else to deal with first. Someone else."

"What do you mean?"

"Before I closed that last chapter, stumbled upon a new endin'."

What was he talking about?

Before she could ask, he continued, "Or maybe it's a new beginnin'. Don't know, never read a book yet."

"You will."

"Maybe. Or can just have you read them to me."

"Or you can listen to audiobooks." She made it sound like she was teasing him, but, in truth, him listening to audiobooks and reading along with the narrator would be good for him.

"Would rather listen to you."

"I'd rather hear your explanation on this new ending. Or new beginning."

"Got a lot to talk about, maybe we should go inside so you can sit down."

What? "Oh no. Now you need to explain this second. I'm not moving until you do."

"Ain't you cold?"

"Shade!"

"At least sit on my sled—"

"Shade!" She wasn't moving an inch until he was done talking.

In the end, Chelle knew he skipped over a lot of details. Like the main reason he was in that house in Georgia and what else happened while he was there besides finding a twelve-year-old boy in a cage. Goosebumps broke out along her skin and it wasn't from the chill in the late October air. It was from the little he did tell her and everything he omitted.

But from what he did say, she knew he went to revisit his past. To seal whatever doors he needed permanently shut. He couldn't move forward until he did that.

Not only for himself but for her. For their future together.

Even so, if she'd known what he had planned, her realization of why he left without a word was correct. She would've fought like crazy for him not to go. One reason being she was sure for him it was like stepping back into the depths of hell.

A hell she wanted to protect him from, even though that might never be possible.

But in the heavy darkness he revisited, he'd become the light.

For a boy who had been stolen. Just like Julian.

"He's stayin' with me... With the club... With us."

"For good?"

"If I can't find his family."

"He has family, Shade."

He frowned. "What?"

"He's got us."

Shade squeezed his eyes shut and whispered, "Fuck, Chelle."

"Isn't that why you brought him home?"

"Home," he breathed, opening his eyes. "Yeah." He went on to explain the conversation he had with Jude about Shade acting as his father and also the conversation he had with Trip.

"Did Trip believe you?"

"Don't think so."

"Will that be a problem for us?"

The corners of his lips curled slightly, and he didn't hide his relief as he repeated, "Us. No, ain't gonna be a problem for *us*. What about your girls?"

"You tell me." Shade knew them well enough now, knew what they were like. And they loved him. Chelle had made up an excuse on why he'd disappeared but promised them he'd be back. At the time, she only hoped that was true.

"Knowin' your girls, ain't gonna be a problem for them, either."

"They always teased me about giving them a little brother. After getting my tubes tied, I never thought I'd become a mother again."

"Might not be easy. He's a twelve-year-old kid who's gonna go through some shit."

"We all go through stuff. And who would understand those things better than you? Are you sure his mother's not out there somewhere?"

Shade blew a breath through his nostrils. "No. Hope to fuck I'm wrong. Hope she escaped or they took pity on her. Somethin'. But from the info I got, not lookin' likely."

"If it happened the way you think it happened, does he

know those details?"

Shade's jaws flexed. "No. Gonna try to shield him from that as long as possible."

"What did you tell him instead?"

"That she accidentally died when she was fightin' them. She slipped tryin' to escape and hit her head on the concrete. Died instantly."

"What really happened to her?"

"Chelle..."

"She didn't die instantly."

His lips pressed into a flat line.

What happened to Jude's mother must be bad, since Shade wasn't sharing those details with her, either. Chelle closed her eyes as her stomach turned. Jude's mother was most likely tortured.

Tortured.

Why was the Earth so full of sick people? What ever happened to humanity? Or had she been living in a bubble? She couldn't wrap her head around all the evil in the world.

Not that she wanted to.

It was bad enough she lost her husband to it.

Shade lost his mother to it. Lost himself for a long time to it, too.

Now Jude was motherless because of it.

No, she didn't want to understand it. She only wished things like that, people like them, didn't exist.

Most likely that wish would never come true.

"Gonna keep lookin', just in case. But thinkin' he's now an orphan."

"Like you were."

"Yeah, Chelle, just like me."

She slapped a hand over her mouth when what he just said and how he said it hit her. "Oh no," she breathed.

Shade shook his head. "Found him before that happened. He got lucky, in a way. Lost his mom but didn't lose anythin' else."

"Oh, thank goodness," she whispered. "I'm still heart-broken that he lost his mother. That has to be devastating for him. But I'm so thankful you found him."

"He's tryin' to be tough about it. But every night I hear him cryin', usin' his pillow to smother the sound."

"I don't even know him yet and I want to hug away his pain."

"Gonna meet him. And then you can hug him. He's gonna need it. From you and from the girls. So, here's the deal... Askin' you to accept us both. A package deal."

He felt the need to ask? "That's not even a question, Shade."

"'Kay then. Next problem..."

She groaned. "There's more?"

"Yeah, this is a big one. Jude can't live in the bunkhouse with me."

How was that a problem? "Were you planning on remaining in the bunkhouse?"

"We either live here with you or I get us a house on the farm. Trip prefers the second choice."

"And if I don't prefer that choice?" she asked. That was a decision for her and Shade to make, not the Blood Fury's president.

"Want what you want."

That was too easy. "I want you."

"Want you, too, beautiful. Nothin' I want more. Leavin' the decision up to you. Want you and the girls to be happy. Don't wanna disrupt their lives. Also, wasn't expectin' to dump a surprise kid on you in addition to you dealin' with my problems."

"I can deal with a surprise kid. I can deal with your problems now that I know what causes them. My concern about living on the farm comes down to my girls. And honestly, the fact your club has sweet butts and who those women are."

If he was surprised at that last part, he didn't show it. "Know my family ain't typical, Chelle, I get it. Includin' the sweet butts and why they're a part of the club. But my brotherhood's tight and it's all I got."

"No, you now have me."

"Your daughters..."

"Love you. They already accept you for who you are. They're smart and level-headed and old enough to see what's in front of them. As much as I wouldn't want them to be in Angel or Crystal's shoes, I also don't want my girls judging them. Angel and Crystal chose to be who they are, what they are, to do what they do. I understand they're not forced. You made it clear that they could walk away at any time, but choose to remain. Too many of us women cut each other down instead of lifting each other up. I don't want my daughters to ever be like that. I want every woman to feel empowered enough to be who they are without fear or judgement. Maybe it'll never happen because it's against human nature." She shrugged. "I don't know. But my hope is for my girls to live in a more accepting and inclusive world. Or at least do their part to make that closer to reality." She lifted a palm when he opened his mouth to speak. "That being said... The problem is, Maddie used to be friends with Angel. My daughters know Crystal, too. I don't want there to be issues between them or for my girls to get any ideas about doing what they do. Maybe once they're out on their own, we can consider moving out to the farm. But for now... I want to keep this house as our home."

"You includin' me and Jude? Or should me and him get our own place on the farm?"

"No. I thought you wanted us to be a family. All of us. I figured you'd want help with Jude."

"Yeah, beautiful, help would be good since I don't know shit about kids."

"You're good with mine."

"They ain't kids. They're young women. There's a difference." He hesitated, then asked, "What about Rick? He gonna give you shit?"

Yes, her brother and his need to overprotect her and the girls.

"He'll either understand or he won't. I'll love him the same either way. I just ask that you give him a chance to accept you."

"Think he ever will? Don't wanna cause problems between you and your brother."

"It's not you causing the problem, it's him. He worries about me and the girls and I love him for that, but once he sees you for who you really are, I have no doubt he'll come around." She was done talking about her stubborn brother. That wasn't a problem they'd solve today. "Now, how soon are you bringing Jude here to his new home?"

Shade shook his head, his eyes serious. "Seen a lot of fuckin' evil humans in my life, Chelle. Also met some good people. You, beautiful, are one of the fuckin' best. So lucky to have met you."

The damaged biker standing before her had his sweet moments and she cherished every single one of them. "Thank Pumpkin."

It was hard to believe that the day she put her cat down, she met the man she hoped to spend the rest of her life with. He might not be perfect, but he was perfectly imperfect for her.

Fate was funny like that.

"Gonna go grab Jude."

"I want to go with you." She was not letting Shade out of her sight. Not yet. "Put your *sled* in the garage and we'll take my car."

"Cage."

She smiled. "Yes, my *cage*."

"Gonna make a great ol' lady."

"Do I get to wear one of those 'property of' cuts like the other ol' ladies wore on the run?"

"You want one?"

"Hell yes! They're badass! And I want everyone to know who you belong to."

"Supposed to be the other way around."

She arched an eyebrow. "Is it?"

He shook his head and smothered his grin.

She grabbed his arm as he turned to put his bike inside. "Hey…"

He paused and glanced back over his shoulder. She tugged on his arm and he turned toward her again.

"Come here," she whispered, tilting her face up to him. He lowered his until their mouths were only a fraction apart.

"Yeah, beautiful?"

"I never responded to your text."

"Noticed that."

"That's because I wanted to tell you in person," she whispered.

"I'm listenin'," he whispered back.

"I love you, too."

Epilogue

FOUND

CHELLE STOOD in front of the French doors and watched flurries fall from the sky, leaving a blanket of white wonder over her favorite part of her home. Her backyard. Her haven. Where her two previously lost souls sometimes tossed a football around when it wasn't too cold.

Jude was teaching Shade how to throw one, though the boy wasn't much better than his "dad," who had never touched a football before in his life.

He'd missed all that.

Even though it could sometimes be awkwardly comical, it helped the two of them forget the reason why they'd met in the first place. If only temporarily.

To get him enrolled in school, Ozzy, on the sly, put Shade in contact with someone who made fake documents. Julian Jones was now on Jude's new birth certificate as the boy's father. They used Jude's mother's real name with the slim hope she was still out there somewhere and she'd resurface one day. Unfortunately, Shade doubted she would.

Chelle constantly scoured online news for any mention of his mother. So far, nothing. No body found, no obituary, no Jane Doe matching her description, nothing.

Even if she was never found, Jude would always have a home with them. But he'd always wonder.

While she searched for Jude's mother, she'd also spend her lunch hour searching articles for Shade's mother, too.

It took her a few weeks, but she finally found something. Not what she hoped, but what she expected.

She kept her eyes on the falling snow as the bedroom door closed behind Shade.

She had asked him to come up to their bedroom for privacy. He probably thought it was for one reason, when it was actually for a completely different one.

She considered waiting to tell him until after Christmas, but Shade couldn't care less about the holidays. It wasn't like he had an opportunity to enjoy them while growing up.

He'd missed out on putting out milk and cookies for Santa, drinking eggnog, decorating an evergreen and waking up early on Christmas morning to rip open gifts. He'd also missed out on holiday meals with family.

Until this year. Trip and Stella decided to start new traditions for the holidays, starting with Thanksgiving dinner on the farm in The Barn. Lots of food, alcohol and, of course, weed. But best of all, lots of laughter, good-natured ribbing, aka busting balls, smiles and fun. Also, plenty of full bellies after the traditional turkey dinner delivered already prepared by the Amish. Homemade pies, free-range roasted turkey, stuffing, fresh cranberry relish and more.

Luckily, Thanksgiving dinner hadn't been an "anything goes" type of party that the club typically had, it consisted of only the patched members, their ol' ladies, their kids and even the prospects. No sweet butts, no hang-arounds, no one but the Fury family. It was truly a "family dinner."

So, she, Shade and Jude went and both Josie and Maddie joined them. Her girls fought over cuddling with Dyna until she needed her diaper changed, of course. Then they had no problem passing her back to Jemma or Tessa. Or even Cage.

Chelle smothered a giggle while watching a badass-looking biker wipe poopy baby butt like an expert. While it was funny, the faces and sounds Cage made to his baby girl to entertain Dyna while he did the dirty deed was endearing.

Chelle witnessed the fact that no matter how tough these bikers were on the outside, they had ooey-gooey centers when dealing with their daughters. She saw it not only with Cage, but with Judge and Daisy.

Chelle turned her thoughts to the package that came early this morning. She'd been waiting for it to be delivered before telling Shade what she'd found.

He stepped behind her and wrapped his arms around her waist, pulling her against him and nudging her hair out of the way to kiss the tender spot where her shoulder and neck met. One hand firmly and possessively cupped her between the thighs and the other her breast.

His actions and the erection he pressed against her ass proved she was right. He thought she asked him upstairs for a quickie.

They might have time for that before they had to leave for the club's Christmas party, but his desire for sex might be squashed after she delivered the news she'd been struggling to keep to herself.

She turned in his arms and planted her palms on his chest. He wore a black long-sleeved thermal shirt which fit him like a second skin along with a pair of worn blue jeans. No boots yet, no belt, no cut. It wouldn't take long for him to get naked.

While she was tempted to put off her news by having the quickie first, she wanted to get it over with.

"I love you," she whispered.

She caught his confusion before he masked it. "Love you, too."

"I need you to sit down."

The confusion was back, but he didn't hide it this time. "Don't wanna sit down. Came up here to fuck you. Unless you want me to sit on the bed so you can ride my dick?"

"I want you to sit on the bed but keep your pants on for now."

He frowned and his hands slid to her hips. "Gonna do a striptease?"

"Not right now."

"Later?"

She avoided rolling her eyes. "Shade, sit down."

"Not likin' this."

She sighed. "Please."

"Jude do somethin'?"

"No."

"I do somethin'?"

"No." She pulled out her bossy mom voice. "Sit."

He reluctantly released her hips and moved to the bed. He stared at it for a few seconds before turning and sitting on the edge.

"I know you didn't want a Christmas gift, but I wanted to do something for you anyway."

"A striptease woulda been good."

She would've laughed but his brow was wrinkled, and he appeared a bit worried. She quickly grabbed her laptop and sat down on the bed, putting it between them.

"We watchin' porn?"

She glanced at him in surprise. "You want to?"

"Want whatever you want."

She shook her head and opened her laptop. "I don't need porn to get turned on. You turn me on by simply coming out of the shower naked and wet."

"Yeah?" He finally smiled but it was lopsided.

She finally let her eyes roll. Hard. "Like you don't know how freaking hot you are."

"Need to tell me more often."

"I show you all the time."

He tilted his head and grinned. "Yeah."

After another quick eye roll, she pulled up the article she had found. She knew he wouldn't read it. It would take too long for him to make out all of the words. They didn't have the time for that and he'd end up frustrated anyway.

"What's that?" He leaned closer and stared at the composite drawing of a woman below the bold heading of the article. It was the kind of drawing police used to identify unknown people.

"What the fuck," he whispered. His eyes went from the woman to her, then back to the woman. "What the fuck, Chelle?"

"Do you want me to read the article to you?"

He didn't answer right away. He only stared at the drawing, then reached out to trace the woman's face with his finger.

That just about cracked her heart in half. She needed to keep herself together.

"Don't know," he whispered.

The uncertainty in his voice made her heart break even more. "I don't have to read it. I can give you a summary, if you want."

He closed his eyes and took a couple of deep breaths. When he opened his eyes again, he shook his head. She could actually hear him swallow. "Read it."

Chelle had to brace herself to read it again. She'd already read it several times and every time she had, she cried for Shade. She cried for Cecelia Bennett.

She cried for Julian Bennett, too. The little boy lost.

"I'm going to do my best to get through it without stopping, but if you need me to stop, tell me."

He didn't answer, only continued to stare at the screen.

She started with the headline of the article and began to read. She did it slowly, which allowed him to follow along if he wanted to and, if not, it made it easier for him to process the words as she read.

Cecelia Bennett had been originally found as a Jane Doe in an alley in Newark, New Jersey. She had track marks in her arms, her legs, in the webbing of her fingers and in between her toes. She'd been found with both recent and old bruises. Her cause of death was a heroin overdose.

Once she was identified by her dental records, law enforcement pieced together that she was the young mother who'd disappeared from a shopping mall with no sign of her, her four-year-old son Julian Bennett, or even their vehicle. Her empty minivan was discovered much later at the bottom of a nearby lake.

The article went on to say no family ever came forward to claim her body, so a Newark funeral home cremated her and put her ashes in the storage closet where they kept unclaimed cremains.

The last paragraph stated her son was never found and was presumed dead. Records showed Cecelia Bennett never married and no father was listed on Julian's birth certificate.

While he hadn't stopped her from reading, he also hadn't made a sound, not even a noise. She wiped away the single tear that had slipped from her eye before turning to face him. His eyelids were shut tightly and his fingertips dug deep into his thighs.

"You okay?"

"Yeah... No." He shook his head. "Don't know."

She placed her hand over his and squeezed. "Do you want to talk about it?"

"Not sure."

"There's a phone number at the bottom of the article for anyone who knows anything about her death, the abduction or Julian's whereabouts." She watched his face carefully when she asked, "Do you want to come forward?"

His jaw worked for a few seconds. When he finally twisted his head, his almost black eyes hit hers. "No. That life is over. This is my life now."

"You might have relatives..."

"That life's over, Chelle."

She nodded, but wasn't sure how true that was.

Over or not, she wasn't done yet. "This bad news wasn't your present, Shade. Because that would really suck for a Christmas gift."

"Wouldn't know."

"Trust me."

"Always," he answered instantly and automatically, like he always did when she said those two words. The first time she ever told him to trust her, he had quickly answered with "always," catching her off guard. While the saying became a habit with having kids, she never thought anyone took it literally.

Shade did.

"I called the funeral home." She released his hand and closed her laptop. "I filled out the paperwork to claim her ashes and I paid for her cremation so they'd release them." She got to her feet, feeling his eyes following her as she moved across their bedroom to her closet. One he never used since he had his own. "They shipped them to me."

She slid open the closet door and grabbed what she had hidden behind a few boxes of shoes. When she turned, his gaze dropped from her face to what she held in her hands. An urn.

Not just any urn. She had picked a pretty red and gold metal one. A gold pendant hung around the neck of it, engraved with his mother's name and the dates of her birth and death.

"Bet they don't put unclaimed ashes in somethin' like that."

"No," was all she said.

His mother deserved something nice after all the ugly she'd experienced. Even if it was after her death. Shade could keep her ashes or spread them, it was up to him.

It might not be a traditional Christmas gift, but at least in some way, she had finally reunited mother and son.

It had been a long, painful twenty-six years apart.

"I only wish the reunion with your mother had gone differently."

"Chelle." He got to his feet and came to her. "Don't know what to say."

"You don't have to say anything."

"Didn't get you a present."

"I got what I wanted already. I have you. I have Jude. My girls are healthy and happy. I don't need anything else."

"Will get you a kitten."

She smiled. "I think Jude would rather have a dog."

"Jude will get a dog, you'll get your kitten."

"After the holidays, we'll go to the Humane Society and pick out one of each. A lot of them are dumped around Christmas. Older dogs beforehand to make room for a new puppy, puppies afterward for being too much work." He didn't need that lecture right now or even at all. He'd never give up on something or someone he loved. He hadn't felt love since he was four and not again until recently, so he knew how priceless it was. She lifted the urn. "Where do you want her?"

"Not where she can watch us."

She rolled her lips under for a second before saying, "Good idea. Then you better put her somewhere where she can't watch you giving me your gift." The man definitely had a gift when it came to pleasuring her. They could squeeze in a quickie if he still wanted it.

He took the urn from her, studied the engraved pendant, took an audible breath, then nodded. "Yeah, need to thank you properly. Also need to come inside you before the party, make sure anyone with a dick knows who you belong to."

"I think everyone knows already." She leaned into him. "Maybe I need to claim you instead. Make sure all the women know who you belong to."

"Only got eyes for you, beautiful."

She believed it. She tilted her head toward the urn in his hands. "Can you...?"

He jerked into motion and put the urn back in the closet, this time on the top shelf. He closed the door. "Just for now. Will figure out what I want to do with the ashes later."

"When you're ready."

He frowned. "Is it fucked up I wanna fuck you even with my mother in the closet?"

"Probably, but I won't tell if you won't."

"Good at keepin' secrets."

That was very true. He was.

"We got time to fuck before we gotta leave?"

They would make the time if that's what he wanted. "For a quickie. Where are the kids?"

"When I came up, Josie was playin' a video game with Jude. Maddie said she'd meet us there."

She glanced at the clock next to the bed. "We might be late."

"Beautiful, you think you need to arrive on time to a club party?"

She giggled. "If it was anything like Thanksgiving dinner? No."

"That's a fuck no."

"Then it's a fuck yes to you giving me your special gift. Did you lock the door?"

He went over to the door and pushed the lock on the knob. "Yep."

"Then why are you still dressed?"

He yanked his thermal shirt over his head and dropped his jeans and boxer briefs just as quickly. He still hid his scars from the kids but not from her. "Ain't dressed. You are. Makin' me think you don't want my dick."

"You'd be wrong."

His eyes narrowed. "Prove it."

She proved it.

They only ended up being an hour late for the Christmas party.

———

SHADE STOOD where he could observe the family who now belonged to him.

Where he could keep one eye on Maddie and one on Josie. Where he could do a quick scan of The Barn to easily find Chelle and also Jude.

They were already two hours into the club's first official Christmas party, not counting the hour they were late because he got lost in a naked Chelle and took his time filling her up with him and his cum.

Every once in a while she'd stop what she was doing—whether she was checking on Jude, talking to her daughters or getting pulled into a huddle with the Fury sisterhood—and look for him. Once she located him, she'd give him a small smile.

A smile that held secrets only meant for him.

He would lift his chin only enough for her to notice and she'd go back to doing whatever she was doing still wearing that smile.

He wished this fucking party was over so he could take her home and fuck her again.

But she fit in well with the sisterhood and he was relieved about that. Not that he doubted she would. She pretty much got along with everyone.

It was also good for Jude to feel included in the Fury family. Ozzy was teaching him to play pool. Once the kid mastered that, darts were next on his list of useless skills to learn.

Jude recently asked Shade if he could hang out at the garage so he could learn to work on vehicles. Dutch said he could become an apprentice and he'd teach Jude to turn a wrench just like he taught Rook and Cage. Shade read between the lines. Dutch would be happy to have some free labor.

What Dutch didn't know yet, was Jude wouldn't be working for free. He'd make something helping the old man out after school, even if it was only enough to buy more expensive video games.

For the most part, Jude was happy, but sometimes he'd still lock himself in his room and, if they listened carefully enough, Chelle and Shade could hear him crying.

They let him work it out in private. Eventually, he'd come back out of his room and act like it never happened. The only evidence being his still red eyes and nose. They didn't push him. If Jude needed to talk, he usually went to Josie since she was old enough to understand since she had lost a parent, too, but not too old in Jude's eyes.

Because of that, Shade had to clue Josie in on a few details but not the complete truth. The pact between him, Jude and Chelle was that no one ever admitted Shade wasn't his real father. If it slipped, they were afraid Jude would end up in the state's hands. It was a secret they'd have to keep until he was at least eighteen, if not longer.

Unless Shade found his mother first.

Unfortunately, he doubted Jude's mother would ever be found.

Shade lifted his head and watched a curvy blonde break away from Stella and Red and head in his direction. The woman had hips and an ass that moved in a way that made it just about impossible for anyone with a dick to not stop and appreciate.

Most of his brothers tried to hide the fact they were watching, since Cassie's ol' man wasn't one to appreciate all of them doing that appreciating.

She stopped in front of him and smiled.

That smile was trouble.

Even so, he'd go along with whatever game she was playing. "Know I love you, right?"

She bumped her shoulder with his. "Doesn't mean I'm still not mad at you."

"Been weeks," he reminded her.

Cassie had broken down in tears the first time she saw him after he got back from Georgia. She had squeezed him so tightly, he thought she would break his ribs.

She plucked at a strand of her long, blonde hair. "I can't forgive you since you caused a streak of gray. And you drove Chelle out of her mind with worry. We all freaked out. But, yes, I know you love me. Just don't let my ol' man hear you say that. I'd give you another bone-crushing hug but I'm sure Judge is watchin us."

Shade found the club's enforcer. Of fucking course he was watching. "Good reason to do it, then."

He grabbed her and pulled her into his arms. The first time Cassie ever hugged him, it had made him stiffen and feel uncomfortable. He wasn't used to someone being so openly warm and touchy-feely.

But since working with her at the crematorium for so long, he was now used to the way she was. He no longer fought her hugs. He tolerated them.

Right.

He more than tolerated them. He just didn't tell her that.

When she gave him her signature Cassie-hug, he put his mouth to her ear and whispered, "Know you know."

She pushed him away, trying to hide her surprise. She failed. "I don't know what you're talking about," she lied and pointed to her head. "I'm blonde. I forget things very easily."

He shot her a look. That was complete bullshit. "Thanks for keepin' that shit to yourself."

"Again, I don't know what you're talking about, Shade." She shrugged. "See? I've even already forgotten this conversation." She leaned toward him and whispered, "You could've told me. I would've helped. Still can, if you want."

"Got it covered with Chelle and the girls."

"They're great," she said with a big, easy smile. "Seeing how responsible and mature Josie and Maddie are gives me hope for Daisy."

"Wouldn't go that far," he teased. Daisy would always be a handful. She would drive some man crazy when she was old enough.

Thank fuck it wasn't him.

Cassie bumped his shoulder playfully again. "When are you claiming Chelle at the table?"

This wasn't the first time Cassie bugged him about it, but he gave her the same answer he always did. "Don't know."

"Have you asked her yet?"

Why was she pushing this today? "No, but she mentioned it earlier. "

A sly smile crossed her face. "Just so you know, we already got her a 'Property of' cut so don't make us rip her name patch off the front and give it to someone else."

Jesus fuck. The women were taking matters into their own hands. Meddling, what they did best.

"What did you get her for Christmas?" When he didn't answer, she breathed, "Shade."

Now he felt like a total fucking piece of shit since Chelle had found his mother and got him her ashes. Gifts and holidays were new to him. He didn't know what was expected. "Not good with that shit," he muttered.

"Then good thing we ladies are. Give her the cut tomorrow morning for Christmas. We already have it boxed and wrapped in Christmas paper with a big bow. When you give it to her, ask her if she'll accept being your ol' lady and when she says yes—and she'll say yes—take it to the table."

Boxed and wrapped? Chelle would know he didn't do any of that shit.

"That wasn't a suggestion," Cassie said in a low warning.

He snorted. "Yes, boss."

She winked at him. "Now, if I could only make that tall, bearded grumpy-looking guy over there—the one scowling at us—call me boss, my Christmas would be made."

"Hold out 'til he does."

Cassie bugged out her pretty brown eyes at him. "I'm not holding out from all that giant goodness!"

Shade barked out a laugh.

"Good to hear you laugh, Shade. Seriously. I'm going to go hug Chelle and thank her."

"Don't you fuckin' dare."

She wiggled her eyebrows and walked away.

Fuck.

He quickly scanned the floor again, searching for Chelle's girls. He found Josie now leaning against one of the pool tables, a cue stick in her hand, a flirty smile on her face as she gazed up at a much taller Ry.

Judge's son had headed back to school after Thanksgiving break and now was home until January.

Why he wasn't chasing Saylor, Shade didn't know. He

spotted Judge's house mouse and Rev's younger sister standing by the bar, her arms crossed over her chest and her narrowed eyes pinned on Josie and Ry.

That wasn't good.

He figured he'd better break up the little flirt-fest because at nineteen, Ry was probably nailing anything with a warm hole.

Shade wanted to guarantee Josie wouldn't be one of them.

He got stopped in his tracks by Easy's loud, "Yo."

Shade glanced at Easy to see he was shouting it to him and not warning Ry, as the brother sidled up to him. "Saylor ain't happy."

"See that."

"She should know Ry's off limits. Probably why he's sniffin' around your girl. Judge will break off Ry's dick if he puts it in Saylor."

Too late. That deed had already been done. Probably too many times to count. But that was Ry and Saylor's secret, no one else's. Instead, he growled, "Gonna break off Ry's dick if he even tries to put it in Josie."

Rev wandered over and noticed the same as they were seeing. "Poor fuckin' Ry. Kid can't stick his fuckin' dick anywhere without gettin' it ripped off."

"Kid goes to fuckin' college, he can fuck plenty of college girls," Shade muttered.

Easy grinned. "Yeah, I should go visit him at school sometime." He nudged Shade. "How about her?"

Shade followed where Easy's attention landed. Which was the bar. Maddie was drinking and laughing. Whip was doing the same with his hand planted on the small of Maddie's back, way too close to her ass, and his crotch pressed to Maddie's hip.

What the fuck.

"Yo, Whip," Shade yelled across the barn. "Twelve-inch distance. Minimum."

With a frown, Whip dropped his hand and stepped back. Maddie also shot him a frown, but Shade answered it with an arched eyebrow. That was all she needed as a reminder. She rolled her eyes and went back to facing the bar and chatting with Angel.

Rev snorted at that exchange and then asked, "You see the fuckin' ring Trip gave Stella?"

"Hard to miss," Shade mumbled. Not because the engagement ring was big, but because it was unique.

It wasn't a diamond since Stella wasn't into those kind of things. The ring was a platinum skull head with two large rubies for eyes. Trip had it specially made for her and surprised her with it. It was badass, but also feminine. It fit Stella's personality perfectly.

Rev said, "He's really working hard on her to get knocked up."

"Sure is," Easy agreed. "Bet they fuck constantly."

"We all fuck constantly." Rev's grin turned wicked as he grabbed his crotch. "Ain't that why we got dicks that get hard?"

"Mine gets hard, not sure about yours," Easy said to Rev. "Heard Billie complainin' about you bein' limp."

"She scares the fuck outta me sometimes."

"She scares us all," Easy muttered. "But ain't that supposed to be the fun part?"

After an answering wince, Rev got back on track. "Trip's plannin' a big weddin' here on the farm, most likely next summer. Plannin' on invitin' all our allies."

Shade turned to stare at Rev. "Yeah?"

"Yeah. Like a weekend-long biker blow-out with the Dirty Angels and the Dark Knights."

Shade didn't know much about those two clubs. Only that the Fury, the Angels and the Knights now controlled all of Pennsylvania west of the Susquehanna River. Trip wanted to stay in good standing with the two well-established MCs, so it made sense to include them at his wedding, with him being the Fury president and all.

"All right, need my annual Christmas Eve cock suckin'," Rev announced, rubbing at his zipper and glancing around The Barn in search of a prospective volunteer.

"Billie's in the back. Think she's suckin' Santa off right now while he shouts 'ho, ho, ho.' You can get in line," Easy suggested to Rev.

"Prefer not to have ornaments hangin' from my balls from those fuckin' hooks. Gonna find someone who ain't gonna maim me. Wanna fuckin' come not cry."

Shade smothered his laugh, while Easy didn't bother as Rev wandered away. The mechanic headed toward where Reese and Reilly were sitting.

Yeah, that wasn't going to happen. Reese would shove the tree topper up Rev's ass if he walked up to Reilly and outright asked for head.

Actually, Shade wouldn't mind seeing that.

"Maddie turned twenty-one coupla weeks ago, right?"

Fuck. Maybe the girls needed to go the fuck home and never come back. Chelle might be right with wanting to keep them off the farm. Josie and Maddie were fresh meat in a room full of horny motherfuckers.

"Brother," he growled in warning.

"Just askin'." He leaned a little closer. "Whip and I decided that later we're going to fight to the death for her. She's fuckin' hot. You gotta notice it."

He noticed. He also addressed the possible issues of them coming to The Barn with the girls. Before the big Thanksgiving dinner and also before today. He might have to have that discussion with them again tomorrow or ban them completely. Maybe he'd gotten his words wrong and didn't make himself clear.

Shade turned to Easy whose eyes were still glued on Maddie. Angel was on the other side of the bar, leaning across it and talking animatedly to Chelle's oldest daughter. The sweet butt's tits were practically falling out of her top and Shade swore he could see her nipples from where he stood. Yeah, he needed to have some words again with both of Chelle's daughters.

"Brother, either of you fuckin' touch her, you'll end up in one of the furnaces turned to fuckin' ash."

"You sayin' Chelle's girls are too good for us?"

"Sayin' they need to get their college degrees and make somethin' of themselves. That's Chelle's dream for them and as a single mom she worked hard to make that happen. None of you assholes gonna fuck that up. Otherwise, I might even let Chelle push the ignite button on the furnace while you're still breathin', if I don't slam it with my hand first."

Easy grimaced. The last time someone was burned alive, it left a mark on everyone who witnessed it. Getting rid of a dead body was one thing, incinerating one still screaming was another.

"What about Jude?" Easy asked.

What the fuck? The kid was twelve, Easy better not be interested in him. Then he *would* be burned alive. "What about him?"

"College. All that shit."

For fuck's sake.... He didn't think Easy had a thing for guys, especially ones underaged, but still... It sucked that Shade's thoughts had gone there automatically.

"Jude wants to stick around, that's up to him. Got six years before he can prospect if he wants that. Might wanna do his own thing and get some fancy degree. He's fuckin' smart."

"You sayin' we ain't smart enough for Chelle's girls?"

"More like smart-ass. Gonna tell you once more, put

Josie and Maddie in the column of un-fuckin-touchables. Right under Reilly, Saylor and Tessa. Yeah? Thought I made that clear at Thanksgivin'."

"She wasn't twenty-one at Thanksgivin'." His brow furrowed. "Hey, d'you think it's fucked up you're closer in age to Maddie than to Chelle?"

This wasn't the first time he'd been asked that, especially after Maddie recently turned a year closer to thirty. "No."

Easy nudged him again. "Guess seasoned pussy's better than unseasoned, right?"

"Brother, outta everyone, you're like blood to me. But that blood could easily be spilled."

Easy grinned. "Only fuckin' with you."

He wasn't, but Shade let it slide. Especially since they both spotted Chelle walking toward them. Her hips weren't quite as round as Cassie's, but they still managed to draw attention. Too much for Shade's liking.

"Fuck yeah," Easy moaned. "Fuckin' lucky bastard. Never thought I'd wanna MILF for my own, but I'm seein' the error of my fuckin' ways."

"Get fuckin' lost."

Easy chuckled, gave him a chin lift, whispered something to Chelle in passing and then headed over to the bar to stand the minimum required distance away from Maddie.

Shade would still keep an eye on her. And him. *Hell*, all of his horny fucking brothers.

"Hi, handsome."

"Hey, beautiful. You good?"

"Yes."

The way she answered didn't sound like it. He wondered if it had something to do with what Easy said to her. "Spill."

Chelle took a breath.

"Chelle."

"That one over there..."

She pointed to a sweet butt with long light brown hair.

Young like the rest of them, except for Lizzy. He was surprised Josie and Maddie didn't know Brandy. But maybe the girl hadn't grown up in Manning Grove.

"Brandy," he told her.

"*Brandy* asked if I breastfed you when you were a baby or if I gave you formula. I guess she was hinting that I'm old enough to be your mother."

Shade blinked, then looked at Brandy, where she was standing behind the bar, now doing Jell-O shots with Lizzy and Ozzy. Ozzy seemed to be working the younger sweet butt with his rough charm, probably for a threesome later.

"Gonna handle it," Shade murmured.

She grabbed his arm and shook her head. "No, I handled it."

"How?"

"I told her I didn't nurse you as a baby, but as a man you can't get enough of sucking on my tits."

His eyebrows shot up his head. "Used the word tits?"

She jerked up one shoulder. "I figured it was appropriate for the situation."

He grinned. Yeah, it was. "Gonna make a great ol' lady."

She glanced up at him. "How am I not your ol' lady yet?"

Fuck. Did she think she was? He shook his head. "There's a process, beautiful."

"I figured the process was done earlier."

"When I filled you with my cum?"

Color shot into her face and she whispered, "When you moved in." She pushed her glasses higher on her nose and fanned her red cheeks with her hand.

Yeah, he'd give her the cut the ladies got her Christmas morning. Earlier, she claimed wearing a "Property of" cut would look "badass." He agreed. Especially if that was the only thing she was wearing.

Fuck yeah, he would fuck her in it tomorrow morning after she opened the present in private.

"We'll get it sorted." When she sank her teeth into her bottom lip, he stared at her mouth. "Wanna fuck you again."

She quickly glanced around. "Here?"

"On the bar's a good place."

She whacked his arm. "Not funny."

"Wasn't a joke. So, what the fuck did Easy say?"

She shot him a bright smile. "That you're a... quote... lucky fucker... unquote."

"Yeah, I am." He hooked an arm around her neck and pulled her into him.

She sighed, leaned back into his chest and pulled his arms tighter around her waist, keeping her hands on his forearms to hold him there.

She didn't have to worry, he wasn't going anywhere.

Cassie might give good hugs, but he preferred Chelle's.

She nudged his dick with her ass. "Are you quietly having a fit about the interest your brothers are giving Josie and Maddie?"

"Ain't you?"

"I figured you had that covered for me. As long as they don't disappear from your sight, I'm good with them being here."

He pressed his nose against the top of her head and inhaled the familiar scent of her hair. "You talk to Rick yet?"

"Mmm hmm."

That answer didn't sound promising. "And?"

"*And* he invited us over for Christmas dinner tomorrow night."

That was unexpected. "Jude and me, too?"

"Yes, all of us."

Thank fuck. "He gonna be a dick?"

She sighed, not one of contentment this time. "Probably."

"Wouldn't care if it was only me, but Jude…"

"It'll get better."

"If it don't?"

"It'll get better," she said more firmly.

He hoped to fuck it did for Chelle's sake.

Shade should make her wear her Christmas gift tomorrow night at dinner. Rick would probably love it.

He grinned and glanced around the room again, checking on her girls, checking once again on Jude. He spotted Trip and Stella standing on the other side of The Barn. Stella was being held by Trip the same way Shade held Chelle.

One of Trip's hands was spread flat across Stella's lower stomach. The man wanted babies badly with his ol' lady. He never hid that fact.

The second Stella agreed, he'd get busy planting one in her belly.

Shade hoped to fuck for Trip's sake Stella would agree soon. She was getting to the age where she needed to decide. Maybe that was why the Fury president was pushing the marriage thing, since that was the normal progression of making a family. First marriage, then kids.

Not that any of them in that room were normal.

Fuck. None of them were.

The Blood Fury was a patchwork of Fury blood and outsiders.

Like him. Like Jude.

Maybe not blood, but accepted all the same.

He'd found his family.

He'd found his woman. A woman who was helping mend his splintered soul.

Chelle turned in his arms and noticed whatever was on

his face as he looked down at her. He usually hid his shit from everyone.

Everyone but her.

After a few moments of unspoken words between them, she pressed a hand to his gut under his cut. "Are you hungry?"

"Always hungry for you."

Her eyes instantly heated. As did her cheeks. Again. He loved that even after being around his rude and crude brothers long enough now, she still blushed so easily. He hoped she never stopped.

"I meant food."

"If I was a starvin' man and had to choose between you and a meal, I'd choose you, beautiful."

"No need to starve, handsome. You have me."

Yeah, the woman fed his soul.

As long as he had her, he'd never fucking starve.

———

"To live every day as if it had been stolen from death, that is how I would like to live." ~ Garth Stein

———

To report suspected human trafficking, please contact your local authorities. In the U.S., please contact the FBI: 1-866-347-2423

———

Keep up with my latest news by signing up for my newsletter here: https://www. authorjeannestjames.com/

———

It's a thin line between love and hate…

Secrets.
Every one of his brothers in the Blood Fury MC has them.
Including Rook.
Especially Rook.
What he's done in his past. What he's involved in currently.
What he still needs to do.
Even worse, what he's tempted to do.
With someone no one expects.
Least of all him.
But resisting her is impossible, no matter how much he tries.
Problem is, his club's on the verge of war, so she's either
with the Fury or against them.
If she's against them, she's against them all.
Including Rook.
Especially Rook.
Which will turn the thin line into an insurmountable wall
dividing them forever.

**Turn the page to read the prologue of
Blood & Bones: Rook**

Blood & Bones: Rook

BLOOD FURY MC, BOOK 7

Prologue

When life kicks you in the balls and drops you to your knees…

RANDY SAT behind the wheel of the 1974 Pontiac LeMans and stared through the windshield. The neighborhood was sketchy as shit.

While he didn't expect a gated, luxury community, the shit-hole house surprised him.

He'd found the Baltimore address along with her name in scratchy handwriting on the back of a torn envelope buried deep in his father's dresser drawer. Under a loaded .40 caliber handgun with the serial number ground off and a full box of ammo.

Randy wondered why those three things were kept in the same spot. Was Dutch planning on coming down here for a final reunion? Did he hate the woman that much?

He wouldn't be surprised if his father did.

They weren't allowed to speak her name in their house. Not since the day she walked out.

441

That was three years ago. When he was twelve and his brother Chris was eight.

Three damn years.

Randy wondered if Dutch knew where she was all that damn time and never told them. Knowing his asshole father, he probably fucking did.

From where Randy had parked the piece of shit Pontiac at the curb, he twisted his head and studied the duplex through the passenger-side window. He had no doubt which one Bebe lived in.

The one with the rebel flag covering the front window.

Randy's lips flattened. *Figures.*

One-by-one, he peeled his fingers off the steering wheel and gritted his teeth. He needed to get the hell out of the vehicle and go up to the door. He didn't drive all this way for nothing.

He didn't risk stealing the LeMans only for shits and giggles.

He was here now. He was doing this.

He was here to find out why.

Why a mother would just up and leave her sons. Never see them again. Never talk to them again.

Forget they ever existed.

He pulled a deep breath in through his nose, held it and blew it out his mouth.

Fuck this.

The driver's door creaked loudly as he forced it open. He had to slam it shut twice to get it to latch closed.

"Piece of fuckin' shit," he muttered, giving the door a good kick. He should've stolen a Corvette or something. However, this vehicle had been easy to pinch and he could start it with a screwdriver. It was why he picked it.

Plus, it wasn't flashy. Like a Corvette.

His goal was to get from Manning Grove to Baltimore and back without getting caught.

By his father or the pigs.

He rounded the front of the Pontiac sedan, dodged the garbage bags piled at the curb, strode over the cracked concrete sidewalk and up the porch steps. The storm door that used to hang on her side of the duplex now leaned against the siding. The screen was busted out like someone had punched it and the wood frame was splintered.

He hesitated for the few seconds it took him to take another deep breath before using the side of his fist to beat on the wood door with the peeling paint and no window or peephole. She would have no clue who was standing on the other side.

She would either answer it or she wouldn't.

"Who the fuck is it?" came from the bowels of the house.

If he answered that question, she might not open the door. Instead, he pounded again. This time harder and louder.

"God-fuckin-damnit! Keep your fuckin' pants on!"

A lock clicked and the door abruptly swung open with an ear-piercing creak.

And there she was. The woman who had pushed him out of her snatch a little over fifteen years ago.

His upper lip curled as he took her in.

Her dark blonde stringy hair had three inches of solid gray roots. She wore frayed Daisy Dukes that showed way too much skin for her age or body size. Her cottage-cheese thighs squeezing out of the bottom of the denim shorts reminded him of a popped zit.

She had on a threadbare T-shirt that told people to "Get Fucked." The neckline had been cut out and sliced down the chest to show off her tits. Ones not contained by any bra.

As she stared at him, she squinted one dull blue eye when the smoke from the Pall Mall swirled into it.

She looked like hell. Way worse than what he remembered.

When both eyes narrowed on him, she yanked the cigarette from her mouth. Probably so it wouldn't tumble from her lips when they gaped open at the sight of him on her front porch.

"Which one are you?"

What a cunt.

Her gaze roamed from the top of his head down to his toes, then back up before she answered her own question. "Randy."

Ding, ding, ding. You won the "Mom of the Year" award for recognizin' your first-born son.

"Got tall," she muttered.

"Yeah, no longer twelve."

"What you doin' here?"

Great to see you, too, Mom. He jerked up one shoulder. "Just in the neighborhood."

She peeked her head out the door and peered around. "Yeah? You know someone 'round here?"

Holy shitballs. "Yeah, I used to. Gonna let me in?"

It would be nice to at least get the chance to drain his snake since he only stopped once to piss in the woods during the four-hour drive.

She took another long drag on her Pall Mall, blew it out the door over his head and stepped back. She jerked her head toward the darker interior.

He guessed that was as good of an invite as he'd get.

She closed the door behind him, turned and raked her gaze over him again. "Kinda look like your father."

"You mean Dutch?"

Hopefully she wasn't going to surprise him by naming someone else instead.

When she ignored his question, he glanced around the tiny living room. He thought she left for bigger and better things. Looking around her place, it was clear she'd missed that mark. By a mile.

More like a hundred miles.

The house she gave up in Manning Grove might not be some big, fancy mansion, but it was a hell of a lot better than this rat trap.

The place was filthy. Worse, it stunk.

Overflowing ashtrays were scattered around the room. Empty beer cans littered every table. The couch had bare patches on the ass-indented cushions and what fabric remained was stained.

He had no idea what color the carpet should be.

He didn't care, either.

Thank fuck she hadn't taken him and Chris with her. He'd deal with Dutch being a dick any day over this hell hole.

After seeing what he saw, he decided he'd rather pee in the woods once he left Baltimore. He might catch crabs by using her bathroom.

"How the fuck d'you get here?" She yanked a corner of the rebel flag away from the window. The cigarette hanging from between two fingers came close to touching the dirty fabric that covered the equally dirty window. He didn't warn her since it would be for the best if this place burned to the ground.

"Your asshole father ain't here, is he?" She peered out, and jerked her chin up at the LeMans. "Whose car is that?"

"Mine."

She let the flag drop and turned on him. "You ain't old enough to own a car." Her brow furrowed and she used a cracked, dirty fingernail to scratch the corner of her mouth, then took another long drag on her cigarette. The ash hanging off the end had to now be an inch long. "You even old enough to drive?"

"You don't know?"

She didn't answer, which was his answer. She didn't even know how old her sons were anymore. Or didn't care. Most likely never did.

She'd forgotten about them both the second she walked out their front door with her shit packed in garbage bags.

The ash finally fell off the end of the Pall Mall and landed at Bebe's slipper-covered feet. Of course, she paid it no mind.

His mother should've stuffed herself into one of those black garbage bags because she was absolute trash, too. She hadn't been like this when she was with Dutch. She hadn't been mother of the year material then, either, but from what Randy remembered, Dutch always rode her ass about taking care of the house and his sons. He would also get on her about her appearance. Randy didn't think she listened to his dad, but the way she had spiraled down since leaving proved he was wrong.

Dutch and Bebe would get into some nasty fights. Both Randy and his brother had learned some really good curse words that way. It wasn't the only thing they learned during their spats. Their parents would fight, sometimes even come to blows, then fuck through their anger. Didn't matter where they were at the time.

Kitchen, living room, bedroom... Even on the front porch one night when she locked Dutch out of the house, accusing him of banging some other woman.

He made her come out of the house and get on her knees to sniff his dick to prove he hadn't, then Dutch bent her right over the porch railing. It had been rough, loud and angry for both of them. It had been like two snarling tom cats fighting.

He and Chris, who were nine and five at the time, watched from the front window while the neighbors watched from theirs.

When Dutch was done fucking her, he forced her to her

knees and made her suck his dick clean. Then he locked *her* ass out of the house for being a bitch.

Someone had called the damn pigs and both of them ended up spending the night in jail to dry out and for a shit-load of minor charges. One of the women from the club had come over to stay with them that night. She slept in their parents' bed with one of Dutch's club brothers and they made a racket, too. Lots of squeaky springs, headboard slamming and screams of "fuck me harder!"

"So, why you here, boy?"

He mentally shook away that memory. "Why does Dad have your address?"

She only stared at him with those dull, empty blue eyes.

He came here for fucking answers and he was going to get fucking answers. "Why does Dutch have your fuckin' address since you left us all behind? Why would he need your fuckin' address?" He was trying not to shout but, by the end, he was shouting.

That made Bebe scowl at him.

Too fucking bad.

"That ain't your business, boy."

"Don't call me boy."

"You're my boy, I can call you what I want."

"You gave up that right the second you walked out on us."

She took one last drag on her cigarette and ground it out in a mountain of butts in the nearest overflowing ashtray.

"Dutch told you I walked out on you?" She glanced around, spotted an open pack of Pall Malls, slid another one out of the pack and tucked it between her lips.

"He didn't have to tell us. We watched it, remember? You had me carry the garbage bags out to your fuckin' car."

"Shouldn't be cursin'."

"A little too late to try parentin', *Bebe*."

She frowned as she tried to light the cigarette with a Bic.

When she couldn't, she shook the almost empty disposable lighter as if that would magically fill it. "Still your mother, still older than you. I can knock you into next week if I want."

She could try. Randy doubted she'd succeed.

"Want the truth?" she asked. After a few more flicks of the Bic, a half-assed flame stayed lit long enough for her to light her smoke.

"What I came here for."

"Thought you knew someone in the neighborhood."

Randy planted his hands on his hips, dropped his head and shook it. No wonder Dutch was always yelling at him for doing stupid shit. He got his lack of smarts from his birth receptacle.

"Your father forced me to leave."

Randy's head snapped up. "No, he didn't."

"The fuck he didn't."

His thumping heart was so loud he had to yell over it to hear himself. "You asked if I wanted the truth. I want the fuckin' truth!"

"That's the truth, boy."

He frowned. "I don't get it."

"Ain't for you to get."

"I'm your fuckin' son. I should know why you left."

"I left because he paid me to."

Randy's pounding heart seized and his ears began to ring. "You're lyin'. Why would he do that?"

"'Cause we fuckin' hated each other. 'Cause he forced me to have you two rug rats. 'Cause I didn't wanna be tied down to you brats. 'Cause I didn't wanna suck his cheating dick anymore. That's why."

He thought she left because she'd had enough of the club after all the shit that went down. The fighting, the killing, the—

"And 'cause I got knocked up by Tinny."

She did what?

He knew they weren't faithful to each other. From the moment he could remember and understand it. He saw them both doing shit with other people. At the warehouse, at the house, in the garage. In their bed.

But...

Randy glanced around the living room again for some signs of a young kid. "I got another brother?"

Bebe shook her head and plugged the cigarette between her lips again. "Fuck no."

"A sister?" When she turned away, he asked, "What d'you do with him?" Or her. His half-brother or sister. Did she keep the new one after dumping the old ones?

"Used some of the scratch Dutch gave me to suck that leech outta me soon's I could."

Randy blinked as he watched his mother pick up open beer cans around the room and shake them. It took her a few tries, but she finally found one that sloshed and she chugged the remainder down.

She kept her back to him when she admitted, "Woulda done that with you two if he woulda let me."

Randy was having a hard time breathing. It wasn't from the stink in the house or the heavy cloud of cigarette smoke, but the fact the woman standing in front of him was supposed to be his mother. She'd never been one. Not once that he could remember. So anything she said shouldn't surprise him.

It still did.

He never should've come here.

She was a piece of shit Dutch scraped off his boot for good reason.

Dutch might not be perfect but at least he wanted his sons. He took care of them. Randy just wished he would've picked a better cum dumpster to grow his sperm in. Not the cunt on the hunt for another can with a backwash of beer.

"You want the truth? Here's the hard truth, kid. He pays me to stay away."

Pays? As in currently pays? No fucking way. "You're lyin'."

"Boy, I ain't lyin'. Ask him. He's stupid enough to think I'd want visitation or custody of you and... and the other one." She laughed. "I never did but pretended to and every time I threaten to hire a lawyer, he sends me more fuckin' dough."

"You're blackmailin' him?"

Bebe shrugged. "I see it as compensation for giving the bastard the two boys he wanted. And ruining my tight pussy when your big heads stretched it. The other one ripped me damn near in half."

"The sons you never wanted."

"You know what kids are?"

"Blood," Randy muttered. At least that was what they should be.

"Parasites who suck your blood. Suck the fuckin' life right outta you. And after I gave him the sons he demanded, he still stuck his dick in our whore of a house mouse."

"You fucked Tin Man!" he screamed, the heat from his fury burning his cheeks.

She most likely fucked a ton of other bikers. Whether from the Blood Fury MC or other clubs. She had no right to judge Dutch for fucking around when she had done the same damn thing.

"Now you know why I left."

"You woulda stayed if he hadn't paid you off?"

Bebe shrugged and flicked the growing ash of her Pall Mall near an ashtray but totally missed. "Why not? Had a roof over my head, food in my belly and plenty of dick to choose from."

Not one of those things she listed included her own flesh and blood.

Randy pressed his lips together and nodded. More to himself than her. Yeah, she didn't leave because she was scared of the shit going down with the Fury, she left because she was a greedy, selfish cunt. And the only way Dutch could get her to leave him was to pay her to do so.

She did that willingly and without a fight.

Bebe got what she wanted.

Dutch got what he wanted.

And two kids got confused. As well as lied to.

"You got any cash, boy? I'm outta beer."

He lifted his head and stared at the woman who used to be his mother.

He dug into the front pocket of his jeans, pulled out a quarter and flipped it at her.

Bebe watched as it fell to the floor at her slippered feet. "Think that's funny?"

"You hear me laughin'?"

Yeah, maybe it was good he came. Got the truth. He could now put the woman out of his head and never think about her again. Maybe tell Chris she was dead.

Because that was what she was. Dead to him. Dead to his younger brother.

"Better take that fuckin' quarter, 'cause that's the last cent you're gonna get from a Dietrich. Tellin' Dutch to never give you a fuckin' dime again. Gonna tell him your threats are empty. Also gonna tell him to shoot you right between the fuckin' eyes if you ever show the fuck up in Manning Grove again. You hear me, you worthless slit?"

Her mouth got tight and her fingers curled into a fist like she was thinking about belting him one. "You don't speak to your mother like that."

His eyebrows shot up. "Wouldn't, if I had one."

He was done.

With her.

With this shithole.

With all of it.

He spun on his boot, jogged out the door, down the porch steps and didn't stop moving until he was in the LeMans and headed north out of Maryland.

He didn't stop until he was forced to.

By the red and blue flashing lights behind him.

He had no choice but to pull over since the Pontiac piece-of-shit would never outrun the souped-up Crown Vics the state pigs drove. Maybe he should've taken the back roads all the way home instead of the interstate.

Too late now.

He slammed his palm against the steering wheel and muttered a curse under his breath as the uniformed pig approached the back of the LeMans with one hand already resting on the butt of his gun.

Randy didn't have to roll down the window since it was already open. The LeMans didn't have air conditioning and, being late afternoon in the middle of August, it was ball-sweating hot outside.

"How you doing, sir?" the pig oinked.

Sir. Randy's tight jaw shifted.

"Need your license, registration and insurance. Assuming you have all that even though the registration plate seems to be missing."

Randy stared straight ahead, waiting. His fury from his *used-to-be* mother still bubbling like lava in his gut. Now he had to deal with a pig of a different kind.

"Must have lost the key, too, since I see you've made your own with a screwdriver. Do I even need to run the VIN to see if it's stolen?"

"Do whatever gets you off."

The pig leaned closer to the window, tilting his head just slightly. "Sorry, I think I missed that."

Randy turned his head slowly and stared straight up at the pig who wore one of those stupid-ass hats on his head with the black strap across his double-chin. Dumb fucks didn't even know how to wear a hat right.

This time Randy repeated it slowly, loudly and in very clear English. "Said do whatever the fuck gets you off."

"Huh. Guess my ears don't need cleaned. I heard you right the first time."

"Yeah, you ain't deaf, just dumb."

The Trooper slid his sunglasses down his nose far enough to peer over them. "How old are you, kid?"

"Eighteen," he lied.

"Must have a glandular problem, then."

Randy grabbed his crotch. "Had no problem fuckin' your mom's hairy snatch. She even begged me for more."

"Why don't you step out of the car."

"Are you askin'?"

"Did I make it sound like I was?"

"Did your sister tell you I throat-fucked her 'til she gagged and swallowed my hot, salty cum?"

A hand reached into the driver's side window so quickly, Randy didn't have time to dodge it. Fingers snatched the collar of his T-shirt, while the pig's other hand grabbed his neck, and he was yanked bodily through the window. He landed hard on the searing hot berm of the road.

After registering the pain, his first thought was that vehicles were driving at a high rate of speed not that many feet from his exposed melon.

As he tried to get up, a boot on his back shoved him back down.

"I was wrong. I do think I need my ears cleaned because I couldn't have possibly heard what I did."

Randy spit a little bit of blood out onto the blacktop in front of him. "Nah. You heard me right. Fucked your mom, fucked your sister, then I blew my load up your daughter's tight ass. It was sloppy seconds, though, you musta gave her the first load."

The boot on his back turned to a knee and the pig's crushing weight made it hard to breathe.

Randy heard a clicking sound before feeling the press of a metal rod to the back of his neck. One of those expandable metal sticks that five-o carried. The one they loved to beat innocent people with. *Fuckers.*

"Good thing you're eighteen. Otherwise, you'd end up in juvie for grand theft, instead. They'll like fresh meat like you in prison. Tight hole. Sweet, young mouth. Just enough hair around your asshole so Bubba can pretend it's a virgin pussy. Hope you like big, black dick."

"Know your wife loves it," were the last words he recalled saying.

He didn't remember anything after that.

Not for a long time.

Continue Rook's story here:
https://books2read.com/BFMC-Rook

If You Enjoyed This Book

Thank you for reading Blood & Bones: Shade. If you enjoyed Shade and Chelle's story, please consider leaving a review at your favorite retailer and/or Goodreads to let other readers know. Reviews are always appreciated and just a few words can help an independent author like me tremendously!

Want to read a sample of my work? Download a sampler book here: BookHip.com/MTQQKK

———

Sign up for Jeanne's newsletter: https://www. authorjeannestjames.com/
Join her FB readers' group for the inside scoop: https://www.facebook.com/groups/ JeannesReviewCrew/

Also by Jeanne St. James

Find my complete reading order here:

https://www.jeannestjames.com/reading-order

Standalone Books:

Made Maleen: A Modern Twist on a Fairy Tale

Damaged

Rip Cord: The Complete Trilogy

Everything About You (A Second Chance Gay Romance)

Reigniting Chase (An M/M Standalone)

Brothers in Blue Series

A four-book series based around three brothers who are small-town cops and former Marines

The Dare Ménage Series

A six-book MMF, interracial ménage series

The Obsessed Novellas

A collection of five standalone BDSM novellas

Down & Dirty: Dirty Angels MC®

A ten-book motorcycle club series

Guts & Glory: In the Shadows Security

A six-book former special forces series

(A spin-off of the Dirty Angels MC)

Blood & Bones: Blood Fury MC®

A twelve-book motorcycle club series

<u>**Motorcycle Club Crossovers:**</u>

<u>Crossing the Line: A DAMC/Blue Avengers MC Crossover</u>

<u>Magnum: A Dark Knights MC/Dirty Angels MC Crossover</u>

Crash: A Dirty Angels MC/Blood Fury MC Crossover

Romeo: A Dark Knights MC/Blood Fury MC Crossover

Beyond the Badge: Blue Avengers MC™

A six-book law enforcement/motorcycle club series

<u>**Double D Ranch**</u>

A six-book MMF ménage series

<u>**COMING SOON!**</u>

Property of Stone (Kings of Anarchy MC: Pennsylvania)

Dirty Angels MC®: The Next Generation

WRITING AS J.J. MASTERS:

The Royal Alpha Series

A five-book gay mpreg shifter series

About the Author

JEANNE ST. JAMES is a USA Today, Amazon and international bestselling romance author who loves writing about strong women and alpha males. She was only thirteen when she first started writing and her first published piece was an erotic short story in Playgirl magazine. She then went on to publish her first romance novel in 2009. She is now an author of almost 70 contemporary romances. She writes M/F, M/M, and M/M/F ménages, including interracial romance. She also writes M/M paranormal romance under the name: J.J. Masters.

Want to read a sample of her work? Download a sampler book here: BookHip.com/MTQQKK

To keep up with her busy release schedule check her website at www.jeannestjames.com or sign up for her newsletter: https://www.authorjeannestjames.com/

www.jeannestjames.com

Newsletter: https://www.authorjeannestjames.com/
Jeanne's Down & Dirty Book Crew: https://www.facebook.com/groups/JeannesReviewCrew/

facebook.com/JeanneStJamesAuthor

instagram.com/JeanneStJames

bookbub.com/authors/jeanne-st-james

goodreads.com/JeanneStJames

Get a FREE Sampler Book

This book contains the first chapter of a variety of my books. This will give you a taste of the type of books I write and if you enjoy the first chapter, I hope you'll be interested in reading the rest of the book.

Each book I list in the sampler will include the description of the book, the genre, and the first chapter, along with links to find out more. I hope you find a book you will enjoy curling up with!

Get it here: BookHip.com/MTQQKK